Praise for Alan Furst

'Hugely intriguing; Furst is in a class of his own'
William Boyd

'Competitors despair. Alan Furst's mastery of the espionage novel puts him beyond any would-be rival'
Literary Review

'A spy novel, a war story, an adventure, a survivor's tale, *Night Soldiers* is all this and more'   *Seattle Times*

'The most talented espionage novelist of our generation'
Vince Flynn

'Furst never stops astounding me'   Tom Hanks

'Intelligent, ambitious, absorbing'   *New York Times*

'Furst's latest excellent spy thriller [is] so elegant and genteel – beautifully written . . . your heart will be pounding with tension'   *Guardian*

'Furst's research is such that one gets the impression he hasn't just travelled, he has time-travelled. He evokes beautifully the haunted, precarious existence of Europeans caught up in the march of war'   *Financial Times*

'Furst's tales . . . are infused with the melancholy romanticism of Casablanca, and also a touch of Arthur Koestler's *Darkness at Noon*'   *Scotsman*

'Mr Furst excels at period atmosphere . . . His characters are wonderfully human: complex and ambiguous, fearful and determined . . . Mr Furst is a subtle, economical writer who knows precisely when to stop a sentence'   *Economist*

NIGHT SOLDIERS

Alan Furst is widely recognised as the master of the historical spy novel. Now translated into eighteen languages, he is the author of fourteen novels including *Midnight in Europe*, *Spies of the Balkans* – a TV Book Club choice – *The Spies of Warsaw*, which became a BBC mini-series starring David Tennant and *The Foreign Correspondent*. Born in New York, he lived for many years in Paris, and now lives on Long Island.

www.alanfurst.net

Also by Alan Furst

A Hero in France
Midnight in Europe
Mission to Paris
Spies of the Balkans
The Spies of Warsaw
The Foreign Correspondent
Dark Voyage
Blood of Victory
Kingdom of Shadows
Red Gold
The World at Night
The Polish Officer
Dark Star
Night Soldiers

NIGHT
SOLDIERS

ALAN FURST

WEIDENFELD & NICOLSON

First published in Great Britain in 1988 by The Bodley Head
First published in paperback in 1989 by Mandarin
First published in paperback by Weidenfeld & Nicolson in 2005

This paperback edition published in 2018
by Weidenfeld & Nicolson
an imprint of the Orion Publishing Group Ltd
Carmelite House, 50 Victoria Embankment
London EC4Y 0DZ

An Hachette UK Company

First published in the USA in 1988 by Houghton Mifflin

1 3 5 7 9 10 8 6 4 2

Reissued 2009 and 2018

A CIP catalogue record for this book is
available from the British Library.

ISBN (Mass Market Paperback) 978 1 4746 1162 6
ISBN (eBook) 978 1 7802 2149 6

Printed and bound in Great Britain by Clays Ltd, Elcograf S.p.A.

MIX
Paper from
responsible sources
FSC® C104740

www.weidenfeldandnicolson.co.uk
www.orionbooks.co.uk

Push out a bayonet. If it strikes fat, push deeper.
If it strikes iron, pull back for another day.

V. I. Lenin
May 1922

Executive order 9621

TERMINATION OF THE OFFICE OF
STRATEGIC SERVICES (OSS)

The Secretary of War shall, whenever he deems it
compatible with the national interest, discontinue
any activity transferred by this paragraph and wind
up all affairs relating thereto.

Harry S. Truman
September 20, 1945

The
Danube River
1934–1945

0   50   100
MILES

0   50   100
KILOMETRES

Dniester River

U.S.S.R.

Prut River

BESSARABIA

Odessa

Belgorod-
Dnestrovskij

Izmail

Galati

Sulina

Sfintu
Gheorgiou

Murigheol

ROMANIA

Lake Murigheol

TRANSYLVANIAN
ALPS

BLACK SEA

CARPATHIAN MOUNTAINS

Bucharest

Silistra

Iron Gate

Ruse

Turnu-Severin

Svistov

Nikopol

DUNĂREA

Vidin

BULGARIA

SERBIA

Levitzky's
Geese

In Bulgaria, in 1934, on a muddy street in the river town of Vidin, Khristo Stoianev saw his brother kicked to death by fascist militia.

His brother was fifteen, no more than a blameless fool with a big mouth, and in calmer days his foolishness would have been accommodated in the usual ways – a slap in the face for humiliation, a few cold words to chill the blood, and a kick in the backside to send him on his way. That much was tradition. But these were *political* times, and it was very important to think before you spoke. Nikko Stoianev spoke without thinking, and so he died.

On both sides of the river – Romania to the north and Bulgaria to the south – the political passion ran white hot. People talked of little else: in the marketplace, in the church, even – a mark of just how far matters had progressed – in the kitchen. *Something has happened in Bucharest. Something has happened in Sofia.*

Soon, something will happen here.

And, lately, they marched.

Torchlight parades with singing and stiff-armed salutes. And the most splendid uniforms. The Romanians, who considered themselves much the more stylish and urbane, wore green shirts and red armbands with blue swastikas on a yellow field. They thrust their banners into the air in time with the drum: we are the Guard of Archangel Michael. See our insignia – the blazing crucifix and pistol.

They were pious on behalf of both symbols. In 1933, one of their number had murdered Ion Duca, the prime minister, as he waited for a train at Sinaia railway station. A splinter group, led by a Romanian of Polish descent named

11

Cornelius Codreanu, called itself the Iron Guard. Not to be outdone by his rivals, Codreanu had recently assassinated the prefect of Jassy 'because he favoured the Jews'. Political times, it seemed, brought the keenest sort of competitive instincts into play and the passionate reached deep within themselves for acts of great magnitude.

The men of Vidin were not quite so fashionable, but that was to be expected. They were, after all, Slavs, who prided themselves on simplicity and honesty, while their brethren across the river were of Latin descent, the inheritors of a corner of the Roman Empire, fancified, indolent fellows who worshipped everything French and indulged themselves in a passion for the barber, the tailor, and the gossip of the cafés. Thus the Bulgarian marchers had selected for themselves a black and olive green uniform which was, compared with Romanian finery, simple and severe.

Still, though simple and severe, they were *uniforms*, and the men of Vidin were yet at some pains, in 1934, to explain to the local population how greatly that altered matters.

It was a soft autumn evening, just after dusk, when Nikko Stoianev called Omar Veiko a dog prick. A white mist hung in the tops of the willows and poplars that lined the bank of the river, clouds of swallows veered back and forth above the town square, the beating of their wings audible to those below. The Stoianev brothers were on their way home from the baker's house. Nikko, being the younger, had to carry the bread.

They were lucky to have it. The European continent lay in the ashes of economic ruin. The printing presses of the state treasuries cranked out reams of paper currency — showing wise kings and blissful martyrs — while bankers wept and peasants starved. It was, certainly, never quite so bad as the great famines of Asia. No dead lay bloated in the streets. European starvation was rather more cunning and wore a series of clever masks: death came by drink,

12

by tuberculosis, by the knife, by despair in all its manifestations. In Hamburg, an unemployed railway brakeman took off his clothes, climbed into a barrel of tar, and burned himself to death.

The Stoianevs had the river. They had fished, for carp and pike, sturgeon and Black Sea herring, for generations. They were not wealthy, but they did earn a few leva. That meant the Stoianev women could spend their days mending lines and nets and the family could pay the Braunshteins, in their flour-dusted yarmulkes, to do the baking. They had, frankly, a weakness for the Braunshtein bread, which was achieved in the Austrian manner, with a hard, brown crust. Most of their neighbours preferred the old-fashioned Turkish loaf, flat and round in the Eastern tradition, but the Stoianev clan looked west for their bread, and their civilization. They were a proud, feisty bunch – some said much too proud – with quick tempers. And they were ambitious; they meant to rise in the world.

Much too ambitious, some thought.

A time might just come, and come fairly soon, when the Stoianevs would have to bow the head – who were *they*, one might ask, to have their damned noses stuck so high in the air? After all, had not the eldest son of Landlord Veiko sought the hand of the eldest Stoianev daughter? The one with the ice-blue eyes and thick black hair. And had he not been refused? A shameful slight, in the watchful eyes of Vidin. The Veiko were a family of power and position; property owners, men of substance and high rank. Any fool could see that.

What fools could and could not see became something of a topic in Vidin following Nikko Stoianev's death. A few leading citizens, self-appointed wise men and local wits, who read newspapers and frequented the coffeehouse, asked each other discreetly if Nikko had not perhaps seen the wrong Veiko. That is, *Landlord* Veiko. For Landlord Veiko was not in the town square that autumn evening.

Colonel Veiko was.

In his black and olive green uniform, marching at the head of the Bulgarian National Union – all eighteen of them present that night. You see, the wise men told each other, to call a landlord a dog prick was to risk a slap in the face for humiliation, a few cold words to chill the blood, and a kick in the backside to send you on your way. That much was tradition. It had happened before. It would happen again. But to say such things to a *colonel*. Well, that was another matter altogether, was it not.

Omar Veiko, in either manifestation, landlord or colonel, was a man to be reckoned with in Vidin. A man whose studied effeminacy was a covert tribute to his power, for only a very powerful man raised neither voice nor fist. Only a very powerful man could afford to be so soft, so fussy, so plump, so fastidious. It was said that he dined like a cat.

This Veiko had a moustache, a sharp, stiff, well-waxed affair that shone jet black against his cream-coloured skin. He was a short man who stood on his toes, a fat man who sucked in his stomach, a curly-haired man who oiled his curls until they brushed flat. A man, obviously, of some considerable vanity and, like most vain men, a close accountant of small insults. A note of sarcasm in the voice, a glance of ill-concealed anger, a rental payment slapped overhard on the wooden desk. All such sins were entered in a ledger, no less permanent for being kept in Veiko's razor-sharp memory rather than on bookkeeper's pages. It was, in fine, the Turkish style: an effete, polished surface just barely concealing interior tides of terrible anger. An Eastern tactic, of great antiquity, meant to frighten and intimidate, for Omar Veiko's most urgent desire on this earth was that people be frightened of him. He lived on fear. It set him above his fellows, content to live out their days animated by less ambitious cravings.

Some weeks later, Antipin, the Russian who pretended to be a Bulgarian, would nod slowly with grave understanding. 'Yes, yes,' he would say, pausing to light a cigarette, 'the village bully.'

'We know them,' he would add, eyes narrowing, head nodding, in a way that meant *and we know what to do with them.*

Colonel Veiko marched his troop into the main square from the west. The sky was touched with the last red streaks of the setting sun. The twenty-five minarets, which gave the town its fame along the river, were now no more than dark shapes on the horizon. There was a light evening breeze off the water and, at the centre of the town square, the last leaves of the great beech tree rattled in the wind, a harsh, dry sound.

The Bulgarian National Union marched with legs locked stiff, chins tucked in, arms fully extended, fingers pointing at the ground. Legs and arms moved like ratchets, as though operated by machinery. All in time to Khosov the Postman, who kept the beat with a homemade drumstick on a block of wood. They badly wanted a drum, but there was no drum to be had unless one went all the way to Sofia. No matter. The desired effect was achieved. A great modern age was now marching into the ancient river town of Vidin.

Colonel Veiko and his troopers had not themselves conceived this fresh approach to parades. It had come down the river from Germany, twelve hundred miles away, brought by an odd little man in a mint-coloured overcoat. He arrived by passenger steamer, with tins of German newsreels and a film projector. To the people of Vidin, these were indeed thrilling spectacles. Nobody had ever seen anything like it. Such enormous banners! Huge bonfires, ranks of torches, songs lifted high by a thousand voices.

The people of Vidin worked hard, squeezed the soul from every lev, watched helplessly as their infants died of diphtheria. Life was a struggle to breathe. Now came an odd little man in a mint-coloured overcoat and he offered them *pride* – a new spirit, a new destiny. Omar Veiko, who could read the wind like a wolf, realized that this time belonged to him, that it was his turn.

First he made himself a captain. Later, a colonel.

The uniforms were sewn up by a tailor named Levitzky, whose family had for generations outfitted the local military: Turkish policemen stationed in the town, Austro-Hungarian infantry going to war against Napoleon, Bulgarian officers in World War I, when the country had sided with Germany. The fact that money passed into the hands of Levitzky, a Jew, was regrettable, but was viewed as a necessary evil. In time such things would be put right.

The uniforms were soon ready. The heavy cotton blouse was olive green, an Eastern preference. The trousers and tunic, of thickly woven drill, were a deep, ominous black. A black tie set off the shirt. Each tunic had a shoulder patch, a fiery crucifix with crossed arrow. The uniforms were received with delight. The heavy double-breasted cut of the jackets made the National Union members look fit and broad-shouldered.

But the caps. Ahh, now that *was* a problem. Military caps were not the proper domain of a tailor – that was capmaker's business, different materials and skills were required. There was, however, no capmaker about, so the job fell on Levitzky.

A progressive. A reader of tracts on Palestinian repatriation, a serious student of the Talmud, a man who wore eyeglasses. Levitzky had an old book of illustrations; he thumbed through it by the light of a kerosene lamp. All Europe was represented, there were Swiss Vatican Guards, Hungarian Hussars, French Foreign Legionnaires, Italian Alpine regiments of the Great War. From the last, he selected a cap style, though he hadn't the proper materials. But Levitzky was resourceful: two layers of black drill were sewn together, then curved into a conical shape. The bill of the cap was fashioned by sewing material on both sides of a cardboard form. All that was lacking, then, was the feather, and this problem was soon solved by a visit to the ritual

16

slaughterer, who sold the tailor an armful of long white goose quills.

Colonel Veiko and his troopers thought the caps were magnificent, a little flamboyant, a daring touch to offset the sombre tone of the uniforms, and wore them with pride. The local wise men, however, laughed behind their hands. It was entirely ridiculous, really it was. Vidin's *petite-bourgeoisie* tricked out in goose feathers, strutting up and down the streets of the town. The grocer preceded by his monstrous belly. The postman beating time on a wooden block. Laughable.

Nikko Stoianev thought so too, standing with his arms full of Braunshtein's loaves on a soft evening in autumn. The Stoianev brothers had stopped a moment to watch the parade – very nearly anything out of the ordinary that happened in Vidin was worth spending a moment on. Veiko marched in front. Next came the two tallest troopers, each with a pole that stretched a banner: the blazing crucifix with crossed arrow. Three ranks of five followed, the man on the end of each line holding a torch – pitch-soaked rope wound around the end of a length of oak branch. Five of the torches were blazing. The sixth had gone out, sending aloft only a column of oily black smoke.

'Ah, here's a thing,' Khristo said quietly. 'The glory of the nation.'

'Levitzky's geese,' Nikko answered, a title conferred by the local wise men.

'How they strut,' Khristo said.

They took great strength from each other, the Stoianev brothers. Good, big kids. Nikko was fifteen, had had his first woman, was hard at work on his second. Khristo was nineteen, introspective like his father. He shied away from the local girls, knowing too well the prevailing courtship rituals that prescribed pregnancy followed by marriage followed by another pregnancy to prove you meant it the first time. Khristo held back from that, harbouring instead

17

a very private dream – something to do with Vienna or, even, the ways of God were infinite, Paris. But of this he rarely spoke. It was simply not wise to reach too far above what you were.

They stood together on the muddy cobbled street, hard-muscled from the fishing, black-haired, fair-skinned. Good-natured because not much else was tolerated. Nikko had a peculiarly enlarged upper lip that curled away from his teeth a little, giving him a sort of permanent sneer, a wise-guy face. It had got him into trouble often enough.

In good order, the unit marched past the grand old Turkish post office that anchored the main square, then reached the intersection.

'Halt!'

Colonel Veiko thrust his arm into the air, held tension for a moment, then shouted, 'Left . . . turn!'

They marched around the corner of the open square, heading now toward the Stoianevs, white feathers bobbing. Veiko the landlord. The grocer. The postman. Several clerks, a schoolteacher, a farmer, a fisherman, even the local matchmaker.

Nikko's grin widened. 'Hup, hup,' he said.

They watched the parade coming toward them.

'Here's trouble,' Khristo said.

There was a hen in the street. It belonged to an old blind woman who lived down by the fishing sheds and it wandered about freely, protected from the pot by local uncertainty over what the fates might have in store for someone who stole from the blind. It tottered along, pecking at the mud from time to time, looked up suddenly, saw the Bulgarian National Union bearing down upon it, and froze. Seemingly hypnotized. Perhaps dazzled by the sparking torches.

Veiko marched like an angry toy – legs thrusting stiffly into the air, heels banging hard against the earth. The hen stood like a stone. What could Veiko do? The local wise men were later to debate the point. Stop the parade –

18

for a *hen*? Never. The National Union had its dignity to consider. It had, in fact, very little else but its dignity, so it simply could not afford the sacrifice. It had to – this became immediately clear to everybody – march through the hen. No hen could stop *them*. So the hen was deemed not to exist.

True to its breed, the hen did not cooperate. It did exist. When the first black boot swung over its head, it rose into the air like a cyclone, wings beating frantically, with a huge, horrified squawk. It could not really fly, of course, so descended rapidly into the scissoring legs of the following rank, which stopped short, legs splayed, arms and torches waving to keep balance, amid great cursing and shouting. The following rank did its part in the business by crashing into the backs of those in front of them.

This happened directly in front of Khristo and Nikko. Who clamped their teeth together and pressed their lips shut, which made the thing, when finally it came tearing up out of them, a great bursting explosion indeed. First, as control slipped away, a series of strangled snorts. Then, at last, helplessly, they collapsed against each other and roared.

Veiko could have ignored it, with little enough loss of face, for everyone knows that giggling teenagers must, at all costs, be ignored. But he did not. He turned slowly, like a man of great power and dignity, and stared at them.

Khristo, older, understood the warning and shut up. Nikko went on with it a little, the issue altering subtly to encompass his 'right' to laugh. Then changed again. So that, by some fleeting alchemy of communication, it was now very plain that Nikko was laughing at Veiko and not at the misadventures of a stray hen.

But the hen did its part. Everyone was to agree on that point at least. For, as Colonel Veiko stared, the hen ran back and forth, just beyond arm's length of the milling troopers, cackling with fury and outraged dignity. Raucous, infuriated, absurd.

19

Thus there were two outraged dignities, and the relation between them, a cartoon moment, made itself evident to Nikko and he laughed even harder. His brother almost saved his life by belting him in the ribs with a sharp elbow – a time-honoured blow; antidote, in classrooms, at funerals, to impossible laughter. Nikko stopped, sighing once or twice in the aftermath and wiping his eyes.

Behind Veiko, the troop was very quiet. He could feel their silence. Slowly, he walked the few paces that separated him from the brothers, then stood close enough so that they could smell the *mastica* on his breath, a sharp odour of licorice and raw alcohol. They always drank before they marched.

'Christ and king,' he said. It was what they said.

It was what they believed in. It was, in this instance, a challenge.

'Christ and king,' Khristo answered promptly. He'd heard what was in the voice – something itching to get out, something inside Veiko that could, at any moment, be born, be alive and running free in the street.

'Christ and king.' Nikko echoed his brother, perhaps in a bit of a mumble. He was confused. He knew what a challenge was, on the boats, in the schoolyard, and he knew the appropriate response, which was anything but submission.

Anything.

But here the provocation was coming from an adult, a man of some standing in the community no matter what one thought of his damn feathers and banners. Between Nikko and the other kids his age it was just a snarly thing, cub feints, a quick flash, perhaps a few punches were thrown and then it was over. But this – this was domination for its own sake, a nasty reek of the adult world, unjust, mean-spirited, and it made Nikko angry.

Veiko saw it happen – the tightening of the mouth, the slight flush along the cheekbones – and it pleased him. And he let Nikko know it pleased him. Showed him a face that most of the world never saw: a victorious little smirk of a face that said, *See how I got the best of you and all I did was say three words.*

The troop re-formed itself. Veiko squared his shoulders, took a deep breath, thrust his lead marching leg into the air.

'Forward!'

From Nikko: 'Yes sir, Colonel Dog Prick!'

Not too loud.

Just loud enough.

An audible mumble particularly native to fifteen-year-olds – *you can choose to hear this or not hear it*, that's up to you. A harsh insult – *khuy sobachiy* – but by a great deal not the worst thing you could say in a language that provided its user with a vast range of oath and invective. It was a small dog, the phrase suggested, but an excited one – dancing on its hind legs in expectation of affection or table scraps.

Veiko chose to hear it. Stopped the troop. Backed up until he was even with Nikko and, in the same motion, swept his hand backward across Nikko's face. It didn't hurt. It wasn't meant to hurt. It was the blow of a tenor striking a waiter, and it was meant simply to demonstrate the proposition *I am someone who can slap your face.*

Veiko returned the hand halfway, to a point in line with Nikko's nose, pointed with an index finger, and shook it firmly twice. Lifted his eyebrows, raised his chin. Meaning *Naughty boy, see what happens when you curse your betters*?

Nikko let him have it.

He could toss a hundred-pound sack of fish onto his shoulder. The shot was open-handed and loud and the force surprised even Nikko. The feathered cap flew off and Veiko staggered back a step. He stood absolutely still for a long moment, the red and white image of a hand blooming on his cheek.

Both brothers went down under the first rush.

There were no shouted commands or battle cries; it was

21

an instinctive reaction, blind and furious, and it no longer had anything to do with military formations or political slogans. It had become entirely Vidin business, Bulgarian business, *Balkan* business.

There was an initial rain of blows, ineffective flailing punches that hit the Stoianevs, the ground, other troopers. Khristo's mind cleared quickly; he tried to curl into a ball, tried to protect head and groin, but he could barely move. There were five or six of them on top of him, and it was a lot of weight. He could smell them. Licorice *mastica*, garlic, boiled cabbage, bad fish, bad teeth, uniforms sweated and dried and sweated again. He could hear them. Grunting, panting, soon enough gasping for breath. Khristo was a moderately experienced fighter – in Vidin it was inevitable – and knew that street fights burned themselves out quickly. He did not thrash or punch. Let them get it out of their system.

Nikko was fighting. He could hear it – his brother cursing, somebody's cry of pain, somebody yelling, 'Get his head!' Damn Nikko. His crazy boiling temper. Punching walls when he got mad. Damn his wise-guy face and his fast mouth. And damn, Khristo thought, turning his attention to his own plight, this fat, sweaty fool who was sitting on his chest, trying to bang his head against the cobblestones. In just about two seconds he was going to do something about it – dig an elbow into fat boy's throat, drive it in, give him a taste.

Then Nikko screamed. Somebody had hurt him, the sound cut Khristo's heart. The street froze, suddenly it was dead quiet. Then, Veiko's voice, high and quivering with exertion, breath so blown that it was very nearly a whisper: 'Put that one on his feet.'

For the first time, real fear touched him. What should have been over was not over. In Khristo's world, brawls flared and ended, honour satisfied. Everybody went off and bragged. But in Veiko's voice there was nothing of that.

They hauled him to his feet and they made him watch

what they did next. It was very important to them that it be done that way. There were four or five of them clustered around Nikko, who lay curled around himself at their feet, and they were kicking him. They kicked as hard as they could and grunted with the strain. Khristo twisted and thrashed but they had him by the arms and legs and he couldn't break free, though he ground his teeth with the effort. Then he ceased struggling and pleaded with them to stop. Really pleaded. But they didn't stop. Not for a long time. At the last, he tried to turn his face away but they grabbed him under the chin and forced his head toward what was happening and then he could only shut his eyes. There was no way, however, that he could keep from hearing it.

The moon was well up by the time Khristo reached home. A shack by the river, garden vines climbing along a stake fence and up over the low roof. With Nikko on his shoulder, a long night of walking. He'd had to stop many times. It was cold, the wind had dried the tears on his face.

The uniformed men had left in a silent group. Khristo had stood over his brother's body. He'd felt for a pulse, out of duty, but he knew he need not have done it. He'd seen death before and he knew what it meant when a body lay with all the angles bent wrong. He had knelt and, slowly and carefully, with the tail of his shirt, had cleaned his brother's face. Then he took him home.

Where the dirt road turned into his house, the dogs started barking. The door opened, and he saw his father's silhouette in the doorway.

*   *   *

The Russian, Antipin, came a few weeks later.

Like the odd little man from Germany in the mint-coloured overcoat, he came on the river. But, the local wise men noted quietly, there were interesting differences in the manner of his coming. The German had arrived by

23

river steamer, with a movie projector and a steel trunk full of film cans and pamphlets. The Russian rowed in, on a small fishing skiff, tying up to one of the sagging pole-built docks that lined the river. The German was an older man, balding, with skin like parchment and a long thin nose. The Russian was a young man, a Slav, square-faced and solid, with neatly combed brown hair. The German had to use German-speaking National Union members to translate for him. The Russian spoke idiomatic Bulgarian – at least he tried – and they could understand his Russian well enough. All along the river, the Slavs could speak to each other without great difficulty.

The German arrived as a German, and his arrival was honoured. The postman's chubby daughter waited at the dockside with a basket of fruit. There had been a banquet, with speeches and copious brandy. The Russian said, at first, that he was a Bulgarian. Nobody really believed him. Then a rumour went around that he was a Czech. Because it was a rumour, there were naturally some who believed it. Somehow there was confusion, and the Russian-Bulgarian-Czech, whatever the hell he was, wasn't much seen around the town. To a few people, the Stoianevs among them, he admitted that he was a Russian and that his name was Antipin. Vassily Dmitrievich. The falsehoods were a *gesture*, he explained, *not serious*, necessitated by the *current situation*.

The German smoked a cigar every night after dinner. It looked peculiar, outsized, in his thin weasel's face. The Russian rolled and smoked cigarettes of *makhorka*, black Russian tobacco, earthy-smelling weed grown in the valleys of the Caucasus mountains. He was generous with it, offering constantly. Poor stuff, it was true. But what he had he shared, and this was noticed.

Of all the points of difference that distinguished the two visitors, however, there was one that absorbed the coffeehouse philosophers a great deal more than any other:

The German came from the west.

The Russian came from the east.

The German came downriver from Passau, on the German side of the Austrian border. The Russian came upriver from Izmail, in Soviet Bessarabia, having first sailed by steamer from the Black Sea port of Odessa.

And, really, the local wise men said, there you had it. That was the root of it, all right, that great poxed whore of a river that ran by every front door in the Balkans. Well, in a manner of speaking. It had brought them grief and fury, iron and fire, hangmen and tax collectors. Somewhere, surely, it was proposed, there were men and women who loved their river, were happy and peaceful upon its banks, perhaps, even, prayed to its watery gods and thanked them nightly.

Who could know? Surely it was possible, and it was much in their experience that that which was possible would, sooner or later, get around to happening. Fate had laws, they'd learned all too well, and that was one of them.

And it was their fate to live on *this* river. It was their fate that some rivers drew conquerors much as corpses drew flies – and the metaphor was greatly to the point, was it not. Thus it was their fate to be conquered, to live as slaves. That was the truth of it, why call it something else? And, as slaves, to have the worst slaves' luck of all: changing masters.

For who in history had not tried it? Put another way: if they had not tried it, their place in history was soon given over to the next applicant. Every schoolchild had to learn the spellings, for their national history was written in the names of their conquerors. Sesostris the Egyptian and Darius the Persian, remote bearded figures. Alexander the Great – one of their own, a smart Macedonian lad, a very demon for the love of a fight like they all were down there, a hundred miles south in what they called the *dark* Balkans. With reason. Charlemagne came through this

25

way, and so did Arpád the Hungarian. (Magyars! A curse on their blood!) Genghis Khan, with his Tatar armies, who believed that babies grew up to be soldiers and that women were the makers of soldier-babies. And acted accordingly. The Romans had come down on rafts, after Dacian gold. The legions of Napoleon were stopped some way upstream. (What? A disaster avoided? Oh how we will pay for *that*.) And at last, the worst. The Turks.

As love can be true love, or something short of it, hatred too has its shadings, and the Turk had stirred their passions like none of the others. It was the Turk who earned the time-honoured description: 'They prayed like hyenas, fought like foxes, and stank like wolves.' The Turk who decreed that no building in the empire could be higher than a Turk on horseback. The Turks who, when they were fed up with local governors, simply sent them a silken strangling cord and had them manage the business for themselves. Now there was a condition of stale palate that a man could envy! Even murder, apparently, would with time and repetition produce a state of listless ennui.

In 1908, after three hundred years of the Ottoman Empire, the Turks withdrew, leaving, alas, only a minor cultural legacy: bastinado, the whipping of bare feet; pederasty, the notion of sheep-herding mountain youths agitated even the pashas' burned-out lusts; and the bribery of all high persons as a matter of natural law. The first two faded quickly from life in Vidin, though the latter, of course, remained. The local wise men would have been astonished to discover people who did not know that greed far exceeded sadism and lechery in the succession of human vice.

The mosques were turned into Eastern Orthodox churches, the minarets painted pale green and mustard yellow, and the people of Vidin were free. More or less. By 1934, the Bulgarian people had enjoyed twenty-six years of freedom over the course of three centuries – if you didn't count military dictatorships. A sad record, one had to admit, but

God had set them down in a paradise with open doors front and back – the great river. Open doors encouraged thieves of the worst kind, the kind that came to live in your house. And when the thieves stole away, to whatever devil's backside had spawned them, they left something of themselves behind.

For historical custom dictated that conquest be celebrated between the legs of the local women, and each succeeding conqueror had added a river of fresh genes to the local population. Thus they asked themselves, sometimes, in the coffeehouse: Who are we? They were Bulgars, a Turco-Tatar people from the southern steppe, chased down here in the sixth century by invading Slavs from the north. But they were also Slav and Vlach, Turkish, Circassian and Gypsy. Greek, Roman, Mongol, Tatar. Some had the straight black hair of the Asian steppe, others the blue eyes of the Russo-Slav. 'And soon,' a local wit remarked, gesturing with his eyes toward the river steamer that had brought the German, 'we will be blond.'

It was remarked, by others there, that he spoke very quietly.

As did Antipin.

In the evenings, in the melancholy dusks of autumn when small rains dappled the surface of the river and storks huddled in their nests in the alder grove, he would roll his *makhorka* into cigarettes and pass them about, so that blue clouds of smoke cut the fish-laden air of the dockside bars. He was, they discovered, a great listener.

There was something patient in Antipin; he heard you out and, when you finished, he continued listening. Waiting, it seemed. For it often turned out that you only thought you were finished, there was more to say, and Antipin seemed to know it before you did. Remarkable, really. And his sympathy seemed inexhaustible, something in his demeanour absorbed the pain and the anger and gave you back a tiny spark of hope. *This is being writ down,* his eyes seemed to say, *for future remedy.*

27

At times he spoke, some evenings more than others. Said things out loud that many of them literally did not dare to think, lest some secret police sorcerer divine their blasphemies. Antipin was fearless. What were dark and secret passions to them seemed to him merely words that required saying. Thus it was he who spoke of their lifelong agonies: landlords, moneylenders, the men who bought their fish and squeezed them on the price. It seemed he was willing to challenge the gods, quite openly, without looking over his shoulder for the inevitable lightning bolt.

'To them you are animals,' he said. 'When you are fat, your time has come.'

'But we are men,' a fisherman answered, 'not animals. Equal in the eyes of God.' He was an old man with a yellowed moustache.

Antipin waited. The silence in the smoky room was broken only by the steady drip of water from the eaves above the window. The café was in the house of one of the fishermen's widows. After her husband drowned, people stopped by for a fruit brandy or a *mastica* at the kitchen table. Somehow, the condolence visits never quite ceased, and in time the widow's house became a place where men gathered in the evenings for a drink and a conversation.

Finally, the fisherman spoke again: 'We have our pride, which all the world knows, and no one can take it from us.'

Antipin nodded agreement slowly, a witness who saw the truth in what others said. 'All people must have pride,' he answered after a time, 'but it is a lean meal.' He looked up from the plank table. 'And they can take it from you. They can put you on your knees when it is to their purpose to do so. Your house belongs to the landowner. The fish you catch belongs to the men who buy it from you. The little coins buried in your dooryard belong to the tax collectors. And if they take them from you, you will get nothing back. These people do with you as they wish. They always have, and it will continue in this way until you stop it.'

28

'So you say,' the fisherman answered. 'But you are not from here.'

'No,' Antipin said, 'I am not from this town. But where I come from they fucked us no less.'

'We are taught,' the fisherman said after a while, 'that such things – such things as have been done elsewhere – are against our Lord Jesus Christ.'

'Perhaps they are right.' Antipin's face was that of a man who acceded to superior logic. 'When they come to take you away, you must remember to call for the priest.'

At this, a few people chuckled. Someone at the back of the room called out dramatically, 'Father Stepan, come quick and help us!' A hoot of laughter answered him.

'A grand day,' another man said, 'when the capon runs to save the cock!'

Antipin smiled. When it grew quiet again, the fisherman said, 'You may laugh while you can. When you are older, perhaps you will see things in a different light.'

The man sitting next to Antipin bristled. 'I'll go to meet God on my own two feet, not on my knees,' he said. 'Besides,' he added, slightly conciliatory, 'there can be nothing wrong with a little laughter.'

'There can be.'

It was said plainly, from where Khristo sat on the edge of a table facing Antipin's end of the room.

'It is a step,' Antipin said, 'to laugh at them. The holy fathers in their expensive robes, the king, the officers. But it is only the first step. We have a proverb . . .'

But they were not to hear the proverb. What stopped Antipin in midsentence was a series of loud bangs against the wood of the door frame on the exterior of the house. A puzzling sort of sound – a pistol shot would have had them all up and moving – everyone just looked up and sat still. A moment later they were on their feet. Glass shattered out of the room's single window – a glittering shower followed by an iron bar, which swung back and forth to finish the job, hammering against the interior of

29

the frame. The men in the café stood transfixed, every eye on the window. The iron bar withdrew. There was a shout outside, something angry but indecipherable, then a glass jug was thrown into the room. It was filled with a brownish-yellow liquid that plumed into the air as the jug rotated in flight. It broke in three when it landed and the liquid flowed slowly across the floorboards in a small river. Stove oil – the reek of it filled the room. The men found their voices, angry, tense, but subdued, as though to conceal their presence. From without, a cry of triumph, and a blazing torch of pitch-coated rope hurled through the window. The fire caught in two stages. First, small flames flickered at the edges of the oily river. Then an orange ball of flame roared into the air with a sigh like a puff of wind.

The earlier banging sound now began to make sense, as several men thrust their weight against the door but could not open it. It had been nailed and boarded shut from outside. The intention was to burn them to death inside the widow's café.

The man near Antipin who, moments earlier, had made clever remarks, leaped into the air and screamed as the fire exploded. Seeing the mob of men shoving and cursing at the door, he rushed to the window and started to clamber through, without heed to the long shards of glass hanging from the frame. The iron bar, swung at full force, hit him across the forehead, and he collapsed over the sill like a dropped puppet.

Khristo Stoianev stood quietly, resisting the panic inside him. His eyes swept about the room, to the door and the press of bodies in front of it, to the smashed window, trying to choose. Before he could move in either direction, a hand took him above the elbow, a hard grip that hurt. It was Antipin, face completely without expression. 'A cold cellar. There must be one,' he said softly.

'Where she cooks.' Khristo nodded toward the kitchen

30

area, separated from the main room by a sagging drape on a cord.

'Come then,' Antipin said.

They brushed the drape aside. There was an old black wood stove, a rickety table, a bent-twig crucifix on the wall. A bin where potatoes and onions were stored through the winter. In order to circulate the air and keep the food from rotting, a square had been cut in the wall, then covered with a metal screen to keep the rats out. In winter, a piece of cardboard was hung over it on a nail to keep out the worst of the cold.

The widow, on hands and knees, was in the act of crawling through the broken-out screen of the narrow square. She disappeared suddenly, with a little cry, and they could see the night outside.

Antipin stopped him with a hand on the chest. 'Let us see if there is a surprise planned. Wait for me to go through, then shout for the others.'

He was a square block of a man, but he moved like a monkey. Grabbing the upper edge of the frame with both hands, he swung out feet first. A few moments later, his face appeared.

'It's safe,' he said.

Khristo moved toward the window, grasped the frame as Antipin had. Antipin raised a palm. 'The others,' he said. Khristo shouted, heard a thunder of footsteps behind him, then went through. He landed on the side of the house facing the river, away from the dirt road.

Antipin peered cautiously around the side of the house, then waved for Khristo to follow him. Up by the road, a group of silhouettes stood beside a farmer's open-bed truck. The shapes were silent, moving restlessly, pacing, turning to one another. In the darkness, Khristo could not see details — faces or clothing. One man detached himself from the crowd and walked slowly down the hill, toward the house.

Antipin, meanwhile, pulled the board away from the

door and a group of coughing men came out in swirls of smoke and cinders. It was not difficult to jerk the nails from the wood, a kick from within would have done it, but the board had been cleverly positioned, across the knob, so that kicks against the door were ineffectual, and no one had thought to kick at the knob, an awkward target.

Khristo watched as the board was worked free of the door. It took him a moment to understand the device, it was too simple. But, when he did understand, something in the knowledge turned his stomach. Somebody, somewhere, in appearance a man like himself, had thought this method through. Had studied the problem: how to obstruct a door when setting fire to a house full of people so that those within could not escape, and had found a solution, and applied it. That there were those in the world who would study such things Khristo Stoianev had never understood. Now he did.

The man coming down the hill was Khosov the Policeman, brother of Khosov the Postman who kept the rhythm for the National Union parades. He was a policeman because no one had known what else to do with him. He was a man whose mouth never closed, who stared dreamily around him, seemingly amazed at a world full of ordinary things. He was slow. Everything had to be figured out. But when he did figure it out – and eventually he always did, especially if there was somebody around to help him – he could be swept away by a blind, insentient rage. At one time he had been much persecuted by children, until he beat one little boy very nearly to death with a broom handle.

The men stood around and watched the house burn. There was nothing to be done about it. A few buckets of water were tossed on neighbouring roofs, to protect the dry reeds from embers floating through the night air. The widow knotted her hands in the binding of her apron and held it in her mouth while she wept, her wet cheeks shining in the firelight. The men around her were silent. They had

32

brought a disaster down on her, and there was nothing to be done about that either.

Policeman Khosov came down the hill and stopped ten feet from Antipin. His eyes searched the crowd carefully; one had better not make a mistake here, as one's fellows watched from the road above. They were counting on him, trusted him to go it alone; he wasn't going to – not if he had to stand here all night – let them down.

One to another, each in turn, he peered at them, his face knotted with concentration, sweat standing on his brow with the effort of it, mouth open as always. Even though it might be you he sought, the sheer agony of the process made you want to help him.

Finally, he discovered Antipin, his eyes widening with the amazement of having got it right. He pointed with his arm fully extended, like an orator.

'You,' he said. 'You, communist, come with me now.' His other hand rested on the butt of a large revolver in a holster.

Antipin made no move. There was a long silence, the fire crackling and popping as the dry roof timbers caught.

'Did you hear me?'

Antipin took a step forward, inclined his head toward Khosov and said, 'What did you say?'

'I said come with me. No trouble, now.'

Antipin took another step. The fire played shadows on his back. He spoke very slowly, as to a child. 'Go back up this hill, you braying ass, and tell your friends up there that their mouths will be full of dirt. Can you remember that?' The 'mouths full of dirt' referred to events in the grave.

They watched Khosov's face. Watched the slow painful process as the information was worked at, disassembled, examined. When comprehension arrived, his hand tightened on the butt of the pistol but it was much too late.

Antipin flowed easily through the space between them and punched Khosov in the heart, a downward motion, as though his balled fist were a hammer. It blew the breath from Khosov's mouth and made him sit down and wrap his arms around his chest. Antipin leaned over and took the revolver from the holster and smashed it to pieces on a rock. Khosov groaned, then hunched over, struggling to breathe. Antipin reached down and put two fingers inside his nostrils and jerked his head upright. Khosov gave a shrill little cry like a hurt animal.

'Now you go up there and tell them what I said. That they shall eat the dirt.'

Antipin let him go and he managed to stand up, still gasping for air. Blood ran freely from his nose and he tried to stop it with his hand. He gave Antipin one terrified glance – this is a thing that makes pain, stay away from it always – then turned and scrabbled up the hill, holding his nose, head turtled down between his shoulders like a child running away from a beating.

Khristo watched him go, then turned to look at the men around him, illuminated by the light of the burning house. They coughed and spat, trying to get the smoke out of themselves. Someone had dragged the man from the windowsill where he had fallen and laid his smoking body on the ground. He had been burned black in the fire, but those who had heard the sound of the iron bar knew he had been beyond feeling anything at all. Up on the road, the group of silhouettes shifted nervously as Khosov the Policeman scurried toward them.

Khristo sensed clearly that this was not the end of it, that it would go on, that each act would become a debt to be repaid with interest. Nikko's death had seemed to him, to his family, a tragedy of bad fate – like a drowning, or a mother taken at childbirth. You had to live with death, God gave you no choice. Today it was your turn, tomorrow it would touch your neighbour; thus people gathered around you, held you up with their spirit, tried to fill the empty place. He now understood that Nikko's death was a tragedy of a different kind. It was part of something else; there was a connection, a design, at first faint, now much clearer.

The unknown intelligence that conceived a method of blocking doors could also see a purpose in the murder of a fifteen-year-old for laughing at a parade.

As Khosov climbed toward the road, a man near Khristo said, 'We had better stand together here.'

The old fisherman took a step back. 'I am no part of this.'

'Go home then,' someone said. 'They know where you live.'

'I do not oppose them. I will tell them that.'

'Then there will be no problem,' the man said, a sour irony in his voice.

On the road, Khosov and the others climbed onto the back of the truck, which stuttered to life and bounced away down the dirt road.

Khristo found Antipin at his shoulder. 'Come with me,' the Russian said. 'Let us take a little walk together.'

They walked down to the river, past the sagging pole docks, to the sand beach below the walls of the old fort, called Baba Vida – Grandma Vida – built by the Turks three hundred years earlier, though some of the inner walls had blocks set by Greek and Roman hands.

It was well after midnight, a stiff breeze blew off the river, they could just make out the dark bulk of the Romanian shore on the other side. Antipin rolled two cigarettes and gave one to Khristo, lit a wooden match with his thumbnail. They bent toward each other to protect the flame from the wind. Their cigarettes glowed in the darkness as they walked along the beach.

'You understand, do you not,' Antipin said, 'that they meant for me to kill him.'

'Who?'

'The policeman.'

'Khosov?'

'If that's his name.'

'Why?'

'Why. To create an incident, to make politics, to give their

35

newspapers something to say: bloody-fanged Bolshevik murders local policeman. Yes?'

Khristo thought about it for a time. He understood it, but it seemed very strange. Events occurred, newspaper stories were written. That the sequence could be staged – events made to happen *so that* stories would be written – had simply never crossed his mind.

'The murder was their alternative, a second scheme to try in case their first one failed.'

Khristo squinted with concentration. The world Antipin was describing seemed obscure and alien, a place to be explained by an astrologer or a magician. Violence he knew, but this was a spider web.

'You see,' he continued, 'they meant for all of us to die in that house. An accident, they would say. Those pigs were swilling brandy and some lout knocked over an oil lamp and whoosh, there it went and too bad. But you see, Khristo Nicolaievich, I repeat only their words. And words may be spoken in different ways. Their fine faces would tell a much different story. The wink, the sly look, the flick of a finger that chases a fly, would give those words quite another meaning. *We burnt them up*, they would say, with pride in their eyes. That's how it is, boys. We take care of our own problems around here. We don't go crying to the *politsiya*. We see something wrong – we go ahead and fix it.'

Khristo nodded silently. Veiko, the others, were like that.

'So, you can see how it works? They had the policeman ready in case we got out of the house. Sent him down to arrest me. Knew very well he was too stupid to manage it. A simple provocation. Right?'

'Right.'

'You are a thinker, that I can tell. You turn the world over in your mind to see if it is truly round.'

Khristo was both flattered and a little uncomfortable to be addressed in this way. One didn't hear compliments.

He took a drag at his cigarette, feeling very much the man. There was something so admirable about Antipin. The local toughs were blowhards, dangerous only in a group. Antipin was strong in another way entirely, he had an assurance, carried himself like a man who owned the ground wherever he stood. The notion that he, son of a fisherman in a little town at the end of the world, could win the respect of such a man was definitely something to be thought about.

'I try to understand things,' he answered cautiously. 'It is important that people understand' – here he got lost – 'things,' he finished, feeling like a bird with one wing.

'Naturally,' Antipin said. 'So you see their intention. Get rid of a problem, let everybody here and about know you got rid of it, and perhaps others will not be so quick to cause problems. Bravery is a quirky thing at best – you know the old saying about brave men?'

'All brave men are in prison?'

'Just so. We have it a little differently – all brave men have seen heaven through bars – but the thought is almost the same.' He was quiet for a time. Somewhere out on the river, in the distance, was the sound of a foghorn. When he spoke again, his voice was sad and quiet. 'We Slavs have suffered. God knows how we have suffered. In the West, they say we cannot be bothered to count our dead. But we have learned about human nature. We paid a terrible price to learn it, because you must see desperation before you can understand how humans truly are. Then you know. Lessons learned in that way are not forgotten. Do you see this?'

He paused a moment, then continued. 'I will tell you a story. When Catherine was empress of Russia – you'll remember, she was the one who fucked horses – she chanced to be wandering one day in a wood some distance from St. Petersburg and found a beautiful wildflower. She was enraptured by it, such a tiny, perfect thing, and so she decreed right then and there that a soldier be assigned to

37

guard the spot just in case, in future days, it should bloom again. Eighteen years later, someone chanced to find that order in a file and went out there, and there was a soldier guarding a spot in the forest, in case a wildflower might bloom, in case, if it did bloom, some shitfoot of a peasant might come along and stomp on it – as if he had nothing better to do.'

Khristo was properly silent for a moment; he loved and respected a story like little else. Antipin bent to the sand, put his cigarette out, slipped the remnant in his pocket.

'Was the flower grown? When they went there the second time?'

'The story does not say. I like to think it wasn't. But the point has to do with being ruled. Being someone else's property. Fifty years ago the landlords owned their serfs, hundreds of them, to do with as they pleased. They would marry them off, one to another, to please their wives' romantic fantasies. We love dolls in Russia, Khristo Nicolaievich, it helps us remember our past.'

'Perhaps it was like that here too,' Khristo said. 'When the Turks ruled us.'

'The Turk still rules you, my friend, except that he has taken off the fez and put on a crown. Czar Boris, your king calls himself. Czar! And he is the toy of the army and the fascist officers' clique that calls itself *Zveno*, the chain link. You are young, and have lived a natural life on this river, perhaps you don't yet understand how these bastards work. You see Veiko and his little army, and you know them for what they are – bullies, drunken piss-bags out for a good time. But when there is fertile political soil, your Veiko will soon be a towering tree. As things stand now, he is the future of this country.'

He paused a moment, cleared his throat. 'Forgive me, there is a demon in me that demands to make speeches. Let me tell you, instead, what will happen here. Your brother

38

died at the hands of swine, and nothing was done. Nothing will be done.'

Khristo's heart sank. A thousand times he had wished that that night could be lived over again, that he could take Nikko by the scruff of the neck, as a wise older brother should have, and haul him away from the ridiculous parade. He had loved his brother well enough, his death was a piece torn away from his own life, but there was more than that. The sorrow of the family had lodged in his father, and he suspected, no, he knew, that his father blamed him for it.

'Do not feel shame,' Antipin said quietly, reading his mood. 'It was not your fault, no matter what you think. You should not blame yourself. I do not grant absolution, I am not a priest. But it is history that I understand, and this thing had to happen. It was *meant* to happen. That it happened to you, to your brother, is sorrowful but you will someday see that it was inevitable. The important thing is this: what will you do now?'

'I don't know.' His voice sounded small. They had reached the end of the beach and stood for a time, the Turkish fortress looming above them, the river running quietly along the sand, white foam visible in the darkness.

'I will presume,' Antipin said, 'to jump history a pace and I will tell you what to do. Do not waste your time with grief. It is a great flaw in our character, our Slavic nature, to do that. We are afflicted with a darkness of the soul and fall in love with our pain.'

'What then?'

'Come with me. East.' Antipin nodded his head down-river.

His eyes followed Antipin's gesture into the darkness, toward the East. His stomach fluttered at the idea of such a journey, as though he had been invited to step off the edge of the world.

39

'Me?' he said.

'Yes.'

'Why?' In wonder.

'Here, in this town, it will go on. You will not survive it. They murdered your brother; they must now presume you to be their mortal enemy, very troubling to keep an eye on. As the eldest brother, responsibility to even the score rests with you. With me or without me, Khristo Nicolaievich, you must go away. You may very well save your family's life, you will certainly save your own.'

Khristo had not meant *why go*. He had meant *why me*. But Antipin had answered the wrong question the right way. It would happen like the old feuds – one of mine, one of yours, until only one stood. Since Nikko's death he had hidden this from himself but it festered within him. Now it had been said aloud and a weight fell away.

'Come with me,' Antipin said, 'and I will teach you something. I will teach you how to hurt them. Hurt them in ways that they do not begin to understand, hurt them so that they cry for mercy, which, by then, I think you will not grant. Your country has a sickness. We know the sickness well because we were once its victims, and we know how to cure it. We have taught others, we can teach you. You yearn to see the world, to move among men, to do things that matter. I was as you are now. A peasant. I sought the world. Because the alternative was to spend the rest of my life looking up a ploughhorse's backside. Come with me, my friend, it is a chance at life. This river goes many places, it does not stop in Vidin.'

Khristo's heart rose like the sun. These were words he had waited all his life to hear without realizing, until now, that he waited. The river, he knew from hours of droning in the dusty schoolhouse, did not stop in Vidin. It rose in Germany, its legendary source a stone basin in the courtyard of a castle of the Fürstenberg princes in the Black Forest. Called the Donau by all German-speaking peoples, it moved through the Bohemian forests to Vienna, crossed into Czechoslovakia at Bratislava, where they named it the Dunaj, turned south through the Carpathians into northern Hungary, divided the twin cities of Buda and Pesth, flowed south into Yugoslavian Serbia, passed Belgrade at the confluence of the river Sava, known now as the Duna, roared through the Iron Gate – a narrow gorge in the Transylvanian Alps – and headed east, serving as a border between Romania and Bulgaria, where it was called Dunărea to the north and Dunav to the south. Then, at last, it turned north for a time and split into three streams entering the Romanian delta, snaking through the marshes to Izmail, Sulina, and Sfîntu Gheorghe, where it emptied into the Black Sea, bordered by the Russian Crimea and Turkey, where the Caucasus mountains ran down to the sea, where Europe ended and Asia began.

'Well,' Antipin said, 'how shall it be?'

'I . . .' He was not sure how to say it. 'I do not think I am a communist.'

Antipin dismissed that wordlessly, throwing it away on the wind with a broad flip of the hand.

'Does it not matter?'

'You are a patriot. That matters. You are not our enemy. That too matters. Some day, we may convince you to be our true friend. All we ask is opportunity.'

They turned and walked back along the sand toward the town, where it was quiet and dark. *So there will be cities*, Khristo said silently, talking to his destiny. He had argued with it, prayed to it – to him it was a live presence, which might or might not heed petitions and curses, but one had to try – damned or praised it depending on what it did with him. Oh but what a trickster it was, this sly eel of a fate that wiggled his life about. He had yearned for Vienna or – someone had to find treasure,

41

else why ever look – Paris. Now he rather thought it
would be Moscow. Turn around then, and face east.
Nothing new in this country. Still, a city. Golden onion
domes, elegant buildings, people who read books and
talked into the night of important things. Like Antipin,
they would understand and appreciate him, encourage
him. His imagination dined on caviar and inhaled the
perfume of the one who sat across the table yet leaned
so close.

'When?' he said.

'Tomorrow,' Antipin said. 'They are done for tonight,
except for the drinking and the singing. Tomorrow is soon
enough.'

What few things he had, Khristo tossed onto a blanket
in a small pile, then he tied the corners together in
a thick knot. At dawn, it started to rain hard, little
streamlets poured off the roof and dripped from the
grapevine that grew above the kitchen window. They
drank tea and ate what remained of yesterday's bread.
His mother embraced him, kissed him on both cheeks,
gave him a smile of love to travel on. His father looked
at him for a long moment, from another world, then
patted his shoulder – as though he would be back in
a few hours – and plodded off toward the docks, walking head down in the rain. His sister, Helena, whose
black hair and fierce blue eyes made her nearly his
twin, reached across the table and touched his face. He
went out into the yard and looked around for the last
time. Helena ran out of the house and took him hard
by the arms. 'This is for the best,' she said, the rain
running down her face, 'but you must not forget we
are here.' He could see she was afraid. 'Promise,' she
said. He promised. She went back into the house and
he left.

* * *

42

At the squatty police station, a yellow building no higher than a Turk on horseback, the old fisherman showed up early and stood solemnly in a corner – one did not sit down and wait for the captain. He had lain awake all night, alternately cursing his luck and praying for deliverance. He had been in the wrong place at the wrong time with the wrong people. He had determined to make a clean breast of it, the authorities would have no question about where *he* stood. At last he was ushered into the captain's office. A hangdog Khosov sat open-mouthed on a chair in the corner, like a bad boy at school. The remains of his pistol were gathered on the edge of the captain's desk. There was, the old man announced, treason afoot, and he would have no more of it. There was a Russian loose in Vidin, spouting revolution and atheism in the cafés. He was prepared to tell them all he knew.

His understanding of the official methodology in such instances was woefully inadequate – 'all he knew' wasn't enough. They'd known of the Russian for a week – such heresies came quickly to the attention of the local gods – and had wired Sofia to find out what to do about him. Though the country was ruled by Czar Boris and his army officers and the future was clear to those with the stomach to see it, foreign policy was ephemeral, and it was hard to know where to put your foot. Russia might be characterized as a wicked beast of a nation, but it was a very large beast, and sometimes it thrashed its tail. Thus, to date, the central administration in Sofia had been silent. As for the old fisherman with the yellowed moustache, him they took down to the basement, to see whether such things as were done there might not stimulate his memory. Their efforts proved fertile and a few hours of it had him, in whatever remained of his voice, making every sort of denunciation. All of it was copied down. Later it was widely believed that it was he who had denounced the Stoianev family.

* * *

43

They moved downriver in the skiff, taken gently along by the current, rowing or poling from time to time, principally to keep warm. They'd rigged a waterproof groundcloth on four makeshift poles to keep the rain from falling directly on their heads, but autumn on the river demanded philosophical travellers – the drizzle often enough blew sideways, and there was every sort of dripping mist and fog. The river itself was wide here, often as much as a mile between shores, as it moved through the Walachian plain. The wheat harvest was long in, on sunny days farmers burned the yellow stubble and columns of thin smoke hung on the horizon. Now and again they would be passed by steam tugs pulling barges loaded down with sand, crushed rock, or timber.

On the Romanian side, there were occasional watch towers. Soldiers with slung rifles trained binoculars on them as they went by. On the Bulgarian shore, stands of oak and beech stood dark and silent. Antipin kept two fishing lines trailing from the stern, and patrol boats took them for fishermen. When the weather cleared, the river dawn was exquisite, a painting at first without colour, shapes in negative light. Then strands of pearl-coloured mist rose from the water, grey herons skimmed the surface, flocks of pelicans took off from the sandbars in midstream, and the hills turned blue, the birches white, the bare willows brown. It was a world of great stillness, and they instinctively spoke in undertones.

Antipin was no less a listener than he had ever been, and Khristo talked for hours. Mostly on the subject of Vidin and how life was there. Who was rich and who was poor. Lechery and drunkenness, religion and hard work, love and hate. It was like most places in the world, really, but Antipin sat and soaked the stories up with scrupulous attention. He was, Khristo came slowly to realize, learning it. On hearing the oft-told tale of Velchev's wife and the borrowed chamber pot, Antipin recalled that Velchev's wife was also Traicho's daughter. Extraordinary. He knew the names of the fascists, the agrarians, the intellectuals who had supported Stamboliiski and the Peasant party.

And he could, it seemed, do anything he turned his hand to and do it well. Cut wood shavings to start a fire, gut a fish, rig a shelter, steer the skiff around the gravel islands that dotted the river. If this was the world he was entering, Khristo thought, he would have to learn very quickly, but the challenge was not displeasing to him. He had been set apart, for the first time in his life, and felt that his fortunes had taken a sharp turn for the good.

They moved past Kozloduj, past Orehovo and Nikopol. Past Svištov, where the Bulgarian poet and patriot Aleko Konstantinov had been stabbed to death, where his pierced heart was exhibited in a small museum. Past the great city of Ruse, the grain port of Silistra. At the border, where the river flowed north into Romania, they pulled over and stopped at a customs shed. Antipin produced a Nansen passport in Khristo's name, with a blurry photograph of a young man who could have been anybody. The Romanian customs officer accepted a *makhorka* cigarette and waved them through. It was, to Khristo, simply one more rabbit from the hat, one more specimen from Antipin's collection of little miracles. He did wonder, once in a great while, what on earth made him worth such grand attentions, but these thoughts he put aside. There was enough of the East in him to take pleasure in the present moment and paint the future white.

Moscow knocked him virtually senseless.

They put him in a house – in pre-Revolutionary times the love nest of a wine merchant – on Arbat Street. But his training class was only just getting organized and they really didn't want to be bothered with him. He had no money, but that did not prevent him from walking, from experiencing, for the first time in his life, the streets of a city.

Winter had come early. The snow and the city swirled

45

around him and, at first, overwhelmed his mind. On the river he had drifted into the easy numbness of a long journey, a traveller's peace, wherein constant motion caused the world to slide by before it could make trouble. Thus he was unprepared for the city, and the sights and sounds drove themselves against his senses until he was giddy with exhaustion.

And though the Moscow of his dreams – grand boulevards, golden domes – was as he had imagined, it shared the stage with a riptide of ordinary life. For every glossy Zil or Pobeda that disgorged important-looking people into important buildings, there seemed to be ten carts pulled by horses: the carts piled high with coal or carrots, the horses' breath steaming from flared nostrils, the red-faced draymen drunk and cursing like maniacs. The streets were crowded with old women in black dresses and shawls, bearded Jews in black homburgs, Mongolian soldiers with flat, cold faces. He saw a woman knocked down by a trolley, a bad fight between two men armed with broken vodka bottles. He imagined he could smell the violence in the air, mixed in with horse manure, coal smoke, and fried grease. A huge, bald, fat fellow urinated at the base of a pensive – chin on fist – statue of Karl Marx. Some militiamen happened along and shouted at him to stop. When he didn't – he called out that he couldn't – they rushed at him. He swung a thick arm, knocked a couple of them sprawling, but the rest ganged him and beat him to the ground with wooden truncheons, then stood there smoking until a Stolypin car arrived to take him away. Khristo saw inside when they opened the door: two rows of white faces in the darkness.

Yet, a moment later, turning the corner into Arbat Street he saw, he was almost certain, a ballerina. His spirit swooped, that such glory could exist on earth. Her face, her whole presence, appeared to have been drawn with a needle-sharp pencil. Hard lines: jaw, cheek, eye, and the suggestion of firm leg beneath the supple skirt as she strode

46

along the street. The women of Vidin started working at the age of twelve and bore children at sixteen. The bloom shone briefly, then vanished. But this was a city and in a city, he reasoned, certain plants flowered in perpetuity. She was surrounded, as she moved along the sidewalk, by her personal theatre: the faces in the crowd that watched her, the borzoi on a thin silver chain that preceded her, and two fat little men in overcoats who toddled officiously behind her. Her eyes caught his own for a moment, then flicked away, but her face remained utterly still. Like a seashell, he thought.

Such treasures were to be worshipped by the eyes alone. Were meant to inspire poems; were surely not meant to be craved after in the ordinary, mortal ways. But, in Moscow, the ordinary mortal ways were, for comrade Khristo, not entirely neglected. Communism was the golden opportunity of the working classes – everyone must share – and the Russian winter was an endless horror of white ice and white sky, demonic, survivable only with the three traditional warmings: the vodka, the tile stove, and the human body. Marike was her name, said as though the *e* were an *a*.

She was a Moravian German from eastern Czechoslovakia, a descendant of one of the Teutonic colonies strung all across Eastern Europe, a nineteenth-century attempt, inspired by religion and empire, to alleviate the tragic lot of the Slav by means of energetic German example. See how large *my* cabbage grows! That it grows on land that used to belong to your uncle we shall not discuss.

At the first wash of her he turned entirely to stone. She blew at him like a wind. She was an intellectual, a Marxist. She was intense, all business. She sang like a dockworker, ran like a soldier, and argued like a drill. God help the man or woman who let a false lick of lumpen deviationism creep into his words – Marike would soon have it out, and with hot tongs at that. She had burned the mannerisms of the ass-licking bourgeoisie from her soul, now it was

47

your turn. There was to be no *diplomacy*, no *gentility*, no *sentiment*.

But the most astonishing aspect of this human storm was the package in which it was wrapped. Where was, one wondered, the dirndl? She had crinkly orange hair drawn back tight and tied with a red ribbon. She had a broad forehead, and a permanent blush to her cheeks. She was full-breasted and wide-hipped, with freckled white forearms that could throw a haybale through the side of a barn.

She boxed him on the bicep to get his attention – it was all he could do not to rub it. 'We are equals,' she said. 'This gives you no rights. Understand? Does not make you my master. Yes?'

Yes. They had stolen an hour on the coarse blanket of her bed in the women's section of the dormitory, where she'd hauled him off in accordance with the banner strung above the inside door of the entry hall:

БРАТСКИЙ ФРОНТ   34 г.,   ПРИВЕТСТВУЕМ!

Brotherhood Front of 1934, Welcome! It was Marike's idea to welcome him, just as it was her idea to bang on his bare back with her fists to urge him to a greater gallop. She chose him openly. Studied him, considered the genetics, the dialectics, the inevitability of history, then let her blue-veined breasts tumble out of her shirt before his widening eyes. Farewell Vidin, thou backwater. Hail to the new order, and if this belt does not come soon undone I shall rip it in half. He was, beneath it all, nineteen and alone and away from home for the first time in his life and he clasped her warm body like a life preserver, then proceeded to a happy drowning. A proletarian coupling, simple and direct, nothing fancy, and without precaution. Should a tiny artillery loader or fighter pilot chance to come tumbling out some months hence, he or she would be another soul pledged to revolution and glad of it. No dreamy slave of love, Marike closed her eyes only at the last, exhaled a huge purr of relief, then casually chucked him off. To work, it meant, enough of such frivolity, a hygienic relaxation had been achieved.

As the winter lay down on the city, harder and harder through the month of November, her appetite grew. They did it in the attic, where the May Day portraits of Lenin, colossal things coloured a vengeant Soviet red, were folded and stored. They did it behind the targets on the basement pistol range. They did it under the table in the kitchen while the cook snored asthmatically in the parlour. The pace and spirit of it never changed – a mad dash to the finish line, first one there wins, as though Revanchist Materialism waited just outside the door to gobble them up. He had heard, over the back fences in Vidin, that there were other paths through the woods, that one could also do this and that. But, on the one occasion when she was squiffed on Georgian brandy and he'd attempted to put theory into practice, his reward was a double whack on the ears. 'Get off your knees,' she said, 'that is an attitude of slavery!' So much for this and that, back to essentials. And the more they did it, the more aggressive she became in daily matters.

Over the salt herring at the long plank dinner table: 'Did you know that Dmitrov is in Moscow? I think I saw him coming out of the Rossaya Hotel.'

'Dmitrov?' Khristo looked at her questioningly over his fork.

'Oh no. This I refuse to believe. *Georgy* Dmitrov. The Bulgarian hero.'

He shrugged. Voluta, a lean-faced Pole with black hair swept back from a high forehead, coughed into his hand with embarrassment.

'Your very own countryman.' She shook her head, lips pressed in resignation at the utter futility of him.

Goldman, a young man from Bucharest, stepped in to save him. 'Dmitrov took part in the great patriotic burning of the Reichstag,' he said. 'His speech at the trial is to be learned in the schools. Now he is in Russia.'

'Oh,' Khristo said. 'Our newspapers lie about such things or neglect them entirely.' As he struggled to learn all the new ideas, he learned also to cover what Marike called his *political infantilism*.

Hitler's speech on that occasion was one of many statements typed on paper slips and tacked to the dormitory wall, waiting in ambush for the wandering eye of the daydreamer: 'This is a God-given signal. If, as I believe, the communists have done it, you are witnessing the beginning of a great new epoch in German history.' In Germany and in Russia, it became clear to Khristo, they were itching to go at it, there remained only the question of time and provocation.

Khristo struggled in his classes. English and French, an impossible snarl of alien noises. Political history and thought, a crosshatch of plots and counterplots, irredentist imperialism, Pan-Slavism, the sayings of Lenin, the revelations of Marx. The world was not as he'd thought.

Tides of confusion pulled at him, but he somehow remained afloat. He was now firmly established in the dormitory on Arbat Street, where he'd been given two blankets and one towel, introduced to a milling crowd of Serbs, Poles, Croatians, Jews, Slovenians and whatnot, forty souls in all, including eight women who had *their own sleeping quarters* – please take note, comrades. He had been handed a schedule of classes and a stack of books printed on mealy grey paper. Do not mark, others must use. Measured for a khaki uniform of heavy cotton. Poked and studied shamelessly by a large, frightening nurse. Drenched with kerosene in case of lice. Assigned a narrow cot between Voluta and Goldman. Told to learn the words to the songs by tomorrow morning, but the lights must be turned off at ten. Inside himself, Khristo was desolate. Not at all what he had expected. He had imagined himself as Antipin's assistant, just a bit important, we'll take him out dancing with us.

It was not to be. A white card outside the office door said

V. I. Ozunov. A bald man with a fringe of black hair, a brush of a black moustache, delicate gold-rim glasses and a dark, ferocious face, who wore the uniform of an army major. Khristo sat hypnotized as Ozunov reeled off a monotone of forbidden sins. The underlying message was writ large: we have you, boy. Now dance to this music. As for threats, we needn't bother, right?

'What has become of comrade Antipin?' Khristo asked, one try for bravery.

Ozunov smiled like a snake. 'Antipin was yesterday. Today is Ozunov.'

End of rebellion.

Yet as much as he struggled and sweated with the languages and the levantine webs of theory, there was one area in which he succeeded. He was, it turned out to his and everyone else's amazement, gifted in the craft.

It began with the affair of the knitting needles. Five students were taken to a classroom and seated around a scarred wooden table. The room stank of carbolic soap. Beads of condensation ran slowly down the fogged-up window, coloured a sickly white by the winter sky above the city.

Ozunov paced up and down and addressed the backs of their heads, his hands clasped behind him.

'On your desk are sealed envelopes. Do not touch them. Also a pair of knitting needles. Do not touch them, either. We presume you to know what they are, much as we presume that you have never used them.'

They laughed politely.

'Good, good. You are not old *babas* after all, though your degenerate love of prattle and gossip might lead one to think otherwise. I am relieved.'

He paced.

They waited.

'Voluta!'

The Pole jumped. 'Yes, Major Ozunov.'

'Turn the letter over. To whom is it addressed?'

51

'To the British ambassador, Major Ozunov.'

'A keen analysis, Voluta. Do we all agree?'

They turned their letters over. All were the same, they agreed.

'What might the envelope contain? Stoianev!'

'A plot?'

'Kerenyi?'

'The reports of spies.'

'Oh yes? Semmers, you agree?'

'Uhh, it is possible, comrade Major.'

'And so, Voluta?'

'A denunciation.'

'Goldman. Your opinion on this matter.'

'Perhaps a false denunciation.'

'Always the Romanian, eh Goldman? You see the complexity, the winding and twisting of political matters, I give you that. But then, could it not be a *false denunciation*? By *spies*? In Stoianev's *plot*? What about that? Or it could be the information, no shock to anyone around here, that Ozunov's students are a blithering pack of donkeys' behinds!' He finished with a shout.

He paced silently, his boots slapping the scrubbed wooden floor, and breathed with a fury. 'The point is, comrades, you don't know. Not such a difficult solution, is it? You don't know because the letter is sealed. It could be birthday greetings from the Belgian consul. It could be a love note from the stable boy. It could be anything. Now, how shall we discover this elusive truth?'

Kerenyi: 'Take the letter out and read it.'

'Brilliant! You shall now all do exactly that. When I give the word, you have ten minutes. Oh, by the way . . .' He stopped, leaned over Voluta and spoke in a conspiratorial whisper. 'Don't tear the envelope. We don't want the gentleman to know that someone is reading his mail. And here's a hint, little as any of you deserve it, use the knitting needles.'

For the next ten minutes, an intense flurry of effort.

52

Ozunov, of course, made it much worse by announcing 'thirty seconds gone' from time to time as they worked. To their credit, they kept at it long after hopeless frustration set in. They pried and poked and stabbed and wiggled at the envelopes. Voluta tried to force up the point of the flap and ripped a groove through the paper. Goldman, after a few moments of intense concentration, staring fixedly at the problem, determined that the knitting needles were a false technology, offered with the intention of misleading them, and picked at the thing with his fingernails. Semmers, with shaking hands, wounded himself in the palm and left red blots on the address. By the end of the ten-minute period, Kerenyi, a tow-headed boy from the Hungarian town of Esztergom, had letter and envelope in shreds and one of the knitting needles bent in a vee.

Khristo Stoianev held the letter in one hand, the envelope, still sealed, in the other. The letter read: *Meet at noon by Spassky Tower.*

Ozunov could feel his heart beating. It was the throb of the prospector finding golden flecks in an ordinary rock. What was this? A magnificent discovery, to be wrapped carefully and delivered, in all humility, to his superiors? Or something else. Something bad. Something very, very bad indeed. He began to sweat. Closed his eyes, reviewed the last few weeks in his mind.

Khristo had discovered the small, unsealed slit at the side of the envelope where the glue line ended. He had squeezed the envelope so that the slit bulged slightly; peering inside, he had seen the fold of the letter within. Carefully, he ran one needle inside the fold, then inserted the second needle between the top of the fold and the upper edge of the envelope flap so that the needles sandwiched the fold of the letter between them. With great patience, he began to rotate both needles, and soon the letter became a tube of paper with the needles at its core. When he had the whole letter, he drew it toward him through the slit.

Ozunov dismissed the others.

Stood in front of his desk. Folded his hands and tapped his thumbs together rapidly. From years of school, Khristo knew this situation intimately and it puzzled him. What had he done wrong? Clearly he had done *something*, they didn't push their glasses up on their foreheads and shut their eyes and pinch the bridges of their noses like that unless you had made a very great botch of it indeed.

'So, Stoianev, tell Uncle Vadim. We'll talk man to man. Yes?'

Uncle Vadim? He said nothing.

'Where did you learn it?'

'Just here. I, ah, it revealed itself. The solution.'

'A lie.'

'No, comrade Major, I must disagree with you.'

'You think me stupid?'

'No sir.'

'Do not use that form.'

'Beg pardon, comrade Major.'

'Do you know, Stoianev, what is done in the Lubianka? In the cellars? What they do with the hoses? It takes no time at all. You will confess that your mother is a wolf, that your father is a dragon, that you keep the czar's dick hidden in a Bible. You will confess that you fly through the air and consort with witches. You will tell them who taught you such tricks – when and where and what you had for dinner. You understand?'

'Yes, comrade Major. I learned it here, just now.'

'I give you one last chance: tell me the truth.'

'From the first moment, it seemed the obvious way.'

Ozunov took a deep breath and exhaled, dropped his gold-rim glasses and settled them on his nose. 'Very well,' he said, 'I must offer you my congratulations.' He thrust his hand forward and Khristo shook it once, formally. 'Now we are both dead men,' he added stoically, and gestured for Khristo to leave the room.

The news travelled. Everyone wanted to be his friend.

He found himself regaining some of what he had lost when abandoned by the admiring Antipin. Even Marike relented. Took his hand and led him down to the warm, dusty boiler room where, on a scratchy blanket, he received a Soviet Hero's reward.

In the following weeks, Major Ozunov himself began to thaw. Khristo and his comrades chased each other through the streets of Moscow. Following each other and being followed. Eluding their pursuers, checking their backs in shop windows, running dead-drops in the parks, brushing hands in fast passes in Krasnaya Presnya Park. At the militia station near the school, the lieutenant said, 'I see Ozunov is at it again.' Denunciations poured in from angry citizens. *I saw them pass an envelope, comrade, just as bold as brass in clear daylight. Foreigners, I'd say they were. And most brazen.* They were broken up into teams, competed in discovering and penetrating each other's operations. Semmers gave Goldman a bloody nose when he caught him stealing a master cipher. A baker reported that a group of hooligans had kidnapped a tall Polish fellow in his shop.

And Khristo won. And won again. It was Khristo's Red Star team that accepted the prize copy of Lenin's speeches. You could dodge through crowds, slither beneath a wagon, crouch down in a phalanx of cyclists, it did not seem to matter. You looked in the reflective shop window and there he was – just near enough, just far enough – doing something or other that made it seem he had lived on this street all his life. Twenty of them chased him into the Bylorussian railroad station on Tverskaya Street. Then, three hours later, trooped back to the dormitory empty-handed. To find Khristo waiting for them in the parlour, wearing a stiff-billed train conductor's cap. They knew him now for what he was, the best among them. They had seen it before, wherever they came from: the best in the classroom, the best on the soccer field, and they acknowledged his preeminence.

For his part, he learned to wear the star and honour

its responsibilities. He encouraged the slow learners, lent a secret hand to those arrayed against him in competitions, and dismissed his successes as pure luck. Major Ozunov, in the hearing of other students, called him Khristo Nicolaievich, which put a seal on his ascendancy. Inspired by all this attention, he even managed to learn a little French.

On the last day of December it snowed a blizzard and he was summoned to Ozunov's private office. Since dawn, kopeck-size snowflakes had drifted down the windless air. Through the major's leaded windows — his office had formerly been the master bedroom of the once grand house — Khristo watched the street whiten and fill.

Ozunov stuffed the bowl of a pipe with tobacco, then lit it carefully with a large wooden match. As the office filled with sweet thick smoke, the major produced a chessboard and pieces.

'Do you play, Khristo Nicolaievich?'

'Not really, comrade Major. In Vidin, there was no time to learn.'

'You know the moves, though. What each piece may do.'

'Of course I know that, comrade Major.'

'Good. Then let us try a game. What do you say?'

'I will do the best I can, comrade Major.'

'Mmm,' he said around the pipe stem, 'that's the proper spirit.'

He offered his closed fists: Khristo picked the left hand and played black.

He had learned the moves, back in Vidin, from Levitzky the tailor, who called it 'the Russian game'. Thus, the old man pointed out, the weak were sacrificed. The castles, fortresses, were obvious and basic; the bishops moved obliquely; the knights — an officer class — sought power in devious ways; the queen, second-in-command, was pure aggression; and the king, heart of it all, a helpless target, dependent totally on his forces for survival.

Khristo had virtually no inkling of strategy, but he resolved to be the best opponent he could. The object of the game, he knew, was not to slay the other king but to put the opponent in a position where he had no choice but to submit. He had overheard one of Vidin's more daring wits describe checkmate as 'all that Russian foot-kissing business'. Khristo's notion of a chess tactic was to sneak a pawn down one side of the board – hoping for a distracted or mortally unobservant foe – and quickly make it a queen. At heart, the strategy of checkers thrown in well over its head. Failing that, he liked to send his castles hurtling back and forth, up and down, in obvious but savage forays, hoping to shock a piece or two from his opponent. The knights he rarely used – they had a herky-jerky motion he distrusted: things shouldn't go straight and then cat-corner.

Ozunov attacked down the left side of the board, giving up two pawns, but pinning Khristo's castle down with a bishop. Khristo wasted two turns hip-hopping his queen around the pawn rank – stopping to take Ozunov's apparently suicidal pawns – for he liked it to have an unobstructed field of fire. Ozunov reacted to this provocation with apparent caution, breaking off his bishop's attack on the castle, drawing the piece back to safety. It was Khristo's theory that a succession of entirely random moves might startle the opponent, give him pause, make him think you had some obscure trick up your sleeve. Ozunov pondered the board, smoke curling upward from his pipe, chin resting on folded hands, intent once again on his own attack. So intent that Khristo had a little flurry of victories, took a pawn and a bishop with his galloping castle, made Ozunov move to defend his king. He seemed, somehow, to have taken the initiative. Perhaps he really could play. He stared out the white window, hypnotized by the slow drift of the snowflakes, then forced his attention back to the game – he could not allow Ozunov to see that his mind wandered. Where was Marike? He'd not seen her at breakfast.

Suddenly, a tragedy. Ozunov's remaining bishop came wheeling out of ambush and snapped up his queen. Damn! Khristo quickly checked his pawns to see which had sneaked farthest down the board. No solace there. Finally, for want of anything better to do, he threatened Ozunov's castle with a pawn. How on earth had Ozunov finagled his queen? His eyes wandered to the piece, lying on its side among the ranks of the dead by the edge of the board. Would he not have taken the bishop with his queen on the previous move if the path had been open? How had he missed it?

The game progressed, snow drifted in the street below, Khristo's forces were slowly picked to pieces. He tried to concentrate, to see the distant implications of each possible move, but the suddenly captured queen obsessed him. From that blow he would not recover, but he wanted at least to see the reason of it. In time, he realized what Ozunov had done. At first he could not believe it, but finally had to accept the fact that Ozunov had brazenly cheated him. Why? He didn't know. Even the strongest had a weakness somewhere – they'd taught him that themselves. Perhaps Ozunov could not bear to lose.

Toward the end of the game, as Ozunov chased his king mercilessly around the board – stopping only to pick off one of the few motley survivors – the Stoianev temper asserted itself. Khristo determined that he would not be fooled quite so easily and, just then, a distraction in the form of a telephone call came to his aid.

Soon enough the game was over, a last faithful knight eliminated, a few helpless pawns standing around like poor relations at a funeral. Ozunov reached over and laid Khristo's king on its side.

'Check,' he said, 'and mate, I believe. You agree?'

'Yes,' Khristo said.

'You dislike to lose, Khristo Nicolaievich?'

'Yes, comrade Major.'

'Then you must learn to play better.'

'I agree, comrade Major.'

'Losing your queen, that's what finished you I believe.'

Khristo nodded agreement.

'A very simple stratagem. Plain as your nose, eh?'

Khristo was not sure how to answer. Ozunov smiled, as though to himself, and poked idly at the bowl of his pipe with a toothpick. 'I knew an Englishman once, a few years after the Revolution, it was my job to know him. We spent many hours in conversation, it was a most pleasant assignment really. There was nothing we did not speak of, women, politics, religion. All those matters that men like to speculate about when they are at ease. From this man I learned a particular thing. *Fair play*, he called it. Not such a simple notion, perhaps, when you probe to find its heart. A kind of code, which each gentleman must honour individually in order for all to benefit. In time I came to understand that it was a good system for those who had more than they needed, for those who could afford to give something away. But I also realized that I had never known anybody like that. Nobody I ever knew could say, "Here, you take it, I do not deserve it. I do not need it so badly that I will cheat and lie to get it." Perhaps some day we may indulge ourselves in that fashion, we may have so much that we can afford to give some of it away, but not now. Can you understand this?'

Khristo looked hesitant. Ozunov laughed at his discomfort. 'Yes, boy, I cheated you. I moved a piece while you were daydreaming out the window, enchanted by our Russian snow. I acknowledge it!'

'But why, comrade Major? You could have won without that.'

'Yes, I could have. You do some things well, comrade student, but you play chess like a barbarian. I wanted merely to teach you something, that is my job now.'

'Teach me what, comrade Major?'

Ozunov sighed. 'I am told Lenin once called it the Bolshevik Variation, simply another strategy, like the

59

Sicilian Defence. It has two parts to it. The first is this: win at all cost. Do anything you have to do, *anything*, but win. There are no rules.'

Khristo hesitated. He had a response to this, but it was very bold and he was not sure of himself. At last, he took the leap.

'I have learned what you wanted to teach me, comrade Major,' he said, opening his hand to show Ozunov the white pawn he had stolen when the telephone rang.

'You're a good student,' Ozunov said. 'Now learn the second part of the Variation: make the opponent play *your* game. And the more he despises your methods, the more you must make him use them. The more he arms himself with virtue, the more you must make him fight in the dirt. Then you have him.'

He gestured with his pipe toward the white pawn lying on Khristo's palm. 'Keep that,' he said. 'A student prize from Ozunov. You have won the copy of Vladimir Ilyich's speeches, now you will have something to remind you, in times to come, how to turn them into prophecies.'

*   *   *

'Wake *now*, please.'

The hand jerked his shoulder. His body rose upright, by itself it seemed, and he suddenly found himself sitting. He struggled to get his eyes open. What time was it? His heart was beating like a drum at being torn from deep sleep.

'You are up? No falling back down in a heap?'

It was Irina Akhimova, one of the night guardians, an immense woman with tiny eyes and a voice like a ripsaw.

'Dress yourself, Khristo Nicolaievich. Quickly, quickly.'

At last his eyes opened. The dormitory was dark, the windows revealed snow drifted over the sill, black night above. Goldman stirred in the next bed. Somebody coughed, a toilet flushed. Ozunov's chess game had kept him awake a long time the night before, his mind tossed on the sea.

'What is it?' His voice was thick.

'Angels dancing on the roof!' Her harsh voice cut through the room. 'How should I know?' She grabbed him by the hair, not so playfully. 'And wear your warmest things, little rooster, lest your manhood become an icicle.'

She let him go with a flourish. He swung out of bed; she didn't take her eyes off him while he dressed. When he visited the toilet, she waited just outside. He wound a scarf around his throat, put on a sweater and his wool jacket.

'Very well,' he said.

She looked at him critically. Reached to a nail above his bed, whipped his peaked cap from it and put it on him, pulling it down as far as it would go. Then she took him above the elbow and led him out of the room. There was a mug of tea for him on the table in the parlour and a man's silhouette in the shadows.

'Here he is,' Irina Akhimova said to the shape, 'and good morning to you.' She left abruptly. The man moved forward and stopped. His body was very still; he stared at Khristo and his eyes did not blink.

Khristo had never before seen anyone like him. He came from an unknown world, and this world, sealed, alien, hung about him like a shadow. His overcoat was finely made, with a soft collar standing upright.

On his head was a fur cap, set at an angle. He was perfectly shaven and smelled of cologne. He had longish, lank black hair, strong cheekbones, dark eyes so deeply set they seemed remote and hidden.

'I am Sascha,' he said. 'Drink your tea quickly and come with me.'

Khristo gulped his tea. The voice was educated and genteel, but there was no question of not doing whatever it told you to do. He put the cup down. The man gestured toward the door.

The air outside was like ice, dead still, bitter with wood and coal smoke. White plumes blossomed slowly from every chimney. The snow was cleared away in a path to the street, where a low black car idled unevenly in front of the building. Sascha opened the back door for him, then went around and climbed in the front seat. The driver was bulky and thick-necked, with a hat like Sascha's set square on his head.

They moved slowly down the street on packed snow. The lights picked out dark bundles, which Khristo knew to be women, wielding shovels. They drove in silence, the driver turning the wheel gingerly as they crawled around the corners. On the horizon, Khristo could see a fading of the darkness, a thin light that he had come to know as the winter dawn. The upholstery in the car had a strong musty smell. Sascha moved the sleeve of his coat back an inch, he was wearing a watch.

Khristo tried to quiet his breathing, to slow it down. He did not want these men to know what he was feeling. The interior handles of the back doors had been removed.

They drove down Kutuzov Prospekt, a grand boulevard, past the Kremlin towers, then into a narrow side street that had been shovelled down to the paving. They passed under an archway, where a soldier with a rifle saluted them, then stopped in a courtyard full of black cars. The driver remained seated. Sascha opened his door and beckoned him out. He moved stiffly, shoulders hunched as he stepped into the sharp air. He had thought that facing death, facing whatever he now faced, his mind would be bright with panic, but this was not the case. Instead, he felt like a man at the bottom of a deep well, a statue, empty of feeling.

Sascha led him through a series of guarded doors until they stood in a grand marble entry hall dominated by a magnificent staircase and a domed ceiling that was a vast concave painting of nymphs and swains in a woodland. Khristo was directed to a small door set into a panel on one side of the rotunda. This opened on an iron stairway which they descended, their footsteps ringing against the walls. It was otherwise silent and very damp, lit, just barely, by dim bulbs in wire cages. Down three flights, they moved through empty corridors that seemed to go on and on, like hallways in a dream. At last, they stopped in front of an unmarked wooden door.

'Listen to me carefully,' Sascha said in a low, even voice. 'We have caught a German spy. There has been a full confession — names, details, places of meeting, everything. You are not implicated in this. We do not *believe* you are implicated, but we do not know so very much of you. If you are to be one of us, we must assure ourselves of your disposition in such matters, so you will have to prove yourself. Now. On the other side of this door. My instructions to you are these: do not think, do not speak, do not hesitate. Only act. Follow directions. Do what needs to be done. You must not be sick, or stagger. Remember that you are a man full-grown.'

Sascha tapped on the door and it opened instantly. On the other side was a large man in white shirt and dark trousers with braces. The man had a cold, plain face and looked at him for a long moment without expression.

The room smelled strongly; musty, sweet and damp. It had no windows, only water-stained floral wallpaper, a rough table and chair, and a carpet rolled up against one wall to reveal a smooth brick floor with a drain at the centre.

The German spy knelt facing a corner of the room. Khristo saw the hands, tied behind the back with brown cord, the head bent forward, the eyes shut, the lips moving silently, skin the colour of dirty chalk.

The man in braces moved forward. He limped when he walked, in felt slippers that did not make a sound on the brick floor. Standing by the kneeling figure, he looked back at Sascha, who nodded affirmatively. Gently, he pushed the head forward until the forehead was only a few inches from the floor, then took the orange hair tied back in a red ribbon and tucked it in front of her shoulder, revealing a white neck.

Khristo felt Sascha take him by the back of the hand and turn it palm up. He had bony fingers, cold to the touch, and a grip like steel. From his pocket he took a Nagant revolver, slapped it hard onto Khristo's hand, then stepped back.

A different pair of men drove Khristo Stoianev back to Arbat Street and the Brotherhood Front of 1934. They too wore watches, conspicuously checking them now and again. But they drove slowly and carefully, and took a long, winding route through the city, which had now struggled to life amid the great snowdrifts. Black bundles – you could not determine the age or sex – shuffled head down, single file, along shovelled paths. The sky was dark and thick, the air still. It had long since stopped snowing. Khristo stared out the side window. They were watching him in the rearview mirror – in the same mirror he could see their eyes shift – and he hid his privacy by looking away.

He felt, had chosen to feel, absolutely nothing. A door had closed inside him. Marike joined Nikko on the other side of it. But he remembered the old story of the man who returns home one day to find his house occupied by demons. He hides in the basement. Each day, the demons put one brick on the trap door that is his only access to freedom. How many days shall he wait to confront them? Khristo would wait a day, many days, he hoped. He had not loved her – never would she have permitted such a thing to happen. Sentimentalism was to be fought at all costs. On her part, making love was only a trick you did for the sake of health or, perhaps, as an appreciative gesture toward a fellow worker. She was, he remembered, demonstratively unaffectionate, as though tenderness in the dance of lovers would betray the honest barnyard essence of their desire. Perhaps, he now thought, this had been her method of deception and had nothing to do with playing the part of worker. He had been naive, he realized, had simply not considered that deception could occur in such matters. Very well. It would happen no more. And, if it did –

now that he knew of Sascha's existence and others like him – it would surely be the last time. Unless you could turn over and fuck in your grave. In this place you could not make a mistake. That was the lesson he had learned in the morning; God only knew what he might be taught in the afternoon. He watched the black figures on the street, their white breaths hanging in the air. What was this place? Who were these people?

The car turned into Arbat Street. In front of his building there was a Stolypin car, puffing black exhaust on the snow as it idled. No one moved to open his door, so he simply sat and waited. Two men in overcoats came quickly out of the building, holding the arms of a man running between them. It was Ozunov. He was barefoot, wearing blue silk pyjamas. He stumbled a little, the two men jerked him upright and his glasses went askew. They stopped at the back of the Stolypin car, and one of the men let him go in order to open the door. Instinctively, he adjusted his glasses. Turned his head. For a bare instant, he stared at Khristo. His face appeared to have somehow shrunk, and his eyes looked enormous. Then the two men hoisted him into the back, as Khristo caught a brief glimpse of other people inside the trucklike compartment. One of the men slammed the door and dropped the steel bar into its bracket. The whole street could hear the clang.

Just at that moment, the door on Khristo's side of the car was swung open by the man from the passenger seat. He nodded toward the building entry. He was apparently forbidden to speak, but the look on his face, a smile without mirth or pleasure, made it clear that they had wanted him to witness this event. The winding trip home had been simply a matter of timing.

Khristo, his arms wide for balance, the peaked cap still pulled down on his head, tip-toed carefully across the ice into the building. Irina Akhimova awaited him just inside. She took him to the small parlour off the dining area, sat him down at a table, and disappeared in the direction of the kitchen. Very slowly, he took off the hat, unwound the scarf. Set them on a chair beside him. Stared vacantly at the wall. It was unpleasantly silent in the room; he could hear himself breathing. He desperately wanted to fall asleep, and he swayed in the chair and bit his lip when his eyelids drooped.

'None of that,' Irina Akhimova said from the doorway. He came to with a snap. 'Soldiers must not sleep at the post.' But the words were somehow tender and there was kindness in her tiny eyes. She beckoned him, led him into the kitchen.

In an iron pot, she was making *pelmeni*, ground pork and onions wrapped in dough and boiled. The air in the kitchen was fragrant; there was a glass of thin, freshly made sour cream set by a plate, he could smell the vinegar in it. Akhimova's enormous back was bent studiously over the pot as she prodded and poked the floating *pelmeni* with a long wooden spoon.

She served him. Filled his plate at the stove, then tilted it over the pot to let the steaming water run off. Placed it before him. Moved the sour cream closer, filled a tall glass with strong tea.

'Will you not join me, comrade Lieutenant?' he asked.

She made a dismissive noise, just the way the older women in his own town did, meaning that it was his moment for grand food, not hers.

It was his victory they were celebrating.

The *pelmeni* were delicious, garlic laid on with a broad lick, the way he liked it. He resisted a powerful urge to gobble, took his time, was spartan with the sour cream until, smiling broadly, she waved him on. He felt the meal bring his soul back to life. Despite the world, despite Marike and Ozunov, despite himself. His body, his heart as well, took the food to itself, became warm and grateful.

And, since the day was meant to be an exemplar, a homily on life as they wished him to perceive it, there was yet one more lesson in store.

'News from home,' she said solemnly when he had eaten as much as he could. She laid a sheet of cheap brownish paper in front of him. He stared at it, perplexed. Nobody in Vidín could have the faintest idea where he was. 'Brought by friends,' she added in explanation.

He recognized his father's schoolboy letters, each one laboured over with a stub of pencil:

My Son,

I greet you. I am happy to hear that you are with friends. Mama and I are well. Last Sunday, at the St. Ignatius church, your sister Helena took wedding vows with Teodor Veiko, the son of Omar Veiko the landlord. I know you will join us in wishing them prosperity and long life. It was a fortunate match. Life here will now go on more smoothly. It is my hope that you are studying your lessons and obeying your teachers, making something of yourself, and that the time will come when you may come home to us. That my blessings find you in good health,

He had signed it 'Nicolai Stoianev' with ceremony, a man who had written very few letters in his life. To Khristo, the message between the lines was quite thoroughly clear. Nikko's affront to authority and his own flight eastward had placed his remaining family in grave danger, and Helena had determined to sacrifice her happiness on behalf of her parents' lives. No Vidin child of his acquaintance would have done any less. He knew of Teodor Veiko, an older man, child of Veiko's youth. A drunkard, a violent man. But Helena was clever, would wind him around her thumb. The rest of the message was this: you cannot come home. That it should arrive on the day when his thoughts might well be expected to turn in that direction was no coincidence and he knew it.

'The news is good?' Akhimova asked.

'Yes, comrade Lieutenant, as good as can be expected.'

She leaned over his shoulder, he felt her bulk near him, and pretended to read the letter for the first time. She squeezed the tender place between his shoulder and his neck. 'Be brave, Khristo Nicolaievich,' she said softly. 'Be a good soldier.'

They had him.

The first step was to comprehend it. The second was to form, in the privacy of his mind, the words themselves – a reading of the sentence. He was held by a system based on the portcullis, a medieval security tactic no less effective for its age. A system of two gates. A visitor entered through the first gate – no questions asked. It locked behind him. He was now confronted by a second gate, held a virtual prisoner in a small space. Above his head, the walls were honeycombed with arrow slits and fighting ports. For the moment, only questions came from above. If the answers were found to be good, they opened the second gate. If the answers – or the stars, or the cast of the dice – were found to be not good, they did not open the second gate. After that, the disposition of the prisoner was more a matter of whim than tactics. The portcullis was a system based on the medieval assumption of evil in all men – again, a notion no less effective for its age – and the certain knowledge that any visitor carried your destruction in his hand, intentionally or not, a spy's gold or the Black Death.

Thus they had him and he knew it.

He could not go home. He could only move in the direction they pointed out – pray God you understood where they were pointing, pray God you did not make a misstep along the path. The lesson of *The Mistake* had been sharply staged for him in the departure of Ozunov. The major had permitted a spy to flourish in his house. Perhaps he was a witting accomplice, perhaps not. But, they said, we have no time to find out. No wish, either. The New Science is ingenious in that way: motive is unimportant.

Why does not matter, only *that*. And the New Science is economical. An arrest, if properly managed, is also a lesson. Thus we make what we have go further, thus we spend wisely.

But they – the masters, the unseen – had incorporated a tiny flaw in their structure. It was endemic, they could do nothing about it. As Oriental rugs are woven with a single imperfect strand – that the weaver not be seen to compete with Allah, who is the only perfection – their system had one defect. It was not perfectly dark. Some light got in. For the more they trained Khristo in their methods, the more he understood their logic. It was a problem they couldn't overcome, but they knew it existed and they watched closely, and watching was their greatest skill.

Thus they had him *but* he knew it.

The way home was closed. They had let him know that with the letter. He realized also that Antipin had operated openly in Vidin on purpose, that secrecy had not been his intention. If the fascists were after you, to whom could you turn? To the East, of course. Now, let us provoke the fascists: they will drive the sheep, we shall have the wool.

That winter, Khristo Stoianev learned to bear weight.

He understood the system in that way: a great heavy mass that pressed down upon you, that kept you struggling and gasping to remain, in any sense at all, upright. It crushed the mind because it demanded every resource, every tag end of memory and cognition, simply to stay afloat. Imagination withered, fantasy collapsed; only some of the strong would survive. There were special rules, special interpretations of the rules, regulations to be adamantly obeyed, regulations to be adamantly ignored, tests – obvious tests and subtle tests and obvious tests that hid subtle tests – provocations to be silently withstood, provocations to be instantly reported, papers to be kept on the person, papers to be written and handed in, papers to be punched at regular intervals, papers to be returned by a certain date, special passes, special permissions, 'open' conversations, guided conversations. If there were a way to hammer a nail into a thought, they would have found it and done it.

To this weight add the weight of the winter. Which bore them all down, Bolshevist and cellar priest alike. A sky that turned black, then grey, then brown, then white, then black again. 'The sun?' Goldman said in an unguarded moment. 'I hear they've shot it.' If they had, it bled snow. The unrelieved whiteness became blinding over time, made a world without feature, a terrible empty blankness where, at last, the concept of *nothingness* – ПОЛНАЯ ПУСТОТА – became brutally real. And, finally, at the centre of it all, was the cold. A cold that shrank you up inside yourself, a cold that collapsed every face to a frown or a snarl, a cold that blew in the wind like a whip or hung motionless in the air like dead smoke. Even to wash was agony, and all stank together. The sex shrivelled back into the body, only alcohol could move the blood, and, with enough alcohol, the cold found new ways to feed itself. An old woman sat on a bench to rest for a moment. You came upon her, thinly glazed with ice, the following morning.

Khristo bore the winter cold as best he could and found ways to bear the other kind of chill as well. Would they, he reasoned, teach you French and English unless they intended to send you someplace where such languages were spoken? They would not. So he bent his back to it. It did not come easily, it did not come quickly, but he simply would not let go until he had a deathgrip understanding of it.

'Good morning, Mr. Stoianev. How is the weather today?'

'Good is the weather. Maybe snows little.'

'The weather is good. Maybe it will snow a little.'

'The weather is good. Maybe it will snow a little.'

'Not *leetle*, little, lit-tul.'

'Lit-tul.'

'Faster!'

'Little.'

By the hour, by the day, by the week. In February he was twenty years old. Goldman and Voluta and Semmers chipped in and bought him a cream cake. The cream was off. He ate it anyway and showed pleasure, licking his lips enthusiastically and humming with pleasure. Later, in bed, he curled around his stomach and fell into a sleep of exhaustion despite the cramps.

It was comradeship, he came to realize, that brought them through the winter agonies of 1934 and 1935. While the blizzards and the system swirled around them and the purges beat like a drum in the background, they held on to each other and rode out the storms. *Perhaps*, Khristo thought privately, *we are the truest communists in Moscow this winter. We share our pain. We share our food.*

The idea had been simple enough: send out an army of Antipins across the mountains and river valleys of Eastern Europe, recruit – never mind how – the young and vigorous. Look for stealth, raw courage, a gift for lies or seduction – you know what we want. Bring them back here. Teach them what they need to know. Make them – one way will work as well as the next – our own. Marxists, patriots, criminals, outcasts, adventurers. Mix it up, boys, you never know what you'll need. They will be *ours*. Poles, Czechs, Serbs, Macedonians, Bulgarians, Croats – our brothers and sisters to the west. War is surely coming, and these seeds will make a harvest in future famines.

It was equally logical to run them through in batches, keep them in a group, for one always wanted to be sure *where everyone was*. In a country of two hundred million souls that covered eleven time zones, you could misplace the damnedest things: entire trains, whole battalions. Sometimes you never did find them. The country had a way of swallowing up what most normal persons would hold to be entirely indigestible objects, it drove some technicians quite literally mad.

71

Thus convenience for the accountants of the system made for the salvation of its inventory – survival could only be managed if they took care of each other. They learned that everyone in the group had something to offer. They learned who the stool pigeons were and fed them on small sins to maintain their credibility so that new, and unknown, informers would not be introduced.

Thus together they learned their lessons.

*   *   *

March, no sign of a thaw, winter giving every sign of an encore, it was their turn to occupy the village of Belov on the river Oka.

An outing! A half-day ride in a rattly wooden railcar, chugging past bare birch groves and black-green forests of fir with snow-weighted boughs. Real countryside: wood-cutters' huts, the occasional farm field in a peculiar shape. The Russians, to everyone's amazement, farmed in oddly configured patches of land, nothing square, perhaps the result of endless divisions of the *versts* among sons over the centuries. But all they saw was new, and that was what mattered. It made their blood run fast after the shut-in winter months in claustrophobic Moscow. They yelled and capered and carried on like kids. Kerenyi managed to free the upper half of one of the windows. Painted – a horrid Soviet institutional green – shut for years, it shrieked as it opened, borne down by Kerenyi's great strength. At last, delicious cold air seasoned with railroad soot came rushing into the car. Hooray! Reaching up through the window, Kerenyi returned with a handful of snow from the roof. A rapid shaping in red hands, then a fat snowball sailed out the open window toward a hut. A near miss! They threw themselves on the other windows, and soon enough they were shelling the scenery amid shouts of triumph and exasperation. Well, you know how it is. It would have to be Iovescu, that appalling snitch, who would get it in the back of the head. Fat-faced goody-goody from the Banat. With vengeful eye he searched the crowd who, as one, raised their shoulders in shrugs of angelic innocence. Finally – wouldn't you know it – he picked on Ilya Goldman, one of the smallest, and chucked a fistful of loose snow at him. There was only one answer to that. The ensuing volley hit Iovescu and everybody else, producing squeals of fury as snow worked under the odd collar. Mayhem followed. In the melee, Karina Olowa, a little blonde thing from Wilno, journeyed stealthily to the platform between cars and returned with a colossal snowbomb which, launched upward, splattered against the ceiling and rained down on various heads. A huge cry arose and that, at last, brought Lieutenant Akhimova and the other officers on the run. Order was restored. They'd used up most of the roof snow anyhow.

In the little village of Belov they took over various thatch-roofed huts – where the Belovians themselves had got to, nobody could say – with wood bunks covered by mothholed blankets. They built coal fires in the stoves, trooped down to the church for dinner, where iron pots of soup were boiling and misshapen loaves of rye-flour bread were set out on long tables. After a winter of potatoes and cabbage and fish-bone soup, the smell of food was thrilling. There may even have been a few private thoughts of home. They built a bonfire that night and sang songs, then trooped off to their respective houses – just like real townspeople – and slept the sleep of city dwellers on their first night in the country.

The next morning, after tea and bread, they went to work.

They were divided into fourteen teams of four – each team designated by a number and given numbered strips of material to pin to their collars. Khristo, Goldman and Voluta were a team, joined by a tall Yugoslavian named Drazen Kulic who, in his late twenties, was rather older than most of the others. Kulic seemed to have lived his life away from the sun – his hair, eyes and skin were almost

73

without colour. Yet he did not fade into the background; his presence was physical, hard, and there was something in the set of his face that was watchful and unforgiving.

The four were designated Unit Eight.

In the first exercise of the day, half the units entered Belov as security police, the other half were given blank-loaded Tokarev pistols, wooden boxes supposedly containing explosives, a notebook labelled *List of Partisan Units*, and signalling flares – contraband to hide in their huts. As counterinsurgency officers, Unit Eight was assigned to search houses at the southern end of the village.

On the edge of town, waiting for the whistle that would begin the exercise, Unit Eight held a meeting. Khristo would be the captain, would have final say in all things, though all would participate in planning and executing operations. Ilya Goldman was appointed intelligence officer and freed from all other obligations. He immediately undertook to make lists of the units they would oppose and cooperate with during the exercises. Goldman, a lover of detail, set himself to annotate these lists – in his own code – with observations on personalities, strengths and weaknesses in each unit.

The first argument began right there. Now that Goldman was intelligence officer, he wanted a staff. Typical! Give him an inch and he took a mile! Goldman waited for the other three to calm down, then explained patiently. Lists took time, and observation. Operational efficiency could be sacrificed, for a day or two, in favour of acquiring data that (A) would be useful in defeating opposing units and (B) could be marketed to other units in exchange for cooperation – thereby increasing the data files and making the potential for trading even more productive.

Khristo was impressed and promptly ordered Goldman to choose a staff. He selected Kulic. Khristo calmly pointed out that Kulic was physically strong, and if there were to be only two of them operating as security police that quality was important, principally for purposes of intimidation but who knew what it might come to – future assignments could well be affected by the outcome of the Belov games, and everybody wanted to do well. Fistfights were not out of the question. Goldman accepted Voluta as his assistant, and the two of them immediately went off and whispered in a corner.

Therefore, when the whistle blew and the designated counterinsurgency units fanned out across the village, Unit Eight was represented only by Khristo and Kulic. Belov had been a reasonably prosperous little place: a small church with a dome, a town hall–police station, and a few small shops – really open market stalls – on the main street, which was surfaced in frozen mud. The sun had come out, beads of morning frost glistened in the roof thatch. Khristo, blank-loaded holstered pistol riding his waist, strode along the main street and saw life anew from a policeman's perspective. A curious sensation, to go anywhere he wanted, to say what he liked to whomever he pleased. There was, he hated to admit it, some distinct comfort in such power.

As other units commenced the exercise, Khristo and Kulic could see that they had adopted the time-honoured forms. The hard-handed banging on the door. Shouts of 'Open up! Security search!' When the doors were opened, they could see people who had recently been self-confident students transformed by circumstance into groups of huddled peasants.

They found their assigned target, the hut of Unit Five, and briefly discussed their strategy. Kulic disappeared around the back, Khristo tapped lightly on a board below the window. The unit captain appeared at the window and gestured toward the door.

'I needn't come in,' Khristo said.

The captain looked puzzled.

'They sent me to tell you that you're in the wrong hut. This one here is supposed to be storage – Unit Five belongs next door.'

The captain nodded and disappeared from the window. Khristo waited, pleased to have the warming sun on his back. It stood to reason that when they moved, their contraband would have to move with them. The captain reappeared at the window and chopped the edge of his right hand into the bent elbow of his left arm, adding, for emphasis, an extended middle finger on the left hand. The universal sign language informed Khristo that his suggestion had been staunchly rejected, so he went and knocked on the door.

The captain opened the door. 'Nice try,' he said acidly.

'Keep a civil tongue when you talk to us,' Khristo said, 'or you're in the stockade for the day.'

No stockade had been mentioned in the rules, but one could never be certain. The man stared at him for a moment, then grunted and stood back. Khristo let Kulic in the back door.

'Lieutenant Kulic will conduct the search,' Khristo announced, folding his arms and leaning back against a wall.

'Where are the rest of you?' one of the 'peasants' asked.

'You'll find out,' Khristo answered, putting as much menace in his voice as he dared.

'All stand up!' Kulic shouted as loud as he could. Unit Five stood, slightly sullen at being addressed so harshly.

'All strip!'

They stood with their mouths open.

'Hurry up. Down to the skin,' he yelled.

'Against the rules.' Her name was Malya. She was tall and sallow and won all the prizes for codes and ciphers. She stood with her arms folded and glowered at them. 'You are state security,' she added, 'not dirty-minded boys.' Her eyes glittered with contempt.

As Kulic took a fast step toward her, Khristo's hand shot out and grabbed his elbow. Kulic shook him off but stayed where he was.

'I'll be back,' Khristo said. He ran out the door and down the street to the town hall, where the officers had constituted themselves a committee of the rules.

He addressed Irina Akhimova. 'Comrade Lieutenant!' He stood at attention.

'Yes, comrade student?'

'We require the search of a female person.'

The officers, five or six of them smoking cigarettes and drinking tea, passed an eyes-to-heaven look among themselves. *Here we go again*, it said. *Another year at Belov and already they are at it.*

Akhimova climbed to her feet, affecting weariness, brushed Khristo ahead of her with hand motions. 'Yes, yes, comrade Security Officer. Lead the way.'

They arrived at the hut to find Kulic and Unit Five locked in a staring contest. Kulic's hand rested on the butt of his holstered gun. Akhimova took Malya out the back door toward the privy behind the hut. In a moment they reappeared. Malya's face was angry, her cheeks well coloured. 'Donkey,' she said to the unit captain. Akhimova handed Khristo a thickly folded wad of paper.

'One current map of the Ukraine, six towns circled,' she said, 'tied to the upper left leg with string.' She took a notebook from the side pocket of her uniform jacket. 'Ten points subtracted from Unit Five. Ten points awarded to Unit Eight. Continue the exercise.' As she walked out, only Khristo could see her face. She winked at him. He glanced out the window. Goldman went scurrying by like a ferret.

So, for a week, it went. They battled among themselves, shadowing each other to clandestine meetings, plotting to suborn their opponents, bending every rule until the judging committee stomped about in a red-faced fury. They ran, in their *eshpionets* kindergarten, every classical operation in the repertoire. Given the preponderance of males, there did seem to be a particular obsession with the honey trap – seduction for the purposes of leverage, the country air had stimulated more than one appetite — but no conquests for *intelligence* purposes were recorded. They planted compromising evidence on each other — Khristo found a curiously whittled wooden dowel in the bunched-up blanket he used for a pillow. Even Goldman, their chief Machiavelli, declined to offer a theory on its intention. They buried it beside the hut and waited. That night Unit Five, led by the Hungarian captain, an officer-judge in tow, kicked the door open and accused Khristo of secreting an ampoule of morphine. The following day, Voluta planted it on somebody else, but he too discovered and removed it before the group was raided.

The classical operations, it turned out to everyone's irritation, often had classical results. Which is to say, no results. They were accustomed, in all their games, to winning and losing, and the frequency of *no decision* calls first puzzled, then annoyed them. They had stumbled on the dispiriting truth about spycraft, which was that few disciplines had a lower incidence of clear victories. 'I bent my brain to get this right!' Goldman whined after some particular piece of treachery had fizzled before his eyes. They shared his frustration. Their coup of the first day had given them an inflated opinion of their abilities. They were now treated to the chilly reality of initial success diluted by subsequent failure. No matter how hard they went at it, a second Great Triumph eluded them. They won points, they lost points, but most of their efforts earned a 'no decision'.

There were serious undertones to this competition. Most of them had been in Moscow for six months or more, and they had discovered that in this egalitarian society some were decidedly more equal than others. Elusive and shadowy it was, but privilege did exist. Being out and about in the city, you'd catch a glimpse, a scent of it. Clearly it was based on rank, one's position in the scheme of things, and their success in the competition, and generally in the school, would ultimately determine that position. But, try as they might, the members of Unit Eight could not work their way into first place on the list posted daily on the door of the church. They fluttered between second and third. That, it seemed, was the way it was destined to work out. Unit Two, a cadre of teacher's pets captained by the infamous brownnose Iovescu, sat firmly atop the heap.

The final exercise was witnessed by the god Petenko himself, driven out that morning in an open staff car, a picnic hamper riding next to the officer who acted as chauffeur. This Petenko was a fabled personage – his telephone calls produced ashen-faced terror in subordinates – who sported one of those battering-ram titles in which the words *deputy, assistant, minister, interior, state* and *security* all appeared. The tolling of a frightful bell. The sort of high but not too high job where the incumbent could snip your balls off without signing for them. Beside the point, perhaps, that he had seven months to live, or that some of his former *castrati* were waiting for him when it was his turn to go to the Lubianka – that day he was the czar.

The assignment: assassinate General X as he enters the captured city. Citizens line the streets. Security is rife. This is a triumphal entry. Citizens and security were composed of the other thirteen units – one unit had to do the job. General Petenko deigned to take the role of General X. His flunkies were enacted (in every possible way) by three members of the judging committee. The part of the car was played by his car.

Unit Eight stayed up till dawn, blankets wrapped around their shoulders. They had been screwed, somehow, placed last on the schedule. By then, every other unit would have had its try, every possible variation, every deceit, trick, diversion and ruse would have been seen and identified. They pounded their heads to come up with something completely new. What made it worse was that their officers, the judging committee in the car and others in the street, were arrayed against them along with all the other units and *they*, of course, were looking forward to

79

it, popping away at their students with blank 7.62 rounds, symbolically slaughtering the incompetent.

For the nineteenth time Captain Khristo asked Intelligence Officer Goldman what assets they had and for the nineteenth time was shown the two pistols Kulic had managed to weasel away from other units. He was, for such a heavy-shouldered brute, a surprisingly subtle thief. In addition, Goldman could make overtures to certain weak links, in other units, in search of covert assistance, but — who could know, they might well be delivering themselves into the nets of somebody's counterintelligence scheme. They themselves had played the traitor too often, in order to discern someone else's intentions, not to know that the prank could just as easily be played back on them.

'It's getting light,' Voluta said. 'What can we do with two extra pistols and a few weak links? Or, really, *five* extra pistols, we'll only need one to shoot the bastard.'

'Weak links cannot be trusted.' Khristo spoke the axiom automatically.

Kulic agreed, nodding sadly. Completed the worn joke: 'Trust the strong even less.'

When, at long last, it came their turn to try the assassination, *weak* was the word for their effort. It was getting on dusk, there were rumours of a splendid supper on their last night. Everybody was tired and cold and hungry — thirteen foiled assassinations made for a long day. Some units had come close, a few points awarded, but nobody had managed a clean kill.

General X rode into town in stately fashion, waving at the assembled multitude from the front seat of the open car. Irina Akhimova, hands choking the steering wheel, drove the car slowly, her face frozen in rigid concentration. Never mind murder, her expression seemed to say, just don't scratch the bodywork. Poor Goldman was caught flat-footed on the roof of the church (by Unit Two guards, of course! — points to them), his 'bomb', a sock full of white flour, still hanging down the front of his shirt. Kulic, absurdly disguised with a home-cut eyepatch, was pounced on a moment later. Voluta, attempting to hide in an open doorway, simply raised his hands. Why get your shirt torn on the last day? At the end of the street, two security guards stepped out of the crowd with Khristo held between them. Truly, a disappointing try, especially from the ever-ingenious Unit Eight. Bomb-from-the-church-roof had already failed, and failed quite miserably, twice that day.

General X stood up in the front seat, became General Petenko, raised his hand for silence. The crowd gathered round for a blessing.

'On behalf of the security workers of this progressive nation,' he trumpeted, 'I wish to bestow on you and your dedicated instructors compliments and congratulations. What I have seen here today is an inspiration to me, to all the proletariat everywhere. Perhaps not an inspiration of craft – for you are beginners, there is still great effort ahead of you – but an inspiration of *effort, seriousness,* and . . .'

Inspired, then, to silence.

Mouth frozen open.

Leaping backward as the electricity of fright jolted his heart. Crossing his hands in front of his closed eyes, turning his head away. A perfect statue of a man in the last instant of life.

Not real death.

Not real bullets.

But the move was so sudden, so blurred, he had no time to sort it out. There was an animal lying along the length of the hood. It had sprung like an animal, without warning or hesitation, and it had landed like an animal, crouched, coiled to spring again. Then it had flung itself flat, both fists spewing flame.

For Khristo, the realization was explosive. *He really thinks he is being shot.* He could see Petenko in exquisite focus – glossy jowls, drooping chin – and the man's terror opened a door in him. What burst through was a bright fountain of

81

rage. *This fat Russian bag of piss and vodka.* Khristo ground his teeth and moaned in his throat and then heard hammers clacking on empty chambers.

There was rather a long interval.

Akhimova, her face a mask, stood up in the driver's seat for no apparent reason. Petenko lowered his arms, came out of hiding. His voice was high and thin the first time he screamed.

'Lieutenant!'

Dropped an octave on the second try.

'Lieutenant!'

Khristo heard Akhimova exhale a long breath.

'Yes, comrade General?'

'This man . . .' He pointed. Khristo could see his finger shaking. Petenko blinked, slowly lowered his hand. *This man* could not be forced to his knees and shot then and there. *This man* was a student, of a sort, reciting his lesson, of a sort.

Petenko cleared his throat. Students in the street murmured to each other. The urgent need to return to normalcy was everywhere. Khristo, careful of the paint, slithered cautiously backward until he stood before the car.

Petenko turned his head a little to one side. 'What is your name, young man?'

'Khristo Stoianev, comrade General.'

'You are Bulgarian?'

'Yes, comrade General.'

'They are proud people,' Petenko said. There was proper admiration in his voice. The working classes needed no national boundaries, they were as one race. The concept had been clearly set down.

His eyes, of course, told a very different story, but only Khristo could see what burned there and he was meant to see it.

* * *

A different sort of train ride back to Moscow. The wooden benches they'd barely noticed on the way out were now discovered to be of a diabolical hardness. Heads drooped. There was coughing and sniffling. They were exhausted, worn down by the intensity of competition, lost sleep, country air, and cheap, throat-searing vodka knocked back, toast by toast, at the farewell party. One of the officers had brought forth a battered fiddle – he did it every year – and all danced and sang. What the Arbat Street officers called *Belovian love affairs* were consummated one last time behind, beneath and, in the cases of the truly brave, inside various huts. Farewell, my pretty one. Life back in Moscow was not so free. Oh, one could manage – clandestine training would serve for other than political purposes – but it wasn't the same, hiding out in the boiler room. Better not to be so forthright. Marike had carried on rather openly, and she'd not been seen since. Sent home, most thought.

Khristo tried sleeping but it wasn't possible. With windows shut tight it was getting close in the train, and he went between cars wanting fresh air and there found Kulic, curled up out of the wind in one corner of the platform. Kulic invited him to sit down and Khristo rested his back against the smooth wooden boards.

In the open air, the rail rhythms were amplified and white smoke from the locomotive streamed overhead. There was a strange sky, common for the Russian spring, with clouds and stars and a probing little wind from the south that stirred the birch groves.

'Well, comrade Captain,' Kulic said after Khristo had settled himself, 'it wasn't for lack of trying.'

'We should have won it,' Khristo said.

Kulic shrugged. 'It is different here.' His voice was without inflection.

The judging committee's decision had been announced at the farewell party. Unit Two and the smug Iovescu had come in first. They had been placed second, just ahead of

Malya and the Hungarian captain and Unit Five. Khristo's unit had been awarded a full score for the assassination of General X – there was no way to deny their success. But the committee had awarded Unit Two the points for capturing Goldman on the roof. Goldman had challenged the decision – it was all a feint, right up to the point when the two bribed security guards had released Khristo's arms – but the challenge was turned aside: a political decision had been made and that was that.

The brownnoses won. That was always the way of it, Khristo thought, and there was a lesson to be learned there if one wanted to see it. Kulic was right, it was different here. Gazing at the cloudy, starry sky, he felt captivity as a slight pressure at the base of the throat and swallowed a few times, but it would not go away. Twenty years old. Life already twisted into a strange, contorted shape, like a tree growing in sand. When he'd been Nikko's age he had harboured a secret contempt for his father. A slave of the fish buyers, the landlords, the Holy Fathers, he'd seemed yoked to his life like a patient ox. Now and then a sigh, but never a protest, never a curse. Khristo had believed one could tear the yoke from one's neck, cast it into the Dunav, be free of the weight that had to be hauled from dawn to dusk every day of the year. He'd believed his father lacked the passion, the human fire, to shed his burden, and he was ashamed to be the son of such a willing beast. Now he knew differently, of course. He'd learned something about yokes.

'Do you hate them?' Kulic cut into his sorrow. Seemed almost to know what he had been thinking.

Khristo shrugged, not trusting his voice. Kulic punched him twice, lightly, on the upper arm. 'Doesn't pay to think about it,' he said.

He didn't hate them. He didn't think he hated them. Though the fury that had possessed him when he'd 'shot' Petenko would bear some thinking about when he could get away alone. But he didn't hate them. He was afraid of them. He was afraid of them because they were, in some sense, madmen. A boat carpenter in Vidin had gone mad with sorrow after his wife died and had spent all his days down by the river building endless mounds of stones, constantly correcting the height of the piles to make them all perfectly even. *They* were like that. They practised a kind of witchcraft and called it science. When you went to get your papers stamped, you slid them beneath a curtain to a waiting official – you were not to see the faces of those who controlled your destiny. Like Veiko, they dealt in fear. *Like Veiko*, he thought ruefully.

Kulic continued, taking Khristo's silence for assent. 'If you cannot go back, best go forward. What else is there?'

'You too?' Khristo said.

Kulic nodded sadly. 'All of us. That's my guess.' He slumped backward and stared up at the sky. 'I was one of the *Komitaji*. You know what that is?'

'The committee?'

'That's what the word means. Called the Black Hand in Macedonia, something else in Croatia – you know how it is where I come from. Back in November, they murdered the king of Yugoslavia in Marseilles, King Alexander. The assassination was managed by a man called Vlada the Chauffeur. That action was accomplished by *Komitaji*. Some call us bandits, others, *partizans*.' He shrugged and spread his hands.

'You knew the people who did that?'

'Not personally. But I knew who they were. My group was active on the river. From the Iron Gate all the way up to the Hungarian border, including the city, Belgrade. And the truth about us was that some days we were bandits, other days, *partizans*. But always *Komitaji*. Bound by the oath of blood. Tradition of centuries – all of that. When we bury our dead, we do not close the coffin until it is in the grave. How is this? the visitors say. Oh, we answer, too cruel to shut out the last glimpse of sky until the very, very end. They like that idea. But the truth is different. *Komitaji* have always hidden guns in coffins, so the king made a law, and now it's a good country to visit if you like to see the occasional corpse being carried through the street.'

He laughed for a moment, remembering a particular national madness that seemed, from a distance, endearing. 'Up on the river we are mostly Serbian,' he said, 'though part of my family is Macedonian. We marched with Alexander the Great, of course, but then all Macedonians will say that. Just as all Macedonians are revolutionaries.'

'Like the Russians.'

Kulic glanced around the platform, though there could be nobody else there. 'Shit,' he whispered. He moved closer to Khristo and spoke in a low voice. 'We are revolutionaries because we cannot stand any man who tells us what to do. The Turk sent his tax collectors, we sent them back a piece at a time. *These people*, they crave to be told what to do. A whole bloody revolution they had, but they never left the church. Not really. They aspire to be priests. Do this, do that, today is Tuesday, all turn their hats back to front. Someone says *why*? They answer *because God told me it is so* and then they give him nine grams.'

'Nine grams?'

'The weight of the bullet, Captain Khristo. What goes in the back of the neck. They worship their Stalin, like a god, yet he is no more than a village pig, the big boar, poking his great snout in everybody's corncrib. These Russians will come after us some day, that is foretold, and we will give them an ass-kicking worthy of the name.'

They were quiet for a moment. Letting the sweet smoke of treason blow and billow around their heads.

'Yet you are here,' Khristo said.

'I deserve no better,' Kulic answered. 'The king sent special police to our town – which is called Osijek, there are hill forts above the river there – and some fool shot them down. This fool hid in people's haylofts when the police came – army police, with machine guns, not the local idiots – but they started poking bayonets into the hay. So the fool moved up into the mountains. But they followed him there as well. One day came a Russian. *We like such fools*, he said, and he had false documents, a Soviet passport, and a train ticket to Varna, in Bulgaria, and a ticket on a steamer across the Black Sea to Sebastopol. So this fool – like all fools he thought himself wise – believed the Russian promises and left the mountains. Now you find him playing baby games with blank pistols, now you find him cheated of his victory, even his victory at baby games. But he accepts it. He takes everything they give out because he has no choice. He is like a bull with an iron ring through his nose. Every day they find a new way to tug on it.'

He threw his hands into the air and let them fall back to his thighs with a loud slap.

For a time they watched the stars floating by, lulled by the engine's steady beat over the rails. Kulic took a small penknife from his pocket and began paring a thumbnail.

Khristo sighed. The night made him sad. The history of Kulic's nation was like that of his own. The fighting never stopped. The conquerors kept coming. Other Kulics, other Khristos, all the way back through time, wandered the world. Away from love, away from home. They were destined to be eternal strangers. Melancholy adventurers, guests in other people's houses. From now on, forever, there could be no peace for him, no ease, none of the small domestic harmonies that were the consolation of plain people everywhere. His pleasures were to be those of the soldier in a distant outpost – a woman, a bottle, a quick death without pain. Those he could look forward to. And, though his heart might still swell with poetry at the fire of a perfect sunset, there would never be the special one beside him to share such joys.

Distracted by a slight scratching noise, he turned to see Kulic lying on his side and carving on the wooden wall of the railcar with his penknife. Kulic stood up, made space for Khristo, pointed with the knife toward the wall. Khristo slid over. The scratching was tiny, hidden away in the extreme corner, only an inch above the floor: БФ 825.

'What is it?'

'B for Brotherhood. F for Front. Eight, two and five for the proper order of finish in the Belov exercises of March 1935. Our group, Unit Eight, won it. Even though they fixed things so that their stooges came out on top. Unit Two should have been second, and Unit Five third. Thus, somewhere in the world, wherever this railcar travels, our victory will be celebrated.'

He stuck his hand out. Khristo stood and grasped it firmly, the hand was hard and thickly callused. Kulic gestured with the penknife in his other hand. 'We could make a blood oath, but pricked fingers are the very sort of thing these sniffing dogs take note of.'

They sat down again. Khristo could see the scratched letters and numbers in his mind's eye. He had read in a history book that the early kings of Greece could not trust their own countrymen not to assassinate them, so they imported, as guards, northerners, blonds and redheads from lands far away where they wrote in runes, scratch writing. These guards, time heavy on their hands, had inscribed their initials on the stone lions that, in those days, kept watch over the harbour at Piraeus. He now understood those men. Even the eternal stranger needs to leave a mark of his existence: I was *here*, therefore I *was*. Even though, after a long time away, there is nobody left who especially cares whether I was or not.

Kulic rested a hand on his shoulder. 'Don't be so sad. Remember what I said – if you cannot go back, go forward. While you are alive there is hope. Always.'

'BF eight, two, five,' Khristo said. He felt better because of what Kulic had done, and he was very surprised at that.

'We tell nobody, of course.'

'Of course.'

Again they sat quietly. It occurred to Khristo, staring up at the Russian sky, that if you had nothing else in the world you could at least have a secret.

* * *

April. Sleet storms rattled the windows. Outside, on Arbat Street, a broken water pipe had revealed its presence as the spring thaw began and a group of workers was breaking up the pavement with sledgehammers. The boiler had been turned off and in the classroom Khristo wore wool gloves and scarf and cap. He could see his breath when he spoke.

'Good morning, Mr. Stoianev.'

'Good morning, Mr. Smiss.'

'Smith.'

'Good morning, Mr. Smith.'

'How did you spend your evening?'

'I read a most interesting book, by the English writer Arthur Grahame.'

'What was it called?'

'Called *That Some Shall Know*.'

'What did this book concern itself with?'

'It is a novel, about conditions of the agrarian poor in Great Britain.'

'And what did you find the most telling scene in this book?'

'The scene where the duke struck the peasant in the face with a riding crop.'

'Why did that interest you?'

'It showed the contempt of the ruling classes for their serfs, and that servitude exists even today in Great Britain, a nation that many in the world wrongly regard as progressive.'

'Thank you, Mr. Stoianev.'

'You are welcome, Mr. Smith.'

89

In the street, the sledgehammers rang against the cement, a slow, steady rhythm.

*　*　*

It was Kerenyi, the Hungarian boy from Esztergom, who found the dog hiding in the cellar. A wet brown thing with sad eyes, half starved, its broad tail sweeping coal dust from the cement floor in hopeful joy.

Kerenyi looked like a ploughboy – even after the medical directorate had provided him with a delicate set of wire-framed eyeglasses – broad-shouldered and shambling, thick-handed, slow of speech, though his father taught mathematics in a school for the children of aristocrats. It had been the elder Kerenyi's political convictions that had sent his son east, convictions turned into actions by the fiery speeches of Bela Kun, the Hungarian communist leader. Even after the students learned of his genteel background they still called Kerenyi 'Ploughboy.' There was a gentleness, a willing kindness, about him that reminded them of those who worked in the earth, those who never complained when the cart had to be pushed.

It was to Ilya Goldman that Kerenyi went after he discovered the dog. Goldman, the son of a Bucharest lawyer, had come to Moscow just as Kerenyi had, for ideological reasons. Kerenyi idolized the Jewish Goldman, who, small, near-sighted, exceptionally clever, embodied for him the idealistic intellectual who would lead the world into the new age.

In the cellar, late at night, Goldman threw his cap against the far wall and the dog galloped across the room and brought it back to him, eyes shining with achievement.

Kulic was brought into the business because he had a friend in the kitchen, a skinny girl who scrubbed the soup pots and slipped him a few extra scraps when she could.

They never did agree on a name. Or a breed. Kerenyi claimed it was part Viszla, the pointer dog of Hungary. Goldman, a city boy, had no opinion on the matter, but

Khristo, after Kulic had dragged him downstairs to show him 'the new student', thought it more retriever than pointer. With most of Unit Eight now reassembled they could not leave Voluta out of it, and it was Voluta who stole the soup bowl that they used as a water dish.

To coordinate the operational necessities – food, water, waste removal, play – they required an operational code name. It was Kulic who suggested BF 825 – the symbolic cryptogram he'd carved on the wall of a railway car. Thus an apparently blank slip of paper Khristo found in his pocket read, when pressed against a hot pipe: 'BF 825 requires a theft of bread from the evening meal.' It was their Codes and Ciphers instructor who had taught them that canine urine would serve, in extremity, for secret ink. She would, they thought, be amused to learn how her instruction was being used – but of course she could not be told about it.

They had the dog for ten days, and they would forever associate it with Kerenyi. As the dog loved all who befriended it, Kerenyi was always prepared to be kind, to lend a hand when he could. Everyone at Arbat Street, student and instructor alike, knew that Kerenyi had no business being there – such ready affection would only get him in trouble, sooner or later – but the instructors were loath to fail him and his fellow comrades spent long hours making certain he could pass his examinations.

One Friday the entire group was marched off to a vast theatre in central Moscow to hear a four-hour speech by Ordzhonikidze, the passionate Georgian from the Caucasus, a prominent leader among the Bolsheviks, and when they returned the dog was gone. Its dish, toy, and piece of blanket were gone as well and the floor had been swept clean of coal dust and mopped with carbolic.

*　*　*

A week later, the weather broke.

The spring rains swept in from the west, warm and

steady. The great snow mounds, blackened by months of soot and ash, turned crystalline, then spongy, and the cobbled streets ran like rivers. The Moskva rose in its banks, people crossing the bridges stopped to watch great chunks of dirty ice spinning past below them. Rain pattered on the roofs, ran down the windows in big droplets, dripped from gutters, downspouts, eaves, and the brims of hats. It was a great softening, night and day it continued, a water funeral for the dying winter.

Late that afternoon, they came for him.

Two members of the school security staff took him to the parlour, then stood politely to one side. The power station had gone wrong again, so the lamps flickered and dimmed and left the corners of the room in shadow.

Sascha was leaning against the back of a sofa, a white scarf looped casually around his neck, hands thrust deep into the pockets of a brown leather coat that glistened with afternoon rain. A cigarette dangled from one corner of his mouth and the smoke, drifting through the soft dusk that lit the parlour, made his presence cloudy and obscure. He raised one hand and flicked the fingers, at which signal the two security officers left the room.

'I am told you do very well here,' he said.

'Thank you, comrade Sascha.'

'I am called Sascha. Only that. Save your *comrades* for those who need them.'

He moved about the room, slowly and speculatively. The end of the cigarette glowed briefly and two long plumes of smoke flowed from his nostrils.

'Tell me, Khristo. Tell me the truth – I promise that your answer will not hurt you. Do you dream? Specifically, do you dream of her? The redheaded girl? Does she reach out to you at night? Or, perhaps, is she under water? Long hair streaming out? She might call out your name. Does she do that? Possibly a private name, a sweet name, that you shared.'

He reached the far corner, turned slowly, moved back toward the window.

'You may tell me, Khristo Nicolaievich. I am, among other things, your confessor.'

Khristo took a beat to organize himself. 'I do not dream of her,' he said.

'Of what, then?'

'I dream of freedom for my people.'

He stopped walking and stared, canting his head over slightly. 'Do you,' he said. Again he began to pace, took his hands from his pockets and clasped them behind his back. 'Well, perhaps you do, after all, perhaps you do. We speak of such things. We speak of little else, in fact. But that it should actually happen . . .' He stopped. Seemed for a moment to commune with himself. 'Maybe they have taught you that, your faithful instructors. Maybe they have taught you to dream in the prescribed manner. Imagine. To tame the dreams.'

'Not that, Sascha.'

'Hmm. Well, don't give up. Keep trying. You must, you know – the proletariat demands it – keep trying. Tell me, what do you think of this:

> *'Ten thousand banners marching,*
> *'neath the reddened sun.*
> *They sing, O hear it,*
> *a leader's glorious name.'*

He waited. Facing Khristo, staring through the drifting smoke.

'It is a poem of inspiration,' Khristo said.

'Yes, oh yes, student Khristo, you do learn well here, they are right to say it. For you do not say it is *inspiring* – you do not know who wrote it, or when, or why, and you could be wrong. Very wrong indeed to be inspired by an improper sentiment. Such errors often cannot be forgiven, and where would you be then? Eh? On your knees in a cellar?'

He waited. Khristo had to answer.

'May I ask who wrote the poem?'

'I wrote it. I am a poet. Can you not look at me and see that? When I was very young, I was obsessed with foolishness, romantic nonsense. My poems were full of herons, birch trees, endless skies, and girls with pretty hands. Now, well, you have heard. Truth found me. Sought me out, perfected my heart. *The plough*, it whispered, *your soul has lost its plough*.'

He stood close to Khristo and took him by the shoulders. The smell of alcohol was overwhelming, as though it sweated through his pores. Khristo squinted as the cigarette smoke burned his eyes. The room was suddenly very still.

'The plough of steel,' he went on, voice persuasive and logical, 'turns our black earth to silver, / thus our Leader's wisdom / Opens our hearts to knowledge.' He drew back and waited a moment, returned his hands to his pockets and waited for a reaction. 'Khristo Nicolaievich,' he said, 'how do you not weep to hear such thoughts?'

When there was no response he took the cigarette from his mouth and dropped it at his feet, where it smouldered in the carpet. Then he walked to the window and looked out. 'This fucking rain,' he said.

He drew the leather coat around his shoulders as though he were suddenly cold, turned toward Khristo and gazed into his eyes. 'Well,' he said, 'we are to be married, you and I.'

Khristo did not answer.

'Yes,' Sascha said, 'it is time you left this house of virgins.'

'I see.'

'But marriage, you know, is a serious business. You will have to be the very best of wives. Obedient and good-natured, ready always to protect the honour of the family. You must never flirt with strangers, or tell our secrets at the village well. And, of course, you must be eternally faithful. That most of all. Do you understand?'

'I do,' Khristo said.

Sascha smiled crookedly at the words, and nodded to himself. 'Yes,' he said, 'I almost believe you. You will give all but a little corner of your heart – a private place, you think.'

Khristo almost answered, then stopped.

Sascha laughed. 'Knowledge is forgiveness, boy, and who among us has not crossed his fingers behind his back? Come along, *bratets*' – the word meant *little brother* – 'and we'll go and see the priest.'

He stepped back and gestured for Khristo to precede him through the alcove that led from the parlour to the door of the house. He followed, and his hand fell affectionately on Khristo's shoulder. Sascha was slim and small-boned, an aristocrat, a man made for drawing rooms, but the force of the blow very nearly drove Khristo to his knees.

It was the same black Pobeda as before, idling at the kerb, shiny with rain. And the same driver, a thick roll of flesh riding atop his collar. This time, Sascha joined him in back. Crawled across the grey upholstery, sank down in the corner of the seat, and closed his eyes. They tore across the city at great speed, the driver banging on the horn with a red fist. The windshield wiper squeaked as it jerked back and forth across the glass. The back end of the car fishtailed alarmingly as the driver bent it into the corners. They bounced through puddles, spewing up huge fountains of brownish water, and people scattered in front of them, flailing and slipping on the wet pavement. An old man, stooped almost double, was startled from a daydream as he crossed the street and dropped a large sack as he hobbled for safety. Potatoes rolled every which way – the car bumped as it passed over them. Khristo turned and looked back. The man was gathering them up from the gutter as best he could. The driver, glancing at his outside mirror, snorted to himself: 'Horseshit in the soup tonight, Papa.'

The rain stiffened, sweeping over them in windblown sheets, and the Pobeda's amber beams seemed useless and insignificant in the dark blue light of the late afternoon. After cutting through a maze of city streets, they turned onto the ring road that surrounded the city, coming up on the occasional truck. The truck driver, knowledgeable on the subject of shiny black Pobedas, would wobble off the road to let them pass.

Some twenty minutes later the car slowed, the driver peered into the gloom, grunted with satisfaction, and swerved between two armoured cars parked in a vee at the entrance to a broad avenue. Khristo caught a glimpse of a horrified white face in the front of the armoured car on his side as the driver punched the accelerator and went sideways through the narrow gap. The slewing turn woke Sascha up.

'Mitya,' he said, 'you drive like a peasant.'

'I am a peasant,' the driver answered.

It was a grand, straight road that led out into the countryside, lined with towering poplars that swayed in the wind, a scene that suggested dispatch riders on horseback and carriages with footmen. Khristo stared out the window. There were police everywhere, wearing rain capes and armed with submachine guns. Hundreds and hundreds of them stamped their feet by the side of the road, snapping to attention as they flew by. A Stolypin car was parked at every intersection. Otherwise it was deserted, not a single vehicle going in either direction.

'Getting an eyeful?' Sascha asked.

Khristo turned away. It was not wise to look around too much – spies were said to memorize details of bridges and railways and police posts. Nobody in Moscow, despite the glare of the summer sun, wore sunglasses. It was not precisely forbidden, but it made people wonder why the eyes were concealed.

'It is the road to Koba's dacha,' Sascha explained, using Stalin's affectionate nickname. 'Twenty miles of it. Three special battalions guard it day and night – even the foxes don't come here.'

Three battalions meant thirty-six hundred men. Day and night. What was it Antipin had said about the soldier who guarded the spot where a flower had once grown?

'Don't forget the bodyguard,' Mitya said.

'Correct,' Sascha said. 'Wherever he is, dear Koba is accompanied by four hundred and two bodyguards. Not four hundred and three or one. The number must have special significance – so special, in fact, that none of us has ever figured it out. Nonetheless, you see how well our leader is beloved, that we protect him so.'

Mitya laughed. 'Big country, big numbers, everything big. When the bad spirits take our hearts and the blood runs high, we hack each other down like wheat, comrade student. Do you see? Koba knows us. Better than we know ourselves. We are all peasants – even the delicate flower in the back seat with you – and every peasant pines for the scythe in his hand. Wha-aaack!' He slashed at the dashboard with the side of his hand. 'And there are eight hundred and four whose single job it is to watch the four hundred and two!'

'Mitya indulges himself,' Sascha said. 'Now today, alas, you do not go to meet the Great One himself. If I were you, I would not be too sad about that. Whom Koba meets, he thinks about, and you are too young to be thought about in that way. No, today is our wedding day, as I have said, and the ceremony is to be performed by Yagoda himself. You know who that is?'

'Chairman Yagoda is the leader of the NKVD,' Khristo said.

'Very good,' Sascha said. 'He is my boss and your boss, so be on your best behaviour. Watch me, and do what I do. Remember that you are one of us.'

Khristo had overheard the instructors talking about Yagoda. It was obvious they feared him. Genrikh Yagoda had been born, raised, and educated in the Polish textile city of Lodz. Like his father before him, he was a chemist by training, and was known as Yagoda the Chemist. He had been Stalin's fist after the Revolution, no less an eminent chekist for being Polish. The great Dzerzhinsky, who had founded the Soviet intelligence services, was a Pole, and two of his notable assistants — M. Y. Latsis and Y. K. Peters — were Latvians by birth. Yagoda, in 1918, had organized and directed the new Gulag system of labour camps. He had disappeared for a time, then, in 1934, had been appointed head of NKVD. It was rumoured that he had plotted the death of Stalin's rival Kirov and had suggested that the assassination be used as pretext for getting rid of the Old Bolsheviks. There were rumours darker yet — his contemporary Bayonov had written that Koch's bacilli, introduced in the subject's food, would produce a galloping tuberculosis and a quick death from apparently natural causes. Thus there were some who would implicate him in Lenin's death as well as Kirov's.

For Khristo, the memory of that evening was never entirely clear. Certain moments stayed with him; every detail, every inflection of voice sharply recollected. Other times were lost in the mists. There were toasts — with different vodkas: Zubrovka, Polish Ostrova, the fiery Pertsovka. Two ounces every time. To Stalin. To revolution. To breasts and pussies. To departed friends. To the great city of Lodz. To Kiev. To Baku in the Transcaucasus. To Lenin. To life. To laughter. To friendship. Slowly the edges of the grand ballroom, all parquet and crystal to please the mistress of an aging prince, dimmed and faded from his vision. He began to feel as though he were sinking — a dizzying descent in both mind and body — into some desert valley at the depths of his soul. A sad and desperate place, arid, cruel, strewn with the bones of old friends and dreams, lost love, the times of childhood. He sank and sank, his chin sought his chest again and again, and he had to haul it upright with greater effort as time and toasts went on. The room swayed and bobbed in a light sea, and faces floated past his vision like ghost ships.

When the drinking slowed, the eating began. Ukrainian pork soup full of chopped red cabbage and garlic, cold peas with vinegar and salt, chicken stewed in cream. These he tasted, then filled up on hunks of black bread with sweet butter, first inhaling deeply of the bread – a time-honoured curative for vodka drinking. The smells of the food made him enormously hungry, but the vodka mustn't, he knew, be tampered with. Let it sit down there and fume, don't make it angry by sending down a lot of chicken stewed in cream – it might not like that. The men in the room with him – there must have been forty – ate prodigiously. Physically, they were all sorts, though Sascha stood out among them in form and finery. There were dark-skinned Georgians with moustaches and oiled curly hair who, like Stalin, spoke a barbaric, halting Russian, a language they'd had to learn in school. Some were pale and beefy, like Mitya, though some grew paler, and some redder, as the evening wore on. It was this group who stood to accept the honour of the toast to Kiev, this group who smacked their lips the loudest over the Ukrainian soup. Sascha, it turned out from the toasts, was from Leningrad – St. Petersburg. The intellectual city, compared to political Moscow. Kirov had been from Leningrad. During the dinner, people wandered about talking to each other, and Khristo recalled odd fragments of conversation. There was an almond-eyed man with a shaven head and olive skin who did something with sugar beets in Kazakhstan. But most were chekists, intelligence officers, and when they talked to each other they spoke in private code – nicknames, obliquities. They laughed and whacked each other on the shoulders. And, finally, there was Yagoda himself.

He took Khristo by the elbow as they went into the sauna after dinner, accompanied by Sascha, Mitya, and several others. They were all roaring drunk by this time.

99

They undressed in the yellow cedar antechamber, a large room decorated with Russian Orthodox icons, old wooden ones from country churches. There was Saint Prokópius with his handful of burning coals. The Virgin of Vadimir. The Anastasis – Christ harrowing hell. Saint Simeon on his pillar. Saint Lawrence racked with fire. Saint Basil. Saint Theodorus. Saint Menas, and the Patriarch Photius. They had the narrow faces and sorrowful eyes of Byzantine saints and bore the marks of time: wood rubbed smooth by handling, brass-coloured halos worn down to the grain. More recent suffering – chips and pockmarks – was also evident.

Khristo hung his clothing on a peg. When all were undressed, Yagoda proposed a blasphemous toast. Raised his glass and called the saints faggots and whores, proposed a list of sexual indecencies and drank to each. Then, inspired, he ran to the wall where his clothing hung and returned with a pair of revolvers. The group shouted and clapped, howled with laughter and urged him on. Yagoda the Chemist, his glasses fogged, thick grey hair curling along the tops of his shoulders, began firing into the icons. The shots were painfully loud in the small room and it was all Khristo could do to keep his hands from covering his ears. Other revolvers were produced. Khristo was offered one and blew a hole in a triptych of the martyrdom of Saint Ephraem. His marksmanship produced a roar of approval.

In the sauna, they sat on cedar benches and Mitya poured a pail of water on the coals, filling the tiny room with white steam. Yagoda peered at Khristo on the bench opposite him.

'This one belongs to you, Sascha, am I right?'

A voice from the steam: 'My very own.'

'And will he do the work?'

'Yes. Quietly too. The mice will never know he's around until it's too late.'

'You think he's a mouser?'

'A good one, if he works at it.'

'Yes, I agree with you. He has the look. Does he have the heart for it, though? That's what I worry about with a good mouser.'

From the steam, a different voice: 'He's the one that blew up Petenko, at Belov.'

'Oh? This is him? The Bulgarian?'

'The very one, Stoianev.'

'Stoianev. Well, I like Bulgaria. A refreshing place, I think, where, it is said, the women do it while hanging from trees. Tell me, Stoianev, is it so?'

'Oh yes,' he said, 'and while they do it, they bay at the moon.'

This produced a gale of laughter and wolf howls.

Yagoda nodded with satisfaction. 'Sascha is a nimble lad,' he said. 'He always finds the clever ones.' He leaned a little closer. He had the elongated face and small moustache of the intellectual, grey, speculative eyes and delicate features. 'Not too clever, of course. That makes people edgy. Now tell me this, and we'll see how clever you really are. Who is it that has eyes like binoculars, ears like telephones, fingers like glue, and a mouth that whispers?'

Khristo shook his head. 'I don't know.'

Yagoda threw his slim hands into the air and his eyes sparkled with mischief. 'I don't know either,' he cried. 'Let's dig him up and find out!'

That he remembered perfectly.

Otherwise, but for two moments that would live with him for a long time, it was all darkness. Drunken shouts, breaking glass, spilled food, rain blowing against the windows.

In the first moment, there was a thickset man in the uniform of a general, who sat against a wall with his legs stretched out before him. He held his right hand tightly over his right eye while blood welled from beneath and trickled down his cheek. All the while he was singing, in a false baritone, an old Russian love song.

In the second moment, the car pulled up in Arbat Street and Mitya let Khristo out. It was a cold, drizzling dawn. Sascha had passed out in the back seat, Khristo looked back at him through the fogged window. In sleep, he had the face of an old youth, fine features blurred, morning beard a blue shadow. Khristo stood unsteadily on the sidewalk. He had been drunk, then sober, then drunk again, and now his head had a spike through the temples.

'You can get in all right?' Mitya asked from the driver's seat.

He nodded that he could. The car pulled slowly away from the kerb.

There was a woman, probably going to work, coming toward him down the street. At first he thought she was an old woman because she was stooped and walked with difficulty, but when he peered through the darkness he could see that she was not old at all, perhaps in her thirties, and rather pretty in a fragile sort of way. Perhaps, he thought, she worked at Food Store 6, which was just around the corner. Perhaps she was a clerk, coming on duty at dawn to check the produce in as it came off the wagons and trucks from the countryside. She had seen the black Pobeda, Mitya at the wheel, Sascha in his leather coat sprawled in the back seat, and Khristo, swaying for a moment on the sidewalk. She stopped, then moved around him in a wide circle, walking close to the wall of the building. She kept her eyes on the pavement in front of her, but then, just for a bare instant, she glanced at him, then looked down again, and he realized that she knew who they were. She knew *what* they were, what *he* was, and she was afraid of him.

From the *New York Sun*, August 23, 1936:

102

MOSCOW, August 20 — President V. M. Molotov has announced that the Soviet Union is sending three hundred volunteers to assist Loyalist forces in the continuing conflict in Spain. 'At issue,' Molotov stated in a speech to the Praesidium, 'is the democratically elected workers and people's government in Madrid. The USSR must take every measure to ensure that oppositionist military units do not overthrow the popularly supported regime of President Manuel Azaña.' The unit of volunteers, who have chosen to call themselves the Brotherhood Front for the Protection of Spanish Democracy, is made up of civil engineers and public health workers and will provide technical assistance to the Azaña government. A Soviet spokesman informed The Sun that many of the volunteers are of various Eastern European nationalities.

Blue
Lantern

In Catalonia, some way inland from the ancient spice city of Tarragona, in the valley of the Río Ebro, lay the village of San Ximene. It was any and all of the villages of Spain, a series of white cubes stacked against the side of a brown hill, outlined sharply by a hot blue sky. To the eye of the traveller, it stood high above the road, somehow remote, and very silent and still. *Go on to the next village*, it seemed to say, *to Calaguer or Santoval, you will like it better there.*

San Ximene, and all the countryside thereabout – the olive and lemon groves, the vineyards, the fields where sheep grazed on stubble after the cutting of the wheat – these belonged to Don Teodosio, of the noble family Aguilar.

It had always been so. Like the blistering sun that dried the soil to dust and the cold wind that blew it away, it was a law of nature, a commonplace of existence. A local maxim had it that on the third day of creation, when God divided the waters and revealed the land, the first Aguilar was discovered there, dripping, awaiting his maker with a basket of figs.

Whatever else might be said of Don Teodosio, or Doña Flora, they were, like their distant ancestor, generous with the Aguilar figs. In rush baskets woven by the maids and seamstresses of the household, the figs arrived punctually every Christmas and Easter. If you were a peasant of the San Ximene region, sometime before the coming of the great holidays you would behold the cream-coloured De Bouton automobile, its body fashioned of tulipwood, rolling to a ceremonious stop in front of your mud-brick house. Miguelito, the chauffeur, would tap twice on the

107

horn – a sound as pure as a heavenly trumpet – and you, your good wife, your shy children, and your esteemed parents would gather, bareheaded, before the whitewashed doorway to receive the gift. Doña Flora – Don Teodosio was too much occupied with grave affairs to have time for such business – would descend from the elegant car, wearing a dove-coloured woollen suit with a foxtail stole, and approach the family, seconded by the chauffeur carrying the basket. She would greet you by name, inquire after the health of all, remark briefly on the piety of the season, and offer blessings all round. Miguelito would hand the basket to Doña Flora, she would in turn hand it on to the head of the household, who would thank her for the gift. Good wife, shy daughters, and esteemed mother would curtsy.

It was deemed, in general, a wise disposition of the Aguilar figs. If, somehow, you had miraculously contrived to dine as richly and voluminously as they did at the great house, the figs would have been just the thing to assure felicity of digestion, for they were infamously purgative. Perhaps they believed up there that all the world fed liberally on salted ham and pink frosted cakes and thereby suffered the attendant constipation – a distemper, like gout and melancholia, reserved exclusively for the rich. No matter the motive for their distribution, the Aguilar figs grew, had grown there for a thousand years, and something had to be done with them. Nobody, certainly, would ever buy them. Thus they came – thick-skinned and pungent, like all the gifts of Spain – to you. It was always nice to have the rush basket – something or other could be done with it.

This year, of course, being 1936, there would be no figs.

Not that they would cease to grow – the gnarled and twisted *ficus carica* had no choice in the matter. The harsh copper sun flamed in the heavens for months, as it always had, the ancient roots sought out what moisture remained in the stony soil of the river valley and, even in civil war, photosynthesis would not be denied. Not, that is, until the shellfire came and blew everything to hell. But, in October of 1936, the shellfire was still a comfortable distance away – more than two hundred miles away, where the Moorish armies of General Mola had besieged Madrid. And – *no pasarán*, they shall not pass – *they* would steal not one more inch of Republican earth.

So there would be figs. There would be lemons as well. Hard, green things certain to produce a gargoyle's scowl on the face of anyone foolish enough to taste them. For the true *limón* – a beautiful, fat, sunny fruit near sweet to the palate, you had to go to Valencia or Tarragona. In San Ximene, alas, they were not so blessed, the fertility of their little valley being most charitably described as *unkind*. The *vino tinto*, red wine, produced in the Aguilar vineyards was reputed to be curative, though exactly what it cured no one could say, lest it be life itself.

There would be figs, come harvest time, but they would no longer be nestled in rush baskets. They would not be bestowed by Doña Flora in her foxtail stole. The glossy De Bouton would never again sound its velvet trumpet at the whitewashed doorways of the San Ximene peasants. Those days were gone forever. The Aguilar figs were embarked on a new destiny.

Thirty-two percent of the total harvest would be retained by the workers and peasants of the San Ximene commune. Twenty-one percent would be donated to the food stores of the Asturian miners' brigades, fighting to the north. Twenty-four percent would be dispatched to relieve the hungers of Madrid, as the fascist noose was tightened around the city's throat, threatening to still its passionate song of freedom. Twenty-two percent of the harvest would travel east – eleven percent for hospitals on the coast, another eleven percent to feed the International Brigades, now flowing into the country from the breadth of Europe. An additional twenty percent would be required, it was

109

felt, for trade with other villages, so that tools and seed, medicine and ammunition, could be obtained. Let the world take note and raise its fist: the San Ximene figs were going to war!

But it would not be easy. There had been defeatist grumbling to the effect that San Ximene had pledged to distribute one hundred and nineteen percent of its fig harvest. How was that to be done?

Work harder! Thus spoke the fiery idealists of the village. An old man, however, his hands frozen to knotted claws by a lifetime of torturing food from the wretched soil, rumbled with laughter at such a suggestion. 'Work yourselves to death, if you like,' he said, 'but you'll not get a fig tree to grow more fruit.' A young peasant disagreed. Was it not the case that some of the fruit spurs were pruned from the trees every spring? Everyone had to admit it was the usual practice to do so. Well then, let them be. At this, the old man stopped laughing. 'If you do not cut some of the spurs, the branches will break in the autumn. You'll have your nineteen percent, it's true, but next year you'll have nothing.' The young peasant nodded, sadly, his agreement. He had to point out, however, that if Franco and his fascists gobbled up their beloved Spain in 1936, who was foolish or greedy enough to worry himself over the fig harvest of 1937? Heads swivelled back and forth between them as they argued. Who was right? What was right?

One timid soul – formerly a laundress in the Aguilar household – wondered aloud if, just perhaps, it might not be the safest course to lower the production goals. But at this *everyone* was aghast, so she fluttered her hands and quickly backed down, her career in political debate over before it began and a good thing too. For the percentages were as rocks or mountains – immutable.

These numbers were, after all, the precious fruits of weeks spent in fervent disputation – intense, talmudic sessions held in the back room of Serreño's Bar that had seen the best minds of San Ximene fully engaged in struggle

– and one didn't simply cast such treasure over the nearest fence. The percentages were *symbols* – a de facto treaty between countervailing forces. And, truly, that they were able to agree on anything at all was simply astonishing.

Consider the opening positions: the PSUC, Partido Socialista Unificado de Cataluña, in which socialists and communists had agreed to agree, wanted to parcel out the harvest down to the very last fig. The technical approach, in which numbers danced formally with contributions to the cause. What value a soldier? Less than a hospital nurse? More than a railroad worker? How many figs to each? It could, if one applied oneself to the dialectic with good will, be determined. It had to be determined – the war went on, and the trees would leave dormancy in a few months. So it would be determined. They would sit there and determine it. Serreño, make coffee!

On the other hand, the Partido Obrero de Unificación Marxista, POUM, had very different thoughts on the matter. These were the anarchists. To them, freedom was all and to hell with your pussyfooting numbers. Do nothing! That was their war cry. Action achieved by inaction. Simply leave the groves open and whoever needed figs could come and take them. Was this great battle in which they were engaged not, when all was said and done, over freedom itself? Could the past – the tyranny of priests, the despotic Aguilars, the brutal Guardia – be forgotten so quickly? Open the groves, open the town, open the world, come to that, and let each individual attain the full flowering of conscience. The ruling of the self by the self, *that* was government!

Clearly, at the beginning, the contending forces had some way to go.

And if, in getting to their common solution, they agreed to distribute many more figs than could safely grow on the fig trees, well, that was considered a very small price to pay.

*

111

Soon enough, there were committees for everything. Not that you could have found a soul under heaven – not a sane one, anyhow – who thought that Spaniards and committees were anything but mutually exclusive propositions, but something had to be done. Just be thankful, they told each other, that the committees were composed of PSUC and POUM and that, San Ximene being innocent of factories and workshops, the CNT – Anarcho-Syndicalist trade unionists – didn't have to be included. They would have hacked down the fig trees, sawn the damn things into boards, and built themselves a Hall of Workers.

There were committees for the distribution of food, for health and sanitation, for education, for grievances, for justice, for the moral improvement of youth. There was a committee assigned to the supervision of Don Teodosio and Doña Flora – held under virtual house arrest since the Nationalist rising in July. This committee immediately gave birth to a subcommittee – known as the Committee for the Carlist Mules – made up of a communist peasant and an anarchist peasant who, responsible for the twenty-six grey beasts belonging to the Aguilar estates, argued politics by the hour while shovelling manure out the barn windows. It was a small irony to call them Carlist mules since they, unlike their former owners, hardly cared whether or not the Bourbon monarchy was restored to the Spanish throne, but small ironies were permitted the men who had to wield water buckets and dung shovels on behalf of the greater good for they surely got little else for their labour.

There was even a committee – an ad hoc unit comprising both mayors, Avena from the PSUC and Quinto of the POUM – that saw to the needs of the convalescent draughtsman. He needed very little, it turned out: the rental of a small cottage at the edge of town, an old woman to clean once a week, some beans and vegetables from the market which he cooked for himself.

He was a small, shabby man, Señor Cardona, self-effacing and painfully polite. In his forties, he suffered from a

112

weakness of the lungs, and came to San Ximene now and again throughout the summer and fall to escape the smoke and dust of Tarragona, where he had a small business that produced engineering designs and specifications. He could often be seen through his window, bent over a table, making long, perfect lines on graph paper with infinite care. 'You must call me *comrade*,' he would admonish them with a shy smile, but nobody ever did. The ancient instincts of San Ximene recognized true gentility when they encountered it, and *señor* he remained. There were some – there always are – who would have had him turn his hand to minor labours for the cause, but their niggling was as chaff in the wind against his self-appointed protectorate, the older women of the village. Thus the mayors, Avena and Quinto, merely shrugged when somebody complained. If the harsh, dry air of San Ximene aided the recovery of Señor Cardona, he would have all he could breathe. Besides, he paid for everything – the pesetas were not unwelcome – and paid, in fact insisted on paying, just a little more than the going rate.

He was, above all, a nice man.

Dark-skinned, with thick sensual lips and a gently curved nose, the brown eyes – soft and deep – of a favoured spaniel, and a few strands of hair combed hopefully across a balding head. He wore always a hand-knit sweater beneath his camel-coloured jacket – the night air was crisp – and the canvas shoes of a comfortable man. He did, it was true, speak an odd Spanish, rather formal and stiff, but that was undoubtedly due to a childhood spent in Ceuta, down in Spanish Morocco. Was there a touch of the Moor in him somewhere? This was suggested, but it did not matter. It was simply impossible not to like him, and he quickly became a pleasant fact of life in San Ximene, appearing every week for a day or two, then going back to Tarragona in his rackety Fiat Topolino.

Though humble and self-effacing, he could not have been entirely without importance, for he was occasionally

113

sought out by two of his employees. In San Ximene, it was a curious notion that something, anything, could be so important that it would not wait a day or two, but Señor Cardona was a city gentleman, and it went without saying that city gentlemen were occupied by matters of considerable gravity.

Los Escribientes de Señor Cardona.

San Ximene rather honoured their part-time resident with such a title – *Señor Cardona's clerks*. It had a bit of a ring to it. Of course, the country was at war, and it seemed that nothing was the same anymore. The men who visited Señor Cardona were proof of that. Clearly, these were not the usual *escribientes*. One might have expected pale, doleful fellows, their spirits turned grey by years of sitting at desks and writing in ledgers. Or minor tyrants, of the fat-assed, preening variety, little lordlings who made life miserable for poor people with their nasty rules and educated meanness.

These *escribientes* were quite another matter. But with so many men fighting at the front, a businessman, it was supposed, had to make do, had to take what he could get. The younger one, with the pale skin, black hair and blue eyes, conducted himself with reserve and courtesy. Some of the village daughters quite liked looking at him, a feminine perception of banked fires warming their curiosity. No, it was the older one who bore thinking about, the older one who caused the local gossips to trail their nets.

The women in black who met at the well at sundown had a ringleader – Anabella was her name, she looked like the get of a mating between a monkey and a sparrow – who led the daily pecking sessions. *El Malsano* she called him, tapping a forefinger against her temple. The unwholesome one. 'He has snakes in his brain,' she said, 'and they bite him.' One of the younger women crossed herself when she said it, though that gesture was now very unwise indeed.

Others were less colourful in their descriptions but gave

114

him something of a wide berth. What sort of *escribiente* walked about in a drunken stupor? His index and middle fingers were brownish yellow with nicotine stains, his lank hair hung carelessly over his forehead, and the lines in his face were too deep for his years, like a film star, perhaps, whose career one day had faltered and died.

He was a Frenchman, probably there was no more to it than that. Serreño had overheard the clerks speaking French as they hauled a bundle of blueprints from the trunk of their long-hooded black Citroën. These were not, however, the same French people so much in evidence at the Aguilar household in summers past. None of that particular grace remotely touched them.

So it went, back and forth, as it does in a small place where people have known one another all their lives, the convalescent draughtsman and his two French clerks, something to talk about.

In the tide of village opinion there was one dissenter, and he made his views known only once and was silent thereafter. This was Diego, the POUM representative to the Committee for the Carlist Mules. One hot, slow afternoon in September, he watched the Citroën crawl slowly up the white street toward Señor Cardona's cottage. When it had passed, he spat out the barn window and nodded to himself, affirming a private theory. 'Russians,' he said.

His co-committeeman, the communist Ansaldo, raised his eyebrows and came to a full stop, his well-laden shovel frozen in midair. 'How do you know that?' he asked.

Diego shrugged. He didn't know how he knew, he just knew. His friend put the shovel back down, stood upright, and sought the small of his back with his free hand. 'If that is so, we are very fortunate indeed.'

Diego wasn't so sure. 'Perhaps,' he said. 'Perhaps not.'

'They will help us against the Falange,' Ansaldo said. 'They will bring tanks and aeroplanes.'

'If it suits them,' Diego said.

Ansaldo lowered his head a little. Diego knew what that

115

meant. 'You are a stubborn man, Diego. Russia is a mighty nation, a great people, and our only ally in this fight. If it is true they are here, you should feel joy to see them.' He was warming up his guns, Diego could tell, for a full afternoon of political cannonade.

'Yes, a mighty nation,' Diego mused aloud. He was silent a while, his mind seeking the applicable wisdom. At last he found it. *Con patienza y salivita, el elefante se coja l'armagita.*

It was an old saying in Catalonia, well tested and well proven over the years. *With patience and saliva, the elephant screws the ant.* But he chose not to say it. Those two were Russians, he was sure of that, and if there were two, there would be more. He had heard that the Soviet Union was sending *health workers* to Spain. He was not sure what health workers would look like, but he was quite sure that they would not look anything like those two. He balanced all this in his mind for a moment, then decided that it was a good time not to have opinions. Maybe later. For the present, the best course was to clean the stables and shut up.

* * *

On October 9, just after midnight, it began to rain in Madrid.

Then, over the Guadarrama range to the west, white flashes lit the sky. A moment later came the long, rolling reports of marching thunder. Faye Berns was jolted awake, came to her senses sitting upright in the narrow bed, her right hand reaching for Andres – who was not there – her left hand resting on a large revolver on the night table. *Boots*, she told herself silently. *Right away. Now.*

She swung her feet over the side of the bed, discovered she'd kicked the quilts onto the floor during the night, reached down and swept them aside, found her right boot. She dropped to her knees, tried to look under the bed, but it was pitch black. The stone floor was like ice – there was no heat in the building. As she reached toward the foot of the bed, she leaned on the quilts and found the other boot muffled within.

The room's small window lit up for an instant. She counted to four-elephant before the sound of the thunder reached her. It was a storm in the mountains, nothing more. There were no sirens, no screams, no machine guns firing from the roof. She took a deep breath and let it out, felt the pounding in her heart ease off, and fell back down on the bed still holding a boot in each hand. Thunder and lightning, not the other thing. She used to love storms. At home, they meant a break in the sweltering, humid summertime, the rain washed down the Brooklyn streets and, for a while, the air actually smelled sweet, like the country.

Andres said that in war you sleep with your boots on. She said they kept her from sleeping. He said that soldiers learned to sleep no matter what. And there you had Andres. Soft as a mouse, but a fountain of righteousness – he lived and breathed it, wore it like a suit of moral armour. Oh, you couldn't do it? That was fine, he understood. You must be doing your best, for nobody ever did less. He would just do more himself. Would do your job as well as his own. Anywhere but here, she would have thought him an insufferable prig and hated him wholeheartedly. But it wasn't anywhere but here, and here, where everything was upside down and inside out, somebody had to be Andres, somebody had to set the example.

It took ten seconds to put on the boots, and with ten seconds to spare you could live instead of dying. According to Andres, who knew about war. But she didn't think this particular ten seconds mattered all that much. From the top floor of 9 Calle de Victoria, formerly the maids' attic, it took about forty seconds to run down five flights of marble stairs to a long, vaulted hallway that led to the street. There was an alcove in the wall about ten feet from the door – at one time a polished mahogany table had stood there, but it vanished into the barricades during the street fighting of

117

July 19 – and that was going to serve as Faye Berns's bomb shelter. Some of the building's tenants took cover in the basement, talking and drinking wine until dawn. This she would not do. Let the Condor Legion blow her to pieces – they would not bury her alive.

Besides, it was the prevailing opinion that the Germans would not attempt night bombing – they were too much in love with their fancy Messerschmitt machines to smash them up on Madrid's surrounding hillsides. The Italian pilots, however, were another story. She'd seen one of them when his plane crash-landed in a beet field just outside the city. Some militiamen in their blue monos – mechanics' overalls had become the uniform of the Republican brigades – had carried him back to the city hanging tied, hand and foot, to a pole, like a wild boar taken in a medieval hunt. Even so, he swaggered. He had a stiff handlebar moustache and he cursed his captors at length and with vigour. When he stood against the wall of an elementary school he refused the blindfold and sneered at the militiamen. But when he fell he just looked like a bundle of rags. They brought a horse to drag the body away, one of the horses that used to do the same job for the bull on Sunday afternoons.

The sergeant of the firing squad had seen her standing there. He made a clenched fist and said, in sad and solemn tones, *'No pasarán, señorita. No pasarán.'* She had come to know Spain, and Spaniards, and she perfectly understood his irony. *Observe this dirty work. Thus our slogans come to reality.* And he was praising her, in his own special style, for not turning away from what had to be done.

Frances Bernstein would have turned away. Faye Berns did not. Frances Bernstein was the daughter of Abel Bernstein, the fierce proprietor of Bernstein's Department Store – Established 1921. The second largest department store, after the mighty Abraham & Strauss, in Flatbush.

Faye Berns came to life midway between Pembroke and Paris, on the S.S. *Normandie*, as Frances Bernstein's

118

well-worn Brooklyn Public Library card stood high on the wind for a moment, then fluttered into the Atlantic to the cheers of a Danish painter named Lars. Frances Bernstein had spent twenty-three years waiting to become Faye Berns. Although near crushed to death by a parlourful of great-breasted aunts with diamond rings up to their wrists, an overstuffed apartment with a twittering canary, and a really very sweet Cornell man named Jacob, she had managed the transmigration of souls. She had escaped.

The canary was called Rabbi Cohen. That was Abel Bernstein, the anticlerical socialist, speaking. He was rich, it was true, but he sold goods of reasonable quality at a fair price to workers. That was his political destiny – *the store*, her family called it – and he accepted it. Picked up the chequebook, took out the fountain pen, let the National Peace Guild and the Brooklyn Committee for Social Justice know where Abel Bernstein stood. When she wrote from Paris that she was going to Spain, had already visited the Comintern offices on the Rue de Lafayette, his letter back to her was a classic. He agreed with her stand. Right was on her side. Now was the time. *But please God for the sake of your mother do not go to Spain!*

In the darkness of the little room under the eaves, Faye Berns became conscious of the ticking of the clock. The heartbeat rhythm of insomnia. *Oh God*, she thought, *now I can't sleep*. She opened her eyes. The room was so dark, the air seemed to fill with dancing grey particles. The insomnia was an old enemy, vanquished by daily hard work and the exhaustion of simply surviving in a beleaguered city. But now it came back, especially on those nights when Andres took his draughting materials from the closet and went away – usually for the better part of a week.

Very well. She had dealt with executions and the Condor Legion, now she would deal with insomnia. She tried to turn on the light, but the electricity was off. Went to the sink in the corner and tried to splash water on her face, but the water was off. Peered at the clock – it was 12:05. She did not have to be up on the roof until 3:30, but Renata was up there now, so she might as well visit. A visitor, she knew – Andres sometimes brought her a cup of tea – helped the hours pass.

She laced up the boots, first pulling hard at the two pairs of cotton socks to make sure there was no crease. Checked the safety on the Llama pistol, then stuck it inside the waistband of her thick corduroy skirt. *Damn Andres*, she thought. What clothes she had not given away were being ruined by the gun. Why could she not have a holster like everyone else? She had stood in line for a day at the armoury to get the pistol, but nowhere in the city could she find a holster for it. She asked Andres, finally. Of course he could get her a holster, it would simply mean that a soldier at the front would do without. Well, did she want it? He tormented her with privilege, as though she would, by the hand of fate, eventually turn into the cosseted little dumpling she had been born to become. Well – her fingers found ribs – she was no dumpling now. Her waistband had more than enough room for the gun. She had long chestnut hair, a nose with a bump, and a wide, generous, impertinent mouth. Her single good feature – the way she saw it – were eyes the colour of pale jade that had raised more than their share of hell. Her beauty, the aunts had always insisted, was inner, and it had taken a number of years, and a number of boys, to pay the world back for *that*.

Over her work shirt she pulled on a heavy grey sweater that her Aunt Minna had knitted as a graduation present – she liked it because it was of sufficient length and bulk to hide the pistol – then tied the red neckerchief loosely around her throat. In a city running out of everything, it was as much of a uniform as anybody had. She closed the door behind her and climbed the iron-rung ladder to the roof.

'Todavía?' Still?

'Siempre!' Always!

120

Sign and countersign, called quietly across the roof, were peculiar to 9 Calle de Victoria — each building had its own passwords. The city was awash with secret signals, codes, posters, banners, *pronunciamenti* painted feverishly on walls — hammers and sickles with drip lines to the sidewalk. The fiery Basque orator La Pasionaria made daily speeches to the city over a network of public address systems wired together through the streets. Her words — *It is better to die on your feet than to live on your knees* — were repeated everywhere. Constantly she reminded the women of Madrid that their traditional weapon, boiling oil hurled from a basin, was not to be put aside when the enemy arrived.

At the top of the hatchway to the roof, Faye Berns paused for a moment and looked out over the city. It was black and cold, the faint outlines of cathedral spires pointed shadows in the darkness.

'Faye?' Bundled in a large, shapeless army coat, Renata moved toward her through the gloom.

'It's me.'

'Can it be time?'

'No. I came for company.'

Studied closely, feature by feature, Renata Braun was something of a covert beauty, subtle and finely made, though the impression left on the world at large was that of a woman whose surface was fashioned by the exigencies of a life lived in difficult times and places. She was fortyish, with salt and pepper hair hacked off short, a delicate nose that reddened in the cold, and severe, gold-rim spectacles that were continually removed so that she could rub the dent marks where they pinched. A Berliner, she carried with her the sophisticated aura of that city and was sharp-witted and sharp-tongued, often to the edge of cruelty. Renata was Andres's friend. Faye was Andres's lover. They had, over a few months' time, worked it out from there, becoming, finally, closer than sisters, a friendship in time of war.

121

Renata took her hands. '*Ach*, ice.'

Faye shrugged and smiled. She had given her gloves away and Renata knew it. She squeezed back for a moment, then put her hands in the deep pockets of her skirt. 'How goes the night?'

Renata made an ironic little gesture with her mouth. 'Very slow,' she said. 'With *der Sphinx* at one's side.'

Faye looked past her, saw the dark shape of Félix, the Belgian journalist who never spoke if he could help it, sitting slumped on an upturned crate beside the machine gun. The position was backed up against the wall of a shed – so that the roof overhang kept the rain off the gunners – and 'protected' by a semicircle of meagrely filled sandbags. The machine gun lay back on its tripod, muzzle pointed at the sky.

'Hallooo, Félix,' she called out quietly. Needling him, knowing he thought her an atrocious American brat, knowing he agreed with those stern Spanish commanders who, echoing Winston Churchill, called the foreigners in Madrid 'armed tourists'.

'The poor thing,' Renata said, shaking her head.

Faye could not see his face, but she could imagine it. A sneer compounded of disgust – specific; and ill-temper – general. Félix was obsessed with doom. He had come to Madrid as correspondent for a Christian Socialist newspaper in Antwerp; then stopped filing stories, stopped doing much of anything. He wanted to leave the city, somehow he could not, yet he seemed to loathe everything about it. Mostly the frenetic tension of the place, which drove people into hilarious, slightly crazed companionship. Live today, for tomorrow we die. You could be married at any militia office in five minutes. And divorced as quickly, though many declined to bother with official sanctions in any way at all. There was an army, a real army, with tanks and planes and artillery, a few miles to the west. When the battle came, everybody in Madrid would simply pick up a gun and walk out to meet it.

Such courage made them saints, of a modern kind, and they knew it. They cared enough about something to die for it, and a sweet, delicious madness blew through the city like a wind. To be a Madrileno was a privilege, an honour. Only a few, like Félix, could find no joy in it.

Or were there, in fact, more than a few.

The Moorish brigades and Spanish Legionnaires of General Mola were aimed at the city in four columns. Mola had been asked, by a foreign reporter covering the Nationalist side, which column would have the glory of leading the attack against Madrid. 'I have a fifth column,' Mola had boasted, '*inside* the city, and it is they who will lead the attack on Madrid.'

This might have been a deception, meant to sow suspicion among allies of wildly different passions: Basques and Catalans seeking their own nationhood, communists of several disciplines, anarchists, democrats, idealists, poets, mercenaries, and those moths who were forever seeking the flame of the hour in which to immolate themselves.

Or it might have been said merely to torment the inhabitants a little. Civil war is not unlike a fight between lovers: each side knows precisely how to infuriate the other. During the Nationalist siege of Gijón, the water supply of the defending Republicans gave out, and they suffered terribly from thirst. Quiepo de Llano, the Nationalist general, went on Radio Seville every night, drinking wine and smacking his lips into the microphone. After that, he boasted of the sexual prowess of his soldiers — the women of Gijón must be ready! It was a powerful station, and all across Europe people tuned in for the nightly show.

Faye and Renata walked for a time, talking in low voices, circumnavigating the rooftop. The rain had stopped, though lightning still flickered over the Guadarrama. They

123

talked about life, laughing at times. At moments like these, Faye felt she was looking down at the entire world, that it was all laid out for her. Her urge for such flights had been dealt with rather summarily at Pembroke – those professors she'd thought to be sympathetic would listen stoically for an hour, then turn her head forcefully back to learning, study, the obligations of womanhood. Everything substantive, hard and demanding. She'd sensed a long line of romantic girls like herself, extending out the doors of the little cottages where the faculty offices were located, sent home to study, marry, pray, bathe in cold water – anything but *life* in its purest, most abstract twirls and adagios, which was what she loved to think about. Renata was willing to talk to her on any level she chose and Faye was more than grateful to be found worthy of such attention: she needed to be taken seriously and she knew it.

'When you are done living for yourself, only then do you learn that living for others is the privilege,' Renata said at one point.

They turned a corner.

'I think that is what I believe,' Faye said. 'I think. But perhaps not. Sometimes I feel I'm like a . . .' She stopped. Moved to the parapet of cracked plaster that closed in the roof. Stared out across the city. Renata caught up and stood by her side.

'Isn't that strange,' Faye said.

'What is?'

'Perhaps it is a lover's signal.'

'What?'

'The blue glow. Over there. Across the street, then one, two, three blocks – no, two blocks, three streets.'

'I don't see anything.'

'Here, look, squint your eyes and follow my finger.'

'God in heaven,' Renata breathed, then turned away quickly, calling 'Félix' in a loud, urgent stage whisper.

He arrived at a trot, sorrowful eyes peering from beneath a wool muffler knotted around his head. Renata spoke to him in rapid French, then pointed. He said a few words back. She gave him what sounded like an order and he turned on his heel and left in a hurry. 'I have sent him for the street map,' she explained.

The blue light moved suddenly, then came to rest in a new, more visible, position. It disappeared for an instant, as a shape moved past it, then glowed again.

'There's somebody there,' Faye said.

'Yes, there is. Have you your pistol?'

'Yes.'

'Give it to me.' She thrust out a hand.

'We'll go together.'

'No! The post may not be abandoned – it must be two to work the gun. Listen, please. When Félix returns, you must remain here. I will go and see about this light. Now please, the pistol.' Her eyes intense behind the gold spectacles, she wiggled her fingers impatiently.

Faye got angry. '*You're* the one on guard,' she said, voice rising. She glanced at her watch, a tiny thing her grandmother had brought from Russia. 'It is two-twenty,' she said triumphantly. 'And I'm the one who's going.'

'Faye, no!' Renata shouted and hurried after her.

Faye opened the door to the hatch, started to climb down. Renata held the door and watched her descend. 'Amen, then,' Renata said. 'Be careful.'

The door clicked shut and she was in darkness. It gave her heart a twinge. She'd expected Renata to argue further, finally to insist on going along. Holding the revolver tightly so that it wouldn't fall through her waistband, she galloped down the marble staircase. As she reached the door, she heard Félix running down the hall, somewhere above her.

*   *   *

Lieutenant Drazen Kulic, Second Section, Fourth Directorate (Special Operations), NKVD, had waited three days for the thunderstorm in the Guadarrama. With the lightning as cover, he intended to make a great flash of his own. Without the storm, the great flash would bring down Nationalist units from everywhere, there would be a *ratissage* – literally 'rat hunt', a counterinsurgency sweep – and he had little confidence in his guerrilla band's ability to elude it. They were not mountain people. They were railroad workers and boilermakers and machinists, UGT communists to a man and very brave, but they did not know this terrain. If they had to move too quickly through the forests there would be lost weapons, excessive noise and sprained ankles. Those who could not keep up would have to be sacrificed and, worse yet, it would have to be done by hand, since a pistol shot was unthinkable. He'd seen townspeople attempt to fight in the mountains of Yugoslavia, and he was damned if he was going to add one more ghastly scene to the tragicomedy of the Spanish war.

Earlier that day, he'd sent his least valuable man down the road. Disguised as a cripple – they'd cut him a primitive crutch from a tree branch – he'd walked up to the roadblock carrying a newspaper packet of dried beans. They'd done the thing right – it was even a Nationalist newspaper, *ABC*, the Monarchist daily – but to no avail. The sentries at the roadblock wanted a password. They were very sorry, they knew how bad things were in the village, that his poor sister needed the *habichuelas*, but – no password, no going down the road. They took the beans, saying they would take them to the sister, but they hadn't even asked her name.

The convent schoolhouse in the village was being used as a Nationalist armoury, logistical support for the Falangist columns in their advance on Madrid. The radio message sent to Kulic's group in the Guadarrama from the Soviet base in Madrid had been specific: *Take the armoury*. Well, he couldn't take it, with twenty machinists, but he could blow it up, and that he intended to do.

He had fourteen time pencils – virtually the same explosive device that had accidentally killed T. E. Lawrence's lover and bodyguard, Dahoud, as he tried to blow up a train. After Arbat Street, Kulic had attended a special school deep in the Urals, and he'd had to read *The Seven Pillars of Wisdom* very thoroughly. What Lawrence did to the Turkish supply columns in World War I, he was now trying to do to Franco's fascists. With time pencils manufactured in 1914. No matter. He would find a way once they broke into the armoury. Theoretically, you could sink a battleship with a candle. Theoretically.

But first he had to get his people down a road. For that, he needed to steal the password. Thus, at 4:00 p.m., as the mountain skies darkened and the wind blew hard from the west, they'd set up their own roadblock two miles east of the Nationalist sentries. Along came two Guardia in a small truck. Kulic's men, acting like normal sentries, had demanded the password. '*Rosas blancas*' came the answer. White roses, a Carlist symbol of purity.

At 10:30 p.m., with the storm very close, a light rain pattering down on the road, they marched to the roadblock, gave the password, and walked into the village. A company of Navarrese infantry was assigned to hold the area and protect the armoury, but the rain had long since driven them back into the Convent of the Sacred Heart, where they were billeted. Kulic set up his machine gun facing the doors of the convent and sent a small ambush team back down the road to wait for the sentries, in case they returned once the gunfire started. A shipfitter, an agile little spider of a man accustomed to riveting in the steelwork of half-built freighters, climbed a drainpipe to the roof and set the convent on fire by dripping gasoline down the chimney. As the soldiers ran out – the sixteenth-century abbot who designed the place knew that the greatest security lay in a single access point

– they were killed. Those who remained inside died in the fire.

The convent schoolhouse – a separate building – was piled to the rafters with rifle and machine-gun ammunition, but what most gladdened Kulic's heart were eighty cases of artillery shells for the Nationalists' 105mm field guns. He now had the power for the explosion, but no lightning. A few minutes after 11:00 p.m., there was gunfire on the road and the ambush team returned, having chased the Nationalist sentries into the forest. At 11:30, the thunder and lightning finally started. By 12:05, after four failures with the time pencils, Captain Drazen Kulic had his big flash. A burning school desk spun brilliantly through the rainy air, high above the village, trailing smoke and sparks before it fell to earth and disappeared from view. Kulic and his band vanished into the mountains. A number of villagers died in the explosion. It couldn't be helped.

* * *

Faye Berns moved through the dark streets of the city, hemmed in by buildings that rose steeply above her, like a corridor in a dream. A small wind, suddenly warm, touched her face. A dog was barking some distance away. She could tell it had been barking for a long time – its voice was almost gone. But, she realized, it doesn't know what else to do, so it barks. A sense of infinite, indescribable loss rolled in from the night and filled her heart.

If I were Catholic, I'd cross myself.

She did it anyhow, quickly, a rapid figure-four in the style of the Spanish women. There was something malefic in Spain, that she knew for a surety, and it was out that night. From the apartments high above her came a sense of restless sleep, disturbance, unquiet, as though every man and woman dreamed they heard a door click open. Spirit wanderers are out, she thought, who cannot find their way home. Perhaps her own ancestors, burned alive in the Inquisition. The blood carried more than oxygen, more than anyone knew and, once the streets were dark and deserted, the bad memories of this place returned. Too many terrible things had happened here. Walking in the centre of the narrow street, she could hear water running in the drains, and with every breath came the chill odour of anciently decayed masonry.

Three streets. Two blocks.

From down here, she would never find the blue light, it was like being in a deep canyon. But she *would* find it. She listened to her footsteps, tried to walk more softly. Her fingers crept beneath the sweater and touched the butt of the revolver. She seemed alone in the world, but maybe that wasn't so bad. The Republican Checa – modelled on, and named after, the Soviet intelligence Cheka – often roamed at night through the neighbourhoods. It was better not to meet them.

Calle de Plata.

Where the medieval silversmiths had kept their workshops. Her cousin Eric, who graduated third in his class at Erasmus High, took jewellery-making at the Art Students League. Now he was a communist. Like Renata and Andres. Was she one too? No, she didn't think so. She was a passionate idealist, in love with the idea of democracy. Certainly she dreamed, like Andres, of a world without oppression and cruelty. She had come to Spain to put one more hand on the wheel that turned toward justice. Were all Jews communists? Hitler said so. Her father grimaced at Hitler's name. 'Why don't you kill him?' he asked the sky. Jews hated injustice, that was what it was. Fania Kaplan, a Jewish girl not much older than herself, with family in Brooklyn, had shot Lenin through the neck because he betrayed the Revolution. But Lenin survived. She would like to shoot Hitler through the neck. They would, she knew, march her in glory up Flatbush Avenue if she did that. Even Mr. Glass, of Glass Stationery, and he was a Republican.

Avenida Saldana.

There was a big market here on Thursdays. An old lady with a moustache gave her something free every time — radishes, parsley. The fishstall man had once picked up a red snapper and bobbed it up and down as though it swam toward her, and everyone had laughed and made Spanish jokes. Now the street was deserted. On the roof of one of the buildings across the street, she had seen a blue light. She had come here to find it. Of course, she could turn around and go back and tell Renata that she couldn't find it. Nobody would be the wiser. In all likelihood, the light didn't mean anything at all, simply one more inexplicable event in this inexplicable country. So go home.

No.

Well, perhaps. But at least, she told herself, examine the buildings.

The numbers ran differently here, but the third one from the corner, 52 Avenida Saldana, roughly corresponded to 9 Calle de Victoria. That meant she might be on the wrong street, because 52 Avenida Saldana was a two-storey factory where they made wooden chairs.

54 Avenida Saldana. That was a possibility. She counted up six storeys.

Number 56 was not a possibility. An old hotel for commercial travellers, it had a steep roof sheathed with green copper. Number 58 was a rather smart private house, with little balconies and French windows, three storeys high.

It had to be 54.

That's good, Faye, you figured it out. Now go home. Report the incident to the Checa, let them worry about it.

She crossed the street. Avenida Saldana was a bit fancier than Calle de Victoria, narrow sidewalks ran along its edges. She stood at the base of the building and stared straight up. No blue light. But on the top floor, just below the roof, a window was open a few inches and, very faintly, she could hear a woman singing. She had heard the song before, mothers sang it to babies to put them to sleep.

*

Good, darling, very good. Her upbringing came through loud and clear. *And brave? In the middle of the night. In Madrid. All alone. With only Nana's watch and a big Spanish gun. Such a gun. Myself, I'd be afraid to touch it.*

Which was probably why, more or less, she simply went into the building and up to the roof. Because the blood did carry more than oxygen. Because there was something there that – when it was crystal clear that retreat with caution was the only sensible path – took the first step and the second step and all the rest of the steps. She had some help, on the order of *I'm an American and I can go anywhere I want,* but she had something a little older than that as well. It didn't precisely have a name, or maybe it had too many names, but it got her up to the roof. And, surprise of surprises, at a time when so much bravery bled itself out into nothingness, it turned out to matter a great deal that she went there. It saved lives.

First she removed her boots. Leaning against a cold wall in the dark hallway, she worked them off and tied the laces together and hung them around her neck. Drew the pistol from her waistband, cocked it, held it before her with a finger hooked securely around the front of the trigger guard. Put her left hand on the wall and walked slowly in her socks up the stairs to the roof, the sound of the lullaby getting closer as she climbed.

The door to the roof was chained and the chain was padlocked.

Breathing hard from the climb, she stood there frozen, so deeply enraged that her cheeks were hot. After all that!

She'd seen her friend at Pembroke, Penelope Hastings of Hyde Park, New York, fiddle a lock with a hairpin. Two problems. She didn't have a hairpin. And it wasn't that kind of lock. It was like a bicycle lock, with a combination. Olive green. Scratched and worn as though it had been well used: first to lock up a bicycle, perhaps at a place like a college where unlocked bicycles were frequently 'borrowed', then to secure a big trunk, which had to travel aboard a transatlantic liner to Europe. *That* sort of lock.

The sort of lock that, if you turned four right, sixteen left, and twenty-seven right, snapped open, though it took one last little jiggle, requiring a practised twist of the hand, to make it spring cleanly.

It was, she was sure, her very own lock, which she'd put in the back of a drawer some months earlier, thinking it was something that she didn't need then but would desperately want the minute after she threw it away. She was shocked to find it, but there was something much too eerie to contemplate in such a coincidence and she had no time to think about it anyhow. Explanations would have to wait.

In the silence at the top of the stairs, she could hear the singing woman one floor down. A child coughed. The woman murmured in Spanish. Then began humming softly, a song without words made up as she went along.

Faye put the lock and the gun between her feet. Slipped one hand beneath the chain, drew it slowly, link by link, across her palm until it was free of the door handle, then laid it silently on the floor, kneeling slowly. Retrieved the gun and held it in her right hand, then put the lock inside one of the shoes hanging around her neck. Took a breath, and pushed gently against the door with her left hand.

The door made one small squeak as it opened. The humming stopped. Faye took a step onto the roof.

She was wound tight as a spring, but not frightened. She didn't think it through, but some part of her mind was trying to let her know that when a door is chained and padlocked on one side, there is rarely anybody on the other side. At least not anybody who wants to be there.

The roof was deserted.

On one wall stood a blue lantern. A device used, perhaps, on a ship or in a railroad yard. She could see the shape of the flame burning behind the blue glass. She went up to it. Opened the little door. And blew it out.

Squinting against the darkness, she peered out over the intervening rooftops but could not make out her own building. Then, close to where she thought it might be, a match flared. The flame lingered for an instant, then disappeared.

Renata!

No signal had been arranged, but she knew absolutely that Renata had been watching the blue light, had seen it go out, and had contrived to make a visible acknowledgment.

Now she flew.

Lantern swinging from her left hand, gun clutched in her right, shoes banging against her breasts, she ran down the stairs and out into the street. Her socks got wet and her feet hurt but she wasn't going to stop for anything. Pumping her arms, hair flying, she tore down the side street, past Calle de Plata, into Calle de Victoria, almost slipping as she went around the corner, into the building past her bomb shelter alcove, up the stairs, up the ladder, onto the roof, rushing into Renata's arms and yelling at the top of her lungs, yelling with triumph.

* * *

In Seville, it was the custom of Hauptmann Bernhard Luders, of the Luftwaffe's Condor Legion, always to have a woman the night before he flew a mission. Such sport maintained the traditions of that city, where Don Juan had been born and raised and where, as a young man, he had observed with horror that the corpse in a funeral procession was his own, and resolved to fight death with lust from that day forth.

It cooled him, Luders said. Left him calm and level-headed for work the following day. It gave him, also, a reputation, and that he enjoyed immensely. He was twenty-one years old, with a small angry face and a small transparent moustache. At his direction, Feldwebel Kunkel, his batman, would sit in a gilded, red plush chair

133

outside the room at the Hotel Alfonso XIII, an apparent guardian of lovers' privacy but in fact an advertisement for the heated *Wurstverstecken* (hide-the-wiener) games being played on the other side of the door.

After midnight, when the officers came upstairs from drinking in the hotel bar, they would nod to Kunkel. He would rise and salute. 'He is in tonight?' someone would always ask. 'Yes sir,' Kunkel would answer, 'but he flies tomorrow.' Ahh, they would nod approvingly, aware of his custom, then add the obligatory joke: 'We shoot by night that bomb by day.'

In response to the joke, Kunkel, a man who understood loyalty at its root, would offer the obligatory response: a slow raising of the hands and eyes to heaven. *What lovers these pilots!*

Luders's latest was sixteen.

Evangelina. *Evangelina.* To Luders, even her name reeked of Spain, of Catholicism, of darkness, ignorance, superstition as black and wild as the unruly bush between her marble legs.

She drove him insane.

He had frolicked a bit at university in Heidelberg, among the properly raised dough-maidens of the city's aristocracy, but nothing had prepared him for what he took to be the true Spanish passion. The Mediterranean *Süden*, the South, tickled his Northern European fantasies to begin with – it was so hot and filthy and poor, one could do anything. *Anything.* The little witch would crawl about the hotel carpet wearing nothing at all, catch hold of his boot and plead with him. It was Spanish, the pleading, but somehow the meaning worked its way through. She was defiled, worthless. He had led her into the Temple of Sin and now she was lost in its vast recesses, a maddened novitiate. She could think of nothing else. Nothing. All day long, devils whispered in her ear, of practices so demonic she dared not speak them aloud. For such thoughts he must punish her. Now. For if he did not staunch this frightful

134

thirst she would tear her hair in frenzy. She sobbed and moaned and wriggled like an eel and begged him to put out the fire that burned her alive.

Poor Kunkel.

He had to sit there and listen to it night after night — and privately wondered how the man ever got any rest. Also, it fell to him to ferry a constant stream of gifts to Evangelina's family, who lived in a neighbourhood that frightened him, in a house that made him ill. He had not joined the air force with such adventures in mind, but what was one to do. Hauptmann Luders wasn't a bad sort, a smart Rhenish lad with a rigid back and a taste for a fight who liked his stinky little cigars. Yet he had plunged into the Spanish mysteries up to his very neck. Ah well, these Condor Legion pilots believed themselves to be of a higher order. Perhaps they were.

At 1:30 a.m., Kunkel knocked discreetly at the door. It was time. Luders disentangled himself from the girl, washed quickly, and arrived at the airfield, a little north and west of the city, a half hour later. There was excellent coffee in the briefing hut, and Von Emel went through the usual drill: weather, situation on the ground – little enough happening, although someone had blown up an armoury in the Guadarrama – and mission. But some things were not as usual. There were two SD types in attendance, from the Nazi party's foreign intelligence service. Small men in expensive suits, sharp-eyed and silent. Luders did not mind the Abwehr – they were military and had kinship with the airmen – but these two made him nervous. They stared at him. The other variation concerned the mission itself. Von Emel handed him a circled street map of Madrid and explained at length.

He rather hurried the takeoff, because he had to reach Madrid while it was still dark. That would require some fast flying, but Luders was an excellent pilot and his Messerschmitt had airspeed tucked here and there that only he knew about. Willy Messerschmitt himself had

135

come to Spain in August, to tour behind Nationalist lines and visit the places where his planes would be tested, and proven. In fact, the 109 was well suited to what Luders would ask of it. The five-hundred-pound bomb slung beneath the belly of the plane didn't slow him down, though it did drink a little extra gas.

Just before sunrise, the dawn no more than a faint blur behind him, he came skimming in over the city from the east. He could not hear the rattle above the engine noise, but a few yellow pinpricks of anti-aircraft fire were evident as he flew over the Paseo del Prado; however, he was really too low, and going too fast, for the Spanish gunners to have any patience with him. He steadied his foot on the bomb-release pedal and kept a light thumb atop the joystick where the machine-gun button was located. You never knew what was waiting on the rooftops — it was wiser to sweep up as you went.

He moved closer to the window, body tensed for action. He had been born with the eyesight of a hawk, and now scanned the dark blocks below until he found what he was looking for. A pinpoint of blue light. From there it was all instinct. He banked hard, came sideways through the turn, the aeroplane slicing neatly through the bumpy air above the city, wound up in a shallow dive with the nose of the plane in perfect line with the beacon.

Then several things happened very quickly. A red flickering that seemed almost to come from the beacon itself. He drove his thumb down hard, but the joypoint, the angle where his tracer bullets came together, was high. He corrected. The red flickers got much larger. There were three figures on the roof — one of them perhaps a woman? Shoved his foot to the floor, felt the plane kick free of its dead weight, then banked hard to the south, laying all the juice he had into the engine.

It took quite some time before he realized that he had a problem. Nothing like a six-second bombing run to ice

136

over the nervous system. But, as he flew over a small forest of pine and cork oak, he discovered that his right foot was throbbing like a giant clock. He looked down, moved the foot, saw a pfennig-size half moon of rushing treetops flanked by two bright red droplets. As sweat stood suddenly on his brow, he clutched frantically, testicles first, at his body. Even as the throbbing became hammering, he breathed a sigh of relief. Thank God, an honourable wound and no more. He climbed to make sure the 109's innards were not damaged, waggled the wings, and headed for Seville.

Something else had gone wrong, but that he did not notice for some time, and by then the Nationalist airfield at Almodóvar was out of the question. He tapped the gasoline gauge, but it refused to change its mind. Actually, he'd been extremely lucky. A bullet had ruptured his gasoline tank, and by rights he should have been blown all over Madrid. As it was, he'd simply showered the rooftops with aviation gas.

He spent only a moment hating himself for not checking the gauge, then concentrated on surviving the error. He needed a field. Not a potato field. Too bumpy — the 109 would hammer itself to pieces before he could get it stopped. Prevailing pilot-mess opinion was that the smoothest emergency landings were made on wheat fields. The ochre patches were detectable from the air and, by late September, the wheat was cut and the ground tended to be smooth, without surprising contours to wreck you just when you should be rolling to a safe stop. And, looking down, he was in luck. Everything was going to work out, after all. The early sun lit up a few yellow squares beneath him and he chose one and hoped it was lucky. He had to keep his attention focused, the foot was beginning to gnaw and bite, and he didn't want to stall on the way down. It would be an excellent emergency landing. He'd fly again as soon as the foot healed, and the aeroplane could be trucked back to Seville. Since there was hardly any gas, the danger of fire on impact was minimal. In a way, his luck held.

It held all the way down the chute to the field. It held as he bounced. It held as he braked with the flaps. Held as the 109 rolled to a stop. Everything seemed to flood out of him at that moment, and he fell back against the seat and let his hands dangle and closed his eyes. The engine had stalled. He turned the key to off. Listened as the birds began to sing again. It had been a woman at the machine gun, he was sure of it now. The long hair stayed printed on his memory. *These Spanish women*, he thought. You had to admire them. Still, it would be wiser to leave that fact out of his report. That was the sort of story that got around and stuck to your career like glue.

He came to suddenly. Had he blacked out for a moment? Somehow he had to find a telephone. Recollecting his error, he wondered idly if he had not been ever so slightly unprepared for the mission. Too much Evangelina, perhaps. A fighting man could not leave his wits in bed. He moved the foot and grunted with pain. He needed a doctor. That thought got him moving, and he shoved the canopy back, grabbed the sides of the cockpit and hoisted himself to a sitting position directly above the wing. And, luck held, here came some people to help him. Peasants, no doubt, in their dark blue cotton shirts and trousers. *These must be the peasants who cut the wheat*, he reasoned, *for they are carrying scythes*. But, he looked around to make sure, the wheat was already cut.

He briefly fingered the flap of the holster holding his sidearm, but there were at least twenty of them, so he threw his hands into the air and called out, '*Rendición, rendición*,' meaning that he surrendered. But at this they only laughed.

* * *

Faye shut her eyes when Señora Tovar, the janitor's wife, soaped her breasts — despite herself, she was very embarrassed to be touched in this way — and the woman noticed and said 'Scha!' in amazement at American notions of privacy. Did this girl not know that it was a woman's destiny to have her hands in everything unsacred, from placenta to horse manure and all that flowed from babies and wounds and old men? That by the time a woman was twenty there was nothing in the world she had not touched? She shrugged, smiled, and moved the girl's delicate little washing cloth to spread lather across her shoulders. Just down the street, at 14 Calle de Victoria, three women were hard at work on her clothing, rubbing it furiously on washboards as the fume of gasoline rose in their faces.

As the glorious hot water poured down on her, Faye bubbled inside. It had been the most exciting day of her life. It had to be shared! But with who? Her parents would be frightened, badly frightened. Penelope Hastings? Penny would be most deliciously envious, but she would, Faye knew, show the letter to her mother, an endearingly foggy society lady who always asked Faye, 'Is there, dear, um, anything you don't, um, eat?' Poor Mrs. Hastings, entirely flustered by the fear of feeding something wrong to Penelope's Jewish friend from college. And poor Mrs. Hastings was just the type, she was certain, who would *simply have to telephone the child's mother*.

The Pembroke alumnae magazine?

Fran Bernstein ('33) pens a note from sunny Spain to say she's enjoying her visit with Bolshevist elements of Republican forces defending Madrid. Recently our Franny shot it out with a Nazi fighter plane and got herself doused with aviation gasoline in the process! A victory celebration followed as ladies of the neighbourhood forced the janitor to turn on the water, at which time shy Fran was unceremoniously stripped down and washed.

Obediently, she let Señora Tovar turn her around and

139

scrub her back. Her eyes still burned; she knew they'd be bright red for days. Andres, of course, would suggest visits to doctors. Would insist.

This was a less than happy thought. She would have to tell him about her bicycle lock, and she knew this would create great stir and turmoil. Clearly, somebody in the building was a traitor, a Fifth Columnist. And a sneak thief.

She had told the excited men of the neighbourhood Checa that she'd found the lock open. One of them, she knew from his cold stare, had not believed her. But he had said nothing. She was the hero of the hour. Not only had she retrieved the lantern, she had helped to shoot up a plane – though the damn thing had flown away to safety – and certainly, everybody said, spoiled the Nazi's aim. The bomb had fallen in the street, breaking every window for a hundred yards but sparing the gas and water mains, which allowed, when the Checa men had been shooed away, the triumphal procession first to Tovar the janitor, then to the aqua tile bathroom on the third floor.

Number 54 Avenida Saldana, it turned out, was a Republican armoury, a secret one. If the blue lantern had been left in place, half the neighbourhood would have gone skyward, and the people in the building – including the humming mother and her child – would have gone with it. When Faye had returned, ecstatic, to the rooftop, Renata had lit the lantern and placed it on the parapet. 'Let us discover who seeks such a light,' she'd said grimly, running the bolt on the Hotchkiss gun and centring it on the trapdoor to the roof. When the plane came, though, it was Faye who grabbed the handles and Renata who fed the belt. Curiously, she had heard nothing. Had seen the twinkling on the 109's wings but had never, she admitted to herself, realized what this meant. Had, in fact, moments later, burned her fingers on a silvery lump half buried in the roof tar, and only then had her mind made the connection that sent a single wracking shiver from shoulders to knees. Renata too had been soaked by gasoline but, being ever and truly Renata, had insisted on her own bathing arrangements.

'*Eres limpio, yo creo,*' Señora Tovar said, stepping back to admire her handiwork.

'*Gracias, mil gracias, señora,*' Faye said, turning the water off and taking a rough, clean towel that had appeared from a hand in the doorway.

The woman waved away the thanks, singing, '*De nada, de nada,*' as she left the room to an uproar of Spanish from friends waiting without.

Faye's bare feet slapped down the marble-floored hallway toward the staircase that led to the room under the eaves. Life was better than a short story, she rather thought, with an O. Henry twist at every turning that caught the heroine unaware and stunned her with the peculiarity of fortune. Could anyone have predicted that in the fall of 1936 a machine gun would buck and vibrate beneath her hands as a German plane swooped toward her from the sky? Not with any Ouija board she'd ever heard of. That her best friend would be a German communist named Renata? No, no, no. That her lover would be a forty-two-year-old Spanish draughtsman from Ceuta named Andres Cardona? No a thousand times!

Oh if they could only see her now.

*   *   *

It was a narrow lane, barely one car wide, that wound its way up to San Ximene, and Khristo drove slowly, conscious of the roadside vegetation – lush and bursting weeds in every shade of purple and gold – as it whispered against the doors of the Citroën.

At this speed he could hear the whirring of insects, could study gates made of twisted boughs that appeared from time to time, guarding dirt paths that wandered off into the fields. Once a week they drove to San Ximene, and he was beginning to recognize individual gates. Each one was built of twisted boughs, crossed and braced in every conceivable style. Once a week was probably too often to visit a safe house, but Yaschyeritsa had ordained the schedule and his word was law. Sascha, after a dreadful week, had at last discovered that vodka could be replaced by Spanish brandy and was his old self again. 'Flies for Yaschyeritsa!' he would call out as they started off. *Not so loud*, Khristo thought, but said nothing. Sascha was a spring river in full flood, which went where it liked.

Khristo loved this car. A 1936 Citroën 11CV Normale. Its long hood suggested luxury, its short, boxy body suggested frugality, and the curved trunk in the rear suggested yet another French preoccupation. The sober black body was accentuated by fat whitewall tyres in open wells and shiny headlamps. The spacious windshield seemed to draw every yellow bug in Spain, but he kept the glass immaculate with wet, crumpled copies of *La Causa*. Soaked newspaper was the thing for cleaning car windows – he'd learned that from a former Riga taxi driver who forged travel documents for the Comintern office in Tarragona. Even the car, he thought ruefully, had a file. The Citroën had been donated to the Comintern by a furniture manufacturer in Rouen. Amazing, really, how the rich in this part of the world worshipped the revolution of the working classes.

He loved driving – he was the first Stoianev ever to operate a motor vehicle. He'd learned quickly, mastered the gearshift after a few head-snapping stutter stops brought on by a popped clutch. It was fortunate that he loved it because he spent a great deal of time behind the wheel. Intelligence operations, he had discovered, consisted principally of driving a car for hundreds of kilometres, sifting through an infinity of reports and memoranda, endlessly locking and unlocking the metal security boxes assigned to each officer, and writing up volumes of agent-contact sheets. In the latter regard, thank heaven for Sascha. The drunker he got, the better he wrote. And he had such mastery of Soviet bureaucratic language – a poetry of understatement and euphemism – that Yaschyeritsa mostly left them alone. That was fine with Khristo.

Colonel General Yadomir Ivanovich Bloch, the illegal NKVD *rezident* in Catalonia – as opposed to the 'legal' military attachés and diplomats under Berzin and the GRU – was secretly called Yaschyeritsa, the Lizard, because he looked like a lizard. He had a slightly triangular head, the suggestion of flatness on top emphasized by stiff hair combed directly back from the forehead. His thin eyebrows angled steeply down toward the inner corners of his eyes, which, long and narrow, were set above sharp cheekbones that slanted upward. Those eyes stared back at you emptily, without expression, watching only to determine if you were easy or difficult prey. Sometimes he licked nervously at his upper lip – the gesture, Sascha claimed, an unconscious throwback to the age when reptiles ruled the earth.

'Flies for Yaschyeritsa!'

Sascha was awake. Where the white boxes of San Ximene towered above them, Khristo rolled to a stop. Sascha brushed the hair out of his eyes and blinked for a moment, then drew the bottle of Fundador from the glove compartment and took a few swallows. Slowly, he twisted the cork back into place, then slapped it dramatically with his palm.

'Now the colonel is ready for agents and debriefings,' he announced. 'The following six measures can be recommended in support of the secure continuance of said operation. One: it is geese who fly the summer night to Sonya's heart. Right, Stoianev? We trap good flies? The best flies?'

'Only the finest. Served by the finest kitchens.'

'Forward, then.'

The Citroën climbed through the tight maze of alleys to the northern edge of the village. The doorways were covered by cloth-strip curtains. Each one, Khristo suspected, with its own pair of watchful eyes. He knew such tiny

143

villages in Bulgaria. They made your heart go fast. Perhaps the next lost little place was the one where they still drank strangers' blood in a toast to forgotten gods.

Still, one had to have safe houses, and it was best to have them in the middle of cities, concealed by crowds, or in desolate, out-of-the-way places like San Ximene. The agent they called Andres was doing a dangerous job: infiltrating the Falange. The *rezidentura* in Tarragona had a long shopping list: names, addresses, planned operations, logistical systems and, ultimately, the discovery of the identities of German intelligence officers in charge of liaison with Franco's Fifth Column in Madrid.

To prove himself worthy of trust, Andres had to commit an act of sabotage against the Republican forces, his own side. Thus he was vulnerable to friend and foe alike, could, at any time, be executed as spy or traitor, depending on who caught him. And this, Khristo thought, was only what *he* knew about. There could be more. The Russians had a genius for these games, a love of darkness, a reverence for duplicities that hid deeper strategies.

They came to a small whitewashed house with a tile roof at the end of a dirt street. A cat was sleeping on the windowsill. In a field across the road a few kids in short pants were fooling with a battered soccer ball. The air smelled like onions fried in oil and sun-heated plaster, and a radio was playing music somewhere nearby. The man known as Andres Cardona was down on his knees in the midst of a wild garden of daisies and fuchsia geraniums surrounding an old, twisted lemon tree. As they drove up, he was yanking weeds from the dry soil and throwing them over the garden fence. He stood up, wiped his hands on his pants and called, '*Buenos días, buenos días,*' in the voice of a man pleased to see his employees. *Ah yes, there you are, fellows, so good to see you, in your absence I've thought of a thousand things we need to do*. All of that in the tonality of a simple greeting, the way he stood, the expectation in his eyes. He was,

144

Khristo realized once again, so very, very good at what he did.

'And the name?'

'Farmacia Cortés.'

'Cortés. Refers to what?'

'The name of the square, I suppose. Though it is near the Cortés.'

'The . . . ?'

'The Cortés. The Spanish parliament.'

'Ah. So it is not owned by a man named Cortés.'

'No.'

'Hmm,' Sascha said, tapping the end of the fountain pen against his teeth. 'Locate it further for me, will you?'

'The Plaza de Cortés is elegant, fashionable. There is a hotel, the Palace – '

'As in English? Not *Palacio?*'

'No. Palace as in English. A fine hotel, quite luxurious.'

'Who stays there?'

'Diplomats. Journalists. Those who seek to approach the Cortés.'

'*Vot eto zoloto!*' Gold.

'Perhaps.'

'Nothing perhaps. It is certain. Comb this one out, thoroughly, you understand, and there would be treasure. Who has a prescription for heart medicine. Who has the clap. Who must have the laudanum syrup every week. More secrets in a pharmacy than in a woman's heart! Better than a bank, my friend. So *specific.*'

'Yes. But one could not comb him out.'

Sascha clicked his tongue and wagged a 'naughty' finger.

'Well yes, if you tied him to a chair and all that, of course. But no other way.'

'Not money?'

'Never.'

'Be sure now.'

145

'I am.'

'He likes women? Girls? Boys? Cats?'

'No. He is purity itself.'

'The pig.'

Cardona shrugged and smiled, a soft gesture that forgave the world everything. 'Would you care to hear about procedure?'

'Oh yes. We like procedure. Khristo, you're getting all this?'

'Yes. Most of it.' He wiped sweat from his face. Because they spoke Russian, the windows were shut tight. The sun beat down on the tile roof and the still air was wet and hot and blue with drifts of smoke. The roll of blueprints he'd taken from the trunk of the car was spread across the table, covered with coffee cups used as ashtrays, half-empty glasses of red wine, and sheets of paper covered with Cyrillic scratchings. One heard rumours of a machine that recorded the human voice on a spool of wire, but it was not to be had outside Moscow.

Cardona lit a Ducado and blew smoke at the ceiling. 'The procedure is to enter the Farmacia Cortés on the Plaza de Cortés between four and four-thirty in the afternoon. Go to the rear of the store, inquire of the clerk — always a young woman in a grey smock — if *el patrón* is available.'

'*El patrón*. The owner?'

'Literally, yes. But it's a grander term in Spanish. The boss.'

'Ah.'

'She goes into the office, then he appears.'

'What does she think you want?'

'Some personal thing, not to be mentioned to a young woman. Prophylactics, perhaps.'

'And do you buy something?'

'No.'

'Isn't that asking to be noticed?'

Cardona pondered this for a moment. 'Such things go

146

on at Spanish pharmacies, it's not so unusual. Men, you know, and their intimate problems.'

Sascha shot an eyebrow and snorted. 'Intimate crabs.'

'Certainly, and everything else. Anyhow, he gives me the time and place of the meeting.'

'His name?'

'According to the tax clerk's office, the Farmacia Cortés is owned by Emilio Quesada.'

'*El patrón.*'

'That's an assumption.'

Sascha sighed. The more they knew the craft, the more they wriggled off the hook. Cardona was exactly right, but it was just such ephemera that drove intelligence people crazy in the long term. 'Very well. Make a note, Khristo.' He turned back to Cardona. 'I don't suppose you'd want to ask the clerk, just once, if Señor Quesada is available?'

Cardona simply smiled.

'Umm,' Sascha said, 'I rather thought not. He comes to the meetings, this *patrón?*'

'Of course he does. But I can't say that. We are all hooded.'

'Describe the hoods.'

'Silk pillowcases, a sort of light brown colour, with slits cut for eyeholes.'

'Tan, would you call them?'

'No, not really. It's what a Renaissance painter would've known as ecru, I believe.'

'Good God.' Sascha held his head and shook it. 'Khristo, make them "light brown". Ecru indeed. Moscow would love that.'

'Each meeting is held at a different apartment, never the same one twice.'

'I suppose you don't go hooded in the street.'

'No. That's done just inside the front door, but the arrival times are staggered, and we leave one at a time.'

'Cautious.'

'Yes.'

147

'And the meetings?'

'Fascist mumbo-jumbo. A red candle burning in the middle of the table. A prayer to start out, a little speech – quite ferocious, really. You know how they are, Christ and blood, Christ and blood, back and forth. Then there's news of the Falange, military victories, piles of dead miners – nothing you wouldn't find in their newspapers.'

'What is their morale, would you say.'

Cardona paused a moment. 'Well, it's hard to tell with the hoods on, but I would say they're pretty scared. Most of them, their political views were well known before the Azaña government took over. They fear their neighbours, co-workers, tradesmen.'

'Does only the leader speak?'

'No. After he has said his piece, an unsheathed bayonet is passed from hand to hand. Each of us holds it and makes a statement.'

'For example.'

'A Republican gang marched into a monastery near Albacete. The monk in charge was tied to the altar and a crucifix was forced down his throat.'

'Others?'

'Nuns raped and murdered, priests strung up in trees.'

'Falangist propaganda, of course.' A muscle ticked briefly under Sascha's eye and he blinked to make it stop.

'Naturally.'

'But they are *conscious* of the gangs.'

'Oh yes. They fear them – with the fear of children – and recite their names. Lynxes of the Republic, Red Lions, Spartacus, the Furies, Strength and Liberty. It is almost as though a constant naming of the terrors will keep them away in the night.'

' "The purpose of terrorism . . ." ' Sascha quoted half the Lenin axiom, a shrug in his voice.

Khristo finished the phrase silently: '. . . *is to cause terror.*' These two, he realized, had something between them quite outside the agent–case officer relationship. They

148

were not the Mitya type – blunt-headed peasants with a red catechism in their mouth and a rifle in their hands. They were intellectuals: they would say the catechism and use the rifle, but they would not delude themselves. Their status demanded knowledge – and admission, no matter how inferential – of the truth.

'Now,' Sascha said, shifting in his chair, 'we come to the blue lantern.'

Cardona drew a deep breath and expelled it slowly. 'I'm still piecing it together.'

'General Bloch was quite pointed in his remarks on the subject.'

'I can imagine. Well, you may tell him that I do not think it mattered that the action went awry. *They* accept the hand of fate, even if General Bloch does not. What matters to them, the Falange, is that I executed the plan. Its failure, I think, will not damage their trust in me.'

'But you've not met with them since it happened.'

'Nor was I scheduled to do so. Tomorrow I go to the pharmacy.'

'Have you any idea what went wrong?'

'Not really. I went to the roof, lit the lantern. Somehow, the lantern was removed, taken to another building, and the attack failed.'

'Another building?'

'Yes.'

'We are told there was an American involved. A woman.'

'Neighbourhood gossip. I have heard it.'

'Find out for me who she is – her name, anything you can learn. There are many Americans who come to Spain now, Moscow perceives this as a critically important opportunity. Thus, if you wish your star to shine . . .'

'I'll do what I can.'

'Tell me, was there no guard at the Avenida Saldana? Did they simply fill up a building with guns and ammunition and leave it there?'

'This is the *Spanish* war.'

They were both silent for a moment, then Cardona went on, leaning across the table. 'A story, if you like. One of the cinemas on the *paseo* is showing *Duck Soup*, the Marx Brothers film. I attended last week, the theatre was packed full. In the row in front of me were three artillery officers on leave. For most of the time they were silent. But then, there is a scene where Groucho Marx is playing a colonel, and he stands before a map and says, "A child of three could solve this problem." He pauses, then adds, "Bring me a child of three." At that, the officers laughed – laughed bitterly, one could say – and nudged each other.'

Khristo and Sascha both smiled.

'Humorous,' Cardona continued, 'it is that. But maybe not so funny when you reflect on what it implies. To answer your question directly I will tell you that the Avenida Saldana armoury was protected by the PQUM, the anarchists, and in all probability the guard had something more important to do and off he went and did it. I carried the lantern up there with a knife in my hand, but there wasn't a soul.'

Dutifully, Khristo tried to keep up with him, writing as fast as he could. Sascha sighed and sat back in his seat.

'Bloch and the others,' he said, 'are getting quite fed up with the anarchists. Quite thoroughly fed up. And given The Great Stalin's attitude toward Trotsky, who sits in Mexico and pulls the strings of his puppets, this lack of discipline is going to receive close attention. I advise you to stay away from them, Andres, if you wish to keep your knees unsoiled.'

'Naturally Moscow is upset. Obedience is everything to them, but this is the way of it and you will not change the Spaniards. They have itched all their lives to stop dreaming, to act, after twenty years of talk. And it is their freedom they love most of all, because it is chained to their manhood. Stick your nose in at your peril.'

150

Sascha held his hand up like a traffic policeman. 'No treason, comrade, it's too hot today.'

'I intend none. But find a way to tell them the truth.' The implied ending of the sentence, *for a change*, hung in the smoky air.

Sascha brought forth a crooked smile, in which all the ironies in his life danced and played. 'Very well,' he said, 'I shall certainly start tomorrow. But, for today, let me first put you on the proper path. We have an alternate plan – not so good as the armoury, but it will have to serve.'

'Of course, comrade.' Cardona smiled.

'Do you have a camera?'

'I know where to get one.'

'Good. Make certain the film is especially light sensitive. Thursday morning, the first Soviet tank column will reach Madrid – an historical moment. It is moving up from the docks in Alicante and will take a route from the east, entering the city on the Paseo de la Infanta Isabella. We are timing the arrival for dawn and taking other measures to ensure that the entry is as secret as possible. What we want you to do is to take a roll of photographs of these tanks. Not the entire roll, of course, shoot the first few frames on something mundane, as though the film were already in the camera. Invent a good story for being out there, in case they ask. Take the roll, undeveloped, to your contact at Farmacia Cortés. The photos must be clandestine in nature, of course, tilted horizons, out of focus – let them see what a brave fellow you are. You'll want to be discreet anyhow, for those tank commanders are country fellows, and they'd as soon make daylight shine through you as anyone else. Make sure you photograph the relevant items – tank numbers, commanders' insignia, the usual drill. It is our intention that the photos soften the blow if your new friends are distressed over the failure at Avenida Saldana, but, most important, we want you to become the keenest sword in the Fifth Column. We want you to glitter in their eyes so that they will show you off to their superiors.

Eventually, we think, you will see a German. Now, need I go back over the ground?'

'No. I understand. And it will be a pleasure,' Cardona said, 'a great pleasure to see a German.'

'Poor Andres. Is he tired of being a Spaniard?'

'In truth, yes.'

'Do not despair, Andrushka, just a little while longer.'

It was dusk – fields shadowed in purplish light, sunset faded to a few red streaks in the western sky – when they wound their way down the hill from San Ximene. Sascha seemed exhausted; he lay slumped against the passenger door and worked hard at the Fundador until he conquered it – a bottle new that morning. It was, Khristo thought, the performance that sucked the life out of him. The role of case officer demanded an actor of extraordinary range: mother's warmth, father's discipline, the acuity of a favourite teacher, the strength of a playing-field hero. Cardona was betting his life that Sascha was good at his job – it was that simple. For months, Khristo had watched him rise to the performance, time and time again.

'Should you not turn on the lights?' Sascha asked.

'I will, in a while. The windshield bugs are terrible here.'

'How can you see to drive?'

'It's a white road.'

'Oh.'

'I'll stop if you want to get in the back.'

'No, I'm better up here.'

They drove in silence. When it was finally dark, Khristo turned on the headlamps and watched moths dancing in the beams. When Sascha spoke again, his voice was thick with exhaustion. 'Save him,' he said. 'I want you to promise me that.'

'Who? Andres?'

'Yes. You promise?'

'Of course. You will be at my side to make certain of it.'

'I think not.'

No point, Khristo thought, in pursuing this. Sascha trailed these hooks until you bit. He was, like other intelligence officers, stricken with an urge to confide. It was too strong, like a devil that beat you over the head with your own secrets until you had to let one out. To relieve the pressure you would tell half a secret, or an old, used-up secret, or boast of the secrets you knew. The cursed things had a life of their own, like weeds they threatened to grow right out of your head into plain sight.

'You've read his file?' The voice picked up a little.

'Not allowed.'

'Shit.'

'The junior officer is confined to knowledge of tactical intelligence. Strategic intelligence is the sole responsibility of senior staff. Section three. Paragraph eight.'

'More shit.'

'I quote you gospel.'

'You are like a market pedlar, Khristo, like a Jew you count kopecks. *Tactical* intelligence. *Strategic* intelligence. The difference between waiters' gossip and ambassadors' gossip. What notions, really. The thoughts of men whose backsides have grown into their chairs.'

Khristo laughed.

'I'm funny. That Sascha, he will make you laugh.'

'Thank God.'

'I'll miss you.'

For a time, Khristo thought he had gone to sleep, but then his voice returned from the darkness.

'Roubenis. That is Andres's true name, Roubenis. Avram Roubenis.'

'Greek?'

'Armenian – at least his father was Armenian – with a Greek name. As for his mother, she was the unhappy result of an *amour* between a German commercial traveller and a Turkish hotel maid.'

'In a word, a little of everything.'

'Just so. Thus he speaks Turkish, Armenian and demotic Greek. Also Russian, as you have seen. Spanish and English, and he can swear handsomely in Arabic. He was first a spy at the age of fourteen, in 1908. He would sneak up on Turkish encampments, listen to the chatter of the guards, and inform the villagers. To hide or not to hide – that was how they fought back.'

'A survivor, then.'

'The word does no justice. A monument, perhaps, to stepping through the fire quickly and going on with life. He was born under the Ottoman Empire, in a little village near Yerevan, Armenia, at the edge of the Caucasus range. Just north of the border point where eastern Turkey meets northern Iran. In the year 1909, the Turks murdered two hundred thousand Armenians – including the father. They cut off his head with a sword. Avram and his mother saw it happen from where they were hiding, in a rooftop cistern.

'The mother was a great beauty – blonde hair like a *Fräulein*, black eyes like an Anatolian Turk. The soldiers would have made short work of her. There was cruelty beyond imagination – in reprisal for an attack against an officer, hundreds were blinded, left to walk around as living reminders. But Avram and his mother escaped. She sold herself to a merchant and he took them west, all the way across Turkey, in a horse and wagon. I believe there was a baby sister who died of cholera along the way. Eventually they reached Smyrna. You know it? A disputed city, first Greek, then Turkish, on the Aegean coast of Turkey. There, the merchant determined that he would enjoy both mother and son in his bed. The mother was cunning. As the merchant undressed, she pulled his shirt over his head and Avram killed him with a brick he had hidden in the wagon. They dragged his body into a marsh and took his gold.

'Soon they were in business. They found a family that made strong gloves from uncured hides to sell to the Greek dockworkers, and bought the business from them. They prospered. Avram went to school, then to university in Istanbul, later in Athens. He became a draughtsman and an engineer. Then, in 1922, it happened again. The Greek-Turkish war, and Smyrna was burned to the ground. Almost the entire Greek population was massacred. Avram rushed home from Athens, where he had a job as a clerk in the office of the civil engineer. But he could not find his mother. She was gone. The house was gone. There was nothing. In despair, he returned to Athens.

'He was a lonely young man. He did his work and lived in a room. One day, he went to a Communist party meeting – it was a way to meet people. In time, he discovered he had a new family, a family that loved and sheltered him but, most important, a family that did not suffer injustice meekly. At party direction, he took a new job, working for a British company contracted to improve the water system in Baku. At this time, Baku was a British enclave protected by Czech mercenaries and White Guards – an imperialist island in a sea of revolution. The British could not resist Avram – his softness, apparent softness, appealed to the bullying side of their nature. He rose within the firm, and reported to the Cheka. There was, on his part, never a moment of hesitation. Spying came to him as making love comes to other men. It is his belief, in fact, that his father may have had relations with the Okhrana, the czar's intelligence service, though his murder by the Turks was haphazard – simply one act in a village slaughter. But Avram knew them, whether they were Turkish Aghas or British officers, he always understood how they worked, where their vulnerabilities lay. Thus he was able to penetrate the Falange – simply by saying the right things to the right people, being patient, waiting for them to come to him. And thus he will find his way among the Germans. That is, if we do not kill him first.'

At first, Khristo did not entirely trust his voice. All through the history of Roubenis there were edges that cut

155

sharply against his own life. He felt ambushed, as though the story had come out of the night and attacked him. There were people in Vidin who had lived under Ottoman rule – and it was something they simply did not speak of. And he had seen his brother die under the boots of the fascists. Poor Nikko. Poor sad, stupid Nikko and his big lip that called the world's bluff. And when the dirty work was done, and the blood long since washed into the earth, both he and Roubenis found themselves in the service of Russia, and that was a locked room – once you were inside. Back in Moscow they had quite a taste for suffering. How well they understood it, used it, made great profit of it. Unconsciously his left hand moved from the steering wheel and traced the outline of the white pawn in his pocket. Poor Ozunov, he thought, this piece of painted wood perhaps his only estate, all that remained of his existence.

Finally, Khristo rose to the baits Sascha had strung for him all day long: 'Why on earth would *we* kill Andres?'

Sascha laughed, a shrill, violent laugh. 'God in heaven cover your ears and hear no more of this!' he cried out. 'This Bulgarian dolt has been with us two years and more, yet he has seen nothing, heard nothing, learned nothing. He still thinks – this trusting child – there must be *reasons*.'

Then the hell with you, Khristo thought and bit his lip to keep the thought from being spoken aloud. He was tired of Sascha, of webs and coils and plots, of lies that sounded like truths and truths used to prop up the lies. He was tired of being afraid. His heart ached terribly and he wanted to go home.

They came to the main road, two lanes wide, that ran along the floor of the valley between the railroad tracks and the river, and turned east toward Tarragona. Khristo drove fast; the hard-sprung Citroën bounced over potholes and cracks, sometimes edging right when a car or truck came toward them. Little towns on their way were dark, though sometimes a cantina was open, light spilling from its windows onto the cobbled streets. The road veered and cornered in the towns, and Khristo downshifted aggressively, making the engine race and sing, making car music in the night. Outside Ribarroja de Ebro, there were dancing lights spread out before them and the red glow of a fire, and Khristo slowed. Then, in the middle of a long curve, a man appeared on the road, and Khristo rolled to a stop when he was clearly in the beams of the headlights.

From Sascha's side of the car came the little popping sound made by disengaging the button and grommet that held a holster flap in place. 'Just let him come,' Sascha said, fully awake and not at all drunk.

But the man stayed where he was, swaying back and forth, his palms held toward them in the universal stop command. The more Khristo stared at him, the less sense he made. He wore a khaki uniform, in the style of Republican officers yet not the same, and he had no insignia at all. His feet and lower legs were wrapped in dirty white bandages that threatened to unravel and his face was webbed with dried trails of blood that seemed to have come from a wound just above the hairline.

'Sorry, gents,' he called out, 'there's no way through.'

Khristo put his head outside the window to see better. 'English?' he asked.

'American,' the man said, squinting in the light.

'What is the matter?' Khristo asked. Phrases from the tattered book came back to him.

'There's bodies and railroad cars all to hell up there. Just before dusk, the Nazis bombed a train. Hit the engine and we went off the tracks.' He pointed at his bandaged feet and said, 'Hospital train.'

'What is it?' Sascha said in Russian. 'He said a bomb?'

'A hospital train was blown up.'

'Ah. That explains the bandages. He is American?'

'Yes. He must be with the International Brigade. Are we supposed to talk to them?'

'No, but we are here.'

The man hobbled over to Khristo's window. 'You're Russians?'

'Yes,' Khristo answered.

'And you speak English?'

'A little, yes.'

He smiled. By the light of the headlamps Khristo could see that his eyes were grey and his face was young and pleasant. 'My name is Robert King,' he said and stuck out a hand. Khristo shook it, reaching over the edge of the rolled-down window.

'How do you,' Khristo said. 'I am Captain Markov.' He had, like all NKVD officers in Spain, a nominal cover supported by one or two documents, a nom de guerre meant only for superficial deception.

'Russians. I've met Italians and Germans and Danes and a Hungarian, but you're my first Russians.'

'Do you need aid?' Khristo pointed at King's forehead.

The man touched the place, winced, looked at his fingers. 'No. Seems to have clotted up. But if you want to help, move on ahead. Go slow, it's pretty bad up there.'

'What does he want?' Sascha asked.

'They need help.'

'Drive slowly.'

As they moved forward, King stepped aside and saluted with a clenched fist and a smile. Khristo returned both.

Sascha took a small notebook and a stub of pencil from the glove compartment. 'He said his name was King?'

'Yes. K-i-n-g I think, like the ruler of Britain.'

'Ah, of course. I remember. And his patronymic?'

'Richard.'

Sascha paused in his writing. 'You're sure that's it?'

'Yes, I'm sure,' Khristo said.

They worked until dawn. It was hard, dirty work, illuminated by torches and flashlights, amid the drifting smoke of small field fires started by the bombing and a ground

158

mist that rose like steam from the river and its banks and blew gently across the road where they laboured.

To avoid the consequences of the periodic flooding of the Ebro, the builders of the railroad had designed an earthen ridge for the tracks. The embankment wasn't very high, perhaps eight feet, but it had added to the velocity of the plunging train and sent the engine and half the cars down onto the road in a tangle of splintered wood and bent iron.

At the start of the bombing run, the train's engineer had two choices: stop the train and have everybody run for the fields or, on the theory that a target in motion is harder to hit, give it full throttle. The engineer had taken the second option – from pure instinct for flight, no doubt – and had been wrong. He'd had no way of knowing that motion in a train is completely predictable, and even less could he have been aware of how moving trains excite bomber pilots, who usually can see little but a column of smoke for their efforts.

But it was most of all, Khristo thought as he heaved on the end of a railroad tie pressed into service as a lever, an intelligence failure. Someone, not knowing the range of the German bombers, had decreed that trains could run during daylight. And here was the result of such ignorance. As they took the wreck apart, pulling away boards, manhandling cast-iron wheel carriages and axles, they came upon the bodies. Most of them, like the American on the road, already wounded and bandaged. Now and then they found one still alive and carried him down to the road, to be taken back to Tarragona by a fleet of private cars and taxicabs called in from surrounding towns. But mostly these wounded, who had expected to live, who had had the luck to survive gunfire or artillery bursts, were dead, twisted into impossible positions by the force of the wreck.

From the survivors, who worked along with local policemen and firemen, Khristo learned they had been fighting against the Asensio column to the west of Madrid, and it had been a nightmare. They had retreated from Navalcarero, across the Guadarrama River, all the way back to Alorcón. They had been, like Republican forces throughout Spain, very brave but poorly armed. The Nationalist field guns had chewed them up from a distance, and forays against the gun emplacements brought them into enfilading machine-gun fire, which mowed them down in long lines. A company of miners from Asturias had arrived to fight by their side, but they had no guns whatsoever and fought with dynamite. When civilians took the field against organized forces, Khristo realized, they learned the simplest tactical truths at brutal cost. And they lost. Lives, armaments, strategic support, positions, and ground – everything. Like the Crusaders of old, they believed the justness of their cause would somehow protect them, and they were equally wrong.

The rescue effort was led – brilliantly, Khristo thought – by the chief of police of Ribarroja de Ebro, who had made his way to the scene in pants, boots and pyjama top. He was a tall man with a pitted face, and he seemed to be everywhere at once. Directing, encouraging, ordering, in total calm and with total authority. When Sascha had tried to explain, using his garbled Spanish, that their mission precluded any possibility of helping in the effort, the man nodded in sympathy and, saying 'Sí, sí, sí, sí, sí,' had taken him by the arm and led him around the Citroën to the trunk. How like those in Moscow, Khristo thought, to teach you French and English and then send you to Spain. When Sascha had refused to open the trunk, the policeman had patted him on the shoulder and, his face full of apology, called for 'una barra' – a crowbar. At that point Khristo stepped in and opened the trunk. The policeman, knowing what he wanted, dug down through the Fundador bottles, Degtyaryova machine pistols, and debriefing notebooks and came up with the car jack and its handle and held them up to Sascha. 'Esta la hora a salvar los vidas,' he said. *'Los procedimientos deben esperar.'* It is time to save lives — procedures will have to wait. Then, summoning the words carefully from a very limited supply of English, he had added, 'You watch or you help — *a mí es lo mismo.'* Sascha stared at him. The policeman, to drive home the point, picked up a notebook between his thumb and forefinger and dropped it back on the pile of bottles and guns. Sascha went pale. Khristo, in response, took off his jacket and rolled up his sleeves, and was rewarded with a policeman's smile.

Three boxcars of live steers had travelled with the train, en route to the markets of Tarragona, and a number of animals had been injured in the wreck. Some of them had managed to make their way into the fields, where they lowed ceaselessly with pain and terror, drawn-out pleading calls from the darkness. The policeman tried to ignore it but he could not and finally, to everyone's silent relief, a detail of surviving wounded had been given pistols and sent off, limping and shuffling, wandering through the mist and smoke, to find the animals and put them out of their misery. Thus there were shouts and pistol reports throughout the long night.

Toward dawn, a train from the east had passed slowly on the remaining track, reinforcements headed for the Madrid front. All wore red scarves. They stuck their heads out the windows and gave clenched-fist salutes to the workers on the road, called out *'No pasarán'* and other slogans. In one car they were singing the 'Hymn of Riego'. Khristo had observed this before — a train of wounded passing a train of new volunteers — and he did his best, with shouts and salutes and smiles, to help them not see what was on the road.

At daybreak they were relieved by a company of infantry quartered nearby and the two collapsed against the side of the car, sitting in the weeds by the side of the road. Khristo stared sorrowfully at his hands, black with axle grease, soot, and dried blood, two nails split all the way to the base, a slice across the palm that had bled itself dry. It had been a long time since he'd really worked, every muscle in his back told him that. He sat quietly, in a kind of stupor, hypnotized by light as the first sun found the river. He watched the mist burning off, the pale green water moving lazily in its autumn flow. It looked so clean to him, the way it changed itself instant to instant, brushing along its banks, running to the sea. He wanted to go up next to it, put his aching hands in for as long as he could stand the cold, but he was too exhausted to move. By his side, Sascha picked with great difficulty at the sealing tape on the neck of a brandy bottle.

'Surely,' Khristo said, 'there will be trouble over this.'

'Oh yes,' Sascha answered. 'Our orders are clear. Do not meddle, do not become involved, NKVD business precedes all else. For me, of course, it no longer matters, so I shall take the brunt of Yaschyeritsa.'

'Sascha, please, for once be real. Truly you are leaving?'

'Recalled,' Sascha said. The word seemed to hang for a long time. ' "Recalled to Moscow." That is the phrase.'

He put the bottle down, reached over and tore up a handful of weeds. 'Let me see, we have here hemlock and wild mustard, chicory, allium, and here is the legendary asphodel, a wildflower of great antiquity. I took a year of horticulture in university. With the famous Academician Boretz. See over there? Those are crown daisies, there is fennel I think, and field marigolds. Good old Boretz, never hurt a fly, couldn't walk without bumping into the ground. But a Trotskyite, or worse, one of Litvinov's supporters. So, that was Boretz. They are going to kill me, Khristo.'

He went back to work on the bottle, at last getting it open and taking a few delicate sips, then offering it to Khristo. The brandy tasted like fire, but the bitter strength of it kicked some life back into him.

'Why do you not run away?' Khristo asked quietly.

'Yes, it occurs to one. But it would be futility itself to try. They hunt you down, my friend, they always hunt you down. And before they dispense with you, they make you sorry you ran. They brought one fellow back to Moscow and let us see him in the morgue, just his face, mind you. One would not think it physically possible to open a mouth that wide.'

Khristo watched him carefully, but his face, coated with oily dirt, was empty. 'What has happened,' he said, 'is that Yagoda is finished. Now it is Yezhov, the dwarf, who runs the service. Yagoda has been accused of murdering the writer Maxim Gorky by spraying poison on his walls. Also, he is accused of complicity in the affair of Kirov. Rumour has it that the scythe is out in Moscow for real – this one will make the events of '34 seem like the nursery. So, fine fellow, what you've seen of Sascha's useless life is what there will be.'

Khristo tried to take this in. The utter lack of drama in Sascha's demeanour somehow acted to balk understanding. 'A dwarf,' Khristo said.

'Yes. The Great Leader exceeds himself in whimsy.'

'My God.'

'The curious part is that I don't care. Oh, later on, in the Lubianka, I shall kick and scream and plead for mercy – hug their boots and all of it. It is expected of one to do that – they demand their theatre. But now, right now, I feel nothing at all.'

'Sascha, this cannot be.'

'Don't worry, I'll await you in hell. There we will keep track of the devils – who works, who doesn't, who makes secret plots with angels. You shall see, it won't be as bad as you think.'

At last the old Sascha. He was relieved. 'Those devils must be watched – they stab the Revolution in the back! Perhaps I should accompany you?'

Sascha smiled gently at his efforts to play along with

the mood. 'Application refused,' he said, 'reapply in thirty days.' He thought for a moment. 'Thirty days in truth, Khristo Nicolaievich. I am only the first to go — there will be others. Many others.'

'You are serious?'

'Yes. In their eyes we have been ruined, you must understand. We have seen the world, and we must not be allowed to tell others what we have seen. Or perhaps we have consorted with the enemy. Who among us has remained pure? Impossible to know, so safety lies in throwing out the whole batch and starting anew.'

Khristo felt his pulse quicken. This was not Sascha the mad poet spinning dreams. This was the Sascha who told the truth. He turned to look back at the river for a moment but heard an odd noise and saw that Sascha was crying, hiding his face in his hands. Beyond him, out on the road, the policeman was watching them. His eyes met Khristo's and he shook his head, slowly, back and forth. He did not understand them, or the world, or the carnage on the road. Nothing.

* * *

'You have achieved virtually nothing, Lieutenant Stoianev.'

Colonel General Yadomir Bloch — Yaschyeritsa — touched the tip of his index finger to the end of his tongue and turned the page. It was brittle, transparent paper that crackled as he smoothed it down on the left side of the file folder.

'Not here,' he said, eyes running over the print. Moistened the finger again, 'Nor here.'

The *rezidentura* was in an old hotel near the docks, and though the curtain was closed Khristo could hear bells and whistles as the night stevedore crew unloaded cargo. The boat had been there for two days, a rusty old Black Sea freighter, its name swabbed out with grey paint.

'As you have no doubt heard, Colonel Alexander Vonets

164

has returned to Moscow at the request of the Directorate, so you will have to carry on, but . . .' Finger to tongue, a new page. 'Mmm . . . yes.'

It was dark in the office, lit only by a tiny bulb in a desk lamp. Shadow hardened the planes of the face, sharpened the angles, cloaked the slanted eyes set deeply in the head.

'Such praise. "Attentive." "Meticulous." "Intelligent."'

A new page, turned back for a moment, then turned again.

'I don't believe it,' he said. He closed the file, rested his chin on folded hands and stared into Khristo's eyes.

For a long time there was only silence, intensified by the low rumble of noise from the docks. 'We have problems, Lieutenant,' he finally said. 'You agree?'

'I am not aware of the problem, comrade Colonel General.'

'*Problems*, Lieutenant, the plural. Don't fence with me.'

'I am not aware of any of the problems, comrade Colonel General.'

'You consider yourself an able officer?'

'I am doing my best, comrade Colonel General.'

Colonel General Bloch seemed to be sitting still, then Khristo noticed that his body rocked slightly, back and forth, as the last answer hung in the air. The longer he rocked, the less true the answer seemed, as though the credibility of the statement melted away with the motion.

'Very well. I choose to believe you, and we have seen your best. The air is cleared, the mystery resolved, this attentive, meticulous, intelligent, able officer has given us his best effort. One cannot ask for more.' He glanced at his watch. 'It is now fourteen minutes after two. The *Neva* will be ready to sail at six-thirty this morning. You will gather your effects and be on it. I will have my aide assign you a berth. Good evening, Lieutenant. I appreciate your frankness.'

With long, thin hands he squared the file, opened the bottom drawer of the desk, and set it carefully among others. Looking up, finding Khristo still staring at him in apparent disbelief, he seemed surprised. 'Dismissed, Lieutenant,' he said and kicked the drawer shut with his boot.

'Comrade Colonel General,' Khristo cleared his throat, 'I believe your criticism would enable me to improve my performance.'

'What performance? You fucking parasite, get out of my office before I have you thrown out!'

Crawl, Khristo's mind told him. *Crawl for your life.* He stood up, came to attention. 'Colonel General Bloch, I entreat you to assist me in the better performance of my duties, that I may better serve the objectives of my service. I entreat you, comrade Colonel General.'

Bloch stood and leaned across the desk. 'How you whine,' he said, 'like your friend Sascha Vonets, of the *prominent* Vonets family. You are all boot-kissers at the last, aren't you. Self-satisfied little kings who drive about the countryside in fine clothes and fuck the Spanish whores, while in Moscow people eat potato peels and give thanks for one more day of existence. Oh you should have heard him. The *intellectual*. What promises he made. The moon and the stars. But it was too late. Too late. Your Armenian spy, Roubenis, sits in Madrid with his American girlfriend and reports on morale. Morale? What morale? These odious little Spaniards have lost their war. They're finished, done with. Because all they've ever done is hold their pricks in their hands and dream of their *freedom* and *liberty*. Generalissimo Franco will give them freedom, all right, he'll free them of their mortal souls and they'll go dreaming to their Spanish heaven. Morale, indeed. Is that what you think we are here for? Is that why Russia feeds you and clothes you with roubles it does not have? You foolish boy, to think we don't know such tricks. At the age of seventeen, I led a mutiny aboard the battleship

166

Sevastopol. We chained the officers to their steamer trunks full of uniforms and threw them into the sea. They too pleaded. A great deal of pleading in 1917, one grew bored with it.'

Abruptly, he sat down. Swivelled his chair away from Khristo and pulled the curtain back from the window. The *Neva*, working lights fixed to her booms and superstructure, stood hawsered fore and aft to the dock. A wooden platform on cables slowly lowered a JSII tank to the quay.

'Sit, Lieutenant,' he said. 'You wish not to sail on the *Neva?* It is not uncomfortable. You might spend a day or two in Odessa before transit to Moscow. No? Not appealing?'

'Comrade Colonel General, my brother was murdered by the fascists.'

'So it says in your file. But then, both my parents were knouted to death by the White Guard. Your parents, on the other hand, have found it expedient to connect themselves to the fascists, by way of your sister's marriage. This too it says in your file. Come to think of it, expediency rather defines you, doesn't it. It was expedient for you to leave Bulgaria in her agony. Expedient to do well at Arbat Street. Expedient to serve Sascha Vonets in his drunken self-pity. Very well. Look out the window. See where expediency leads.'

'What must I do, comrade Colonel General, to improve my performance?'

'Go to Madrid. The time for safe houses is over. Find this Roubenis and put your boot up his ass. He attends these Cagoulard meetings – the Falange in their hoods. Well, enough of that. Put some men in the street. Find out who these people are, where they live, get their *names*. Wire those names to me – there must be ten, at least. Use the wireless at our consulate, in Gaylord's Hotel near the Retiro Park. We'll take care of it from there, believe me. The American girl. I want to know

167

who she is, what of her relationship with Roubenis. Take her to bed if you have to – if Roubenis objects, tell him to get out of your way. She must have American friends, or English. Get me something I can use. I wish to hear no more meowing about *morale*. Is this understood?'

'I understand, comrade Colonel General. I will do it.'

'When? How many days?'

'Twenty days. A fortnight.'

'I will hold you to that.'

'It will be done, comrade Colonel General.'

'You leave here at five o'clock sharp this morning. I will assign you a sublieutenant – observe his commitment, you can learn something from it. Now, before you go, one small matter. Tell me, Stoianev, you have heard me referred to by a certain nickname?'

'No, comrade Colonel General.'

'A stupid lie, but let it pass. The name in question refers to a particular reptile. Let me just point out to you that it depends, for its survival, on a special principle, which is that its prey always believes itself to be beyond reach. Keep that in mind, will you?'

'Yes, comrade Colonel General.'

'Now get out.'

By the time Khristo reached his tiny room, in another dockside hotel, his hands were shaking. Looking in the mirror, he saw that his face was grey with fear. He sat on the edge of the bed, drew his Tokarev from its holster and stared at it for a time, not entirely sure what he meant to do with it. He noticed, finally, an unusual lightness to the weapon and ejected the magazine. Sometime in the last twenty-four hours somebody had unloaded it. He ran the bolt back and inspected the chamber. It was empty as well.

*   *   *

In the Guadarrama, Thursday had come to be known as Día de las Esposas, Wives' Day, in the course of which the guerrilla band of Lieutenant Kulic did those chores that, in normal times, would have fallen within the province of their wives – excepting, of course, the happiest chore of all, which would have to await their return to home and the marriage bed. They shook out and aired their blankets, sand-scrubbed the cooking utensils, washed their clothing and hung it in the trees to dry, and for the grand finale washed themselves – swearing a blue streak in the icy mountain water and splashing each other with childish glee. Kulic's time in the Serbian mountains had taught him the critical importance of domesticity in the context of *partizan* operations. Being dirty and uncared for, men quickly lost respect for discipline, and operations suffered accordingly. As Kulic phrased it to himself, the more you lived in a cave, the less caveman behaviour could be tolerated.

They had found the deserted village quite by accident, but it was perfect for a guerrilla base: no road led there, the approaches were well covered by dense tangles of underbrush, and it lay high enough in the mountains that radio communication with Madrid Base could be maintained on a more or less regular basis.

There was not much left of the village: a few huts – all but three open to the stars – built of dry-masoned stone native to the mountains. They often speculated about the place – perhaps it had been the home of the early Visigoths, western Goths, who had populated Spain in ancient times. It was not difficult to imagine. They would have hunted bear and wild pig in the mountain forests, with spears and dogs, and worn wolf pelts against the weather. Or perhaps another race, unrecorded and unre-membered, had died out in the village, the last survivors wandering down onto the plains to become part of other tribes. In any case, with time the piled stone walls and weedy vines had achieved a harmonious truce, leaving the village a sort of garden gone wild and an excellent hideout.

On the Thursday following the destruction of the Nationalist armoury, while most of the band was occupied with housekeeping, there was a small commotion at the perimeter of the camp. Kulic, walking down the hill to see what the shouting was about, found his two sentries with rifles pointed at Maltsaev, the political officer from the Madrid embassy.

He was a dark, balding young man with bad skin and a sour disposition, a man much given to sinister affectations. He wore tinted eyeglasses and a straw hat with top creased and brim turned down, and spoke always as though he were saying only a small fraction of what he actually knew. He had arrived alone, on horseback, having left his car in the last village before the mountains, some twenty kilometres distant. Thus it was immediately apparent to Kulic that this was anything but a casual visit. To protect his city clothing during the journey, Maltsaev had worn an immense grey duster coat, which, with the hat and glasses, gave him the look of a Parisian *artiste* of the 1890s. An appearance so strange that Kulic was a little surprised his lookouts had not dispatched him on the spot.

They sat together on a fallen pine log at the edge of a small outcrop above the village. From there, they could watch the guerrilla band shaking blankets and capering in the stream, and strident voices – cursing, laughing, joking – rose to them. This was Kulic's thinking place. When the sun came out, the scent of pine resin filled the air and blue martins sang in the trees.

'You don't have it so bad,' Maltsaev said, looking about him.

'It is Día de las Esposas today,' Kulic answered, taking off his peaked cap and smoothing his hair. 'We rest and gather our strength. It is a little different when we fight.'

'One would suppose so. Now look here, Kulic, I won't

170

beat about the bush with you. My mission is not a happy one.'

'It's a long ride up here.'

'Too long,' Maltsaev said ruefully. 'And I'm a city boy, a Muscovite, I admit it.'

He took off his left shoe and pulled the laces apart. From the pocket of his duster coat he produced a razor blade and began cutting open the leather tongue, finally revealing a yellow slip of paper. 'And I had to come through the fascist lines,' he added, in explanation.

'A nervous time for you, then,' Kulic remarked.

'Yes. And I am unappreciated,' Maltsaev said. 'My poor backside has no business on a horse.'

He handed the paper to Kulic, then pressed the layers of the shoe tongue back together again as best he could. 'Of course,' he said, almost to himself, 'one may not carry glue.' Kulic noted that he wore fine silk socks.

'What's this?' Kulic asked, studying the paper. There were four names on it. Four of his men.

'We have discovered a plot,' Maltsaev said.

'Another plot? Shit on your plots, Maltsaev, these men are not Falangistas.' He thrust the paper back at Maltsaev, who was busy putting on his shoe and declined to take it.

'Nobody said they were, and please don't swear at me. Give me a chance, will you. You field commanders have short fuses. A little bad news – and boom!'

'Boom is what it will be,' Kulic said.

'Shoot me, comrade, by all means. There'll be ten more tomorrow, Spetsburo types, Ukrainians – just try reasoning with them.'

'Very well, Maltsaev. Say your piece and ride away.'

'If that's how you want it. These four are members of POUM – there's no question about it, we have copies of the lists, right from Durruti himself.'

'Durruti? The anarchist leader? He claims these men?'

'Well, from his office.'

'And so?'

Maltsaev made his hand into a pistol – bent thumb the hammer, extended index finger the barrel – then pulled the trigger with his middle finger.

'Are you insane? Is Madrid? Moscow? These men are fighters, soldiers. You don't execute your own soldiers. Only for cowardice. And these are not cowards. They've stood up to gunfire, which is more than I can say for some people.'

'Yes, yes. I'm a coward, please do abuse me, I don't mind. But you must take care of the problem – that's an order from Madrid.'

'Marquin, the second name on this list, climbed to the roof of a convent and poured gasoline down the chimney, which enabled us to blow up a Falangist armoury. Is this the behaviour of a traitor? Besides, all these men are of the UGT, not the POUM.'

'Kulic . . . no, *Lieutenant* Kulic, you've been given an order. Have a trial if you like – just make sure it comes out right. The sad fact is that the POUM – Trotskyites, to give them their proper name – are fouling up this war. Sometimes they refuse to fight. They won't take orders. They roam about like a herd of wild asses and cause everybody trouble. Generalissimo Stalin has determined to purify the Spanish effort, and Director Yezhov has ordered that the POUM be purged. These four men claim UGT association, but their names appear on POUM membership lists obtained by our operatives in Barcelona.'

'You're ruining me – you know that, don't you?'

'Four men amount to nothing.'

'You believe the other sixteen, having witnessed their comrades' unjust executions, will fight on?'

Maltsaev thought about that for a time, studying the ground, pushing a pebble around with the toe of his shoe. 'Your point has merit,' he said. Then he brightened. 'One could report, ahh, yes, well one could report that the disease has spread throughout the group, and it was determined to be of no further operational use. I could

172

try that, Kulic, if it would help you. They would transfer you elsewhere, but your record would be clean at least. Better than clean, now that I think about it. Fervour. That's what it would show. It's just the sort of thing Yezhov likes, you know, going it one better.'

Kulic stared down the hill at his men. A word to Maltsaev and they'd all be dead. Julio Marquin, the spiderlike little shipfitter who'd climbed the convent drainpipe, was poking at a pot of rice over a bed of coals. They cooked by day – there could be no fires at night in the Guadarrama. The fool! Why had he gone and gotten his name on the wrong list? He despaired of the Spaniards, their instinct for survival had been eaten alive by their political passions. The Spanish Legion, under Yagüe, had a regimental hymn announcing to the world that their bride was death, and the Republican side was no better. Thus they slaughtered each other. What did it matter if four of them went to heaven early? His own pride was in his way, surely. How he protected his men. Took every care to protect them, to keep them from getting hurt.

He recalled, suddenly, that he'd killed his first man when he was fifteen, in a tavern brawl in Zvornik. Such strength and determination it had taken to do that. Where was it now?

'Well,' Maltsaev said, 'how shall it be?'

'The best time,' he took a deep breath, 'is during battle. All sorts of things happen. It could not be arranged for all four at once, of course, but over time, in a few weeks say, they would be honourably slain in action against the enemy.'

'I'm sorry. I appreciate your thinking, but it just won't do.'

'Who gave this order, Maltsaev?'

'I can't tell you that and you know it.'

'Then you do it.'

'Me? I'm a political officer. I don't shoot anybody.' He took off his straw hat and examined the inside of the

173

crown; the leather band was sweatstained and he blew on it to dry it out.

Kulic knew he was trapped. He wanted to cut Maltsaev's throat. But then they would all die. The Ukrainians would come and, once they arrived, all the talking was over. So it was four now, or twenty-one tomorrow.

He stood up. 'Sergeant Delgado,' he called. Delgado stood up naked in the stream. He was a boilermaker by profession, a man in his forties. His arms and neck were burned by the sun, the rest of his body was white.

'Yes, comrade?' the sergeant called up the hill.

'I need a patrol of four men,' he answered in his rough Spanish. He called out their names. 'To gather wood,' he added.

'We have plenty of wood,' the sergeant responded.

'Sergeant!' Kulic yelled.

Nodding to himself that officers were crazy, Delgado picked his way delicately among the rocks in the streambed and went off to gather the patrol.

Maltsaev was finished blowing on his hat. 'You'll see,' he said, 'everything will work out for the best.' He put the hat back on, carefully adjusting the angle of the brim so that his eyes were shaded from the sun.

They went up the mountain to gather firewood. Kulic was armed with his pistol and, slung over his shoulder, a Spanish bolt-action Mauser rifle, the basic weapon of the Spanish war. The four men were not armed, the better to carry the wood. They chattered among themselves, liking their holiday, drawing pleasure from the work detail. Now and then they looked over their shoulders at Kulic, but he waved them on. At last he found what he was looking for. A small glade, an utterly peaceful place where no people had been for a long time.

They began to gather wood, snapping dead limbs off fallen trees, bundling up twigs and sticks for kindling.

They worked for an hour, tying the wood with hempen cords in such a way that it could be harnessed to their shoulders, leaving their hands free. It was the way he had taught them to do it. He knew, also, that once they were laden in this way, it would be nearly impossible for them to rush him successfully.

When they were ready to go, he held up a hand and unslung the rifle, holding it loosely at port arms. They stood there for what seemed like a long time, watching him, their faces slowly growing puzzled. One of them finally said, '*Capitán*?' – a term of honour they had granted him.

'I am sorry,' Kulic said, 'but I must ask you to sit down for a moment.'

Carefully they knelt, balancing their loads, then sat, lying back against the wood bundles.

'I am told, by the Russian who came to the camp this afternoon, that you are members of the organization known as POUM, an anarchist group. Is this true?'

'Our politics are complicated,' Marquin answered, making himself spokesman for the group. 'We are members of the UGT, the Communist party, but we have all attended meetings of the POUM in order to hear the thoughts of comrade Durruti, who is a greatly gifted man and a fine orator. "If you are victorious," he has said to us, "you will be sitting on a pile of ruins. But we have always lived in slums and holes in the wall . . . and it is we who built the palaces and the cities, and we are not in the least afraid of ruins. We are going to inherit the earth. The bourgeoisie may blast and ruin their world before they leave the stage of history. But we carry a new world in our hearts."'

Kulic was impressed with the speech. 'You can remember all that?'

'All that and more. So many of us do not read or write, you see, that memory must serve us.'

'But you are not members.'

'No, but we do not disavow them. They too are our brothers in this struggle. We attended their meetings, before we came out here to fight the fascists, gave them a *gordo* for the coffee, signed petitions in favour of freedom for the working classes. Can this have been wrong?'

'I am afraid so.'

Sitting next to Marquin was a fat man. How he had managed to remain so, despite forced marches and the unending physical demands of *partizan* life, Kulic had never been able to figure out. He had, when he spoke, the piping voice of a fat man. 'Then we are to be shot,' he said.

Kulic nodded yes.

Two of the men crossed themselves. Marquin said, 'We are ready to die, it is in the nature of this work we do. But to die dishonoured, by the hand of our leader . . .' The pause became a silence as he realized that nothing he could think of would finish the thought.

'You are not dishonoured, and I myself do not understand this, and I do not agree. I am, like you, a soldier, and I have been given an order, and because I am a good soldier, I will carry out that order even though I believe it is wrong. All I know is that we are involved in a great revolution. It began a long time ago, far from here, and it will go on for a long time after we are gone. The POUM is in the way, it would seem, of victory in Spain. A sacrifice will have to be made. That is everything I can say.'

One of the men struggled suddenly to get up but the wood borne by his shoulders held him back, and the fat man, seated next to him, put a hand on his shoulder, making it impossible for him to move. 'No, no,' the fat man said, 'let it be. Our enemy is not in this place.'

Marquin spoke up, his voice absolutely calm. 'I wish to be the first,' he said, 'but I want to stand up.' He wrestled the load of wood from his shoulders and stood. Straightened his *mono* overall so it hung properly, combed his hair into place with his fingers as though his photograph were about to be taken. His eyes looked directly into Kulic's. Kulic worked the bolt on the rifle and brought it to his shoulder, sighting on the man's heart. He had never known the name of the man in the tavern in Zvornik – that had all happened too quickly for any but a perfectly instinctive reaction. The man had rushed at him with a piece of wood, Kulic had plunged a knife into the very centre of him, he had seemed to swell up suddenly to the size of a giant, then twisted away, wrenching the knife from Kulic's hand and falling upon it so that the steel hilt banged against the cement floor. After that there was only the sound of the last breath rushing from his lungs. Kulic tightened his finger on the trigger. The Spanish Mauser was a simple weapon, made to work for a long time, and there was nothing delicate about its mechanism. The trigger was on a hard spring and it had to be pulled with force.

Slowly, Kulic lowered the rifle. He forced the bolt back and, as the ejected cartridge spun into the air, caught it cleverly in his right hand. Then he put it in his pocket.

Slowly at first, and then more rapidly as they understood what was happening, the other three men unburdened themselves and stood up. Kulic nodded his head toward the west. 'Portugal is that way, I believe.'

'But we have no guns,' one of the men said.

'You will draw less attention without them,' Kulic said.

He was not to hear Marquin speak again. The man studied him as his friends walked slowly west along the curve of the mountainside. There was no gratitude in his eyes. Perhaps a veiled smile, perhaps the faintest hint of contempt. It occurred to Kulic then that Maltsaev might have been right in ways he had not understood, but it was much too late to have thoughts like that so he turned his attention to other matters.

He waited until he could no longer hear the departing men and, when the forest was again silent, waited another twenty minutes, sitting with his back against a tree and smoking a cigarette. He enjoyed the cigarette immensely. When it was finished, he took the clasp knife from his pocket, used it, then put the cartridge back in the rifle, stood up, and fired into the air. This act he repeated three more times. His remaining men could make a small but important difference behind the lines in this war, but they could not keep a secret. As the echo of the final shot rang away down the side of the mountain, he shouldered the rifle and headed for the camp. Looking back for a moment, he saw four bundles of well-bound firewood arranged in a line in the middle of a clearing. Whoever might chance to come this way would find them and think himself lucky that day. In all likelihood, he would make no sense at all of the Cyrillic letters and numerals carved into the trunk of a pine tree. БФ825.

*   *   *

At five in the morning, Khristo made his way to the Citroën, parked in front of the hotel. Across the street, the *Neva*'s stacks showed curls of dark smoke as the boiler room got up steam for the 6:30 departure. He had not really slept – Yaschyeritsa's face and voice hammered against his consciousness all night long– and had climbed out of bed in the last hour of darkness with a sick stomach and hot, sandy eyes. At the car, the new sublieutenant awaited him, sitting at attention behind the wheel.

'Good day to you, Lieutenant Stoianev. Allow me please to introduce myself. I am Sublieutenant Lubin, reporting for duty.' It was rehearsed and formal, a squeaky little whine of a voice. Khristo took a step backward and stared at the boy in the car. He had the face of a malevolent baby – a grossly overfed baby – with rat-coloured hair combed and pomaded to a stiff pompadour that rose above his glossy forehead and tiny china-blue eyes. A mama's

178

boy, Khristo thought, perhaps seventeen, who would sit on Yaschyeritsa's knee and tattle at every opportunity.

'Yes, hello,' Khristo managed. 'Usually I drive,' he added.

'Begging your pardon, Lieutenant Stoianev, but I have been instructed, by Colonel General Bloch, that as junior officer it is my duty to drive the car. Let me assure you that I have been trained extensively in the proper driving of automobiles.'

At a steady twenty-five miles per hour they left Tarragona at dawn, Lubin holding the wheel with both hands and driving like a puppet, correcting – Khristo counted spitefully – eight times in a single slow curve. They would be all day getting to Madrid.

'Stoianev. I believe that is a Bulgarian name?' Lubin said.

'Yes. I am Bulgarian.'

'Then you will not have heard of my family. My father is associate director of the All Soviet Institute of Agronomy. Leonid Trofimovich Lubin is his name. Is it known to you?'

'No,' Khristo said, 'I don't know it.'

'It is not important.'

As Khristo stared glassily ahead at the endless road, however, he did recall something of the All Soviet Institute of Agronomy. Sascha had one evening told him the story of one of its most prominent members, O. A. Yanata, the Ukrainian botanist who had set up the first chair of botany at the Academy of Sciences. He had proposed to the academy that certain chemicals could be used for the destruction of weeds. This was an entirely new concept, since the only known method to date was continual use of the hoe. A lengthy political investigation of Yanata was instituted, at the end of which he was accused of attempting to destroy all the harvests of the Soviet Union by the use of chemicals and was subsequently tried and shot.

At the end of an hour, Lubin pulled to the side of the

179

road and stopped. He got out of the car, walked around it three times, then returned and drove away.

'Why did you do that?' Khristo asked.

'A rule of driving, Lieutenant,' Lubin answered proudly. 'To maintain concentration, one must dismount the vehicle hourly and exercise lightly.'

Khristo put his head in his hands.

* * *

Buenas noches, mis amigos. Buenas noches, todos los peleadores bravos que puedan oír ma voz. Y buenas noches, Madrid. Hay veinte horas, y la hora para el jazz hot. La selección primera esta noche es una canción del Norteamericano, Duke Ellington, llamada 'In a Sentimental Mood', *con Louis Vola tocando el violón, trum-trum-trum, Marcel Bianchi y Pierre Ferret en guitarras, Django Reinhardt en la guitarra sola, y, entonces, el grande Stephane Grappelli tocando el violín. Gusta bien, todo el mundo, gusta bien.*

The Emerson, in a tan wooden case with white dials and a little light that made the station band glow green, played best on a table beneath the window. Faye angled it slightly to the left, then fiddled with the tuning knob until the signal came in clear. Andres had gone out to yet another meeting, she was exhausted, and she was going to wrap herself up in a quilt, listen to the radio, and read a Djuna Barnes novel that Renata had discovered somewhere. All day at work, mailing out fund-raising letters for various defence committees, she had planned to spend the evening this way. She really liked the Ellington song, it boded well for the radio programme, and for her private evening. Lately too many people, too many rumours, too much jittery bravado. The antidote: spend some time alone, doing things one liked, the more the better, and do them all at once. She would have made herself a cup of tea, but lately, inexplicably, there was no tea to be found. She would go to bed early, she didn't have to man the machine gun until 5:30 the next morning, and that was hours away.

'In a Sentimental Mood.'

The music that Django Reinhardt and Stephane Grappelli made was very spare – compared to the lush crooning of the big bands it was thin and plain, hardly anything at all. The rhythm guitars and bass plunked away on the same note; a one-two, one-two beat on the chord that changed rarely, and the tempo of it was peculiar. Should you dance to it in an embrace, you'd have to move quickly, a foxtrot in a hurry. But if you danced apart, like the Charleston, it would be much too slow for the dancers to do any tricks at all.

Soloing above the rhythm was first Reinhardt, a Gypsy guitarist with three fingers burned off in a wagon fire, then Grappelli, a classically trained musician who played nightclub violin – take away the other instruments and he sounded like a violinist at a wedding – all perfumed sentiment. Reinhardt's playing was jazzy; long, rhythmic runs, the perfect counterpoint to the too-sweet violin. The two men were, Faye thought, opposites bound together, tenderness and cold passion. She wondered if they liked each other.

The record had been made at a bistro in Paris called Le Hot Club. Listening to the song, she could see it. Dark and smoky and close, a tiny dance floor, a thin woman in pearls with vacant eyes, barely dancing. Faye looked up from her book, head propped on elbow, and had at that moment a premonition: there would come a day when this song would bring back everything of her time in Madrid. It made her – a bizarre trick – long for a past that was still in the future. She burrowed deeper into the quilt, returned to her book.

Sometime during the last flourishes of the violin – Grappelli playing notes that sounded like musical tears, a crazy kind of sadness that wasn't serious at all yet hurt in a special way – the door opened.

Andres came in but she did not see him, not really, she saw the man who stood by his side. Immediately she began writing short stories about him, because his presence came to her in metaphors. *Eyes like tank slits.* He had blue eyes hidden away in there, and black hair and pale skin and square hands. He wore a dark blue shirt buttoned at the throat and a soft grey suit, and when he leaned over, formally, like a Slav, to shake her hand, she could see an automatic pistol holstered at his waist.

Andres was so dear to her, he approached her always like a clumsy man asked to hold – but only for a moment or two while its owner was occupied – a priceless glass vase. She lived in this body every minute of every day, it was just herself. But to him she was treasure. He ran his soft hand along her body and said *silk.* To be glass and gold and silk was a great honour, she knew, but she also knew it took living up to.

The curious thing about Andres was that he was two people. Quite distinctly two people. Andres at a distance was a malleable, hesitant man who moved invisibly in the crowd. But when he spoke, he changed. He was, then, the opposite of malleable and hesitant. Spending time alone with him in a room, you met the strange thing that lived inside him: a fierce and clever animal, a beast that might hunt you down if it decided you'd somehow hurt it.

For some reason, Andres had not expected her to be there. He was unpleasantly surprised and his eyes moved around too much. For the sake of appearances he introduced the other man, but gobbled his name so that it was simply a syllable or two. The man took her hand briefly – here and gone. His face seemed closed with tension. The two of them, Andres and his friend, made together a magnetic field of such exclusionary force that she was surprised her very body did not fly right out the window.

But they could go to hell.

She too fought in this war and what she had learned about war was that slowly but surely it sucked your strength right down to the marrow. She held this ground.

And her forces were arrayed about her. The jazz on the radio, the quilt, the book, the bed – the two men would attack at their peril.

So they left. Andres mumbling something or other, the Slav honouring her with a little bow. His eyes were curious, she noticed, finding everything in the room, taking a few notes, and finding her as well.

* * *

Toward the end of October the weather turned sunny and soft for one last spell before the fall rains set in and during that time the city of Madrid began to die.

The consulate people at Gaylord's Hotel managed to find a cot for Khristo and set it up in a hallway, and there he snatched a few hours' sleep when he could, couriers and code clerks and military attachés rushing past him at all hours of the day and night.

Lubin, whining incessantly of his family connection, was nonetheless dispatched to a nearby apartment building where a junior officers' dormitory occupied the upper floors. His days were filled with researches through Madrid's birth and marriage records, land-ownership deeds and tax rolls, as he built up dossiers on a long list of Spanish citizens compiled for him by Khristo and Andres. 'These individuals represent the gravest threat to world socialism,' Khristo told him, 'you must get me everything you can. And tell nobody what you are doing.' The names had been picked at random from Madrid telephone directories. Lubin, naturally, wanted to tail them from home to office and wherever else they went, but Khristo warned him that these dangerous persons must not be alerted to NKVD interest.

At the consulate, Khristo had a day-by-day view of the war, and visitors represented a cross section of the Soviet intelligence and military elite. Walter Ulbricht, head of the German division of the NKVD, passed through, as did no less than three Russian marshals – Konev, Malinovsky, and Rokossovsky – who had come to Spain to learn all they could of German tactics and, most especially, the capabilities of German aircraft and weapons. People at the consulate also kept track of the other side. Admiral Canaris of the Abwehr was known to be based near Madrid, sent to Spain by Hitler to study the effects of aerial bombing on a civilian population. This had never before been tried in Europe – Mussolini had used the tactic in Abyssinia but that proved nothing – and the Germans urgently wanted good intelligence on the subject. Thus, beginning in late October, the bombing of Madrid began in earnest. What happened when you bombed a hospital? A school? A column of refugees on a road? With the aid of the Condor Legion pilots, flying Junkers-52 and Heinkel-51 bombers, these questions were soon answered.

By October 20, in an attempt to relieve the pressure being applied by Mola's four columns, Republican forces attacked the town of Illescas, west of Madrid. Singing and chanting slogans, some fifteen thousand fighters rode out from staging areas on double-decker city buses to attack Moroccan and Spanish Legion forces under Barrón. The Republican forces fought bravely for three days and gave not one inch until, on October 23, they were outflanked by a relief column of cavalry under Tella that came north from Toledo, and they had to retreat back to the city. Seeing the bloody, exhausted fighters returning, the city's population began to feel that the end might be nearer than anyone would admit.

This same Nationalist cavalry column was then confronted, in the streets of Esquivias, by Russian tanks under Pavlov. A Republican victory was sorely needed, and this was one way to get it. But the tanks – impossible to manoeuvre in the narrow streets – could not hurt the cavalry, and the horsemen could not hurt the tanks, so the confrontation was at best a draw.

But for those who could read the signs, two particular

events signalled the beginning of the end: the national gold went out, and the refugees began to flow in.

The gold, some sixty-three million British pounds in value, was taken first by rail to Alicante, then on to Odessa by Russian freighter. Those who were responsible for guarding and counting the gold soon disappeared. Some time later, the Soviet Union announced major gold strikes in the Urals and, for the first time, began to sell gold on the world markets.

The refugees from outlying towns fled to the streets of Madrid and there set up housekeeping, amid pigs and goats and dressers and mirrors, building small fires to cook whatever food they could lay their hands on. There was, it seemed, less available every day.

The battle at Illescas was plainly audible on the streets of the city and, on October 23, Azaña, the prime minister of Republican Spain, fled the city in secret – his cabinet was not told he was leaving. He made his way to Barcelona, as close to the safety of the French border as possible, and declared the government of the country officially relocated. The exit of Castello, the minister of war, was even less illustrious. He went mad and had to be carried, foaming at the mouth, from his office. The rest of the government would stick it out for two weeks, then they too would head east. They left the city in a caravan of cars, loaded down with state ministers, bureaucrats, government records, wives and children and pets. A little way outside Madrid, the caravan was halted by a group of hooded men carrying rifles. *Go back*, they were told, *and lead the people of Madrid in their hour of crisis*. The caravan turned around, went west a few miles, turned again, and, achieving maximum speed, went barrelling through the roadblock.

The city would fight on, under siege, until March of 1939, when Madrid fell and the Spanish war ended.

*   *   *

185

Sascha arrived in Moscow on the ninth of November. Mitya was waiting for him, in a light snow, at Paveletski station. On the train ride north from Odessa he had in essence said good-bye to himself, a teary, miserable business as the train crawled across the southern steppe. In his colonel's uniform, he stood in the doorway of the passenger car as it crawled into the station, floating past a sea of anxious white faces in the waiting crowd. Then the train ground to a halt with a great hiss of steam, and the people behind him began to press – politely; one did not shove a uniform – to get off. He braced himself to attention, then stepped onto the platform. Somewhere in his imagination he had expected to be shot then and there, before his foot touched the earth of Moscow. But the reality was a sudden bear hug from Mitya and affectionate obscenities shouted in a blast of garlicky breath.

Mitya drove him home. His apartment, in a quiet little street behind Kutuzov Prospekt, was untouched. In the car, he had obliquely referred to Yezhov and the new purge, but Mitya had waved him off. Gossip, gossip, old women's tales. Yes, there had been changes, a few fools had managed to get themselves shot or sent off to the Siberian camps, but they *stole too much*, conspired for advancement *beyond what was good for them*, or *screwed the wrong people's wives*. Not to worry. They had put Sascha up for an Order of Lenin, Second Class, for his service in Spain, and he was certain to get it. Everybody knew Yaschyeritsa was a bastard. He would stay in Spain forever – nobody wanted him back. Not to worry, not to worry.

On Monday, he went to work at the NKVD complex on Dzherzhinsky Square. All were delighted to see him. There were six daisies in a water glass on his desk. His boss, General Grechko – a ham-fisted peasant with a sprouting mole on his nose – pounded him on the shoulders and called him all the old affectionate names: *Sascha my poet! My dreamer! My Chekhov!* Took him into his cluttered office and closed the door, knocked back a few shots accompanied by

186

heartfelt toasts and told him *yes, the medal would go through, even those pansies in Section Nine wouldn't dare stop it!* Sascha must learn to squeeze himself small so that Yezhov, all four feet ten inches of him, could give him the requisite hug and kiss when it was presented.

So for a week.

And he relaxed.

And then they took him.

According to the rules, it was to be done a certain way; each step in the process had been worked out, laboriously, over time, and thousands and thousands of arrests had fined the system down to a jewellike perfection. Instance: at the moment of arrest, the criminal must be beaten. From the *moment*. He opened the door to his apartment and they were waiting on the other side, and they hit him in the kidneys so hard he saw a black sun haloed by white lights, came to his senses on the parquet floor of his living room and threw up and for that they kicked him behind the knees. They showed him a fury he had not believed possible, and they knew all the places to hit, wasting not a single punch. It was the ferocity of Russia itself, for that was who he had betrayed, and it had a thousand fists. The intention was that he understand this lesson from the beginning. They threw him into the car like a weightless doll, and there they started on him again. The car was an old GAZ M-1 and the back seat smelled of what they had, these past several months, been using it for. Pushed face down on the seat, he offered to confess then and there. Confess what? a voice asked. We already know. And they beat him all the way to the Lubianka. According to the rules. They wished him to understand that he had crossed a line, that he was a nonperson; all his *special friends*, relatives, bosses, no matter who had protected him all through his life and career – they no longer mattered. He was no longer *somebody*. Now he was nobody. Crossing into an endless darkness peopled by other *nobodies* that nobody could help.

They beat him with fury because the German ideal, the

slow, nasty, pants-down business so dear to the hearts of the Gestapo on their western border, was repugnant to them. Sadism was despised as an integral aspect of fascism. This was righteous workers' anger, justified. Thus, after some endless, numberless group of nights in a wet cell, when the interrogator beat him up, he did it with a leg torn off a chair. The book of instruction said to do that very thing.

So, on the day when they would finally permit him to talk, when it was convenient for them to listen to him, he talked. They guided. It was, clearly, volume they wanted, they were sweeping with the big broom this time. Under Yagoda it had been a flick here, a flick there, specific enemies, definite plots. The *Yezhovschina* – Yezhov terror – wasn't like that. A big net, lots of fish, clean 'em out boys and get ready for the next batch.

He tried to give them Yaschyeritsa, but they just laughed at that. So he gave them Stoianev, the Bulgarian. Not much, but something. Those Bulgarians had too much Turkish blood for their own good, and it made them plot and scheme like pashas. Who else? They knocked out a tooth over Mitya's name. He was theirs, and they knew better than that. Sent him back to the wet cell and cut off the fishhead soup for two days so that without food he began to hear buzzing flies that didn't exist. When they brought him back he offered them Roubenis, the Armenian presently posing as Andres Cardona. Who had not delivered Fifth Column names because he had secretly gone over to them, with Stoianev's cunning assistance as conduit directly to the Nazis. *Good! Good! More of that.* But the names of some old schoolmates at Frunze military academy did not much excite them. They had, apparently, already mined that vein. Finally, at the end of his strength, when he knew for a certainty he had begun to die, he gave them General Grechko, his boss, who had manoeuvred Stoianev to an assignment in Spain for the very purpose of collaboration with *Hitlerite elements*.

Suddenly, the interrogation ended. They left him alone

in his cell, in an area where the guards wore slippers so that the prisoners could not hear them coming. They had what they wanted, what they'd wanted all along – Grechko. The others were merely spice in the soup.

* * *

In the basement of Gaylord's Hotel in central Madrid, in the code room, Khristo Stoianev closed his eyes with relief. Took a deep breath and let it out slowly. Read the cable again. Yes, it was true. Yaschyeritsa had, one day before the deadline, let him off the hook. He would be part of the operation known as SANCTUARY. He was instructed to work with Roubenis in this *new effort*. The leader of the operation was expected the following day, Captain Ilya Goldman. Good luck. Good hunting.

They used two cars. In the Citroën, Lubin sat behind the wheel with Andres in the passenger seat. Khristo and Ilya Goldman were in the back. They'd taken the Degtyaryova machine guns from the trunk and held them across their knees. In the second car, a dark green Opel Kapitän parked across the street and up the block, sat four Spaniards in black suits. They were members of SIM, the Servicio de Investigación Militar, the Republican intelligence service most closely controlled by the NKVD.

The building in question was a four-storey white house with a marble portico in the elegant diplomatic area near the parliament buildings. The Finnish flag, a blue cross on a white field, hung limply in the early morning drizzle. A tarnished brass plaque beside the front door was inscribed EMBAJADA DE FINLANDIA. The last of the Finnish diplomatic staff had cleared out some days earlier, when the Republican government had left the city.

'It moved,' Lubin said. 'I am certain of it.'

All of them stared up at a curtain hanging at a window on the second floor.

'It looks the same to me,' Khristo said.

'I beg to differ — '

'Shut up, Sublieutenant,' Ilya said. 'It does not matter if they see us. The phone line is dead.'

Lubin opened his mouth to argue, then thought better of it. Khristo was amazed at the changes in Ilya Goldman. He had become a captain, which meant he had proven himself to somebody powerful, and authority had settled comfortably upon him. He was still the same Ilya, near-sighted, physically slight, with the sharpish features and prominent ears of a rodent — not a rat, but a child's pet mouse. Women were irresistibly drawn to him, Khristo knew, finding him easy to pet, perfect to smother, adorable. Yet, Khristo was certain, among all the Brotherhood Front of 1934 his was the mind that moved most easily among the twisting trails and alleyways of the intelligence craft. Khristo found himself blunt and obvious by comparison. 'I am a Jew,' he had long before explained to Khristo, at the Belov exercises, 'survival in the shadows is nothing new to us.'

'There. It moves again.'

Lubin was right. Damnable ambitious brat. The curtain shifted slightly, then closed quickly.

'At last,' Ilya said, 'we've got them thinking.'

Andres lit a cigarette. 'One could stir the pot, perhaps.'

'Exactly,' Ilya said. 'Khristo, you're the one who looks like a bloodthirsty bastard. Go say good morning to our Spanish brothers.'

Khristo left the machine gun on the floor. Walking diagonally across the pavement to the Opel, he kept his eyes from wandering to the second-floor window. But he had the sense of being watched, of being onstage. He just hoped they didn't panic in there and open up on him. Ilya had insisted, of course, that they make doubly sure they had *adequate reason to presume*, and that they didn't, by error, bag a sackful of Finns. Ilya had learned the Soviet ways in his heart — one required an *incident* in case the roof fell in. A moving curtain, by itself, wouldn't do.

The man in the driver's seat of the Opel rolled down the window as he approached. His face was pitted, and he wore a thick black moustache and sunglasses that hid his eyes. The SIM were brutal types, they were proud of it, using for their executions the Vile Garrote, a slow strangulation device of medieval invention. The victim was seated in front of a post and a metal collar was tightened slowly around the throat until death by ligature occurred – a three-hour death.

'*Buenas días,*' Khristo said to the man.

'They will see you, you know,' the man said coldly, eyes invisible behind the dark glasses.

'That's the idea. We want to agitate them.'

A voice from the back seat: 'We will be pleased to go in there and *agitate* them.'

'In a while,' Khristo said. 'Let's see some evidence first.'

'At your pleasure,' the driver said, his voice heavy with boredom. They were here for action, would have had the door down and the victims spreadeagled long before first light.

Khristo walked back to the Citroën, his face, hidden from the SIM car, soured with disgust. Ten minutes later, the door of the embassy opened cautiously and a man came out.

'There he is!' Lubin cried. 'A Fifth Columnist, certainly.'

Walking down the street, the man was a caricature of forced insouciance. Despite himself, his eyes darted to the green Opel. Once he had been fat and sleek, an arrogant bully, showered with cologne and pious as a priest. Now he was unshaven and bleary-eyed, the waistband of his trousers folded beneath his belt to take up the slack.

Ilya cranked his window down a half inch, a signal to the other unit. As the man turned the corner, one of the SIM people slid gracefully from the Opel and followed him. The curtain moved again.

'Now,' Ilya said.

In a tight group, the four moved quickly to the door

191

of the embassy. Khristo held the Degtyaryova loosely by his side. Simultaneously, the SIM men scampered around the building toward the rear door. From the back of the building came a pounding on the door and shouting in Spanish. Andres and Khristo moved to one side of the front entrance, Ilya and Lubin to the other.

Ilya reached over and knocked politely, calling, 'Open, please,' in Spanish. For thirty seconds nothing happened. He armed the Degtyaryova and knocked again and repeated the *please*, and this time the door flew open. An old man with white hair stood with arms akimbo, a crowd of people surged and whined and prayed behind him.

'Gently, father, gently,' Andres said from Khristo's side.

'Please,' the man said, 'do not hurt us.'

They forced the crowd back from the door, closed it, and stationed Lubin in front of it, his Tokarev held before him. Lubin's face was flushed with excitement and his eyes were wild, a strand of hair had come loose from his pompadour and lay across his forehead. 'Back, back,' he said in Russian, 'move from the door.'

'*Los Rusos*,' a woman screamed.

Lubin brought the pistol to bear on the woman. The old man reached cautiously for his wrist, to push it down. Lubin shot him twice and he folded in half and tilted over sideways onto the floor. Lubin whinnied, a burst of nervous laughter, then clamped his hand over his mouth to stop it. The frightened crowd rushed against the opposite wall, several of the women tore the crucifixes from around their necks and held them up before their faces.

Ilya spoke to Khristo in tones of barely controlled anger: 'Take that thing away from him, will you?'

Khristo caught Lubin's wrist and forced his arm down. Lubin turned and seemed to be looking at him but his eyes were sightless with excitement. 'Sublieutenant Lubin,' Khristo said, emphasizing the rank, emphasizing that there *was* order, even here, 'give me your weapon, please.'

Lubin opened his mouth to speak and the laugh poured

out again. With difficulty he controlled it, shutting his eyes.

'Now,' Khristo said.

'I cannot, Lieutenant.'

They both looked down at the hand, which was frozen shut on the pistol. Khristo took hold of Lubin's chubby fingers and forced them open, one at a time. From the back of the house came the sound of splintering wood as the SIM men ripped the door apart. Lying on the floor, the old man pointed at Lubin. There was red foam on his lips. 'You will walk in blackness,' he whispered. 'Forever and forever. I curse you. I *curse* you.' Lubin giggled and Khristo smacked him on the ear, which turned bright red. The SIM man with the pitted face came downstairs, a baby in the crook of one arm. His other hand towed a woman along by the hair. 'This one was upstairs,' he explained, 'trying to throw her baby out the window.'

After some confusion, they got everybody sitting on the floor of what had once been the reception area of the embassy. Ilya managed a count. The SIM men had things to say in a Spanish that none of the four NKVD could understand, but the people sitting on the floor turned grey and lifeless. They sent Lubin back to the Citroën, one of his fingers swollen to double its size, apparently broken by Khristo. Finally, a moving van rolled up to the back door and the SIM took charge of their prisoners.

Driving back to Gaylord's Hotel, Ilya informed them that Operation SANCTUARY would continue, though it would be more efficient than it had been that morning. All over Madrid, Nationalist supporters and Falangists were hiding out in embassies, under diplomatic protection. So, now that they'd cleaned out the first group of refugees from an abandoned embassy, they were going to staff it with Soviet intelligence officers playing the part of Finnish diplomats. Taking the enemy into custody would be a lot cleaner and simpler that way. The SIM, he continued, had a similar operation going at the southern edge of the city: a tunnel, which supposedly travelled below ground all the way to Nationalist lines, in fact went only a few hundred yards, then surfaced in the midst of a courtyard where a gang of SIM operatives was waiting. Word was now being spread among the Falangist cells that their members had been betrayed to the enemy, they should flee to the Finnish embassy, where they'd be protected, or use the tunnel that reached the Nationalist lines.

The shift in policy made sense to Khristo. Using Andres against the Falange was a long-term operation. The new approach was clearly intended to accelerate and intensify the covert effort against the enemy inside the city. Mola's four columns were sharpening the pressure on Madrid; SANCTUARY was clearly an NKVD response. When Yaschyeritsa had lifted the deadline for the effort against the Farmacia Cortés group, Khristo's relief had been tempered by a nagging anxiety: perhaps they were, for their own reasons, manoeuvring him. Now, he felt, he could relax. He hoped silently that they did not ask him to serve as a Finnish diplomat – he didn't think he had the stomach for it. He didn't look like a Finn, he told himself, he was dark, not fair.

* * *

Buenas noches, mis amigos. Buenas noches, todos los peleadores bravos que puedan oír ma voz. Y buenas noches, Madrid. Hay veinte horas, y la hora para el jazz hot . . .

The young woman played with the radio until music flowed into the little room below the eaves. Andres said, 'It is the singer Bessie Smith. You will like it.' Khristo didn't exactly like it, it made him sad. The voice of a blues singer, stark, with only a piano, bass and drums to fill in the spaces, reached through the crackle of the nighttime static and touched his heart. He could not understand the words, but the sorrow of it was all too clear. *Enough grief for one day*, he thought. The nasty scene at the Finnish embassy refused to leave his mind, and he

194

and Andres had decided to drown their war in a bottle of Spanish gin.

They'd split the cost of the bottle and taken it back to Andres's garret at 9 Calle de Victoria. For him to be there, with Andres and his American girlfriend and the German woman called Renata, was very much against the rules. But he was tired of the rules. He was tired of a lot of things. He stared at the bottle, which had a Spanish matador on the label, his expression rigid with pride of manhood, indifference in the face of death. For Khristo, the more he drank the gin, the less he liked the matador.

Andres's girlfriend was called Faye – it was her idea to play a card game called cribbage. The four of them sat around a small table with a pegboard at the centre and tried to make their cards add up to thirty-one. Such achievements were rewarded by the advance of a small stick in the pegboard. He had no idea if he was winning or losing – he did know that the smarmy matador on the gin bottle had nearly destroyed what little mathematical ability he possessed. Renata, his partner, looked at him in despair from time to time.

The four of them spoke English as they played – it turned out to be the only language they had in common other than Spanish, which they had to work at all day long. The American girl had already stifled a giggle at his peculiar diction and he'd looked up sharply, only to be signalled by Andres that no discourtesy had been intended. She certainly was different. Had caught him staring at her at one point and had stared right back. God save her, he thought, from ever visiting Bulgaria, where such looks had meanings he was sure she didn't intend. Did she? No.

'I went to University City today,' she said casually. For a moment, the game stopped dead. There was heavy fighting in the university area, where one of Mola's Moorish columns had breached the city's defences. The Army of Africa, Franco's original striking force, had already captured the bus and tram terminals in the suburbs.

'What?' Andres looked at her with horror.

'You heard me.'

'Perhaps you want to be killed. La Pasionaria will announce it on the streets – a courageous death, our American sister, *no pasarán*.'

'Well, they asked me to go at work. So I went.'

'Why? Who asked you?'

'A woman at work was pregnant, the baby started coming early and the labour was very bad. So they sent me to bring back the husband, who was holding the College of Agriculture.'

'What a war,' Renata said.

'I met a group of British machine-gunners – I'm playing the jack of clubs – and they told me the Moors have been holding the College of Medicine for several days.'

'Really?' Renata said. 'That I had not heard.'

'It's true.'

Renata put a five down on the jack, and moved their peg.

'This fellow, an Oxford man, by the way, told me the Poles in the Dabrowsky Brigade won it back for an afternoon. A shambles, they said. The Moors built fires in the hallways and roasted the laboratory animals on their bayonets and ate them. Now they'll all get rare diseases. The Poles chased them out by putting hand grenades on the elevators and sending them up to the floor they were holding.'

Khristo shook his head in disbelief. 'What a war.' He echoed Renata, knowing the phrase must be correct.

Faye smiled grimly. 'Fifth floor,' she said. 'Travel accessories, kitchenware, hand grenades.'

'What is?' Khristo asked.

'Oh, you know. Department store elevators.'

'Ah,' he said, feigning knowledge.

It was his turn to play. He tried to concentrate, but the cards in his hand made no particular sense, a random collection of numbers and pictures. From across the table,

196

Renata said, 'Forward, comrade. And we shall gain a final victory.' He looked up from his cards, but her smile was gentle and encouraging. The telephone rang, the jingling of a tiny bell in two short bursts. All four reacted to the sound. It rang again. Andres moved toward the corner, where it was mounted on the wall.

He picked up the receiver and said, '*Sí?*' Listened for several seconds, then said, '*Momentito, por favor.*' Left the handset dangling from its cord and walked over to Khristo and said quietly, in Russian, 'Someone wishes to speak with you.'

Khristo carefully laid his cards face down on the table. A tiny muscle below his eye began to run like a motor. Nobody, *nobody*, knew he was there. He searched Andres's face for a sign but the man's expression had gone cold. In that moment, they silently accused each other of betrayal. Then Khristo pushed himself away from the table and walked the few steps to the telephone. He'd become acutely conscious of his surroundings: the silent people in the room, the music on the radio, the rhythmic echo of distant artillery. He held the receiver carefully in his hand, listened to the hum of the open line, and at last said '*Sí?*'

'No names, please,' said a voice in Russian. He knew the accent, the edgy nasal tone. It was Ilya Goldman.

'Very well,' he answered in Russian.

'I have just cast your horoscope. It says tonight is a good time to travel. It says start as soon as possible. I take this to mean right away.'

'Very well. Thank you for telling me.'

'Your friend is born in the same moon.'

'I understand.'

'The time may come when we should meet again. Is it possible?'

'Yes. Yes, it's possible. In the north, I think.'

'A good choice. How can we manage it?'

'Our old sign. The one we used with the dog. Initials and numbers. You recall?'

197

'Ah, yes, very well. Where might such signals appear?'

'Matrimonial ads. In the newspaper.'

'Sorry to see you go, my friend.'

'Join us.'

'Soon, maybe. Not now.'

'Good-bye, then.'

'Good luck.' The connection broke.

He hung up the phone carefully and turned to face the others. Faye saw his face and said, 'My God, what is it?'

'They come to arrest us,' he said in English. 'Me and Andres. But they will take you also.' He turned to Renata. 'And you.'

'The Falange?' Faye said, incredulous.

'No,' Andres said. 'Not the Falange.'

*　　*　　*

They kicked down the door some twenty minutes later — about the time it took to drive from Gaylord's to the Calle de Victoria. Maltsaev and three assistants, with several more waiting in cars below. The radio was playing jazz and there were cards lying about on a small table and a half bottle of Spanish gin and ashtrays full of cigarettes. One of the men silently unplugged the radio and carried it down to the car. Another one found some women's clothing from America, and he too left. When his comrade in the automobile saw that he went up himself, but there wasn't much left — a combination lock and he didn't know the combination, but he took it anyhow, perhaps it could be traded. Maltsaev went to the telephone but the cord had been sliced in two. Señora Tovar, the janitor's wife, was brought up the marble stairs with her arm bent nearly double behind her back. She cursed them all the way. These tenants were Fifth Columnists, she was told. But she knew better. Told Maltsaev to let her go or the women of Madrid would hound him to his grave. He nodded briefly and his men released her. They went up to the roof and found Félix and beat him up a little, but he didn't seem to know much of anything. At last, when they'd removed everything they wanted, they tore the apartment to pieces, but found nothing. Maltsaev and one of his men were the last to leave. 'Too bad,' he said. The man nodded in agreement. 'One has to learn, of course, who warned them. General Bloch will want someone.'

'Perhaps his sublieutenant, Lubin,' the man suggested.

'A logical choice,' Maltsaev said. 'Flies for Yaschyeritsa.'

'What?' the man asked.

Maltsaev dismissed him with a wave of the hand. Such idiots one had to work with in this profession. At least the other one, Kulic, the one in the mountains, would be well fixed. He'd made sure of that. The night's work wasn't entirely wasted. Now for Lubin. The family was powerful, but that could be overcome with a confession. He'd get that in a hurry, he was sure.

* * *

They could go west to Portugal. The Russians would not expect that because it meant crossing battle lines, then working their way, by bluff or stealth, through hundreds of miles of Nationalist-held countryside. They could go south, through Republican territory, and buy passage on a boat across the Mediterranean to Tangiers, a French possession. They could go northeast, to Port-Bou, the Pyrenees crossing point to southwestern France. But this mountain pass was Republican Spain's only major overland border access and would be subject to exceptionally heavy surveillance. Crossing the Pyrenees on the smugglers' routes was not appealing – too many travellers were never heard of again when they attempted that route.

The Russians would use the telephone – the system was operated on contract by American personnel from American Telephone and Telegraph and worked well, for both sides, throughout the war – to alert NKVD units throughout the country, but both Khristo and Andres doubted they would have sufficient time to activate Republican forces.

They also doubted the Russians would tell their allies that intelligence officers had gone missing.

They decided to travel north. Khristo had overheard, at Gaylord's, that the Spaniards were arming fishing boats in Bilbao and using them to bring food into Spain from French coastal ports. Bilbao was two hundred miles away, it would take all night, but the fastest way out of Spain was the best.

Dawn found them still trying to get out of Madrid.

It was a night of madness in the streets. Buildings unaccountably on fire, fire trucks skidding on streets wet with a slow, persistent rain that had started at dusk. They tried the Gran Via but found it blocked by Russian tanks brought up into battery position, their steel sides shiny in the rain, engines muttering and backfiring. Some streets were blocked by refugee campsites — tarpaulins or rain capes rigged upright with broomsticks to keep out the rain. Khristo saw a couple making love under a blanket on a brass bed in a house made of wooden crates. On one of these streets they hit a cat. Khristo slowed instinctively, then realized they could not afford to stop and stepped on the accelerator. When it was almost dawn, they were forced to halt at an intersection as private cars being used as ambulances sped past, coming from the direction of University City. The drivers rang cowbells, mounted on the roof, by pulling on a rope. While they were stopped, an old man approached the car. He wore a formal business suit, with waistcoat decorously buttoned, and carried a tightly furled umbrella on his forearm. His beard was clipped to a precise triangle and a pair of pince-nez sat squarely on the bridge of his nose. He looked, Khristo thought, like a professor of Greek and Latin.

He peered in the window and greeted them as brothers and sisters in freedom. 'I have been to war tonight,' he said, 'and I have been wounded.' He half turned and Khristo could see blood seeping from a small wound at the back of his neck. 'So,' the man said cheerfully, 'it's the hospital for me!' He saluted them with his free hand and disappeared around a corner. A little later they saw, they thought, one of the infamous Phantom Cars, packed with militiamen who arrested and executed suspected Fifth Columnists at night. A rifle barrel protruded from a rear window. Then, when they were almost out of the city, a Checa unit on bicycles stopped them.

Khristo chatted with their leader, holding the Tokarev below the sightline of the driver's window. He was free. It had come slowly, but when comprehension overtook him his spirit soared with excitement. It was as though a hand had let go of the back of his neck and for the first time in years he could raise his head and see the horizon. So they would not take him back.

The Checa man at the window was very slow – he had all the time in the world. But Khristo drew an invisible line for him and waited for him to cross it and die. Yaschyeritsa would get no more satisfaction from him than dancing on his grave. The man talked on and on. It was interesting about his job that he got to meet so many different kinds of people who walked about in this world, who would have ever imagined that on this rainy night in November he would engage in conversation with a citizen of Soviet Russia, now that was why he found this job so very interesting. Finally Andres leaned across from the passenger seat and whispered that they had only an hour to spend with these girls here before they had to return to the fighting. The man's face slid gradually into an immense leer. He winked, stood back from the car, and waved them through. Lascivious shouts of '*Viva la Rusia!*' followed them down the street.

For a time they travelled on the main road to Burgos. But they began to see men in suits standing by cars parked beside the road, so they moved onto the narrow lanes that went through the villages. In some nameless place in the vast wheat heartland north of Madrid the car stopped. They opened the hood and looked inside, but none of them knew

201

anything about cars. The engine gave off a blast of heat that shimmered the air above it. It ticked in the silence and smelled of burnt oil. A small man appeared from nowhere, riding a bicycle with an infant in the basket. They spoke to him in Spanish but he did not understand Spanish, or perhaps he was deaf. He pointed to his ears again and again. He smiled at them. Showed them his baby. Then, almost as an afterthought, he reached into the engine and did something to something and signalled Khristo to start the car. It started. The man refused to take money, waved to them as they moved off. In the car they made plans for what they would do in Paris. What they would eat. Where they would go. Madrid, it began to be clear once they were away from it, had been a prison. Soon they would be in Burgos, it wasn't so far from there to Bilbao. They would get on a fishing boat and sail away to freedom. The car stopped again, on a tiny road bounded by uncut wheat rotting in the fields.

There was nothing for miles. Khristo's hand shook as he raised the hood. He wanted to throttle the engine hoses until the Citroën bowed to his will. This had never happened to him before, the car had always run perfectly. They decided to walk, to march cross-country taking only pistols and whatever else would fit in their pockets. They started out, Andres sang a song to get them moving along. Suddenly, a German spotter plane appeared and swooped low to have a look at them. Faye waved to it and smiled. It disappeared over the horizon and they ran back to the car – some cover was preferable to being caught in the open. The plane returned and buzzed the car, then left. Khristo, for no particular reason, turned the ignition key one last time for luck. The Citroën roared to life and he very nearly wept with relief.

At dusk, they worked their way around the outskirts of Burgos. Found a shack with an ancient, hand-operated gas pump, and bought fuel from a suspicious peasant woman in black who overcharged them mercilessly. They had to pool their remaining pesos to pay her – Khristo had been kept on a small living allowance, most of his NKVD pay *banked safely for him awaiting his return to Moscow*. The woman watched all this with an eye like a hunting hawk. She went into the shack to retrieve some coins for change, and Khristo and Andres whispered briefly about doing away with her. They saw her watching them through a window. Andres looked about and discovered there were no telephone lines going into the shack, then realized suddenly that all she wanted to do was steal their change. They drove away without it. The road began to climb through forests and the Citroën stuttered and threatened to stall. Khristo pushed the gas pedal to the floor; the car faltered, then roared ahead. Bad gasoline, they thought, watered. Late at night they came to the Río Nervión, which ran eight miles to the Atlantic. They easily found the fishing boats, which had 101mm fieldpieces mounted fore and aft. Andres got out of the car and wandered down the street of dockside bars, sailors' haunts with anchors and sextants and curling waves painted on their signs. Khristo, Faye and Renata stayed in the car, too tired to talk, the burst of energy that had seen them through the long night had waned suddenly, replaced by depression and exhaustion. Khristo time and again caught himself fading out. 'Where do you suppose he is?' Faye asked at one point.

Khristo shrugged. Told himself to keep watch, knowing how vulnerable they were. The American girl fell asleep, her head sliding along the upholstery until he felt its weight settle on his upper arm. In her sleep she turned slightly toward him, until the place where her mouth rested grew warm with her breath. He remained very still and fancied he could hear, in the rise and fall of her breathing, the progress of her dreams.

They were all asleep when a hand banged hard on the window. Khristo came to his senses in terror, then saw it was Andres, with a sea captain. He didn't look like a sea captain, he was wearing a suit and tie. He had got married that morning, Andres explained. Khristo got out of the car and went with them to a bar down a little alley between warehouses – moving the Tokarev to the side pocket of his jacket and keeping his hand on it. The bar was only twelve feet long, with five stools. They drank a glass of wine and made their offer: the Citroën and two Degtyaryova machine guns in exchange for passage to France. Yes, good, the man said. He could take two of them for that. Which two would it be? He asked too much, they protested. He thought not. The Russians had come around, he explained, looking for them. The licence plate and automobile were just as they had described. He had, this very day, become a married man. He now had responsibilities. And it was his wedding night. If he was to spend it on the high-running sea of the Gulf of Vizcaya instead of the high-running sea of the marriage bed, he must be well paid. The three of them returned to the car, Andres suggesting that the women carried extra pesos. Khristo saw his game without prompting. They would put a gun in this one's ear and solve the problem that way. Back at the car, they told Renata and Faye about the captain's demand. Andres suggested that the two women should go by fishing boat, he and Khristo would find a guide and use the smugglers' trails across the Pyrenees. Faye took a little watch off her wrist and held it up to the captain. He took it in his hand. Listened to it tick. It was Russian, she explained, brought to America by her grandmother. All that time, she said, it worked perfectly. The captain agreed to take them and put the watch in his pocket.

They reached France the following day, wading ashore at the fishing village of St.-Jean-de-Luz. Shoes in hand, they walked up a narrow beach of brown pebbles to a low seawall. There was a policeman sitting on the wall, he had taken his hat off and set it on a page of newspaper to keep it from the tar, and was eating an apple with a small knife, and he arrested them.

*   *   *

Marquin and his three compatriots very nearly did reach Portugal. Their method was simple enough. They walked only at night. They walked near the road — so as not to lose their way — but never on it. They stole only vegetables, never chickens, to keep local anger to a minimum. A few missing vegetables, they knew, were not worth an encounter with the authorities. A mile short of the Portuguese border, their luck ran out. The army was running things in that region, and they were discovered sleeping under a bridge. The first interrogation was superficial, but in time they were taken by truck to a unit of Nationalist intelligence and there placed under the care of a Moroccan corporal named Bahadi, who specialized in getting answers to any and all questions. Marquin lasted the longest, about an hour. When the officer in charge was satisfied that he had everything he could get, they were taken out and shot in a courtyard. Never, following the session with Bahadi, were four men happier to die.

Thus the story of Kulic's mercy made its way to Nationalist intelligence headquarters in Toledo, and was there submitted for analysis to Oberstleutnant Otto Eberlein, one of the unit's Abwehr advisers. Eberlein, recruited by the NKVD in 1934 under motivation of political idealism, passed the information to his contact in Toledo, a nurse in a podiatrist's office — by 1938 he had surely the most pampered feet in Spain — and from there it soon enough reached Colonel General Yadomir Bloch, who called Maltsaev and told him to take care of the matter. Maltsaev simply moved the appropriate information back through the system to Nationalist intelligence: a time, a date, the name of the town — Estillas — then had Madrid Base radio Kulic and assign the mission.

From the beginning, the attack on the police station at Estillas went badly. He had two men sick with high fever and dysentery and they had to be left at the deserted village. Which meant he was down to fourteen souls. And the ammunition situation was beginning to pinch. Madrid Base had been informed by radio of the executions and sickness, and the need for resupply, but had confirmed the original order. Someone, somewhere, apparently thought that the Estillas police station was a critical target, and his was not to reason why. Still, a daylight attack. And with reduced forces. And with morale, after 'justice' had been dealt to the four POUM traitors, at its lowest ebb. He was close, at one point, to cancelling the mission and accepting in return whatever Madrid decided to do to him. Only one factor kept him from that. An initial reconnaissance persuaded him that Estillas was a rather easy place to attack. Just behind the police station lay the town cemetery, a place frequented only on Sundays, when the townspeople came out to place bunches of flowers on the gravesites. Scheduled to strike on a Wednesday afternoon, the raiding party could move up close before making themselves known.

They got as far as the cemetery, then all hell broke loose. Somebody knew they were coming. Because once the unit was in place, well spread out and awaiting his signal, the mortars and machine guns started in. And the mortars had been zeroed in. Accurately. *Betrayed*, he thought. The first shells raised enormous dirt plumes in the cemetery, smashing headstones to splinters and blowing the dead out of their graves — a fountain of whitened bones rising in the air, then raining down on the heads of the guerrillas. The sergeant, a brave man, stood up and waved the men forward. Machine-gun fire stitched him across the belly and he died howling. Kulic fired twice, at nothing in particular, then a blast concussion picked him up and slammed him senseless against the earth. His mind swayed back and forth, a sickening, dizzy rise and fall from one part of consciousness to another, and he found himself crawling. He meant not to be taken alive, felt around for his rifle but it had disappeared. He heard some of his men weeping, managed to get to one knee before the next shell came in, felt the shrapnel take him all along the left side, knew his left eye was blinded, knew nothing more after that.

*   *   *

In Catalonia, some way inland from the ancient spice city of Tarragona, in the valley of the Río Ebro, lay the village of San Ximene. In the late summer of 1938, a company of Nationalist infantry moved into the town and took it without a shot being fired. By then, the conquest of the province was no longer an issue, and nobody wanted to be the last to die. As the troops marched in, a little winded because the village stood high above the road, a few people lined the narrow lane, waved tiny Monarchist flags, and gave the cheer heard now all across the country. '*Han pasado,*' they called out. '*Han pasado!*' They *have* passed. Don Teodosio and Doña Flora and Miguelito the chauffeur were ceremoniously released from captivity. Both mayors, Avena from the PSUC and Quinto of the POUM, were ceremoniously shot. There wasn't much else to do, so the captain ordered his men forward. They had liberated San Ximene, and he felt they ought to go on, to Calaguer or Santoval, before nightfall. Marching out of the village in good order, they passed through an orchard of fig trees. A sergeant was sent to reconnoitre, but there was no fruit to be had. The sergeant was a country man, and told the captain that the trees had not been pruned. Branches had broken off under the weight of the fruit, disease had spread into the trunks from the open wood, and that was the end of the San Ximene figs.

The World
at Night

'Steady on!'

'Dear boy. Trod on your paw, have I?'

'Damn near.'

'I am sorry. Can't see a thing with the lights off. Candle are lovely in a ballroom, but they do keep one in shadow.'

'Bloody Frenchies. If it ain't a knife 'n' fork they can' work it.'

'Not the power, actually. One of Winnie's *effects* I think Makes it funereal.'

'Mmm.'

'I'm Roger Fitzware.'

'Jimmy Grey. West Sussex Fitzwares, is it?'

'*C'est moi.*'

'Mmm. Been in Paris long?'

'Live here, actually, most of the time.'

'Do you. I'm just in from Cairo. Over at the Bristol.'

'How do you find it?'

'Service gone to hell, of course, and full of Americans.

'In Cairo on business?'

'Little of everything, really.'

'Hot as ever?'

'Yes. Damned filthy too.'

'Dear old thing.'

'Not my sort of place, all those little brown men running, about and stabbing each other.'

'Oh well. One puts up with the little brown men. For the sake of the little brown boys.'

'*Mmm.* Wouldn't know about that.'

'Ah, here's the lovely Ginger.'

'Roddy Fitzware! You promised to call — Who's this?'

'Ginger Pudakis, meet Jimmy Grey.'

'Delighted. Mmm. Yes, well, think I see somebody I know. Good to have met you, Fitzware.'

'See you.'

'Roddy! You are exceptionally bad. You terrified that poor man.'

'Oh well, it *is* Paris, after all.'

'Not here, my lamb. Here is a little corner of a foreign field, and that fellow, if I'm not mistaken, is something or other to Viscount Grey.'

'The 1914 man? "The lamps are going out all over Europe, we shall not see them lit again in our time." That the one?'

'Yes.'

'The lamps are certainly out here.'

'Where's Mützi?'

'Home. In a great snit.'

'Oh Roddy, you mustn't be cruel.'

'Me! Ginger dear, I've been an absolute bishop, really I have. But he sneaked out while I was having me nap, taxied off to Gabouchard and bought himself the most impossible tie. Couldn't let him wear it, could I, not to Winnie and Dicky's. Had a sunset. Some dreadful peachy pinky sort of thing they sold him. Poor Mützi and his filthy *Boche* taste, he can't help himself at all. When I left he was playing Mendelssohn on the Victrola and mumbling about *Selbstmord* or some such thing. Ending it all.'

'Too sad. All for a tie.'

'Told him not to get blood on the curtains.'

'You're a horrid man, you really are.'

'*C'est moi*. Care to step onto the balcony?'

'And what would you do on the balcony?'

'Think of something, dear girl.'

'You probably would.'

'Speaking of that, where's old Winnie and Dicky?'

'Grand entrance at midnight, one is told. From the ballroom elevator.'

212

'Too bad Mützi isn't here to see this, he quite loves the Teutonic style. Draped candles, urns with cypress, roses painted black. Nobody actually dead, is there?'

'Heavens no. On the stroke of midnight, Winnie Beale turns thirty-nine. It's a funeral for her youth.'

'Ah.'

'Really, one must love the Americans.'

'You married one, my dear, so you must. Whatever became of Mr. Pudakis?'

'In Chicago, as always. Where he does something with meat. Bloody old Europe didn't agree with poor Harry.'

'Hello! Something's up, the music's gone queer.'

'It's the funeral march. Is it? Yes, I think it is. Sounds a bit odd from a jazz band.'

'Speaking of odd, *regardez* the elevator.'

'Good God. Now that is courage.'

'Ain't it though? Throw yourself a birthday bash and make an entrance entirely bare-arsed. *Bravo Winnie! Hurrah!*'

'Well, not entirely bare-arsed. The hat is from Schiaparelli, my sweet, the pearls are Bulgari, and the little catch-me/fuck-me shoes are made by a little man in the Rue des Moulins.'

'Still, rather a decent set of flanks . . .'

'Now Roddy, don't be boring.'

'Tell me, dear girl, who's that hard-looking gent presiding over the salmon?'

'Him? You know him. It's Mario Thoeni, the tenor, though one wouldn't exactly say hard-looking . . .'

'Gawd not him. The *waiter*.'

'Oh who knows. Some dreadful Slav from Heininger. Winnie finds him decorative.'

'She's right, you know. He's quite thoroughly decorative.'

'Roddy Fitzware, you're not to poach!'

'Dear girl, wouldn't think of it.'

*

All his life he had handled tools, but this one had its own special set of perfections. It was made of silver, with a pleasing weight that sealed it to the hand, a broad filigree surface ending in a rounded point and a subtle edge of just the proper sharpness. He pressed it down through the pink flesh of the salmon – choosing a natural striation for the cut – deftly balanced the portion atop the server, then slid it neatly onto the maize-coloured plate. With ceremony, he laid the server on a silver dish and took up a small ladle. He swirled it twice through the thick *sauce diplomat* – as though to banish some godlike impurity – then, from the left, drizzled a thin river to the salmon slice, paused to anoint the top with a decorative pool, as in a garden, then ran the river to a perfect delta on the other side of the plate, stopping just short of the thick gold banding. With a tiny silver trident, he fashioned a triangle of capers on the dryland north of the river, then, the dénouement, placed two black truffle 'rocks' at the edge of the garden pool. White-gloved hand turned beneath the plate so that the intrusive thumb barely rode the edge, he proffered the master-work, eyes down, speaking the words '*Merci, madame*' in a soft undertone.

That afternoon, carrying silver trays of hors d'oeuvres covered with brown paper upstairs to the kitchen that served the ballroom, he had observed the Beales' chef preparing the *sauce diplomat*. Fish stock, cream – too thick to pour, it had to be spooned from the bottle – lobster butter, brandy and cayenne. Now, in a crystal bowl by his right hand, the sauce's combined scents drifted up and tormented him. Normally, when he worked at the Brasserie Heininger, he could manage a discreet sample somewhere between kitchen and dining room, but here one was in the public eye.

For a moment, there was no one to serve – a group of rosy-cheeked men favoured the roast – and he gazed out into the crowd with the particular dead-eyed, unseeing servant's stare he'd been taught, suggesting that only the ritual of the salmon could bring him to life. Yet he did see.

A clever play. Written out moment to moment by the guests themselves as they moved about the polished black linoleum in candlelight. Each one, he thought, achieved a sort of glossy sainthood in a special and individual way. Yes, there were trembling hands and bulging eyes and mighty bosoms and shiny pates. No different than Vidin, really. Yet here, by way of some magical process these people had thought up, the common pranks life played upon the body mattered less. The old ladies had big rings and naughty eyes. The fat men were highly polished and told jokes. The chinless girls laughed and shook their little breasts. The wispy young men with wispy moustaches leaned over cleverly and seemed watchful and intelligent. Thank God, he thought, for Omaraeff. Who had brought him to such spectacles.

He served a plumpish, fair-haired man who seemed lost and friendless and on his way to being very drunk in a very depressing way. Then a tall dowager with heavily rouged cheeks who glared down at him with apparent anger. That he would dare to serve her? Perhaps. These were, for the most part, English people, a tribe that swathed its rituals in mystery and seemed perpetually annoyed at the world, offended, perhaps, at humanity's never-ending attempts to discover what they wanted.

He did not care. He had only salmon to offer, and *sauce diplomat*. The American woman, Winnie Beale, floated through the room, principally nude and entirely without shame. Clothed only in social position. Which, curiously, sufficed. He had served her table at Heininger several nights in a row – during the opera season, late suppers at Heininger were virtually compulsory – and Omaraeff had informed him that he was now to work at private parties in the Beale mansion on the Rue de Varenne.

Informed him on other subjects as well. Told him, for instance, that Winifred Beale had in fact begun life as

215

Ethel Glebb, daughter of a trolley motorman in a smoky Ohio town on a lake. Worked as a telephone operator. Contrived to meet, and ultimately marry, Dicky Beale of Syracuse, the heir to an immense fortune acquired by his grandfather through the manufacture of stove-pipe.

Omaraeff knew everything.

Had thus prepared him for the inevitable grappling match, precisely foreseen and described. The summons to the house. The taxi ride across a rainy Paris afternoon with a tray of *langoustines* on his lap. The maid's direction to 'bring them upstairs.' The small library that overlooked the Rodin gardens. The flowered cotton shift so accidentally open. The sly look, the giggle, the teasing wordplay of a young girl. The balletic sweep into his arms. The rolling around on the Oriental carpet. 'Meet the attack,' Omaraeff had said, 'respond to each sortie, but do not advance. Should she wish the cannon rolled out and fired, let her see to it, but do not permit yourself to be provoked. A single sign of passion on your part, dear Khristo, and you will work here no more.' Those instructions he had followed to the letter. She was, up close, frightfully plain. Her face apparently beaten into neutrality over the years, so oiled, patted, painted, baked, kneaded and creamed that it ultimately had neither expression nor feature. It had become a blank canvas, to be turned into whatever she wished. The act was not consummated. She let him up. Kissed him like a fond aunt. He became again the waiter, smoothed his hair, busied himself for a moment with the arrangement of *langoustines* on the tray, then returned to the restaurant by Métro, pocketing the cab fare.

Some of the guests were dancing. A clickety-clack step to the fast foxtrot produced by the band, four American Negroes who performed most nights at Le Hot Club. The leader, chopping rhythmically at the white piano with thick fingers, was called Toledo Red, his trademark, an unlit stub of cigar, clamped in his teeth as he played. The dancers leaned their upper bodies together, eyes vague, flopping about like unstrung puppets. Khristo watched for a time, seeming to look through them, in fact studying their dance in the smoked-glass mirrors that lined the walls. He noticed that the curtains – black for this occasion, normally violet – had fallen open at one of the tall windows, and he thought he could see snowflakes drifting slowly past the glass. It was the last week in March.

'Hallo there, Nick.'

He snapped to attention. '*Madame*,' he said, bowing slightly.

'A bit of salmon?'

'*Bien sûr, madame.*'

He took up the silver salmon knife. She was so pale and pretty, this one, like a movie star, a fragile flower in the last decline, dying in the final reel. She was often at his table at Heininger and, as the champagne bottles emptied – 'More shampers, Nick!' they would call out – her cheeks blushed red and she became excited and clapped her hands and shrieked with delight at anything anybody said.

'*Merci, madame.*'

'Thanks ever so much.'

Nick.

At the internment camp near Perpignan, where the French had detained him while the socialist government chased its tail in circles over what was to be done about the Spanish war, Khristo had decided to become a Russian. He was alone at the camp; his three fellow fugitives had fled into the night, having decided that safety lay in ignorance of each other's intentions. Renata and Faye Berns had been released almost immediately. Andres had been held for a day, then produced a Greek passport from the lining of his jacket and was freed.

But Khristo was officially without documents – the Russian passport with the nom de guerre Markov was nothing but a danger to him and now lay beneath four inches of earth in a Spanish field – so was designated by French officials a Stateless Person. A Russian, he believed, could more easily lose himself in a city like Paris. A Bulgarian would stand out; the Parisian émigré community from that country was not large. But the plan did not work. The League of Nations official who finally processed him, in the last week of 1936, was a Czech, and Khristo dared not try to fool him. Thus he left the camp under his brother's name, Nikko, and the last name Petrov, common in Bulgaria. The English patrons of the restaurant had shortened Nikko to Nick.

The camp had been a vile place. The internees spent their days shuffling around the barbed-wire perimeter or playing cards – the deck made of torn strips of paper – for cigarettes. They huddled around stoves made of punched-out petrol tins and plotted endlessly in a stew of languages. After more than a month of it, Khristo had thought seriously of escaping. The Senegalese troops who guarded them sometimes did not bring water all day long and the inmates were tortured by thirst, pleading through the wire while the guards stared at them curiously. Sometimes a gate was left open – a clear invitation to escape. If one were caught, however, deportation back to Spain was automatic.

Yet he'd had, in the camp, one great stroke of luck. He'd met a Russian called Vladi Z., a soldier of fortune from an émigré family in Berlin, former harnessmakers to the czar's St. Petersburg household. Vladi Z. had worked for the Comintern, smuggling guns into Spain through the mountains. He'd taken to putting a bit of money aside for himself, but greed overtook his sense of propriety and he'd been caught at it. Snapped up by the Checa in Barcelona, he had managed to escape, bribing his guards with gold secreted 'where the sun never shines'. After some days spent wandering helplessly in the Pyrenees, he had crossed into France at Port-Bou with a group of American journalists. There he claimed German citizenship, but he had shed his passport in fear of the Checa and thus was interned. No matter, he confided to Khristo, his family in Berlin would soon have him out. 'You must go to Paris,' he said, 'even the devil won't find you there.' He had assumed, without being told, that Khristo was on the run. 'In Paris,' he continued, 'one sees Omaraeff. A Bulgarian like yourself. A great man. Headwaiter at the famous Brasserie Heininger. Tell him Vladi Z. sent you and give him my greatest respects. And if, perchance, you are some provocateur chekist piece of filth, then we, *we*, you understand, will have you in the ground by sundown.' On the train north, Khristo's heart had pounded with excitement. Watching the winter countryside roll past, he touched the Nansen passport in his pocket a hundred times and hoped and dreamed more than he'd ever dared. Paris. *Paris*.

* * *

The song ended; the dancers broke apart and applauded themselves. Toledo Red shifted the cigar stub to the other corner of his mouth and banged out the introduction to 'The Sheik of Araby'. There were squeals of anticipation from the dance floor as the saxophone player, a great fat fellow with a gold-toothed grin, draped one of the Beales' monogrammed damask napkins over his head in a make-believe burnoose. Winnie Beale had reappeared, after her dramatic entrance, dressed in emerald *crêpe de chine* and now began dancing her own version of the desert slave girl – Valentino's beloved in a Balenciaga gown.

She gave Khristo an affectionate leer as she swept past him. Strange, he thought, these people of the night who glittered in the world of Heininger and the Beale mansion. Mood-swept, arrogant, insecure, yet at times unbelievably kind. They were the gods and goddesses of this city, from the smoke-filled jazz dens on the Rive Gauche to the chauffeured caravans that moved through the Bois de Boulogne at dawn. Yet they took a curious, backhanded pride in knowing a simple waiter. He had become, of all things, a minor feature of this world. Nick.

Stranger still, he cared for them. He was younger than most, yet they played at being his children. 'Nick, my button has torn loose!' 'Be a good fellow, Nick, and help Madame with her lobster.' And even, 'Oh Nick, I feel so blue.' They had, it seemed to him, bad dreams — bad dreams they did not understand. Premonitions. And they sensed, somehow, that he did understand. That he knew what was coming. And that, when it came, he would remember their affection for him, that he would protect them. They would never admit that *they* were the Jews of Berlin, the aristocracy of Russia, the wealthy Spaniards trapped in Madrid and forced to flee to the Finnish embassy, yet, deep down, they sensed that the world as they'd known it had only a little more time to run.

'Dear boy?'

Again caught in reverie, he was startled, and looked directly at the man standing before him. He was on the short side and quite handsome, with thick, reddish-brown hair swept across a noble forehead. His eyes at first seemed exhausted — dark and shadowed — then Khristo realized that makeup had been used to create the illusion.

Looking down quickly, Khristo reached for the salmon server.

'Not necessary, dear boy, I've had me supper.' He handed over a business card.

'Give us a call, will you sometime? I'm a photographer, in a sort of way. Like to take your portrait.'

Then he was gone.

A fine, dry snow was falling on Paris as he walked home from the party. It dusted the cobblestones pale and sugary and hardened the yellow beams of the streetlamps into severe triangles — like a painted backdrop, he thought, for a street scene in a nightclub act. He watched a boulevard turn silver before his eyes, and some trick of the light made

220

the spires of the churches seem disconnected, floating free in the windless night air. All for his hungry eyes, he thought, all this. He had only to open his heart a little and the city breathed itself into him, sent him climbing in a perfect, pointless, nighttime elation to a height that no sorrow could reach. A pair of policemen, rubber capes black and shining, rode past on their bicycles. A window of the Hôtel St. Cyr squeaked open and a young man in gartered shirtsleeves stared up at the sky. Framed in the oval window of a taxi, idling at a corner of the Rue de Rennes, a man and a woman kissed lightly – lips barely in contact – then moved apart and touched each other's faces with the tips of their fingers. At the all-night café on the Rue des Écoles he saw a group of well-rouged old ladies, bundled into the collars of their Persian lamb coats, gathered at a table near the bar. Each one had a tiny dog on her lap or in the crook of her arm. From the way the women leaned across the table, they seemed like conspirators in a plot. It was, after all, well past three in the morning. What brought them together like this? *The Affair of the Little Dogs*, he thought. The oddest conspiracy of 1937, a year of conspiracies.

But nothing here was what it seemed. Even the grey stone of the buildings hid within itself a score of secret tints, to be revealed only by one momentary strand of light. At first, the tide of secrecy that rippled through the streets had made him tense and watchful, but in time he realized that in a city of clandestine passions, everyone was a spy. *Amours.* Fleeting or eternally renewed, tender or cruel, a single sip or an endless bacchanal, they were the true life and business of a place where money was never enough and power always drained away. And, since the first days of his time there, he had had his own secrets.

It was a long walk. From the Rue de Varenne in the Seventh Arrondissement, the heart of Paris fashion, to the rented room on a street of Jewish tailors and little shops that made eyeglass frames, out past the Place République, not far from the Père Lachaise cemetery. It took him about two hours, usually, though he could make it last somewhat longer than that and sometimes did. He was accompanied, for a time, by Marko, the bartender, and his nephew Anton, who washed the crystal and the china service. All three carried parcels wrapped in brown paper and tied with string – though Khristo's was rather heavier than the others'– the 'extras' of the waiter's profession. The *sous chef* had done the wrapping in the manner of *pâtisserie* clerks, who could fold paper into cones of sufficient strength that an elaborate pastry would survive a child's trip to the store. Nestled inside the packets were slightly crumbled slices of *pâté* of wild duck in a game jelly, white asparagus spears, and thick cuts of tenderloin beef from the Limousin, carved to the English taste. In addition, Marko kept a bottle below the bar to receive the remnants of the brandy service. The Beales had provided their guests with an Armagnac, a select vintage of 1896, and all three took sustenance from it now and again as they walked.

They judged the party quite successful. Not a single fistfight and only two slaps – reportedly of political, not romantic, origin and therefore hardly worth discussion. The tulip-shaped elevator remained cranky, but no horrified shouts from between-floor guests had had to be attended to. Nobody jumped out a window, or set fire to the curtains, or tried to drink champagne by pouring it over female undergarments and squeezing them out like Spanish wine sacks. It was the Americans who drank from shoes, under the curious impression that romantic Europeans did such things. The chef, according to Anton, who worked in the kitchen, had been at his very best. Whistling and winking, he had performed with casual speed, directing his staff like a lion tamer in good humour. And hardly a curse all night long. This unusual sweetness of temper was attributed by the Beale staff to his near ceaseless screwing of one of Madame's maids, a recent development. But which one? The shy little redhead from Quimper? Or the fulsome

222

Italian, Tomasina, with haunches that could hurl a man into the air? Speaking of which, what of the naked Beale woman? Would the society columns consider it thrilling or déclassé? 'I served her champagne,' Marko said, in his sturdy Slavic French, 'and her left tit looks toward Prague.'

Together, they walked nearly the length of the Boulevard St.-Germain, then Marko and Anton headed for their rooms by the Gare Austerlitz, the railroad terminal, while Khristo used the Pont de Sully to cross the river. Tomorrow night, he thought, he would take the Pont Marie. Well-learned instincts forbade the use of the same route night after night. One varied daily habits at every opportunity, one made prediction of time and place as difficult as possible, one did not, after all, shed Arbat Street quite so easily. His journey took him through the Marais, the Jewish quarter, a good place to quicken the footsteps. As the situation for Jews in Europe grew darker, the streets of the Marais seemed to him more and more like a maze, a trap. At the northern border of the district he paused to warm up by the exhaust vents of a baker – who had fired his pine bough ovens an hour earlier – then headed for home.

A battered little Simca crawled up the Rue du Chemin Vert behind him, rather too slowly for his taste, and he stepped into a doorway and let it go past – eventually viewing the absurdly besotted driver with some amusement. But one had to be alert. *Do not forget everything*, was the way he put it to himself. And he had not. He read the Russian émigré papers, like thousands of others, with a hopeful heart. To the east, the NKVD – in fact the entire Soviet *apparat* – was stinging itself to death like a tormented scorpion as Yezhov, the redheaded dwarf, rolled down purge upon purge. Good! Let them rip each other to pieces, he thought. Let them sink into the swamp of bureaucratic confusion until not a single file remained in place. The simple defection of a junior intelligence officer would drift endlessly down their lists to the bottom of a clerical sea.

Or so he hoped – though in fact he knew them much better than that. He had changed the parting of his hair, grown a thick moustache (all the Brasserie waiters in Paris had to be well furred in some fashion; it emphasized the sense of midnight devilry the proprietors wished to encourage), and, with remorse, destroyed the clothing he'd worn in Spain. Now he had an old sheepskin jacket, bought at a *marché aux puces* on the outskirts of the city. Beyond that, there was fatalism. Refugees from Eastern Europe and Germany now came to Paris in a steady stream, he was but one among them. He worked hard at being *Nick the waiter*, hid his money behind a loose light fixture in the hallway outside his room, and kept all acquaintance – with the exception of the Omaraeff connection – emphatically casual. He didn't need much. He had his work, he had the city, and he had a great deal more than that.

In the room, he undressed slowly, then made sure the shutters were firmly closed. The window faced east and the pale light of the winter sunrise would leak in through the slats, creating a shadow light that seemed to him peaceful and timeless.

She was, as usual, pretending to sleep. But, if her eyes were closed, how did she sense the moment he was ready to enter the bed? Because it was, always, this very moment she chose to stretch and twist in such a way that she shaped her body for him in the softened outline of the blanket.

'Aleksandra?' He spoke softly, standing by the bed.

'I am sleeping,' she said, unbothered by this, or any other, contradictory statement.

He slid carefully between the sheets next to her. A moment later, just as sleep began to take him, her hand came visiting.

'You are moving in your sleep,' he whispered.

'I am having a dream.'

'Oh.'

'A terrible dream.'

'What of?'

'That certain things, indescribable things, are to happen to me, just at dawn, it is far too wicked even to describe ... my heart beats ...'

'Very well. You must go back to sleep.'

'Yes. You are right.'

'Aleksandra?'

'What?'

'It *is* dawn.'

'Oh no! Say it isn't!'

Who was she?

He was not entirely sure. Her passport gave her family name as *Varin*, probably French, possibly Russian, and she claimed it was not the true family name anyhow. What he did know was that she wanted to be a mystery to him, wished him to see her as a creature of the Paris night, a manifestation, without the claustrophobic bonds of family or nationality. It was self-conscious artifice, transparently so, but she refused to leave its shelter.

'Who are you, truly?' he'd asked more than once.

'Ah,' she'd say, *triste* as a nightclub singer, 'if only one knew that sort of thing.'

She spelled her name in the Slavic form, implied exotic connections – emigrant communities in distant corners of Europe, Trieste perhaps – and claimed that her spirit, her psyche, was Russian. In support of such claims, she owned a few rich Russian curses that were occasionally hurled his way. She was small, waiflike, unsmiling, with a thick shag of muted blonde hair that whipped her forehead when she shook her head and cool, deep, enormous eyes like a night animal. Her colouring he found strange – dark beneath pale – as though a shadow lived inside her. She had a hot temper, would go to war on the slightest provocation.

But there was also in her a peasant sharpness that he found very familiar, an echo of his part of the world. She could leave the room with a few sous and return with the most extraordinary amount of stuff. She spoke a tough Parisian street French – calling him '*mec*', pal, when it suited her, in a hoarse, low voice – and bits and pieces of English she learned at the *cinéma*. Would surprise him with lines memorized from American movies in which men with pencil-thin moustaches duelled over business deals and won the heiress. 'Now see here, Trumbull,' she would say, black beret pulled down over her mop head.

She had been born in the countryside, she said, somewhere in the South of France, but of a family, she claimed, from *elsewhere*. Arrived in Paris at sixteen, alone, without money, and survived. Her father, according to the time of day, had been a gangster, a poet, or a nobleman. She had never met him, she said, and had few memories of her mother – carried off by the influenza epidemic of 1919. She had been raised by an aunt, or rather, a woman who called herself *aunt*, or, perhaps, a woman who had known her aunt. None of her stories was ever told the same way twice and he finally gave it up – acknowledged inconsistency the only effective defence against a trained interrogator – and consigned her to the present moment, which was where she wanted to be in the first place.

He had met her in a bookstore where she worked, lost in a billowing blue smock. She had fierce little hands, and he could not take his eyes off them as they whisked piles of books into order. She challenged him – *What are you looking at?* – he met the challenge. She demanded coffee. They went to a café. He waited for her after work. Eventually, they returned to his room. The following day, she appeared at his door with a cardboard suitcase. 'I have brought a few things,' she'd said.

She had, in her own way, taught him to be her lover. Using for instruction a great range of pouts and swoons and sly looks, attacks and retreats, an entire ragbag of

226

stratagems. She teased him until he growled, then ran away. But not too far. Led him, subtly, to such special silky places as made her sing and showed him how, by example, to play lovers' games.

She seduced him. Sometimes this way, sometimes that. With rainy-day melancholy or by getting absurdly drunk on two glasses of wine. 'Did we do something vile? I swear I don't remember.' She was clever at being 'naughty' and making him 'mad'. Sometimes, pretending to immense modesty, she let him have a peek at something he wasn't supposed to see – quite by accident, of course, a stolen glimpse. She played at being his captive, squeaking for mercy. Or at being his captor, in the voice of a disciplinarian schoolteacher. At times, she was partial to costumes. Not intentional ones, it just happened that he would discover her in garter belt and silk stockings while she was *looking for her earrings*. Other times, he would get in bed to find her in the chaste cotton shift of a schoolgirl, on which occasion she chose to address him as *uncle*. She taught him this and she taught him that until at last it dawned on him that the only way a man ever becomes a lover is at the hands of a woman.

Of her former lovers, whoever they might have been, he had no time to be jealous. The world seemed intent on rushing off its cliff, so, like everyone else, he lived for the moment and hung on tight. The lipstick grew crimson, hairdos were twisted about in bizarre shapes, and in some dresses a woman simply could not sit down. Affairs begun on Friday were over by Wednesday. And every woman in the world seemed to want him, sensing, he guessed, what went on in the little room. At Heininger, the screechy English girls pressed apartment keys into his hand, absolutely bent on having it off with the working class, and an evil-looking Slav at that. He smiled wistfully and returned the keys, regret for the lost opportunity showing clearly in his expression, hoping that such chivalry would spare him their anger.

If he was tempted at all, it was the French women who caught his attention, especially the ones a few years older than he. It was the single glance on the street that undid him, gone in the very last instant before it actually meant anything. His eyes would roam hungrily after them as they trailed their wondrous perfume away down the avenue, leaving him to sniff great nosefuls of Parisian air. What *was* that?

But Aleksandra, who smelled like soap, or lemons, or someone who had just been in the hot sun, was more than enough for him, so he prayed at one church only and, soon enough, woke to discover that love had got him.

* * *

In Vidin, the March wind blew in hard off the river, rippling the surface of the water and flattening the reeds that grew by the wooden dock. A few snow patches remained on the dirt street that ran past the waterfront shacks of the fishermen, and the two old people in dark clothing, a man and a woman, moved carefully around them, bodies bent against the wind. The woman wore a black shawl over her head and the man held his cap on with his hand. It was Sunday, and they were going home from mass. At the path that led through the garden to the house, they stopped. The woman pointed to a small skiff tied to a post among the reeds and said something to her husband. He shook his head, then shrugged. He did not know, he did not care. When they went into the house, there was a stranger sitting at the plank table near the stove. He wore the wool cap and clothing of a river fisherman. He stood up politely as they entered. 'Please forgive me,' he said in Russian, 'for coming into your house without invitation.'

The woman recognized him then – he was the man who had taken Khristo away from Vidin – and her hands flew to the knot of her shawl. The old man stared at the stranger.

'Who are you?' he said.

'He is the Russian,' his wife said. She let go of the knot, but her mouth was tight with anxiety.

The old man continued to stare. Finally, as though he remembered, he said, 'Oh yes.'

The woman opened the door of the stove, inserted a few sticks of oak branch and prodded the fire to life with an iron poker. She poured well water from a bucket into a kettle on the stove and spooned black tea into a battered copper samovar. Almost immediately, the room grew warm and smelled sharp and sweet from the wood smoke.

The Russian spoke gently to the old man. 'Won't you sit down?'

The man sat, took off his cap and placed it carefully on his knee, as though he were visiting the house, and waited for the other man to speak. From the wind, there were tears standing in the corners of his eyes.

The Russian walked to the window, stood to one side, and looked out. 'I came inside,' he explained, 'so as not to be seen by your neighbours. We know how things are going down here – I don't want to cause you trouble.'

The woman waited by the stove for the water to boil. 'You will have tea,' she said.

'Yes. Thank you,' the Russian said, and sat down. 'I've brought you a letter. From your son.'

'From Nikko?' the old man said.

The woman shifted the kettle noisily on the stove.

'No,' the Russian said. 'From Khristo.'

The old man nodded.

'Shall I read it to you?' the Russian asked.

'Yes, please,' the woman said, her back to the room.

He reached inside his wool jacket and took out a square of paper, unfolded it carefully and smoothed it on the table. 'There is no date, of course,' he said, 'but I am permitted to tell you that it was written last week.'

'I see,' the old man said. His eyes narrowed and he nodded wisely, as though he well understood such complicated matters.

229

' "Dear Papa," it begins, "I greet you. I write in hope that you and Mama and Helena are in good health and that the fishing is good this year. I am well, though I work very hard, and there is a lot to learn. I am successful at my school, and my superiors are pleased with my progress. All here join me in hoping that the day may soon come when I can return to see you. Please kiss Mama for me. Your son, Khristo." '

The old woman walked over from the stove and the Russian handed her the letter. She could not read, but she held it up to the light, then touched the writing. 'Thank you,' she said to the Russian.

'Look.' She showed the old man the letter. 'It is from Khristo.'

He stared at the paper for a time, then said, 'That's good.'

'He's doing very well indeed,' the Russian said, taking the letter back. 'Better than most of the others.'

'And he is in Russia?' the woman asked.

The Russian smiled, apologetic. 'I cannot tell you where he is. About that I am sorry, very sorry, because he would be proud for you to know it.'

'Oh,' she said, disappointed.

They were silent for a time, then the Russian relented. 'He is in the place where he has always most wanted to go. But you must not tell anybody that.'

The woman returned to the stove, the water was just beginning to boil. 'We do not speak of him,' she said.

'But you can surely guess,' the Russian said.

She thought for a moment. 'He is in Vienna? Khristo?'

'Perhaps,' the Russian said.

'Or Paris?'

The Russian spread his hands in helplessness, he was not allowed to tell.

'How he dreamed of such places,' she said, shaking her head. She poured a thin stream of steaming water into the samovar. 'We have never been to Sofia, even,' she added.

She left the tea to steep and went to her husband and squeezed his arm. 'Nicolai,' she said, 'did you hear that? He is in a great city. Vienna, or Paris, or somewhere.'

The old man nodded. 'That's good,' he said.

*   *   *

He woke at noon, lit a Gitane from the packet on the night table, then lay back on the pillow and watched the blue smoke curl up to the ceiling. There was a neatly spun web in one corner of the ceiling, a small spider fussing at its centre strands. Max, Aleksandra called him. Their house pet. Cigarette smoke seemed to affect Max, provoking him into a spasm of housekeeping. On the top of the dresser, the food from the party was laid out like a miniature buffet – though Aleksandra had pretty much done for the asparagus. The other item he'd brought home was lying, tossed casually aside, in a nest of string and brown paper.

Aleksandra had gone off to work, at the bookstore near the Café Flor on the square in front of the church of St.-Germain-des-Prés. It was a communist-surrealist-anarchist-dadaist bookstore, a true Rive Gauche jungle of wild beards, curved pipes, black sweaters and sloe-eyed girls who stared. A serious place, at the geographical centre of the city's artistic and political whirlpool, decorated with clenched-fist posters of all sorts. According to Aleksandra, all the local celebrities – Picasso, Modigliani, Jean Cocteau, André Breton – were seen there, as well as at their customary tables at the Café Flor.

Cigarette in hand, he rose naked from the rumpled sheets, padded across the cold floor, and opened the shutters. Above the rooftops, the sky was sharply blue, with white scud racing in from the Brittany coast. There was a pale girl who lived in a room across the street, Khristo had once waved to her as she shook a dust mop out the window, and she had waved back. Her shutter was closed this morning. By opening the window and leaning well out, he could see down into the street. Women with long breads in string bags. School kids in their uniforms coming home for lunch. One of the Jewish tailors, in yarmulke, black vest and rolled-up shirtsleeves, put his cat out the door of his shop. The air smelled like dust and garbage and garlic and March weather. Not a sign of last night's snow.

He put on pants and shirt and went down the hall and used the toilet, then returned to the room, adjusted the shutters so that he could still see a slice of sky but no one could look in, and took the pistol from its brown paper nest. He lit another cigarette and propped it on a Suze ashtray and went to work. Broke out the magazine and examined it in the light. It was a 9mm automatic of Polish manufacture, designated wz/35 for the year of its design, called the Radom after the works where it was made. Large and heavy, it had an excellent reputation for dependability. He played with it for a time, discovering that what seemed to be the safety was in fact a slide lock that facilitated field-stripping the weapon. He took it apart, checked for burrs in the metal, found everything smooth and oiled. The wooden grip was scratched and nicked – the pistol had obviously been well used.

He had purchased the pistol at Omaraeff's request – one couldn't say no to one's friend *and* boss – and it had been easy enough to find. He'd gone to the Turkish quarter, well out the Boulevard Raspail at the farthest reaches of the city. Found the right café on the second try. Struck up a conversation with a man named Yasin (or so he said) who, for six hundred francs, had returned with the Radom after only a twenty-minute absence. Khristo now rewrapped the package, glanced at the clock on the table, finished dressing, and headed for the Métro.

Omaraeff had told him they would be having lunch at a place called Bistro Jambol – a pleasant coincidence since Jambol was the name of a town in Bulgaria. But, when Khristo opened the steam-fogged door of the restaurant, he realized with horror that it was no coincidence at all. The smell of the *agneshki drebuliiki* – lamb innards grilled with garlic – came rushing up at him, along with the realization that he was standing in a roomful of expatriate Bulgarians while holding in his hand a Polish pistol wrapped in brown paper. He broke into a sweat. Of all the stupid places to go! Half the Paris NKVD would be hanging around. He took a small step backward, then a hand closed around his elbow. He looked behind him to discover a tiny waiter with slicked-back hair and a milky eye. 'Omaraeff?' the man said. Khristo nodded dumbly. The man had a grip like a pair of pincers – he felt halfway to the Lubianka then and there. 'Upstairs,' the man said in Bulgarian, nodding toward a rickety staircase on the far wall.

At the top, tables were packed together on a balcony. 'Nikko!' Omaraeff was beckoning violently. 'Over here.' He moved sideways through a sea of people – eyes rising to meet his own – talking, gesturing, observing his progress, all without missing a bite.

'*Zdrasti!*' Omaraeff greeted him as he sat down. 'May you live a hundred years – don't eat the lamb.'

Khristo stared at the hand-scratched Cyrillic on the ragged piece of paper that served as menu. A waiter filled the cloudy glass at his side with yellow wine that smelled like resin. 'What, then?'

'Try the *shkembe*.'

Beef kidney cooked in milk. He ordered it, and the sweating waiter flew away. The room was dense with clouds of strong smoke from the black tobacco.

Omaraeff smiled. 'Just like home, eh, Nikko?'

'Yes,' Khristo said. 'Just like home.'

Omaraeff described himself, with a smile, as a *circus Bulgarian*. His enormous head was shaved smooth, and he wore a grand Turkish moustache, waxed to a fine point on either end. He looked like a strong man in a circus, an appearance that gave him great cachet as the headwaiter at Heininger. To this, for luncheon, he had added a pale grey linen suit and waistcoat, set off by a lavender silk tie fixed in place by a stickpin of ruby-coloured glass, the entire

233

ensemble overlaid by a cloud of cologne that smelled like cloves. He took a long sip of the resinous wine and closed his eyes with pleasure. Suddenly, a dramatic melancholy fell upon him. 'Ah Nikko, how sadly we wander this world.' He raised his glass before Khristo's eyes, a symbol of good times gone away.

'That's so,' Khristo said, not wanting to be impolite. But he could see Omaraeff, in his mind's eye, taking supper in the Heininger kitchen before the late evening crowds arrived. A slice of white Normandy veal washed down with a little Chambertin. Surely he made the most of his exile.

'Mark my words, boy, our time is coming soon enough.'

The *shkembe* arrived, a vast plateful of it, reeking of rose pepper and sour milk and the singular aroma of kidney. Khristo poked it about with his fork and ate a boiled potato. 'I've brought you a Radom,' he said, gesturing with a glance toward the brown parcel by a dish of raw onions.

'Good. It will speak for us. Speak to the world.'

'Oh?'

'Mm,' Omaraeff said, his mouth full of stew. He swallowed vigorously. 'The *Bolsheviiki* press us too hard, eh?' He wiped his mouth with a large napkin and lifted his glass. 'Czar Boris!'

'Czar Boris,' Khristo repeated. The wine was thick and bitter.

Loud voices flared suddenly to life. He looked over the railing of the balcony and saw two old men with white beards who had risen abruptly from their table, upsetting a plate of yellow soup, which splattered on the floor. 'A prick on your grave!' one of the men shouted. 'And on yours!' the other answered, grabbing him by the throat. Diners on all sides cheered as they choked one another. Waiters came rushing in to separate them, the table went over with a crash, several people wrestled in a heap amid the spilled food on the floor.

Omaraeff shook his head with admiration. 'Look at that old fart Gheorghiev, will you? All for honour. *Hit him,*

Todor,' he called over the balcony. *'Break the bastard's head!'* He turned back to Khristo and punched a thick index finger into the brown package. 'It's come to this now. You'll see.' His fingernails were perfectly trimmed and had the opalescent shine produced by a suede buffer.

'Perhaps you ought not to tell me too much, Djadja Omaraeff. Some things are best done in secrecy.' Everyone called Omaraeff *Uncle.*

'Not tell you? Not tell Nikko? Hell boy, you are the one who's going to do it!'

'I am?'

'You'll see.' He raised his glass. 'Adolf Hitler.'

'Adolf Hitler,' Khristo repeated.

They waited at a corner of the Boulevard St.-Michel, the *flics* would not let them cross the street. Close ranks of marching men and women swept past them, chanting and singing.

Omaraeff wore a topcoat that matched his suit, and the stiff wind toyed with the flaps as he stood at the edge of the pavement, eyes smouldering, hands jammed in pockets as though he feared they might reach out and smack a few heads. Khristo was bundled in his battered sheepskin jacket, and they looked for all the world like a well-to-do uncle and a wayward nephew, the latter having just recently been treated to a morally instructive lunch.

'And which are these?' Omaraeff asked. His voice floated on a sea of contempt.

'Medical students, I believe. The stethoscopes . . .'

'Ah-hah. *Doctors.*' The word spoke volumes.

A young man with an artist's flowing hair turned to them and raised his fist. 'Red front!' he called out proudly. A thin fellow by his side added, 'Join us!' His friend completed the thought: 'Bring peace and mercy to all mankind!'

Khristo imagined them in a room with Yaschyeritsa and smiled sadly at the thought.

'Come on,' the young man urged, observing the smile.

A group of women in uniform – white hats and grey

235

capes – marched below a banner stretched across the street: NURSE WORKERS FOR SOCIAL JUSTICE.

Omaraeff growled deep in his throat. 'Go look up Comrade Stalin's rear end and see if you find justice,' he said – Khristo laughed despite himself – 'and powder his balls while you're at it.'

The nurses wore their hair severely cut, and their faces were plain and pale without makeup. He found them very beautiful. 'Comrades,' one of them called out, 'have courage.' *So God speaks to me*, Khristo thought. He would need courage to contend with Omaraeff. You might know a man fairly well, he realized, then suddenly he revealed his politics and turned into a werewolf before your very eyes. Could not one be just a waiter?

The nurses were followed by the municipal clerks, angry, shabby men and women with grim faces. One imagined piles of tracts in their houses, learned by rote, and shotguns in closets. *The day is coming*, their eyes said. They would, Khristo knew, rule the world under Bolshevism – formerly despised, at last triumphant, paying back a list of slights that reached to heaven.

'Who have we now?' Omaraeff asked.

'The clerks of the city.'

'They look dangerous.'

'They are.'

Omaraeff was tight-lipped. 'You see what we face. When the marching begins, the next thing is throwing bombs. Well, we'll put a stop to that. Trust Djadja. For a long time I averted my eyes. This is not my country, I reasoned, let them go to hell in their own way, what do I care?'

'What has changed?'

'Everything has changed. Now there are strikes, here, in England, even America. And posters, and parades. And those NKVD devils are everywhere, *stirring the pot*. You know who I'm talking about?'

'Yes.'

'Well then, you must share my view.'

236

'Of course,' he said. Unconsciously, he shifted the packaged Radom to his other hand.

'One might use it right now,' Omaraeff said. 'And to good effect.'

'Well . . .'

'But I have bigger things in mind.'

There was a stir across the boulevard. A man in the crowd had shouted something that reached the marchers' ears, and one of them strode menacingly toward his tormentor. A policeman stepped out into the street and swung his cape – weighted with lead balls in the bottom hem. The marcher danced away and made an obscene gesture with an adamant thrust of both arms. The marchers, a battalion of streetsweepers, some of whom carried their brooms like rifles, roared their approval.

They were followed by the salesgirls of the *grands magasins* in their grey smocks. In their midst marched Winnie and Dicky Beale, arm in arm, faces set in pained but hopeful expressions, perfectly in keeping with the emotional atmosphere of the march. They were, Khristo noted, smartly dressed for the occasion. Winnie Beale had on a worker's peaked cap, properly tilted over one eye, and the squarish, broad-shouldered suit offered by Schiaparelli that was popular for communist events. Elsa Schiaparelli had journeyed to Moscow in 1935 to observe the workers' styles that would, it was felt, now take precedence in the fashion world. Dicky, careful always not to upstage his furiously *engagé* wife, had merely replaced shirt and tie with a turtleneck sweater beneath his London suit.

Omaraeff shook his head in patient sorrow. 'Lambs,' he said.

A half hour later, they stood across the street from an elegant six-storey building on the Place de l'Opéra, amid commercial luxury of every sort – marble banks, furriers, jewellers, and *sociétés anonymes*. Money and discretion mingled in the afternoon air. The restaurant interiors were subdued and richly decorated, and the shop windows showed the latest colours, Wallis Simpson Blue and Coronation Purple. The people in the street were perfectly barbered and smartly dressed, their complexions slightly pink after long, elaborate lunches.

Omaraeff gestured toward the building with his head. 'There it is,' he said. 'Murderer's gold.'

'That building?'

'Yes. The top floor is owned by a firm called Floriot et cie. It is a gold repository, for those whose faith in banks did not survive 1929 – the Credit Anstalt failure and all of that. In such times it can be very comforting to have some gold locked up in a private vault.'

'I see.'

'What you do not see is that the NKVD sells its gold there.'

Khristo's response was brusque. He was, for a moment, an intelligence officer once again, and asked the intelligence officer's eternal question: 'How do you know?'

'Friends, Nikko. Friendship is our gold. The newspaper kiosk on the corner is owned by an old man called Leonid, who was a banker in St. Petersburg until 1917. Now he stands in his stall for sixteen hours a day, selling newspapers. And he is forced to watch Russians, coming and going at all hours, with black satchels. It is not so farfetched to say that it is his gold, formerly, that passes before his eyes. A cruel irony, but what can he do? He can come to Djadja Omaraeff, that's what he can do. And he has done it.'

'And what do you propose?'

'I propose to take it from them.'

'And the pistol?'

'Just in case. One may meet unfriendly persons anywhere, even in the Opéra.'

'Who is to plan it?'

'That's you, Nikko my boy.'

Khristo shook his head. He felt like a man sliding helplessly down a sheer slope toward the cliff that would kill him. 'How would I know such things, Djadja? I am only a waiter.'

'Not a bad one, either, I've seen to that. What else does one know? Well, you are Bulgarian – but you are not in Bulgaria. Perhaps you do not like the situation there, the way the political wind blows. Yet you do not sit in the lap of the reds, either. You were in Spain, Vladi Z. has told me that, and I doubt you fought for the Falange. You are quiet, in great possession of yourself, everybody's acquaintance, nobody's friend. Marko the bartender tells me you take a different bridge across the Seine every night. And, at last, I ask you to get me a pistol – a test of friendship – and you do get it. And not at a pawn shop, either, I'll wager. What is one to think?'

Khristo was silent.

'Just so,' Omaraeff said, and patted him affectionately on the shoulder.

A cab dropped them off in front of a tiny nightclub called Jardin des Colombes – the Garden of Doves – in a cellar near Montparnasse. One panel of the mirrored wall opened onto a long corridor, full of turnings, that led to a small steam room. They were the only patrons. An old woman took their clothes and gave them towels, turned the steam vent up and shuffled away. They had reached the nightclub in the last hour of the afternoon, as twilight gathered in the side streets, already late for work at the Brasserie.

Omaraeff wiped the sweat from his shaven head and waved concern aside. 'You are with me,' he said grandly, 'so you need not worry. Marko will get everything under way, and Papa Heininger never shows his face until ten. Relax, my boy, relax. You'll work plenty in this life. Breathe deeply, take the steam inside yourself, let it cleanse this dirty city from your heart. Ach, Nikko, I was meant to live a country life – a little farm, a little wife, someplace in the mountains, where the birds sing at night.'

'Birds don't sing at night, Djadja.'

239

'On my place they would.'

'Will you permit me to advise you on this matter?'

'No! Nikko, no, please. Don't spoil this lovely steam.'

Khristo sighed and lay back on the bench until his head rested comfortably against the wall – the wood was spongy and soft from years of steam. Every man has a destiny, he thought, and this must be mine. Everyone in Vidin believed that life worked in that way. A man might kick and thrash and struggle all he liked – it counted for nothing. The old Turkish saying had it right: so it is written, so it shall be. Even now his mind toyed and played with the building on the Opéra. The elevator. The hallways. Time of day. A crush of people. Where a car would go. How many couriers could be taken. If he read Omaraeff properly, the crime was a gesture of politics. Very well, a small act would suffice. Just pray God there was not a river of greed running silently beneath the enterprise. That would make it dangerous. The Russians would not trust their couriers, of course. Their consignments would be small. There would be watchers. They bled the gold wherever in the world they could get their needle in, and there was no point in turning it into roubles. Dollars, pounds sterling, Swiss francs – that's what they would want. With that, one might actually buy something. There was so much timing to do. Did they wait at the embassy to send the next courier until the last returned? Or was it a telephone signal? Oh why did not some great devil come to the surface of the world and suck them back to hell? Aleksandra! We must fly.

'A little refreshment? Something to drink, perhaps?'

He opened his eyes. 'No, thank you.'

'You think too much, Nikko. You'll wear out your brains if you're not careful.' Omaraeff stood, adjusted the towel at his waist, walked to the opposite wall and knocked twice, then returned to the bench. 'I have arranged a small entertainment,' he said, a slight edge to his voice. 'Just something among friends – men of the world. You understand?'

240

Oh God, whores, he thought. Omaraeff went too far —
what he didn't need in his life right now was a dose of the
ferocious Parisian clap. 'I understand perfectly,' he said in
what he hoped was a soothing voice. Let Omaraeff disport
himself as he would – he had agreed to enough stupidity for
one day, job or no job. One could always unload trucks at
the market. The door opened and two naked boys appeared,
perhaps fourteen, dark, sullen-faced, possibly Arab.

'Ahh,' Omaraeff said lightly, 'golden youth.'

One of the boys walked toward Khristo and sat on his
knee. 'Get off,' he said. The boy did not move for a moment,
then stood obediently.

'Dear Nikko, I fear I have insulted you.'

'Of course not. Every man to his pleasure.'

'Yes, yes,' Omaraeff said. He took the other boy by
the waist and turned him back and front, like an artist
contemplating a sculpture. 'Perhaps next time, little one,'
he said, dismissing him with a wave.

'We must be paid,' the boy said coldly in guttural
French.

'You will be paid,' Omaraeff said. His voice sounded, for
a moment, faded, used up. The boys left the room. Omaraeff
lay back against the wall and closed his eyes. 'So you see,
Nikko my boy. Gold is everything.'

The Brasserie Heininger was quite mad that night, Khristo
virtually ran from the moment he put on the waiter's
uniform until the first light of dawn. It was a sumptuous
place. One ascended a white marble staircase to find red
plush banquettes, polished mirrors trimmed in thick gold
leaf, and burnished copper lamps turned down to a soft
glow. The brasseries had been started by competing beer
breweries at the turn of the century and they retained a
Victorian flavour, each one designed to be that ever so
slightly vulgar place where one could behave in an ever
so slightly vulgar way. A place where a glass of champagne
might find its way down a daring cleavage. The waiters

241

were blind to it, their expressions unchanging grins. 'Be merry!' Papa Heininger insisted. They were always on the move, carrying silver platters of crayfish, grilled sausage, salmon in aspic. It was all far too overdone to be anything but deliciously cheap. A place to let your hair down.

That night they had singing Germans, a table of fourteen, heavy red faces bawling out duelling songs as shoulders were thumped and backs thwacked with huge glee. They had an attempted suicide in the Ladies' Room. A Portuguese countess slashed her shoulder with some scissors, then howled for assistance before her dress was ruined. This was followed by a brief but excellent fistfight between two wine brokers from Bordeaux. Two American heiresses indulged themselves in a hair-pulling contest – something to do with a husband, one gathered from the accompanying shrieks. His Most Royal Highness the Prince of Bahadur descended the long staircase on his backside, a series of breathtaking bumps that ended with His Highness roaring with laughter – thank God – on the floor of the lobby.

A night of madness, Khristo thought.

Spring was coming, war was coming, perhaps nothing mattered very much. At dawn, in the room, Aleksandra sat pensively by the closed shutters, grey light spilling over her small breasts, the smoke from her cigarette rising lazily in the still air.

Very quietly, he probed to see if he might get another job. There was no question of staying at Heininger if he denied Omaraeff assistance – the *padrone* system demanded favours in return for favours, that was just the way life was. But the search proved useless. Paris was a village, in some ways no bigger than Vidin. Everybody knew everybody, through some connection or other, so if it happened that you were not known, you did not exist. The peculiar French mentality, a system of locks and gates and weirs so joyously flowing in the matter of sexual undertakings was, in the area of jobs and money – as the proprietor of a small bistro on the Rue de Rennes put it – *plus serré qu'un cul de guenon*. Tighter than a monkey's backside. Who were you? they wanted to know. They hired, it seemed, only cousins. First cousins. Before word of his research could reach Omaraeff, he gave it up.

And went to work.

Not committed to it, not really. Expecting along the way the usual impossibilities that snagged the vast percentage of all proposed clandestine actions. Ozunov, at Arbat Street, had cautioned: 'Nine times out of ten the answer will be no. And of course you'll not be given any such thing as a reason.'

But so artfully fickle was the life of 1937, it seemed to Khristo, that the great snag absolutely refused to reveal itself. The operational people turned up by Omaraeff were not at all the corps of baboons he'd feared. In fact, they did quite well. Pazar, the cab-driver, perhaps an Armenian or a Turk; Justine, the stunning French wife of a Russian *chocolatier*; Ivan Donchev, a quaint old gentleman born in Sofia who had lived forty years in Paris, a retired bookkeeper who wore a rosebud in his lapel every day of his life.

He ran them under a cover that was marginal at best, but you couldn't just tell people what was going on. It would give them, if nothing else, a story for the *flics* if everything went entirely to hell. He presented himself as a confidential agent in the employ of a man who ran a courier service. The couriers had taken to dawdling, visiting their mistresses or gambling or drinking or *something*. One had to know. Therefore these couriers would be closely observed on their routes. The story fooled nobody, of course, but it was there if they wanted it.

In his heart he had to admit that he was happy in the work. He was slightly horrified to find it so, but there was no denying what he felt. The incessant grovelling of his job as a waiter had begun to grate on him, and he could foresee a time when he would come to hate it.

Aleksandra noted the change immediately – her barometer was perilously accurate. 'You seem awfully pleased these days,' she remarked, head canted at an inquisitive angle. 'Perhaps you have another lover? Surely her bottom is cuter than mine.' Such impossibilities were duly and demonstratively denied, but she'd sensed that something was going on. 'I am thinking of starting a business,' he told her. Oh? Did he think that rubbing shoulders with café society made him one of them? No, no, nothing like that. He wished to better himself. 'Ah,' she said. She believed she had some facility in the making of fashionable *chapeaux*, perhaps a small store, in a reasonably good neighbourhood, where she could set up as a milliner. Her chum Liliane had done that very thing, her *friend* had arranged it. The bookstore was boring. The beards breathed Marxist endearments in her face. It was dusty among the shelves. She sneezed. Her wage was a humiliation. A business would get them out of this room into something more suitable. She would learn to cook. She would have a fat *bébé*. In no time at all, they would be the most *grands* of *bourgeoises*.

At which point she laughed wildly and grabbed the tip of his nose so hard in her savage little fist that his eyes wept and he knocked her hand away. 'What are you doing, *petit chou?*' she asked, hard as nails and smart as a whip. 'Money,' he said, 'it concerns money.' She lit a cigarette and turned away. 'Well, then,' she said. But he knew she meant to find out the truth of it.

There were four couriers moving from the Soviet embassy to the Floriot gold repository. They had no schedule, though charts were endlessly drawn up that clocked them and their visits. The operation seemed to him a hurried one. That made sense. What with Stalin and Yezhov attacking the Kulaks, the ongoing purges turning up treasure troves in walls and chimneys, and the infusion of Spanish bullion, there was a great deal of gold that needed converting.

The observers were extremely faithful. Pazar sat by the hour in his cab, even when customers in the rain beat on his doors with umbrella handles and called him every sort of scoundrel. Justine shopped herself to exhaustion, wearing out two pairs of shoes but never once complaining. Old Ivan bought coffees for his cronies in a café across the street until he had to submit a plea for funds – and what oceans of *l'express* did to his digestive system a gentleman would not care to describe. They called the couriers A, B, C and D.

B was a sad-looking fellow, with heavy jowls and downcast eyes, nicknamed Boris by the observers. He seemed to all of them so terribly unhappy, as though someone he'd loved had died. He stared at the ground as he carried his satchel through the streets, apparently caught up in a dialogue that went on in his mind. Sometimes his lips actually moved. To test his personality, Khristo ran a prostitute at him one afternoon on the Rue de la Paix, as he returned from making a drop at Floriot. But Boris merely snarled under his breath and avoided her with a wide swerve.

Apparently, the job would have to be done right on the street. The couriers were chained to their satchels, but a small channel-lock bolt cutter could sever the chain quickly enough.

Otherwise, things went more or less well. There were the normal irritations, of course, especially the grave communications problem they experienced. Khristo determined, at that point, that one simply could not be any sort of spy in France because it was impossible to use the telephones. But, all in all, there was nothing very troubling – unless you counted the ham sandwiches. They all had to eat while on the job, and soon discovered that the grand establishments of l'Opéra itself would quickly deplete the operations fund provided by Omaraeff. But Pazar found a family café hidden away in a side street where a reasonable ham sandwich could be obtained – eaten on the premises or carried away. Khristo had lunch there, in the second week of April, and the proprietress made an offhand remark that rang a bell.

'Suddenly all the world eats ham sandwiches – one can hardly keep the stuff in stock anymore.' Someone else, it seemed, was eating ham sandwiches.

But he couldn't spot them, though he gave it a try, and he hadn't the personnel to run surveillance on the gold repository *and* the café, so he gave up and left it a question mark. Since the intelligence craft ran so close to life, it was subject to life's coincidences, thus one had to be a good soldier and march ahead, no matter how the hair on the back of the neck might rise.

Spring came the third week in April. Blue rain slanted against the building façades and water streamed down the gutters, the parks smelled of earth when the sun came out for a moment, and a great unvoiced sigh seemed to rise from the city as a green cloud of buds appeared on the trees lining the boulevards. Aleksandra took her entire two-week salary off to the pawn shop and emerged with a radio that worked, like a bad mule, if you beat it. The radio stations competed with one another to intensify the seasonal torment, sending out the saddest songs imaginable from Piaf and the other café singers. Khristo discovered one station that played, sometimes, American jazz, and they listened to Billie Holiday and Teddy Wilson's 'I Must Have That Man' and Artie Shaw's sinuous 'Begin the Beguine'. Such music made both of them feel sexy and ineffably sad in the same moment and they made love like lovers in gothic novels. Meanwhile, the city's deep political malaise, its sense of doom, was now conjoined with the pangs of April and some were overheard to call this time *our final spring*.

In the mornings, Khristo smoked Gitanes and collated observer reports to the sound of the pattering rain. He could find no firm structure in the courier system. They were never together. They took the same route from embassy to repository and home again. The walk took about fourteen minutes. Once at the Floriot repository, the couriers were held up for twenty minutes or so for the

246

inevitable clerical ceremonies – a highly developed French specialty – then took another fourteen minutes to return. During the forty-eight-minute round trip, other couriers sometimes started off on their routes, but all four had never yet operated simultaneously. He studied the covert photographs his operatives had taken. Four unremarkable men in baggy suits. Probably armed. To take one of them would not be too difficult – a kidnapping off the street by hooded toughs. If they found a safe place to hold him, they might reasonably wait the remainder of the forty-eight minutes to see if another courier started out, but each variation on the theme would, of course, substantially increase the danger. There would be police, a lot of them, and they would arrive quickly.

For the finale of the surveillance, old Ivan was sent to the top floor of the building with a pair of gold candlesticks while one of the Russians was subjected to the clerical hocus-pocus. Ivan attempted to haggle over the price and made a thorough pest of himself for a time sufficient to observe an exchange through the security grille, then took his candlesticks and went off in a huff. The banknotes were delivered *en paquet*, but the Russian – the sorrowful Boris, as it happened – insisted on counting the money, and Ivan had silently counted right along with him. It came out to more than ninety thousand francs. At the equivalent of $14.28 U.S. an ounce, the European standard, he had converted almost twenty pounds of gold.

One wet afternoon, Khristo walked with Omaraeff in the Parc Monceau – two black umbrellas moving slowly along the gravelled path – and reported to him at length. Gave him a summary of his findings and a set of photographs. After some desultory conversation, they shook hands and parted. At the gate to the park a blind veteran, the breast of his old corporal's tunic covered with medals, stood silently in the drizzle holding a mess-kit plate before him. Khristo put a one-franc coin in the plate and the man thanked him solemnly in an educated voice.

He had an hour before work, so he bought a *Figaro* and stopped in a café and ordered a coffee. He put a sugar lump on the miniature spoon, lowered it just beneath the layer of tan foam, and watched it break into tiny crystals. He was glad the business for Omaraeff was done with; he believed he'd carried it off reasonably well, without getting his hands too dirty. From here on, they were on their own. The surfaces of the café windows were steamy, people going by in the streets looked like shadows.

The front pages of *Le Figaro* were dense with reports of a world in flames: Japanese bombers taking a terrible toll of the Chinese population in Manchuria, the Spanish city of Guernica virtually obliterated by the German pilots of the Condor Legion, Nazi storm troopers in Berlin, standing outside Jewish-owned department stores with rubber stamps and inkpads and forcing shoppers to have their foreheads stamped. Mussolini had made a major speech in Libya, voicing Italian support for Islamic objectives. Bertrand Russell had advised the British public to treat German invaders as tourists, stating, 'The Nazis would find some interest in our way of living, I think, and the starch would be taken out of them.'

The local news concentrated on the particularly horrible murder of an Austrian refugee up in Montmartre. The refugee, Hugo Leitzer, had been a resident of one of the cheap hotels in the district used almost exclusively by prostitutes. At four in the afternoon he was seen to stagger through the lobby with an icepick driven fully into his chest. He had managed to run out into the street, where he'd collapsed to his knees and pulled the weapon out as cars swerved around him. A 'heavy man in his forties, wearing a sailor's sweater', had run out of the hotel, retrieved the icepick, and stabbed Leitzer 'at least six times' before the eyes of horrified onlookers. By the time police arrived, the man had disappeared and Leitzer had bled to death.

The story was accompanied by a passport photo of Leitzer. It was Kerenyi, the blond Hungarian from Esztergom known as Ploughboy, who had trained with Khristo at Arbat Street.

He was exhausted when he got back to the room the following morning. He peeled off his clothes and dropped them on a chair, then slid carefully under the covers so as not to wake Aleksandra. But she was only pretending to sleep.

'You are so late,' she said. 'I fell asleep waiting.'

'It's madness there. Everyone orders champagne at dawn. With strawberries. Of course the old man doesn't chase them away – he shakes them by the ankles to make the last sou fall out.'

'Strawberries? In April?'

'From a greenhouse.'

'Like roses.'

'Yes. The price, too, is like roses.'

'Did you bring me some? You may feed them to me in bed.'

'Sorry. The patrons ate every last one.'

'Swine!'

'They pay the rent.'

'Little enough. They live like kings – we crawl in the dust.'

'Aleksandra . . .'

'I'll say anything I like.'

'Oh yes?'

'Yes.'

'Final warning.'

'I tremble with fear.'

'You shall.'

'No! Get your –'

'Bad . . . little . . . girls . . .'

'Help! Stop!'

He very nearly did. Would have, had she not let him know, silently, that she wished to be courteously ravaged. How she owned him! He marvelled at it. Rejoiced in it

249

even as their mood, their simultaneous appetite, began to shift.

Next, she was hungry. It meant they had to get dressed all over again and go out in the rain, joining the early workers in the café on the corner. Every eye went to Aleksandra as they entered. She peered out at the world from beneath a yellow straw hat – a 'boater', with circular crown and flat brim – wore a green wool muffler looped around her neck, and was lost in the immensity of Khristo's sheepskin jacket while he made do with a heavy sweater. To top it off, she was smoking a thin, gold Turkish cigarette. The workingmen in the café acknowledged her entrance with great affection. She was so *titi* – the classic Parisian street urchin, given to storm-blown passions yet impossibly adorable – towing her coatless lover into a café so early in the rainy morning, so delighted with her own eccentricity yet so vulnerable – blonde shag hanging down to her eyes – that every one of them felt obliged to desire her. For she was, if only for a moment, some girl they'd once loved.

Khristo and Aleksandra seated themselves at a small table by the window, shivering as the warm air drove out the chill, inhaling the luxurious morning fog of strong coffee, tobacco smoke and bread.

'Two breakfasts, please,' Khristo said to the owner when she came out from behind the bar.

She was back in a moment with bowls of milky coffee, a *flute* – the slimmest loaf with the most crust – cut into rounds, and saucers of white butter and peach jam. It took both hands to hold the coffee.

They polished that off in short order and ordered two more. '*Pauvres!*' said the owner from behind the bar, meaning *you poor starving things*, a fine Parisian irony twinkling in her tight smile. It was her divine right as *propriétaire* of the café to make fun of them a little – *I know why you're so hungry.*

To the second breakfast she added, unbidden, two steaming bowls of soup. Last night's, no doubt, and all the better for having aged. When these did not appear on the bill, Khristo began to thank her but she tossed his gratitude away with a flip of the hand. It was her right to feed them, to play a small role in their love affair. These were some of the sacred perquisites of the profession, to be dispensed at her whim.

Aleksandra took his hand on the way back to the room, tugged him off in a new direction just before they reached the door of their building. Steered him to a small park in the neighbourhood, but it was too wet to sit down.

When he pointed this out, she accused him of being unromantic. He sighed and went off to a *tabac* and returned with a newspaper, which he divided and placed on the wet bench. She took his hand again as they sat with the rain misting down on them. 'We will certainly catch cold,' he said.

'Lovers don't care about a little rain,' she said.

He turned her face toward him and kissed her on the lips. 'I am in love,' he said softly, sliding his arm beneath the sheepskin coat and circling her waist, 'but I am getting wet.'

'Some ferocious Bulgar you turned out to be. Whose ancestors rode the steppes.'

'Those were Mongols.'

'Oh? Well then, what did the ferocious Bulgars do?'

'Stayed dry,' he said, 'when they could.'

Back in the room, they rubbed each other dry with the rough towels the landlady provided for a few francs extra each week. Khristo looked up as heavy footsteps moved down the corridor past their door. 'Who is that?' He was used to the light step of the spinster, a retired piano teacher, who had rented the room at the end of the hall.

251

'A new tenant,' Aleksandra said. 'Mademoiselle Beckmann has gone to join her sister in Rennes.'

'Oh?'

'Yes. Madame told me yesterday when she came for the rent. The new lodger is called Dodin. I saw him move in.'

'He walks like an ox.'

'He looks like one as well. He is broad, wide as a door. And he has big red hands, like a butcher. He tipped his hat to me.'

'He sounds strange.'

She shrugged. 'Sit down and I will dry your hair. God made you too tall.' He sat on the bed while she rubbed his head with a towel. 'He is just a man who lives in rooms,' she said.

'So do I.'

'Well, he is the sort who does, I mean. You just happen to.'

'Perhaps we should find another room.'

'Because of Dodin?'

'No, not exactly. A change of scene, perhaps.'

'I like it here,' she said. 'It is ours.'

'As long as he doesn't bother you.'

'Don't worry about that.' She adjusted his head by pulling on his ears. 'I am used to big oxes.'

She had small breasts, they moved as she dried his hair and he touched them. 'Be good,' she said, wriggling away from his hands. But he pulled her down on the bed next to him and, when she began to say the sort of things that always provoked him, when she began to tease him, he stopped her and made love to her in a way that was not their usual fashion. He made love to her from the heart, and when it was over she had tears in her eyes and he held her so tightly that his hands hurt.

*　　*　　*

On the first day of May the weather sparkled, bright blue and perfect, a day just barely warm enough to leave one's coat at home. Ivan Donchev set his homburg at the proper angle and gave the bottom of his waistcoat a final tug. In the hallway mirror, his image was precisely as he wished: an older gentleman but well kept, shoulders set square, chin held high. He had only a minor role in the day's drama, but he meant to play it flawlessly and with style. Outside his apartment building, he stopped at the flower cart and bought his usual rosebud, white for today, and adjusted it carefully in his buttonhole.

He considered a taxi, but it was May Day and many of the drivers would be marching. Huge demonstrations and parades were expected in central Paris, busloads of police had been drawn up since before dawn in the side streets off the Rue de Rivoli. So he walked. It took him more than two hours but he enjoyed every minute, flirting with the passing ladies, patting the occasional dog, swimming easily in the stream of city life as he had done for forty years. He barely remembered Sofia, where he had grown to manhood, yet distance and time had somehow contrived to strengthen his patriotism. Besides, one could not exactly say no to Omaraeff. When something went awry in the émigré community, Djadja was the court of last resort and almost always found a way to put things right, thus he was not a man to be casually turned aside.

Just after 3:00 p.m., Ivan Donchev took up his position on the Place de l'Opéra, in front of Lancel, its windows superbly decorated with gold and silver and Bakelite jewellery nesting among dozens of spring scarves. When the door opened, one could smell perfume. He quite loved this store, though its merchandise was well beyond his means. The women who swept in and out of its doors were delicious, he thought, each one showing off her own special flair. He was, for women in general, a very good audience, offering now and again an appreciative nod and a tip of the hat, which sometimes drew a smile in return.

253

Some blocks away, in the direction of the Rue de Rivoli, he could hear snatches of song and the occasional roar – quite muted by the time it reached his ears – of a huge crowd. Now and then, the high-low song of a police siren cut through the low rumble of the marchers. Omaraeff had, he was certain, chosen to act on May Day for two reasons: the evident symbolic value, as well as the fact that police cars would be well snarled up by the demonstrations. He strolled back and forth in front of the store, glancing at his watch, a man anticipating the reappearance of a woman occupied with shopping. He looked about him, discreetly, but could identify none of his confederates. That was all to the good, he thought, it indicated a professional approach to the matter.

At sixteen minutes past the hour, the man he awaited came toward him from the Rue de la Paix. His mouth grew dry, and he felt his heart accelerate. *Be calm*, he told himself. What he had to do was simple, there was no question of making a mistake. The man with the black satchel moved at the pace of pedestrian traffic. He seemed, as always, terribly morose. He slumped, his shoulders sagged, his jowls drooped, his eyes were lost behind thick, ill-fitting eyeglasses. Well, he would be even less happy in a moment, Ivan thought.

As the courier walked past him, Ivan gathered his wits and rehearsed himself one final time. He let the man go by, waited as he gained some small distance, then ran after him at a trot. 'Wait a moment!' he called out in Russian, waving his hand. The man hesitated, paused, then looked over his shoulder at Ivan, hurrying to catch up with him. 'Please, sir, a moment,' Ivan called. From a taxi parked by the kerb and from the doorway of a restaurant, two men appeared. He had never seen them before but there was no mistaking their trade. They were thick, bulky men who moved gracefully. One of them grabbed the courier's left arm. The courier swung his satchel. A woman screamed. Several people started running. The other man grabbed the satchel but the Russian was strong and swung him around. Ivan stood motionless, watching the drama. The three men struggled for a moment, all tangled up with one another, it seemed. A loud voice demanded that the police appear at once. A woman coming out of Lancel lost a shoe, then stood hopping on one foot, trying to put it back on. From the driver's seat of the taxi a hand appeared, holding an automatic pistol. There was a flash and a crack, then another, then three or four more in rapid succession. The courier leapt into the air as Ivan watched, transfixed. Then a bee stung him in the armpit and he began backing away hurriedly. What a moment for such a thing to happen! He saw the courier on the sidewalk, a handful of pamphlets sprayed across his chest, his satchel gone. The other two men were disappearing into the taxi as Ivan turned away and trotted off. A siren approached in the distance.

He was, at this point, supposed to go home. But he didn't feel well. His left arm was numb, and he had now come to realize what had happened to him. Still, it couldn't be terribly serious, and the most pressing need at the moment was to remove himself from the immediate area. There was a small cinema just off the avenue and he paid and went in, letting the usher guide him to a seat on the aisle and remembering to tip him.

Of the movie he could make little sense. A man and a woman lived in poverty on a barge that sailed up and down the river Loire. They were lovers, but the anguish of the times was driving them apart. The girl was called Sylvie. She had hooded eyes and a down-curved, unhappy mouth. When she lit a cigarette, she watched the match burn almost to her fingertips before blowing it out. This she did continually. Her lover was called Bruno — was he German? — a rough sort who wore a sleeveless undershirt and a neck scarf. Only one thing interested him, that was clear. But he was too much the primitive for Sylvie, a barbarian who thought himself clever.

Ivan kept moving about in the seat, trying to get

comfortable. His skin felt clammy and there was a hot point beneath his shoulder blade that seemed to move about, as though the bee had burrowed well in and was now building a hive. He checked his watch. Amazing! Only fifteen minutes since he had hailed the courier. Much too soon to be out on the street. He settled himself back in the seat and tried to concentrate on the film. A vagabond, a stooped old man with a wild beard, had joined the couple. Sylvie kept staring at him from a distance, as though she had encountered him in a past life. Bruno noticed this but said nothing about it. He drank wine with the vagabond, who began to tell a story about a travelling circus.

The movie was definitely making him drowsy. A dog at the edge of the river barked at the moon. The vagabond cleaned his nails with a long knife. Bruno grabbed Sylvie by the arm and the camera showed his fingers pressing into her skin. It didn't matter much to Ivan. His chin kept dropping onto his chest, then he would snap awake. The idea of an old man sleeping in a movie house in the middle of the afternoon was very depressing, simply not the sort of thing he would do, but there seemed to be no way to avoid it. They didn't find him until after midnight, when an usher came down the aisle to wake him up and couldn't.

* * *

On his way to work, Khristo saw the headlines:

DIPLOMATE SOVIET ASSASSINÉ
LA MORT A VISITÉ L'OPÉRA!
JOUR DE MAI EST JOUR DE MORT POUR DIPLOMATE
SOVIET

There were photographs. It took him a moment to recognize 'Boris', a dark shape tossed carelessly on a grey pavement. He stood in a small crowd in front of the kiosk and read the secondary headlines and lead paragraphs.

256

Trotskyist pamphlets had been found on the body of Dmitri Myagin, assistant cultural attaché at the Soviet embassy. Ivan Donchev, a Bulgarian citizen but long a resident of the city, had been discovered dead of a gunshot wound in a movie theatre near the site of the assassination. The DST, the French internal security service, was treating the death as associated with the Myagin shooting. All émigré groups in the city would be questioned regarding the incident. An anarchist splinter party, LEC (Liberté, Egalité, Communité), had claimed credit for the action. The Soviet ambassador, in a written statement, had decried violence and murder in the streets, and lawlessness in general, as maladies of an oppressive capitalist system. What would be said to the grieving widow? The fatherless children?

Khristo, standing in the sunlight, went cold. Fools. Who could not accomplish a simple street robbery without killing. And old Ivan – what in God's name had Omaraeff been thinking of, to permit an innocent like that in the vicinity of an action? The assassins reportedly fled in a taxi. Was that Pazar? In his own taxi, perhaps? It was unspeakable. Nobody could be that stupid. There had been a good chance that a simple, quiet robbery might not even have been reported by the Russians – one little crime was nothing compared to their obsession with gold – for it would have imperilled the operation at Floriot. But murder, in front of witnesses, in the middle of the afternoon, in a good neighbourhood, with obvious Balkan overtones – that would stir up the newspapers for weeks and the police would be forced into making a serious effort.

And the searching finger, he knew, would be scratching at his door soon enough.

The Russians would find a way to break into the investigation – the Paris NKVD residency surely had its friends in the DST. Perhaps his passport photo was being studied by the police right now. His assumed identity would not hold up under scrutiny – Omaraeff had seen through it easily enough.

In addition, the death of Kerenyi on a Montmartre street still gnawed at him. He wasn't at all the type to look for a fight in a whorehouse. He too might have defected – from Spain or wherever they had sent him after Arbat Street – and hidden out in Paris. If the man who'd killed him was a Spetsburo assassin, evidence pointed to a desire for publicity. An *icepick*. The Russians knew all about newspapers. Perhaps they were sending a message, trying to panic other fugitives in Paris.

Perhaps they had succeeded.

He was ice cold, but a droplet of sweat ran down his side, and there was a claw in his stomach. He had money, hidden in the light fixture in the hallway outside his room. Perhaps they could run. Where? Into Germany? Into Spain? That was madness. Holland, then, or Belgium. Very well, then what? They would have to work soon enough. That meant permits, and police, and no Omaraeff to smooth the way. But if the murder of Kerenyi had been NKVD work – and the more he thought about it the more he knew he had to make that assumption – it was intended to flush the game, to make the rabbits run. Thus, if he ran, he was playing into their hands. They would snap him up.

And he knew what came next.

By the time he was pounding up the Rue du Bac, a few blocks from Heininger, the blackness had come down upon him hard. Everything he had so carefully pieced together, from love and work and a few tenuous dreams, was trembling in the wind. How flimsy it was, he thought. Built on sand. How he had deluded himself, that he could make what he wanted out of his life. It wasn't so.

'Dear boy.'

He stopped dead and looked for the voice. It came from an open two-seater, a forest green Morgan parked at the kerb. Recognition arrived a moment later – the reddish hair swept across the noble brow, cool eyes shadowed with dark makeup. The man who had given him his card at Winnie Beale's birthday party on the Rue de Varenne.

258

"Lo there, Nick. Come sit with us a minute, will you?' It wasn't precisely a request. He walked around the back of the car and climbed in. The upholstery on the bucket seat was worn smooth with time and care and smelled like old leather.

'Roger Fitzware. Remember me?' They shook hands.

'Yes,' he said. 'At Madame Beale's house.'

'You were going to come round and get your picture took, you bad boy.'

Khristo shrugged. 'I am sorry,' he said simply.

'No matter, no matter. Everybody's so blasted busy these days. Even old Nick, eh?'

'Yes. Even now, I was going to work.'

'Oh let's steal a minute, shall we? First of all, you must say "congratulations." '

'Congratulations, Mr. Fitzware.'

'Plain Roddy, dear boy. And I thank you. Seems I've got me a job. Of all things! The old family back in Sussex would absolutely perish from the shock if they heard, but there it is.'

'I am glad for you.'

'Thank you, thank you. Sort of a society column kind of a thing, it seems, fellow wasn't all that clear about it. "Just a few titbits, dear boy," he says. "The odd *item*, y'know, who's been with who and what did they do and what did they say and so on and so forth." You know the sort of thing?'

'Yes, I think so. Tit, bits.'

'That's it!'

'And from me you want . . . ?'

'Titbits, dear boy. Just as you said. You're in the way of finding out all sorts of things, aren't you. One goes here and one goes there and one finds old Nick choppin' up a salmon, eh? It's a natural, that's what I say. Here you are, having to listen to every sort of prattle all day and half the night, now here's the chance to make the odd franc at it. Oh say yes, Nick, I'd be truly grateful.'

259

'I'm sorry, Mr. Fitzware. I must not do such things. My job. . . .'

'Dear boy! Don't even think it. You must, y'know, really you must.'

Khristo – not Nick the waiter at all – gave him a long look. Fitzware sat casually, half turned, at the wheel of the Morgan, his dark blue blazer – double-breasted and stoutly made – hung perfectly, and the striped tie meant something, though Khristo wasn't sure exactly what. A man who had everything he wanted, yet his face was tense and pale, in fear, evidently, that he would receive no titbits.

'I must?'

'Yes, well, damn it all, Nick, there it is. You must.'

'Be your spy, you mean.'

'Dear boy, such language.'

'But that is what you mean. Who goes in bed with who. What people say when they drink too much. Who doesn't pay their bill at the restaurant. That is what you want from me. And you will pay for it.'

Fitzware, in one fluid motion, produced a thin pack of hundred-franc notes from somewhere, laid it on Khristo's knee, and patted it twice. 'Smart lad,' he said, in a voice entirely different from the one he always used.

Khristo picked up the banknotes, wet the tip of his thumb, counted them – there were twenty – folded the sheaf twice, to make it a thick wad, then reached across the car and stuffed the money in the breast pocket of Fitzware's blazer.

'Well. Now you've surprised me, Nick. And you can't imagine how difficult it is to surprise me.' His eyes were wide and unmoving, like an insulted cat.

'I'm sorry, Mr. Fitzware. But I must go to work now.'

'Last thing. Have a look in the glove box, will you?'

Khristo turned the knob and the wooden panel fell open. There was an envelope lying flat on the felt interior. He opened it up and looked at the photograph. Saw himself sitting on a wooden bench, wearing only a towel, with a naked boy on his knee.

'Shocking, eh? Not to worry, Nick. Your little secret is safe with me. *Honi soit qui mal y pense* and all that, love makes the world go round, variety the spice of life. Dear boy, one couldn't guess what goes on in wicked old Paree.'

Khristo smiled. Stopped himself just short of open laughter. 'Omaraeff is yours?'

'Oh, who is anybody's anymore, really. Just that friends do each other favours now and again. Makes the wheels run smooth.'

He handed the photograph to Fitzware. 'To remember me, you keep this, *dear boy*,' he said.

'Don't you realize . . . ?'

'This trick works, Mr. Fitzware, only if there is somebody to show the picture to. Who will you show? Omaraeff? Papa Heininger — what would he think of you, to take such a picture? — or perhaps my lover? She would be surprised, perhaps, or a little sad maybe, or she might laugh. With her, you see, it's hard to tell. Goodbye.'

He got out of the car and closed the door carefully. Walked away leisurely down the street.

'Damn your eyes,' he heard behind him. Again, not the usual nasal whine, not at all. Real British fury — a voice he'd never in fact heard before. The heat of it surprised him.

At Heininger, a few minutes after five, he saw Omaraeff enter the restaurant, a newspaper folded under his arm. His face was rigid. Khristo stared at him, but he refused to make eye contact. The regular patrons, who filtered in just before midnight, were excited by the news of the moment and the waiters found themselves momentary celebrities. 'Uh-oh, here comes Nick. Quick everybody, under the table!' He grinned at them tolerantly and shook his head — these grinning aristocrats who kidded him with their hands formed into children's revolvers. In honour of the assassination they called out *'Nazhdrovia!'* as they guzzled their champagne and tried on a variety of Eastern European accents for his benefit. Omaraeff stood at attention before the roast with a long knife, directing an assistant to wrap up a nice fatty rib for the deerhound of a favoured customer, and accepted the tireless joshing with a thin smile. Later that night he sliced his thumb to the bone and had to be taken off to a doctor.

As Khristo hurried to and from the kitchen, his mind wandered among the small, insignificant events of the past week. Simply, there were too many of them — he felt like a blind man in a room full of cobwebs. There was Dodin, the new lodger. The blind veteran in the Parc Monceau with an educated, cultured voice — wearing a *corporal's* tunic. Small things, ordinarily not worthy of notice. The death of Kerenyi. Sad, surely, and perhaps without meaning. The clumsiness of the gold theft. Ineptitude could be, he knew, an effective mask for intentions of great subtlety. He feared that something was gathering around him, strand by delicate strand, and that, when its presence was at last manifest, it would be one instant too late to run for freedom.

At three-thirty in the morning he went home, walking quickly, head down. Reaching his building, he felt a stab of panic — foreknowledge — and rushed up the stairs to the room. He threw open the door to find darkness and silence. He was silhouetted, framed in the doorway, and he flinched, moved sideways against the wall just as the timed light in the hallway went off with a pop. In total blackness, he closed his eyes in concentration and raised his hands before him. He could hear, faintly, the sound of laboured breathing. A match flared and a candle came to life. Aleksandra, dark-under-white skin glowing amber in the tiny flame, moved toward him in a trance. A piece of rope was knotted low on her waist. She stared at him blindly, lips drawn back, teeth exposed. As in a dream, her hand reached out, fingers curved into talons, and she spoke very slowly, in English shaded by the harsh accents of the Balkans. 'Velcome to my castle,' she said.

Later, as he lay awake in the tangled bedding, he heard the heavy footsteps of the new lodger as he walked down the corridor.

The next day, and for a week thereafter, in the section of *Le Figaro* where various Bureaux de Matrimonie listed the virtues of their clients, the following advertisement appeared:

> #344 – Monsieur B.F., a prosperous gentleman own-ing 82.5 *hectares* of farmland in the Haut-Vienne, wishes to meet a woman of honesty and sincerity. Monsieur B.F. is recently widowed and quite youth-ful in appearance, and will treat all enquiries with discretion. Please write, describing desirable arrange-ments for meeting, to #344, Bureau de Matrimonie Vigeaux, 60 Rue St.-Martin.

He received four responses. The first three were hand-written notes on inexpensive formal paper. Annette scented hers with *eau de violettes* and would meet him for tea at the house of her mother. Françoise, age thirty-nine, wrote in purple ink, including precise directions to her family home near Porte d'Ivry. Suzi suggested dinner at any restaurant 'of good standing' he might choose. The fourth letter was typed. 'Iliane' would be pleased to meet him on the third Sunday in June, at 2:00 p.m., at the Père Lachaise cemetery, by the crypt of Maria Walewska – Napoleon's Polish mistress.

*   *   *

Moving down the gravel paths among the black-clad French families, a small bunch of anemones in his hand, he saw Ilya Goldman standing contemplatively by the Walewska tomb, a small, grey temple-like structure with an iron railing across the front. Even from a distance, Khristo could see the changes. Formerly boyish and exuberant, Ilya had grown older than his years. He wore a well-cut suit with a white handkerchief in the breast pocket, a soft grey fedora, and a black mourner's armband. His hands were clasped behind his back. Up close, there were lines of fatigue around his eyes, and when Ilya greeted him — they spoke Russian, as always — he seemed to animate his face with effort. They shook hands warmly, embraced, then spent a moment without words staring together at the Walewska tomb.

'Well then,' Ilya said at last, 'what is the report from SHOEMAKER?'

'SHOEMAKER?'

'Yes, we are using professions, lately, for operational names. Even Banker and Moneylender. Out of deference to me, I think, the latter is not simply Jew.'

'Ah. Who am I, then?'

'A countess, of obscure origin and terribly poor, alas. With a French fascist for a lover, naturally. Very gamy stuff. Their views on lovemaking are quite . . . unusual. You would enjoy reading about it.'

'You've had somebody watching the Matrimonials all this time?'

'Oh yes. Since the day after you left Spain, in fact. Don't be too flattered, though. We have many hands, and the busier they are kept, the less mischief they cause us.'

'Ilya, I must ask you. Are they getting close to me?'

He didn't answer for a time. 'They are looking, I can promise you that. Looking hard. But I am not in the Paris residency, you see, and I don't know what they're doing here. For the purposes of SHOEMAKER I am permitted to travel. Now, at my *rezidentura* — Copenhagen at the moment, but I may be moved any day – you are safe enough. We have a very long list. Since the *Yezhovschina* purges we seem to leak defectors everywhere. Finding them takes a cursed amount of time.'

'And you? How safe are you?'

He shrugged. 'Who can say, who can say. They've shot ninety percent of the army generals, eighty percent of the colonels.'

'Who will fight the war?'

'There won't be one. Stalin will keep us out of it, I can promise you that. We haven't the officers to fight a war. There are some who say that the doubt cast on the loyalty of the army – generals' plots and what have you – was in fact the work of German intelligence, Reinhard Heydrich and his so-called intellectual thugs. Quite good they are, quite, quite good. Meanwhile, on our side, the old guard is just about gone. Berzin, who ran things so well in Spain, was recalled 'for discussions'. He went, thinking that all could be *explained*, and they killed him, of course. All the Latvians, in fact – Latsis, Peters, the whole crowd. The Chekist Unschlikht is dead. Orlov has defected and is said to be writing a book. A grand housecleaning has been undertaken. All the Poles, Hungarians, Germans. We're to be quite thoroughly Russian in future.'

'Will they purge Romanians?'

'Like me, you mean.'

'Yes.'

'One would suppose so, though here I am. Hard to say for how long. However, I do not intend to die. And that's where you come in, my friend. The time may come when I will need your help. I sleep a little better having a friend on the outside, someone I can trust, for the day when I have to scamper.'

'You saved my life in Spain. Anything you want . . .'

'Thank you. They realized you had been warned – Maltsaev and his pals – but they stuck that one on Lubin.'

265

'Did his family connection save him?'

'No. They died too. One is never quite sure which way it will go.'

Khristo mused for a time, then shook his head. 'We should kill him, Ilya. Somebody should.'

'Stalin? The Great Father? Yes. Will you do it, Khristo? Die for the good of all mankind?'

'If I thought one could actually get at him, perhaps I would. By joining the Guards division or something of that sort.'

'A little late for you to join the Guards division.'

'He must be insane. A mad dog.'

'No, you are wrong about that. That's what Europe thinks – those who aren't in love with him. Here he might be mad, but in truth he is no more than that lovable old character, the wicked peasant. I'm sure you've known one or two. He hits his neighbour on the head, steals his gold, rapes his wife, and burns his house down. Who knows why. If he is reproached, he swears that a fiery angel forced him to do it.'

They strolled for a time, two acquaintances in mourning, through the maze of pathways lined tightly with the tombs of aristocrats and artists, some of which had received Sunday flowers.

'What of the others?' Khristo asked.

'Well, Kulic is alive.'

'Was he arrested?'

'No. He was blown up by a mortar shell in the Guadarrama, leading an attack of partisans. The Germans had him for a time, but we found a way to get him out. A Yugoslavian fascist group, the Ustachi, asked to collect him for interrogation. They are Croatian and Kulic is Serbian and the Germans appreciate such differences, so they released him and we got him back.'

'How?'

'It's our group – this particular band of Ustachi. You know this business, Khristo. One needs a little of everything.'

'He must be well regarded.'

'Somebody thinks he might be of use. Otherwise . . .'

'And Voluta?'

Ilya paused for a moment. 'Probably I shouldn't tell you.'

'Well, don't if you can't.'

'No, it doesn't matter. You of course recall that girl, Marike, at Arbat Street. You knew her somewhat, I believe.'

'Yes.'

'One day she disappeared. Well, it seems that somebody had hidden a list of the names of the Brotherhood Front of 1934 in a most ingenious place – scratched on rubber, washed down the sink, but the rubber was just heavy enough to stay caught in the trap. Marike's bad luck was that some fool tried to get rid of a condom in the sink – no doubt the throne was occupied and he was in a hurry – and *that* stopped it up but good. Next, an unfortunate miracle: a plumber actually appeared one day and unplugged the drain. He knew what he had, went and barked his head off in the right places and down came the counterintelligence types. They pinned the thing on Marike, I don't know why, and away she went. Ozunov as well, of course. Later, much later, they found out some other way that it had been Voluta all along. Now, the best part. He was a priest! Part of a Polish nationalist movement called NOV, made up of priests and army officers. Not fascists – though Moscow would certainly call them that. Patriots, I think, in a conspiracy to preserve Poland as a national entity. They are very much on our Watch List, because they are very dedicated and have enjoyed some significant success. Witness Voluta: he penetrated the Arbat Street training facility, noted every personality and physical description in the place and then, when he was assigned to the *rezidentura* in Antwerp, simply got off the train and has not been seen since. The problem

267

with this NOV is that it spreads among the priests – I mean outside Poland, among other nationalities – and there is reason to believe that the army officers have made similar connections. This is not exactly the Polish government, you understand, but a conspiracy that hides in its shadow. Thus our assets in Warsaw can do nothing about it. Our friend Voluta is quite a famous priest in Moscow.'

'My God,' Khristo said, truly amazed that he'd been deceived along with everybody else. 'I never thought . . .'

'He was very much in himself, you'll remember.'

'Yes. And always helpful, willing to do more than his share.'

'Priestly, eh? And we suspect that this NOV shares information with Poland's dearest ally – British intelligence. Heaven only knows where it might go from there. I expect we are all quite famous by now.'

'Where do you think he is?'

Ilya smiled and spread his hands to include the entire world. They walked for a time, past the tomb of the Rothschilds, the graves of Daumier and Corot and Proust.

'Do you know the Mur des Fédérés?' Ilya asked, standing by the cemetery wall.

'No.'

'The last of the Paris Communards died here, in 1871. They fought all night among the gravestones, then surrendered at dawn. The soldiers put them against this wall, shot them, and buried them in a common grave.'

'Are you a communist, Ilya? In your heart?'

'Oh yes. Aren't you ?'

'No. I just want to live my life, to be left alone.'

There was a moment's silence, then Ilya said, 'Now, a matter of some delicacy.' They turned and began to walk again, their steps audible on the gravel path.

'What is that?'

'This business of the assassination of our courier.'

'On May Day?'

'Yes.'

'What about it?'

'The *rezidentura* here is frantic – they are under the gun, believe me, Moscow is entirely outraged. They've sent in thugs from everywhere, specialists, and activated every net in Paris. So far, no fish.'

'Perhaps that was why it was done. To see who showed up, to learn from the activity.'

Ilya looked at him sharply. 'The old Khristo,' he said. When there was no response, he went on. 'Anyhow, they really *want to know*. What's come in to date is the usual plateful of crumbs – White Russians, phony princes, Cossack doormen, a Mills grenade with Stalin's name painted on it – but Yezhov's not buying any of that.'

'And so?'

'If you should happen to hear something . . .'

'Then what?'

'I believe you mentioned being left alone to live your life?'

'Yes.'

'That's what.'

Khristo spoke carefully: 'I asked you earlier if they were getting close to me. Is this your answer?'

Ilya shook his head violently, like a wet dog. 'No. Do not misunderstand me. I said they were looking for you. I don't know they are, I assume it. But you had better assume it as well. A favour might turn the pressure off, though nobody can guarantee it – not me, not anybody. On the other hand, what have you got to lose?'

They talked for an hour after that, reminisced: Arbat Street, Belov, Spain, Yaschyeritsa, Sascha. Then they parted. Khristo returned to the room. Aleksandra wasn't there. It was Sunday – she'd mentioned something about a picnic in the park. But he had talked to Ilya longer

269

than he'd intended, perhaps she had given up on him and gone to the *cinéma*. That was probably what she'd done, he decided.

He waited for her, smoking Gitanes, watching the square of sky in the window turn slowly from blue to dark blue, from hazy lavender at sunset to the colour of dusk, and then to night. At first, he expected her to return, and waited. Later, for a time, he hoped for it. The hour for him to go to work passed unnoticed. He paced the room, moving from the battered armoire that served as their closet to the open window. He would pause there and look out, sometimes seeing, sometimes not. The shops were closed, their metal shutters pulled down. A few people hurried along the sidewalk, one or two cars went by. Sunday night, and everyone was locked up in their apartments, hiding from whatever it was they hid from on a Sunday night. He could smell potatoes frying and the damp scents of the Paris street. It was so quiet that sounds of clinking plates and bits of conversation – once a laugh – floated up to him. Then he would turn away from the window, move to the foot of the bed and back across to the armoire. At one point he opened it, found all her clothing in place, including the white Marlene Dietrich trenchcoat – a fashion necessity that spring in the city – her pride and joy. But it had been warmish in the afternoon, she could have worn only a sweater. In the drawer of the night table she kept a box of small things she believed to be valuable. Bits and pieces. A silver button, an American coin, a cameo of Empress Josephine from a souvenir shop. Her perfume was heavy on the treasures, as though she had once kept the bottle among them. On one of his trips past the small mirror, he discovered a red, angry mark on the skin beside his eye, realized it hurt, realized he had put it there himself. He looked at his hands, knew for a certainty that if he had a gun

270

he would kill himself. She was lost, he knew; he had lost her, he would not see her again. He lay down on the bed, on his side, and drew his knees up to his chest and pressed his fingers hard against the sides of his head to stop the pain behind his eyes, but that didn't work.

Later, he woke up with a gasp, dizzy and lost, and felt the weight of sorrow return to him. Discovered the side of his face was wet. He forced himself off the bed and started searching the room, but he missed it on the first search, found nothing out of the ordinary. A ten-franc note hidden in a shoe, that was all. At 1:30 in the morning he opened the door and listened for a long time at Dodin's room down the hall, heard only silence. He kicked the door open, went over the room slowly and carefully, as he'd been taught, but there was nothing there at all, only dustballs beneath the bed. Nothing in the drawers. Nothing in the armoire. Nothing taped anywhere out of sight. Nothing. He tried to close the door, but the lock mechanism wouldn't work anymore where he'd sprung it, so he simply left it open. He checked the light fixture in the hall, took his money out, and put it in his pocket. That was all he could do.

He went back to his room and watched the night as the hours passed by. Sometimes he swore revenge, quietly, under his breath, a stupefying and obscene anger that meant nothing. At dawn, moving mechanically, he began putting his own things into a pillowcase. When everything he wanted was there and he was ready to go — though he didn't know where — he forced himself to search the room once again. He willed his mind clear and did the job as he knew it should be done: an inch at a time, starting in a corner and expanding outward and upward in imaginary lines of radiation. He got down on his knees, the lamp by his side wherever the cord would reach an outlet.

He found it an hour later. There was old wainscoting by the door, poor-quality wood with the varnish flaking off, and as he moved the lamp the shift of angle in the light revealed the marks. He moved his fingers across the wood, confirming what he saw. She had, after all, left him a message. He sat down heavily and cried into his hands for a long time. He didn't want anyone to hear him. Time and again he touched the wall, traced, with agonizing slowness, the faintly marked outlines of the four scratches her fingernails had made as she'd been taken through the door.

* * *

The guys out in Clichy absolutely loved it when Barbette came around. They'd run their *poules* off and set him up at one of the tables at Le Maroc or the Dutchman's place on Rue Truot that everybody called the *cul de cochon* and let him buy them drinks all night. He was the strangest thing they ever saw out there – where *people* didn't come unless they had to, and then always in daylight – because he had the money and he liked to spend it and he liked to spend it on them. He was tall for a Frenchman, and he stood straight up and looked at you with those little dark eyes that always seemed to catch the light and he had a big, false laugh. You could tell him you just stole your mother's teeth and he'd laugh. Even his name, Barbette, what did that mean? A nickname? The word meant 'little beard' and he had one of those, a devil's beard, from sideburn tight along the jawline sweeping up to join the moustache, so closely pruned he must have nipped it with scissors every night.

But a *barbette* was also a nun's veil that covered the breast, and that expression in turn was used in slang to mean sleeping on the floor or guns firing in a salvo. The word sometimes referred to a water spaniel – the efficient sort that always brought in the kill. They asked him, in their own way, but all they ever got was that laugh. They didn't really care – he was the kind of guy you liked even better because he wouldn't tell you what you wanted to know. It meant he wasn't in the habit of running his mouth, and that mattered to people out in Clichy. Johnny LaFlamme and Poz Vintre and Escaldo from Lisbon and Sarda, the deafmute who watched your mouth when you talked and knew what you were saying. They were all the family any of them had and they looked out for one another in their own way and they could smell a cop three blocks off. Barbette was no cop. But he wasn't one of them, either. He was something different.

The girls all said he was crazy, that he went for the *petite soeur* like a maniac who'd been marooned on an island. Maybe a bit of a showoff, they said, and he really liked that fancy stuff – nothing standing up – that went on all afternoon and left them worn out for their real work at night, down in the Rue St.-Denis near Les Halles or up in Montmartre. But the guys put up with it. Barbette was always good for a touch when you came up short and he never asked for it back. Everybody had to have one of those long coats like they had in *Little Caesar* or *Public Enemy* – and you couldn't steal those. The great Capone, they fancied, would have told them they looked just right.

Then one day he went off with Escaldo and Sarda and when they showed up again they were richer than they'd ever been. Sent away the rotgut the Dutchman dished up under the name *vin rouge* and ordered the real stuff – for themselves and everybody else. One couldn't ask questions. But the new wealth came from Barbette and it put matters in an entirely new, and very interesting, light. He'd gone from putting money in their bellies – drinks and whatnot – to putting money in their pockets, and that made him really important, no longer just a guy who came around. They were a little jealous of Escaldo and Sarda – why not me? – but they had nothing but time and maybe it was their turn next. Escaldo and Sarda, in the beginning, didn't say all that much. Sarda couldn't – not without a pencil and paper, and who wanted to bother with that – and Escaldo wouldn't. He looked like a pimp, dark and slick and vain, and he kept one of those Portuguese fish-gutting knives strapped to his ankle. You didn't press him too hard, the girls had found that out pretty quick. As for poor Sarda, his face was carved into deep lines from trying all his life just to do things that everybody else took for granted. When he got agitated, he made noises in his throat and privately they all admitted they were a little bit afraid of him. So, for a time, the wine flowed and the beef sizzled and everybody just shut up and waited patiently.

But in families everything comes out eventually, and Escaldo got drunk one night and let them in on part of it. He was, also, under some pressure to explain things. Some smart guy figured out that maybe Barbette banged the girls so hard to prove he wasn't a fairy, which meant maybe he was, which meant that Escaldo and Sarda had sunk to a level where it was definitely *out* of the family. Escaldo couldn't afford to let too much of that go on, so he sang.

The money they had now, he explained, was only the beginning. There'd be more — maybe a lot more, maybe the *big one* they all dreamed of and talked about. Barbette had taken them to an abandoned farmhouse somewhere to hell and gone outside Paris and he'd shown them these, ah, things, and run them through a little schooling and let them, even, use them a few times. *Bon Dieu! Quelles machines! Quels instruments!* His eyes glowed as he talked, and it only took a few more glasses of marc to get the whole story out in the air.

Les machines à écrire de Chicago.

There it was, now they had it all. Chicago typewriters. That's what Barbette had to show them on the broken-down farm outside Paris. Escaldo spread his long coat apart and took out two little pimp cigars and lit one for Sarda and one for himself. Did Bottles Capone, Al's brother, or Jake 'Greasy Thumb' Guzik have anything they didn't? *Not anymore.*

Machine guns.

Around the table, nobody could say anything for a long time, thinking about that.

* * *

Khristo found a room deep in the Marais, on a dark side street off the Rue des Rosiers. It was an ancient building, narrow, seven flights to the top floor, with rusted iron pipes crossing the ceiling and a small window on a courtyard where it was nighttime from dawn to dusk. He rented the room from an old Jew bent in the shape of a *C*, with black sidelocks, beard, coat, and hat. 'Who wants you, little one?' the man asked in Russian. 'I don't understand,' Khristo answered in French. The man nodded to himself. 'Oh, pardon me then,' he said in Russian.

The thought of Aleksandra's things in the treasure box, left to be pawed by the landlady, haunted him, but a return to the room was out of the question. Surely they had him spotted at Heininger as well, but it was less likely that they would snatch him there. He considered finding Yasin again, in the Turkish quarter out on the Boulevard Raspail, and acquiring another weapon, but he put it off. Ilya had given him a telephone number – that was his best weapon now. Had Ilya set him up? Kept him at the cemetery while Aleksandra was taken? Perhaps. Perhaps Ilya had been set up to set him up. At least he knew where he was now. On the NKVD chessboard, all his moves known and predicted, hostile knights and bishops dawdling while he figured out how to move onto the very square where they wanted him. Somehow, it didn't matter. Fate was fate. He would play the game out to checkmate, they would all meet again in hell.

Sweating in the late June weather, he stood in a telephone *cabinet* at the neighbourhood post office while the call was put through. They answered on the first ring. He merely said, 'I want a meeting.' They told him to be at the church of St.-Julien-le-Pauvre at 6:30 the following morning.

*

For early mass, Ilya was in worker's clothing, a copy of *L'Humanité*, the communist daily, folded under one arm. Khristo watched him move slowly down the aisle, kneel briefly, then enter the pew. They were virtually alone, the place was empty except for a few shawl-covered women in the front row and a priest who sped through the rite in mumbled Latin. The high ceilings held the church in soft gloom as the first sun touched the tops of the windows.

'You are very quick,' Ilya said, speaking in an undertone. He glanced at Khristo suspiciously. 'Twenty-four hours,' he mused. 'Have you considered a career in this business?'

'I want her back,' Khristo said, his voice tight with anger despite an attempt at neutrality. 'Do what you like with me, but let her go.'

'Who?'

'She calls herself Aleksandra.'

'I'm sorry,' Ilya said, 'I know nothing about this.'

'You lie,' Khristo said.

'No. Not true.'

'I may just cut your throat right here, Ilya. You're close enough to heaven for a speedy trip.'

'Khristo!'

'Blasphemy? You don't like it?'

'Stop it. I don't know what you're talking about.'

'To hell with you, then.' He stood, began to move down the pew toward the aisle.

'Khristo, wait, please,' Ilya called in a loud whisper.

He remained standing, but moved no farther.

'They are outside. All over the place. They'll cut you down.'

'In front of a church? In the street in broad daylight?'

'Yes, of course. Just like Myagin.'

'Good. You'll die first.'

'You think they care?'

Khristo sat down again and shook his head in disbelief. 'You feel no shame, Ilya. How do you do it?'

'Don't attack me, Khristo. I am trying to help you. Fold up your scales of justice and put them away and don't make judgments. I know nothing of this Aleksandra, but I promise to do whatever I'm able to do. There are so many of us, you see, each one under orders, and it is all compartmentalized, so one doesn't always know – '

'Enough! We're here to bargain . . .'

'We are not. There is no bargain.'

'Then what?'

'Give us Myagin's murderer, Khristo.'

'First the girl.'

Ilya gestured *no* and closed his eyes for a moment. 'Please,' he said gently.

'Omaraeff,' Khristo said.

'Who is he?'

'The headwaiter at Brasserie Heininger. A Bulgarian.'

'For God's sake, why?'

'I don't know. Patriotism, perhaps. There is a chance the British are involved.'

'And you? Are you involved?'

'Marginally, Ilya. I did a small favour, then I walked away from it.'

'You didn't like the plan?'

'No, Ilya, no. I had something. For the first time in my life, just living like a plain man. Working at a job. Coming home to a woman. Nothing I did mattered at all. It was a joy, Ilya. Incomprehensibly a joy.'

'I am sorry.'

'Can you get her out?'

'I don't know. You remember how it is – all blind passages. But I swear to you I will try. I have friends, I'm owed favours. But I must be discreet.'

'Can I walk out of here?'

'No. I must leave first. Then you will be left alone.'

.He thought about the signal, its simplicity. All Ilya had to do was let him go first, and he would be dead in a few seconds. 'God help you, Ilya,' he said.

'Let me help you first. If this Omaraeff is pressed, will he sing your name?'

'A certainty.'

'Very well. That I can fix.'

'I don't care.'

'So you say, but I want you alive. For the other . . .'

'You must,' Khristo said, pleading.

Ilya nodded, looked at Khristo for a moment, then stood. 'Good-bye, my friend,' he said and offered his hand.

Khristo did not take it.

Ilya shrugged, tucked *L'Humanité* beneath his arm, and walked up the aisle.

He saw them as he left the church – some of them. One in a car. Another reading a newspaper in the little park that surrounded the church. A tourist couple – at seven in the morning! – taking pictures of the Seine on the other side of the *quai*. His picture too, no doubt. As he turned north, a car pulled out of a parking space and trailed him. It was the battered Simca that had appeared one night in early spring as he walked home. He remembered the driver, drunk and grinning as he aimed the car up the middle of the street. They had, he realized, been with him for a long time.

How long? Had Vladi Z., his companion in the internment camp, been one of them? If so, they had been *running* him, an unknowing provocateur, since the day he left Spain. And he had fled from Madrid after a telephone call from none other than Ilya Goldman. Yet Yaschyeritsa's threats had been real enough. Or maybe not. Had they tried to panic him that far back?

A bullet-headed thug, with pale hair sheared to a bristle, swung out of a doorway and matched his pace. All sorts of specialists, Ilya had said, were now operating in Paris. The city would be crawling with them. He knew that NKVD search brigades, the sort of units that descended on suspicious activity in the villages, could be ten thousand strong. Not that they would try anything like that in

278

France, but they had people in abundance and they used them abundantly.

He wanted to go to the bookstore where he had met Aleksandra, and he wanted to go alone, so he lost the cars by taking the Métro for two stops. That left him with Bullet-head and a fat-faced man in the Moscow version of a business suit. They stayed with him as he wandered around the back of the Fifth – the university quarter – among students hurrying to early class at the various *facultés* of the Sorbonne scattered through the district. He entered one of the classroom buildings and moved through the corridors and up and down the staircases in a tight press of humanity. When he finally left the building, Fat-face was gone. Perhaps he had given the whole thing up, Khristo thought, humiliated by student derision at his colossal suit, and defected to the registrar. Khristo glanced behind him – not even deigning to use the standard shop-window-as-mirror – and saw that Bullet-head was sweating up a storm, the last man left. A passenger got out of a nearby taxi and Khristo waved it down. Then watched through the rear window as the NKVD man ran in frantic circles looking for another. He rode three blocks, paid the driver, and stood back in a doorway as Bullet-head sailed by in his own taxi, terrified, surely, that such an expense would not be approved by his bosses.

Later that morning, Khristo stood in the bookstore, browsing among the thick, uncut volumes on surrealism and Marx. On the far wall was a poster, in livid red and black, celebrating the Republican effort in the Spanish war. There were stark crosses above graves and a shadowed face of great determination and strength looking into the near distance. In fiery letters, lines from the poet John Cornford were spread across the paper. Cornford, a poet and Marxist from Cambridge, had died at twenty-one, a machine-gunner in one of the international brigades. 'Nothing is certain, nothing is safe,' the lines read. 'Everything dying keeps a hungry grip on life / Nothing is ever born without screaming and blood.' —

He watched the clerks in their blue smocks, moving about the store. How had Aleksandra fitted into this milieu? Her politics, he knew, were the politics of survival, her own survival. Larger questions were not germane — theories bored her; passions belonged in bed, not on the speaker's platform. Her absence stabbed him suddenly, and he said her name silently and dropped a book back onto a table.

'Captain Markov?'

At that name — his cover in Spain — he froze.

Turned slowly to the source of the voice and found Faye Berns. His first impression of her was long hair, washed and shining, and jade-coloured eyes, lit up with recognition, meeting his own. On second glance, he saw that her face was sallow and exhausted, that life had not been easy.

'Did I startle you?' she said.

'Yes,' he said, 'a little.'

She took his arm as they crossed the street to a café. The touch, at first, made him feel guilty, as though it desecrated his sorrow, as though it betrayed Aleksandra. But he could not deny its warmth, he could not deny how good it felt. They sat beneath a striped awning and drank cup after cup of coffee. She told him the story of her life those past few months, her eyes shining with unshed tears as she spoke.

Andres had died.

He had spent a long time dying, as doctor after doctor paraded through a rented apartment near the Parc Monceau that her father had paid for. Their plan, originally, had been to travel to Greece, where Andres had friends who would take them in. Perhaps they'd get married; at times they talked about it. Somehow, the tickets were never bought, there was always something else that had to be done. Renata Braun had left Paris in February, promising to write as soon as she was settled. They waited anxiously for a letter as the weeks went by, but it never arrived. Then Andres came down with a fever.

At first they ignored it. The Paris damp – one had to grow used to a new climate. But the fever was stubborn. Various doctors were consulted, medicines of all sorts were prescribed, but nothing seemed to work. Slowly, the sickness grew worse, until she had to stay up with him all through the night, sponging the sweat from his body, changing the wet sheets. At times he fell into a delirium, shouting and whining, often in languages unknown to her. He was in Anatolia, he thought, and pleaded with her to hide him from the Turkish soldiers – he heard them coming up the stairs. She would go to the door and look out, reassure him that they had just left. She said anything that came to mind, anything to calm him, because his terror broke her heart. She wept in the bathroom, washed her face, went back to the bed, and held his hands until dawn.

In times of clarity, he told her the truth about himself in great detail – where he had been, what he had done. His only regret, he said, was that the one thing in his life he had cared for, the Communist party, had turned on him. She argued with him about it – one could always care for humankind, could work for the oppressed. It had nothing to do with a printed card. But this line enraged him – she did not understand, he claimed – so she dropped it.

He became sly and strange. Would hide his medicine spoon among the covers so she couldn't find it and accuse her of telling the concierge his secrets. When she cleaned the apartment in the morning, he would not permit her to leave his sight. On his good days, he spoke of marriage. Passionately. They must have a child, he said, to continue his work. He begged her to bring a priest, a rabbi, whatever she wished. She told him it would be wiser to wait until he felt better and was his old self again. Her hesitancy angered him, and he accused her of infidelity.

281

Then, with the coming of spring, he seemed to grow stronger. She took him on outings to the Parc Monceau, where he would walk with a jacket over his shoulders and lecture her on a range of political matters. He read the newspapers avidly and explained to her the historical implications of every event. Now, instead of hostility and suspicion toward her, he began to plot revenge against certain individuals in the Comintern who he believed had betrayed him. He became obsessed with the Russian poet Ilya Ehrenburg, claimed he was under strict NKVD supervision, and planned to write an article for a Parisian quarterly – the *Nouvelle Revue Française* – exposing Ehrenburg for what he was.

But then, suddenly, on a day when he'd planned a visit to a museum, on a day when he'd made a telephone call, eaten an omelette, laughed at one of her jokes, he died. She returned from shopping and found him sitting on the couch with an open book in his hand.

The tears came when she finished the story, and she was hunting through her purse when a waiter appeared with a clean white handkerchief, handed to her silently. 'My God,' she said, 'I will miss this city.'

'I am sorry,' Khristo said, 'for Andres. And for you. For what happened. If my English was better . . .'

'Oh please,' she said, 'I understand. And I didn't mean to cry in front of you. It's just . . . When I was sixteen, I used to daydream about a lover dying, to make myself feel sad, I think. But then it happened. It actually happened.' She looked around for the waiter, in order to return the handkerchief, but he was busy at another table.

'I think he wants that you keep it,' Khristo said, searching for a word. 'It is his . . .'

'Gift?'

'Yes, a gift.'

She nodded that she understood and blew her nose. 'Tell me about yourself,' she said.

He shrugged. 'Some bad things, some good.'

'Andres explained to me about not telling people about yourself, how important that was, so I understand.'

'Yes,' he sighed. He wanted to tell her everything, resisted a desire to go on and on in riddles, telling but not telling, like Sascha. 'What for you now?' he asked instead.

'I am going home,' she said. 'To America.'

'Ah. For the best, no?'

'I don't know,' she said, uncertain. 'Maybe. But the tickets are all bought and there's no turning back now. I was in the bookstore looking for something to read on the boat – I really don't want to listen to a bunch of Americans gossiping about their adventures in wicked old Europe.' She made a face at the thought. 'Anyhow, I go up to Le Havre today on the train, I'm there overnight, board the *Normandie* tomorrow, seven days at sea, then it's New York.'

'What train do you take?'

'Five-twenty from the Gare du Nord.' She was silent for a moment, not happy at the prospect of travelling. For a moment it seemed like she might cry again, a shadow crossed her, then, instead, she managed a gloomy smile. 'How like Paris this is – to meet an old friend a few hours before going away forever.'

'Some day you will come back here.'

'Do you think so?' There was a real ache in her voice when she said it.

'I do,' he said.

'Funny, I don't even know your name. I don't suppose it's actually Captain Markov.'

'Khristo is my name. Then Stoianev – like your "Stephens".'

'Khristo,' she said.

'Yes. I have not heard it said for a long time. I use another name now.'

Her eyes suddenly lit up and she smiled to herself.

'Is funny?' he asked.

'No. It's just that my name isn't Faye Berns, not really.'

'Ah,' he said, 'you have a cover.'

'My name is Frances Bernstein,' she said. 'But that sounded too much like just another girl from Brooklyn, so I changed it to Faye Berns.'

He waggled a finger at her in mock reproof. 'Too much like true name,' he said. 'Very bad espionage.'

She fell silent in wonder at all that had happened to her, her eyes sought his and he realized suddenly that he was the last link to a life she'd lived in Madrid and Paris, that saying good-bye to him was saying good-bye to that. 'I don't think,' she said sadly, 'that I can ever tell anybody what happened to me here. I don't think they would believe it. And I know they wouldn't understand it. Most people pretend that exciting things happened to them – I'll have to pretend they didn't. That's what I should do, isn't it?'

He nodded in sympathy, it was a trap they shared. 'Better that way,' he said.

They ate lunch together. And he followed her around Paris for most of the afternoon while she worked her way through an extraordinary list of last-minute errands. He kept an eye out, from time to time, for surveillance, but none appeared, and they were going to places where he'd never been before.

When all the items on her list were crossed off he helped her load a large, battered trunk into a taxi, then into a compartment on the train. He went down to the platform when the conductor blew his whistle, and she leaned out the top of the open window. 'Can I write you a letter sometime?' she asked, her voice rising above the echoing noise of the vast, glass-domed station.

He thought for a moment. 'I don't know where you could send it,' he said.

'You may write to me, then. If you like.' She produced a fountain pen, shook it, and scratched a name and address on a scrap of paper.

He took it from her and put it in his pocket. The conductor sounded two short blasts on his whistle and swung himself on board. There was a loud hiss of decompression and a cloud of steam billowed onto the platform. Khristo reached up with both hands and she took them in her own. They remained like this for a moment, then the train lurched forward and they let go.

* * *

The twenty-fourth of June was the first warm summer night of 1937 – the sort of night when everything was possible, when any dream could come true. Dusk was hazy and soft, as always, but the usual evening chill never appeared. Everyone in the city came out of their apartments, music spilled from the open doors of cafés, and the strollers, excited by the gentle air, made animated conversation and filled the streets with a music of their own. The clouds were low and dense that night, shutting out the stars, and the city felt like a lovely private room where a party would soon begin.

When Khristo arrived at the brasserie, it was a madhouse. Papa Heininger, glasses askew, was glued to the telephone as reservations poured in. As he spoke, he made soothing gestures with his unoccupied hand, as though to placate the invisible caller. 'I am desolated, but I must tell you that His Excellency's usual table is simply not available at midnight. He may have it at one, or there is table fourteen – a quite estimable location in my opinion.' He nodded and soothed, nodded and soothed, as the caller spoke. 'Yes, I agree . . . Yes, *most* unusual . . . Just for tonight, of course . . . Please thank His Excellency for his understanding . . . Thank you, good-bye.' He hung up and patted his brow with a folded napkin. 'Djadja!' he called out to Omaraeff, standing over the reservation book with pencil at the ready, 'Count Iava will take number fourteen tonight. Move the Germans!' Omaraeff asked where, for they hadn't a spare inch of space in the entire establishment. Papa Heininger waved his napkin in the air. 'Must I do the thinking for the entire world? I don't care where you put them. You may seat them in the toilet for all I care. Tell them it is more efficient so.'

So the night progressed.

The florist arrived with sprays of Bourbon roses, fat, decadent-looking things in shades of maroon and lavender. The baker arrived with baskets of loaves. A party of Americans arrived too early, expecting to be fed. They were, despite some shouting in the kitchen, accommodated. The Beale party of six came up the marble staircase at 10:30 – early for them – but the magical night had excited them beyond fashion. Slowly, the sound level grew to a magnificent bedlam – the music of forks and plates, the ring of crystal glasses touched in toast, manic conversation, unbridled laughter, shouted greetings to friends at far tables. The huge mirrors glittered red and gold, the waiters ran to and fro with trays of *langoustines* and bottles of champagne.

And everyone was there.

Kiko Bettendorf, the racing driver. The Duchess of Trent, accompanied by Harry and Hazel, her deerhounds. Dr. Matthew O'Connor and his 'niece', Miss Robin Vote, charming and melancholy as always in her tuxedo and bow tie. The mysterious Mlle. M. – tonight with both her lovers. There was Voyschinkowsky – 'The Lion of the Bourse' – with a party of twelve. Fum, the beloved clown of the Circus Dujardin. Ginger Pudakis, Jimmy Grey, Mario Thoeni – the tenor, and Adelstein – the impresario – guests of Winnie and Dicky Beale. The Prince of Bahadur was accompanied by his Austrian nurse, who showed to advantage in a million dollars' worth of the Bahadur royal emeralds. There was Kreml, the ammunition king, squiring the immense Frau Kreml, her mother, her sister, her cousin, and that nice woman from the hotel who was teaching them bridge. Count Iava. The Baroness de Ropp. Miss Catherine Fetwick-Mill. Mr. Antonio Dzur.

286

Monsieur Escaldo, of Clichy.

His silent associate, Monsieur Sarda.

And their mentor, the handsomely attired Barbette.

Escaldo and Sarda, in their long gangster coats, fedoras pulled down on their foreheads, Thompson guns held at the hip, caused great stir with their arrival. First of all, they did not have a reservation. Simply swept past Papa Heininger, Mireille the hat-check girl, and Omaraeff the headwaiter without a word. When they entered the dining room, they provoked an instant burst of excitement. Was life not sufficiently *fantastique* on this magical night? No, apparently not. For here were real 'American' gangsters, a spicy addition to an evening that had already established itself as thrilling and glamorous. *Vive le grand Capone!* someone shouted, and glasses rang as other voices joined in the toast.

With a cinematic flourish, Escaldo and Sarda raised their weapons and pulled the triggers. Muzzle flashes danced and glittered at the ends of the barrels and the great room dissolved into splinters, a confusion of colour and motion, screams and raw panic.

Khristo was on the floor before he knew what was happening. A man in a cape jumped to his feet and sprinted for the exit, knocking him backward, first into a table of four, then onto the carpet. He heard the rounds buzzing over his head and burrowed down as the mirrors lining the walls dissolved in silvery showers of glass. These were *sub*machine guns – in effect, rapid-fire pistols using the same .45-calibre bullet as the American military sidearm – so, even though they were fired into the ceiling and upper walls, whatever they touched virtually exploded, and diners grovelling below the volleys were covered with plaster and mirror shards.

It was a miracle that nobody was actually killed. Count Iava, having secured table fourteen for the evening, found himself pinned to the carpet by its weight, and nearly choked to death on a mouthful of baby lamb. Kiko

Bettendorf, survivor of the Death Curve at Frelingheissen Raceway, would require fourteen stitches to repair the gash in his scalp. Frau Kreml, hiding beneath a table cloth and believing herself the object of a robbery, dislocated two fingers in a fruitless attempt to remove her rings. Ginger Pudakis stood up, a foolish thing to do, and had her forehead creased by a spent round that ricocheted from the ceiling. She then fell backward against a chair, blood trickling down her face. From where he lay, Khristo saw what happened next, though he was not able to think about it until later. Of all the people in the room, amid the shrieking and the gunfire, it was Winnie Beale who acted with courage. Seeing her friend hit, she leaped forward, from a position of relative safety on a banquette, and covered her friend's body with her own.

Barbette had disappeared, having elected to wander in search of Omaraeff, who had vanished from his usual position at the front of the room. Since he was the true object of this operation, Barbette was anxious to find him. He had not left the restaurant – Barbette had made sure of that. Nor was he in the Men's Room. He was, however, in the Ladies'. In the last stall where he'd gone to hide, his legs bare, a red waiter's jacket gathered around his ankles in imitation of a skirt.

Barbette stood at the entry to the stall, the door held open by his left hand, a 9mm device of no particular distinction held loosely at his side, and contemplated the seated Omaraeff, who was bent well forward, his face hidden in his hands. Barbette's mouth twisted in sorrowful irony.

'Oh Djadja,' he said, not unkindly, 'women do not take their skirts down to use the toilet, they pull them up. Is that possibly something you would not know? Yes? No? Or is it just the strain of the moment that's confused you? Yes? Tell me, my friend, you must say something.'

Omaraeff just shook his head, refused to uncover his face.

'Poor Djadja,' Barbette said. From where he stood, the top of Omaraeff's shaven skull offered a particularly tempting aspect and, without further discussion, he raised his hand and completed his mission. Omaraeff rocked back, then collapsed forward, still seated, his upturned hands resting motionless on the tile floor. It was a small facility, the ladies' W.C. at the Brasserie Heininger, with marble walls and ceiling, and Barbette's ears rang for hours thereafter.

* * *

Roddy Fitzware's favourite place in Paris was the centre window table at the Tour d'Argent. He loved the view of the Seine, best appreciated from the sixth-floor restaurant, well above the heads of the tourists. He loved the serious atmosphere – one came here to dine beautifully, period – which stimulated a deep, formal serenity in him, made him, he felt, his best self. Here he could do without the absurd eye makeup and stylish effeminacy that cloaked his persona in the café society in which, by direction, he'd taken up residence. He loved the *caneton*, and he loved the *turbot*. When it came time to spend some of His Majesty's Secret Impres't Funds, the Tour d'Argent was where he liked to go. One had to scribble the odd voucher, of course, so he couldn't just simply dine. He had to do His Majesty's business.

His Majesty's business arrived on the stroke of 1:15. Fabien Théaud, a stiff-necked young Frenchman, surely somebody's nephew, who moved in the upper circles of the DST – the French equivalent of MI5. In other words, a cop. But, Fitzware thought, a cop in a very good suit. He watched him march resolutely toward the table, chin raised, nostrils pinched, mouth slightly drawn down, as though the world disgusted him.

Fitzware stood, they shook hands formally, in the French manner – a single, firm pump – and Théaud seated himself with ceremony. To the left of the elaborate luncheon setting on Théaud's side of the table lay a brown paper parcel neatly tied with string. The Frenchman politely ignored the package. He had been treated to these lunches for more than a year and had learned to accept Fitzware's sense of theatre. Revelations were not to be made in the first act.

Once ritual courtesies were done with and after the service of the wine, Fitzware came to the point. 'Your people,' he said, 'must be in a frightful uproar this morning.'

'Oh?' Théaud seemed legitimately surprised.

'Last night's madness – the little war at Heininger.'

'Hardly a war. No one shot back and only the headwaiter was killed. In any case, nothing very interesting for us.' Théaud waved it away.

'Really?'

'*Les gangsters*. Some sort of stupid criminal nonsense. Perhaps an extortion, perhaps a war between butchers for the beef concession, one can only imagine the truth of it. The *préfecture* already has the two machine-gunners. Trash. Low-grade pimps from Clichy. As for the headwaiter, shot in the toilet, I think that was what the Americans call a *rub-out*.'

'Nothing much for you, then.'

'No. The police and the justice ministry will see to it.'

'Some prominent people injured, one reads.'

Théaud indulged himself in a mighty Gallic shrug accompanied by an explosive '*Pach!*' Then smiled grimly. 'The American socialite? The German racing driver? *These people*. They come to Paris to be decadent, by accident they come upon the real thing, and then they howl. Good stuff for the newspapers is all it is. As for Heininger's, I wouldn't try to go there for a week or two if I were you.'

'They will close down, then?'

'Close! Heavens no. You won't be able to get in the door.'

Fitzware smiled ruefully. 'In any case, your efficiency is admirable, to have the assassins so quickly.'

Théaud brightened visibly at being complimented for efficiency. 'Nothing to it, *mon vieux*. In the British phrase, 'information received'. The criminals were sold out almost immediately. They won't talk, of course – that would be to violate the code of the underworld. So what they'll get is a nice quick little trial and, if they don't give us the murderer of the headwaiter, the services of Dr. Guillotin. Truly, I don't believe they'll mind all that much. There is some honour to it in their society.'

'In some countries they would be considered merely accessories.'

'Perhaps. But this is France, and here they are murderers.'

For a time they turned their attention to the food and the wine, then Fitzware asked, 'May I ask the state of your progress in the matter of the Russian courier?'

'Ach, you'll ruin my lunch. A nest of snakes is what that is. Informants and counterinformants, power struggles in the émigré community, lies and wishful thinking and false confessions and rumours and every sort of unimaginable nonsense. I fear that one may be forever lost to us.'

'You have found it,' Fitzware said simply.

Théaud looked at him suspiciously. 'Yes? I cannot believe my luck would be that good.'

'But it is. Just to the left of your *plat de salade*.'

'This package?'

'Indeed. It is a Radom.'

'Oh. A Radom. And that is . . . ?'

'An automatic pistol of Polish manufacture, a very serviceable weapon, greatly prized east of the Oder. You'll find that it killed Myagin and, by accident, Ivan Donchev, the old man in the movie theatre.'

Théaud raised a hand and halted him right there. Called for the wine waiter and ordered the best Montrachet they could bring up. 'Thus,' he said dramatically, 'to those who serve France.'

Fitzware inclined his head in a seated bow. He was clearly enjoying himself. 'There's a bit more,' he said. 'The gun was obtained from a Turk, called Yasin, in the quarter out by Boulevard Raspail. The man who bought it is called Nikko Petrov, a Bulgarian, presently employed as a waiter at the Brasserie Heininger. There. Now I feel I have served France.'

Théaud's face collapsed. 'Oh no,' he said, 'you must not do this to me.'

Fitzware was stunned.

'You are telling me – if I were not deaf as a post and entirely unable to hear you – that some connection exists between the Myagin murder and last night's frolic at the brasserie. Tit for tat. A plot in the restaurant results in the murder of a Soviet diplomat, thus the NKVD returns the favour by shooting the headwaiter and causing general consternation in the brasserie. They would assume, of course, that Heininger would not survive such an incident, being insensitive, for the moment, to café society's appetite for scandal. If that is, indeed, what you are telling me, I do not hear it. You did not say it.'

'In God's name why?'

'*Politiques*. Four days ago, as I am sure you are aware, Camille Chautemps, a radical socialist, succeeded Léon Blum, a plain old un-radical socialist, as the premier of France. This is, therefore, no time to anger our most formidable ally, the USSR, by accusing them of upsetting a bunch of rich foreigners in a restaurant. Not with Chancellor Hitler sharpening his teeth on our doorstep, it isn't. My dear Fitzware, I think I am going to weep. With frustration. Right in front of God in the Tour d'Argent. You have solved our most pressing case and taken it away from us in the same breath.'

Fitzware bit the end of his thumb and thought for a time. 'Well, then, may I suggest you don't solve it? You may come part of the way, surely. Pick up this Petrov character, drop a curtain around him – matters of national security, trial *in camera* – and let it stand there. The Heininger connection need not come up, as long as you keep him well away from the newspapers. And, in the case of the brasserie, at least

292

you know what happened. That might mean something or other later on.'

Théaud drummed his fingers on the table. 'Perhaps. It becomes complicated, one has to find a way through, but it's possible. There are those in the Ministry of Justice who would unravel the whole *affaire*, and they will have to be deceived. But it would not be the first time, and we could at least clear the internal accounting. One might ask, however, what this Petrov is to you, that such a fine lunch is served on the occasion of his, ah, delivery.'

'Well, there one has to proceed by indirection – too much information will only confuse the issue. Let us say we are always anxious to be in your good books, and we know that he damaged one of our operations. For his own purposes, he traded one of our people to the Russians for someone he wanted back. Our operative had been of significant value, helping us to acquire information about the NKVD in Paris and elsewhere, a surprising amount of information. This Petrov found a way to ruin him, shall we say. You're not going to feed *him* to Dr. Guillotin, are you?'

'We might. If the Russians found out he was involved in the Myagin business we'd almost have to. But, on the other hand, execution always turns out to be a noisy business – the official sort of execution, at any rate. Still, if there's a way . . .'

Fitzware thought for a moment. 'Oh well, serve him right if you did.' The Montrachet arrived.

* * *

The cranes fly like summer nights,
   their shadows on the sun.

No, not quite.

The cranes fly like summer girls,
   here but an instant, then . . .

293

No. One saw girls in the sky. Ridiculous.

The cranes fly, like cranes.

No. Now his mind was tormenting itself.

The cranes fly like . . . How, in fact, *did* the fucking cranes fly? That was his problem. He'd never seen a crane or, if he had seen one, he didn't know it was a crane. *Someone* had surely seen the cranes flying, for the accursed image had worked its way into the Russian mythos and stuck there like a dagger.

He leaned back in the hard wooden chair and sighed, looking out through the wire at a flat field of weedy grass. Above the guard towers, the sky seemed to stretch to the end of the world. Sascha Vonets was not meant to be a poet, that's all one could say. It was just that his stubborn soul had, somehow, got into the habit of making soulful noises, and one had to do something or other about that, so his instinct had always been to chop up the thoughts so that they trickled down the page instead of marching, margin to margin, like a shock battalion.

He put the mutilated poem in a desk drawer and went back to his account ledger. The question was: what should the numbers say? This was harder, even, than cranes. One lived or died with this. So one had *better get it right*. Problem was, what did Brasovy want? To lie, the better part of the time, to tell Moscow what it wanted to hear just as he told Brasovy what he wanted to hear. Yet there had to be variation, otherwise the whole enterprise was simply too obvious, even for those straw-headed statues back in the Central Administration Office. Some days, one had to tell the truth so that, most days, one could tell the necessary lies. The analysis was correct, all right, but which day was today?

The production norms for the Utiny gold fields, in the Kolyma River region midway between the East Siberian Sea and the Sea of Okhotsk, were in no way possible to fulfil. In winter, the temperature fell to sixty degrees below zero and the wind blew like a demon's rage. The workers lived on translucent soup and a few ounces of gritty bread and died like flies. The work sucked their first strength out of them in a matter of weeks. After that, they began dying – not too fast, not too slow – and their ability to shift rock and sand declined rapidly. The previous spring they'd eaten a dead horse. The horse had been dead for a while, when they found it, and they ate the maggots as well. Others had received a barrel of axle grease for their wheelbarrows, and they'd eaten that down to the wood. Some ate Iceland moss, just to put something in their bellies. When they failed to meet the scheduled production norms, dictated by Moscow, they were stripped and watered down and left to freeze in the cold – though not quite to death. In summer they were tied naked to a pole so that the mosquito swarms could eat on them for hours. But what drove them crazy, they said, was the sound of it. The falsetto whirr in the ears.

He had learned, somehow, not to know of such things.

He had built a wall and lived behind it.

He had survived. It was his grandmother who'd kept him out of the execution cellars in the Lubianka. There went the jewellery, the candlesticks, the silver, everything she had put by to survive in bad times. They had sent him east – to the northeast corner of hell, to be precise – with a thirty-year sentence. But he was alive. And he had a debt to pay, a debt to *them*, and by God's grace he would stay alive long enough to pay it. To make them cry out in anguish, as they had made others cry out. To make them burn, as they had made others burn. To cut their hamstrings, as they had cut millions, and watch them come tumbling down.

The cruellest thing he had to admit to himself was that, in some strange way, he had never been happier. Suddenly, in this necropolis of ice and flatness and dead grey light, he had a reason to live, for the first time in his life. At last, there was something he wanted. He wanted to hurt them as they had hurt him. How simple and childlike life turned out to be once it was pared down to the basic elements.

And the funniest part of it – if anything could ever be funny again – was that they had been right!

There they were, killing left and right on pretext. On the phantom basis of a hostile glance, an indiscreet word, a beard drawn on a poster, anything, and, the greedy swine, leaving *him* alive. The one who had truly spied on them and, better yet, continued to do so. Drunken old crazy poet Sascha wandering about in a daze with his absurd heart dragging behind him on a chain, this posturing fool, this *poseur*, was digging up their buried secrets every chance he got.

First he had done it in Moscow, long before he'd gone to Spain, in Dzerzhinsky Square itself. Little nighttime trips to the files. What's old what's-his-face doing lately? This? Hmm. That? My, my. The other thing? Dear me. We'll just write that down, in a private little code of our own, and make it into a word, and remember that word.

And one could remember, once they were set into metre and rhyme, a thousand words.

When he had first arrived at the camp, they had assigned him the job of general labourer. He was supposed to shift seven cubic yards of gravel a day. Wet gravel. He spat on his hands and set to it; it meant survival, a man was capable of anything when pressed. He shovelled till his muscles rang, till his heart squeezed like a fist. Worked as the mucus ran from his nose and his breath rasped and whistled. The trustee came around just before they were marched back to the camp. Vonets, he wrote, 503775, two yards.

No!

Yes. Truth was, perhaps a little over three, but one's production had to be *shared*, with 'others' – he'd get used to it, they had a system. What was he worried about? At that rate, he wasn't going to last anyhow.

He had managed to become a trustee before death got him, but it had been a close thing. One by one, he'd worked his way through the camp NKVD, looking for the right one, the one in whom a spark of ambition still glowed. And, at last, found him. *I am*, he'd said, *a writer of reports*. The old trick had worked again, just as it had back in Moscow. He couldn't fly a damned crane to save his soul but when they needed drivel, and they *needed* drivel, he was their boy. Fair-haired.

Transportational facilities on the above date were diminished by the reduction of one unit necessitating a restructuring of production goals on said date.

Which meant the horse had died.

They made him a clerk.

That meant he lived in a room with four beds and a stove, that meant he worked in an office where they stoked logs into the stove as though tomorrow would never come, that meant he got a fishhead in his soup every night and twelve extra ounces of bread a day, which meant he could stay alive, and, in turn, *that* meant he could plunge the knife into their hearts and twist with all his might. In time.

It meant, most important, that he had something to trade, because the little diary he had kept for so long had to grow, had to stay current, or it would be worth nothing. In the Kolyma it was as though time had stopped. The wind moaned in the fir trees and the world was white. Blank. Yet, somewhere, life went on, operations continued, changed, assumed new shapes, involved new people. All the little details kept piling up and he had to have them, he fed on them, and they kept him on fire and alive.

So. He watched the new arrivals. The chekists were easy to spot, in their leather coats and boots and their smug, well-fed faces. They'd been interrogated, all right, but they'd put that nightmare behind them in the transit camps, on the cattle cars, and they came into the camp expecting to be treated, well, at least decently. They were, after all, party members.

Then it was the gravel. Or pulling a sledge piled with rocks by means of ropes around their shoulders, like beasts.

297

And that's when Sascha would come around. Could they, perhaps, use a bit of help? A friendly hand? They could? Well, he'd see what he could do. They should hang on, meanwhile, drive that shovel into the wet gravel, take the weight on their forearms, grunt with the effort of it a thousand times a day. He was working on it. The old man responsible for counting the shoes was fading fast, on his last legs – how would they feel about doing such a job? Not too demeaning, counting shoes? He watched their eyes warm with anticipation, their tongues hang out like dogs'. *Soon, soon,* he would tell them. Just get up at four tomorrow morning in the icy blackness and slurp up a few ounces of soup and have at it one more day.

And by the way, stop at my room sometime for a little chat.

He didn't really have to ask them. So grateful were they for even the chance to hope that they spewed it all out – if for no other reason than to make themselves of sufficient importance in his eyes to be allowed to count the shoes. *Oh yes, I was the one who got hold of Bakir, in Istanbul, the minister of armaments. Greedy bastard. Had his hand out all the time until I told him how things were. He's still ours, of that I'm sure. I'm the one who nailed him down.*

One more new memory word. Entered, in case his mind should fail him, in an account book nobody ever looked at. As the months went by, the facts piled up. *Well, Hitler really listens to his astrologer, you know, and I'm the one who went and found Borov, our own astrologer, who tells us every day what Hitler is being told.*

The collection grew and grew. It would make quite a thick book when he finally got around to writing it all out. Perhaps he would make it into a poem, he thought, a patriotic poem or, even better, a patriotic poem dedicated to the NKVD itself. There it was. With each word keyed to the names and places that should have remained forever secret.

But it wasn't time for that yet. He would content himself

298

with research until a certain opportunity presented itself. Then, when the moment came, he was going out. His NKVD encyclopedia would buy him out. And then, whoever got the lists – the names, the places, the money, the deeds – whichever intelligence service that turned out to be, they would be the sword. His sword.

And he would sit back and watch them cut.

* * *

On the twenty-third of July, at 3:25 in the morning, Khristo Stoianev was arrested by personnel of the Direction de la Surveillance du Territoire – the DST. The apprehension was smoothly accomplished. As he headed toward the Marais on foot, going home from work, he was stopped at the foot of the Pont de Sully. Two well-dressed men came from nowhere, flowed to either side of him and took him gently by the upper arms. He did not resist. At the other end of the bridge he could see two men leaning against either side of the parapet wall. Some distance away, up and down the Quai de la Tournelle, were two idling Citroëns. As he was led to a third automobile, one of the detectives informed him that he was under detention for violation of Subsections 104, 316, 317, and 318 of Article 9B of the Criminal Code of 1894, revised, Part XII.

He had no idea what all that meant. Later on, a ferret-eyed man who claimed to be his *avocat*, defence counsel, explained the charges as having to do with procurement of a weapon in aid and abetment of a felonious homicide. There were other accusations, which the *avocat* referred to as 'nieces and nephews'. Going to procure the weapon, paying for it, and failing to report the transaction to the provincial office of taxes and registrations.

The DST Citroën did not turn across the Seine toward the Palais de Justice but stayed on the Rive Gauche, headed, he speculated, for the École Militaire district. The detectives ignored him; they spoke quietly among themselves about the new rules regarding compensation received for working on holidays and Sundays. They were preceded and followed by other cars, and they drove cautiously along the empty boulevards.

Khristo used his last twenty minutes of freedom to watch the nighttime city slide past the car window. The air was warmish and still, and the summer heat made the aroma of the streets sharp-edged and uncomfortably sweet. It was the hour – appropriate for arrest, he thought – when the city cleaned itself. Large trucks hauled away the garbage, the market squares were hosed down, and old women scraped at the cobblestones with brooms made of twigs.

He said good-bye, in his mind, to Aleksandra. Since the night of the brasserie shooting he had telephoned the contact number for Ilya many times, but the call was never answered. It was not disconnected, it simply rang, in some empty place somewhere – he imagined an anonymous trading company – and there was no one present to pick up the receiver. But he was wrong about this, for he had tried the number (*just once more*) in early July and reached a busy signal. He knew, intuitively, what that meant. There was somebody by the phone, somebody under orders not to answer it. He imagined the Russian clerk, love-struck in Paris, chancing one little telephone call to a special friend. He had also gone back to the Matrimonials in the newspaper, phrasing the BF 825 signal in a number of ingenious ways, but the only response had been letters from lonely women who wanted to be married. He had also watched the newspapers for discoveries of the unidentifiable bodies of young women. There turned out to be a lot of those, poor souls dragged from the river. Times were hard, people got tired of their lives.

He was tired of his own. His stomach twisted in knots over what lay ahead of him in a French prison, but somehow he could not bring himself to feel 'trapped' or 'captured.' He was already in prison – a prison of borders, passports, false names, and de facto nonexistence – a citizen of nowhere. He remembered the train ride back to Moscow from Belov, the dark realization of a homeless, wandering future. So it had been written, so it had turned out to be. Cruel of the fates, he thought, to let me taste this place, to know it, and then to take it away.

They moved slowly past the grand buildings of the École Militaire and drew up to a gate with a bored *gardien* slouching against a sentry box. As they rolled to a stop, Khristo saw a green Morgan parked across the street, the driver's face obscured by shadow.

A chain was removed, the detective manoeuvred the car past concrete bollards and parked in a courtyard with shrubs and flowers around three sides. In the building above him, almost all the windows were dark. He got out of the car and asked if he could smoke a cigarette before going inside and they allowed him to do that, lighting up with him and smoking in silence.

When he could see the first edge of dawn, a fading darkness in the eastern sky, he put the cigarette out and took a last breath of free air before they led him across the gravel courtyard into the building.

* * *

In the fall of 1937, in Cell 28 of the 16th Division, at the Santé prison, Prisoner 16-28 received two letters.

The first was signed by his 'Aunt Iliane' – Ilya, clearly enough – who informed him that she was healthy, in general, though suffering the usual complaints of age. The farm was running well enough. Rain had split the tomatoes, but what could you do about the weather? They had been shorthanded throughout the grape harvest, since his cousin Alexandre had left. She had personally taken Alexandre to the station, Iliane reported, her health seemed fairly good – considering all she'd been through – and she was now travelling abroad. Of course, nothing had been mentioned to cousin Alexandre about his present circumstances – Aunt Iliane knew she would find that painful. As for him, she hoped he had seen the error of his ways, and she prayed daily that he would be spiritually reborn. Her arthritis made writing painful – he should not expect another letter anytime soon. She closed by imploring him to have courage. At first, she said, the family had been very angry with him. Now, when they saw what had become of him, while they did not exactly forgive him, they felt that justice had been served.

The second letter was from Faye Berns, in response to a letter he had sent her. She was heartsick that he was in prison – could anything be done? Could he receive money, or clothing, or books? He must write and tell her.

As for her, in some ways it was wonderful to be back in America. In others, not so wonderful. She felt dislocated, a little at sea. Her house looking out over Prospect Park seemed to have shrunk, her parents had gotten old. They had three Jewish refugees from Germany staying with them. A chemist from Berlin and his wife, who suffered from a nervous condition brought on by experiences with Nazi police officials. She paced the living room all night long, but what could anybody say to her? And an architect from Dresden who had been awarded the Iron Cross in the Great War. Even so, the Nazis had closed up his office. All the German Jews were in a very difficult situation – only the lucky and clever ones could leave the country now. A most curious thing had occurred when the three refugees docked at Ellis Island for immigration processing. A well-dressed man had appeared and offered to buy their clothing. All of it – even the underwear and socks. Not only had he paid them, he had given them excellent American clothing in exchange. After that experience, who could convince them that they were not in the promised land?

Her own news was that she was engaged to be married. His name was Leon, he was from Brooklyn, and he was finishing up law school at New York University. He was a very good and decent fellow who would take excellent care of her – really, he gave in to her a little too much. Her father more than approved of the match, since Leon

302

shared his political views and, well, a lawyer. Even the owner of Bernstein's, the second largest department store in Flatbush, thought the seas would part for him. On consideration, they probably would, Leon was just that kind of person. She had not yet told him of her 'other life.' Perhaps she wouldn't, she wasn't sure he would understand it. He was very anxious to have children, once his practice was established. Children? Well, that would be another adventure, certainly. She had seen a few of her friends from Pembroke, and most of them already had their first child.

She closed the letter by saying she hoped he would write again. Their day together had been very important to her. She thought of him often.

He read the letter many times and spent a long time considering his reply. Finally, he chose not to write back. What would be the point? In July, after three days in a detention cell, he had been taken to a small room and 'tried'. The judge had apparently come in from a country house and was wearing white shoes, as for a garden party, beneath his robes. Over a fifteen-minute period, several documents had been read aloud in rapid, legal French. Then the judge sentenced him to spend the rest of his natural life in Santé prison.

Prisoner 16-28 was, in the French custom, isolated in his cell. This was believed to encourage penitence, which was, after all, the intent of a penitentiary. Cell 28 was six feet long and four feet wide. A bed folded up against the wall in the daytime and there was a chair, chained to a ring in the wall. There was a toilet, and a water spigot for washing. The cell was painted brown halfway up the wall, then yellow to the ceiling. In the door was a Judas port that served two purposes: surveillance once an hour and food three times a day, almost always mashed lentils and black bread. Drinking water was poured into his 'quarter,' a tin cup that held a quarter of a litre, at mealtimes. Twice a week, for one hour, he was taken into a courtyard and allowed to walk the perimeter and converse with other prisoners. For the rest of his time he remained alone in his cell, allowed one book a week. These were usually boys' adventure stories with morally improving points of view or, sometimes, religious tracts. Behind a fine mesh grille was a window made of thick, opaque green glass that bathed the cell in a milky light yellowed by the colours on the walls.

In one corner of the window, however, was a hole about the size of a one-franc piece, with a fine web of fracture lines about it – something had been poked through the wire mesh by a former occupant. Khristo was thankful to the man, whoever he had been, because it meant he could see a tiny piece of the sky over Paris. At dawn, when the bell woke him up, it was the first thing his eyes sought and, again and again, in the course of the endless days, he spent hours staring at it. Sometimes it was a pale and washed-out blue, after a rainfall, perhaps. Other times it was a vivid blue, which meant cool, sunny weather. Sometimes it was grey. Sometimes, the best of all times, a part of a white cloud could be seen.

Plaque
Tournante

Brush your teeth with Deems
Your smile needs those gleams!

Robert Eidenbaugh leaned back in his swivel chair and promised himself for the hundredth time to oil the squeak. Bister, the poisonous little snake in the next cubicle – the *corner* cubicle, from which he could see both Lexington Avenue and East Forty-second Street – could hear him every time he sat back in the chair. He'd said so, one day at the water cooler: 'Heard you squeaking away this morning, Eidenbaugh. Leaning back again?' Clearly, he meant *leaning back* in both the physical and metaphorical senses of the expression.

Bister had done well at Princeton and wore a bow tie – just a little frivolous for the J. Walter Thompson advertising company – and definitely saw himself as a man on the way up. Following his remark, he'd shot a furry eyebrow and smiled coldly, confirming his own wit. Confirming his own progress in the world. *Bister* didn't lean back. *Bister* stayed hard at it all day long, pounded his typewriter, talked on the phone, went to meetings – he quite loved meetings – or thought up ways to apple-polish Mr. Drowne, the copy chief. *Bister* was on the way up.

He was not. After the snotty remark at the water cooler, he'd let the conical paper cup fill to the brim and, just about the time the great bubble broke the surface with its characteristic *blurp*, squeezed the sides violently so that a miniature waterspout leapt into the air, narrowly missing Bister's dazzling brogans on the way down. 'Sorry, Bister,' he'd said as the little man jumped backward, 'do you melt?'

But Bister was correct. He did sit back in the chair–*squeak* –and gaze out onto Lexington Avenue, eleven floors below. It was December, and it was snowing. Soon it would be Christmas, which meant that 1941 was almost over. Good! Next there'd be 1942. Hooray! During which time he would undoubtedly do exactly what he'd done in 1941, which was very damn little.

For the last year, the only thing that had truly engaged his attention was the war in Europe. The high point of his day had become the morning delivery – just after the milk – of the *New York Times*. Over coffee he would read of Polish lancers attacking German tank units. Of the rules of the German occupation: Poles forbidden to ride in taxis, carry briefcases, have their teeth filled with gold, use railroad waiting rooms, walk in parks, call from phone booths, enter athletic events, or wear felt hats. But it wasn't only the Germans, the newspaper told him. Forty Russian divisions had invaded Poland from the east, along a thousand-mile frontier. The Russian armour flew white flags, and the tank commanders yelled down from their turrets that they'd come to help the Poles fight the Germans. Thus they were unopposed.

When it came the turn of France to be subdued, he was enraged. He had spent his childhood in France and the thought of the jack-booted Nazis striding arrogantly down the streets of Toulon, where he'd played as a child, was nauseating to him.

Guilt pricked him and made him lean forward over the hateful Remington as the chair complained. *Brush your teeth with Deems / Says the girl of your dreams!* Not so bad. But then they'd need a *girl of your dreams* in the layout, and he knew that old Dr. Deems – a dentist from Rye, New York, before he became a tooth powder millionaire – wasn't having anything quite so daring in his advertising campaign. There would be a sparkling illustration of the tooth powder can – an example of which sat on his desk – in its brand-new blue and white colours. The art director had tried for a dream girl in one of his mock-ups, but Dr. Deems had labelled the notion 'prurient'.

Prurient!

Brush your teeth with Deems / It's prurient, it seems.

Pretty good, he'd have to share that with his friend Van Duyne when they met for breakfast on Sunday.

Squeak. He watched the snow wander aimlessly past the window. Tonight would be dinner with his fiancée, whom he didn't especially like, and her visiting parents, whom he absolutely detested. Her broad-bottomed 'Daddy', whom she 'utterly adored', was a shoe manufacturer from Dayton, Ohio, and a rabid isolationist. 'War in Europe?' he'd said at their last dinner, a two-hour nightmare at Longchamps. 'Don't bet on it, kiddo. Not for us.' He'd paused to attack his roast beef, then added, 'You know who wants *that*,' while tapping his nose and winking. Jews, he meant. The International Zionist Conspiracy to embroil the USA in a foreigners'war.

Maybe, he thought, *if I move very slowly.* He tried to get back to the typewriter without communicating his ennui to Bister, but no, it would have to be oiled. *Brush your teeth* – oh why in God's name had he slept with the girl? A hot August night at the Walker vacation house on a Michigan lake, the Walkers gone off to their bridge evening at the public library, alone in the house, a little necking, a little petting, a little more, the way her breathing changed, then the sudden, caution-to-the-winds disencumberment of her Helen Wills tennis costume, blousy and Grecian . . . and then the rest of it.

Followed by a year of assumptions on her part which he found, in his general malaise, difficult to resist. Of course they were engaged – thus the way was cleared for an encore of the summer lovemaking – of course the wedding would be in June. Suddenly, it seemed to have gone long past the point where he could say that they weren't quite right for each other. Long past. She would scream, she would weep, she would be so terribly *hurt*. That he'd *used* her. No, he couldn't face it. He would marry and have it over with. What was he waiting for? The Walker clan had money, he'd be rid of Bister. The sobering responsibilities of family life would brace him up, steady him down – one couldn't stay single forever. And his own family would surely approve.

He glanced at the calendar on the wall. December 5. Friday. Friday? Friday! Suddenly, his joy was crushed by an ominous shadow that filled the opaque green glass panel beside the open door to his cubicle. That could only be Mr. Drowne, who liked to loom up above his victims before he pounced.

'Say Bob?' He leaned his upper half around the door frame.

'Yes, Mr. Drowne?'

'Got that Deems copy all tied up?'

'Working on it, sir.'

'Read me what you have there.'

'Uh, I'm only, ah, *formulating* here.'

'Bob . . .'

'Brush your teeth with Deems, Your smile needs those gleams!' The affected perkiness in his voice sounded shrill and desperate.

Mr. Drowne shook his head mournfully. 'You're not selling smiles, Bob. You're supposed to be selling taste. Mint. Remember mint?' He reached over and picked up the open tooth powder can and rapped it twice on the desk. A little cloud of minted smoke puffed up through the holes.

'I'll keep after it, Mr. Drowne.'

'Plans for the weekend, Bob?'

'I'm going to the football game on Sunday. Giants versus Dodgers, at the Polo Grounds.'

'Yes, well, enjoy yourself, but do make certain that finished copy is on my desk when I come in Monday. Okay? If that means a little elbow grease on the weekend, well . . .'

'I'll get it done, sir.'

310

Mr. Drowne produced his usual departure sound – the sigh of the oft-betrayed man – then trudged off to his next victim.

Out the window, the snow drifted down onto the Christmas shoppers hurrying along Lexington, carrying green and red parcels. The shop windows had wreaths and little silver bells on granular snow. Above the glass panel in front of his desk, the face of Bister rose slowly, like a sea monster. 'Formulating, Bob?' His eyes glowed with spite.

Eidenbaugh grabbed for a weapon, and Bister disappeared instantly with what could only be described as a *chortle*. He looked down at his hand and saw that he'd picked up the desktop nameplate that had been a gift from his parents on the occasion of his graduation from Columbia University, seven years earlier. ROBERT F. EIDENBAUGH, it said. Fitting, he thought, very fitting. An intended symbol of his success in times to come, it now mocked him and his too-long tenure as a copywriter. Bister was right. He wasn't going up. He wasn't going anywhere.

His father had been a captain in the American Expeditionary Forces, arriving in France in 1917 and fighting in the battle of Château-Thierry. It had been a hellish experience, one he did not speak of easily. Yet he had fallen in love with France, and in 1921, when his oldest son was eight and the youngest three, he had taken the family off to live first in Paris, then in Lyons, finally settling, six months later, in a small rented villa on the outskirts of Toulon, the Mediterranean port just east of Marseilles. Arthur Eidenbaugh was a naval architect and was able to find a position – a minor one, initially, little more than a draughting clerk – with an engineering firm associated with the Toulon shipyards. Elva Eidenbaugh was formerly a schoolteacher from Wiscasset, Maine, and no stranger to hardship. She made the money stretch and set the tone of family life – which was to be a permanent adventure, with all setbacks perceived as challenges to character and sense of humour.

They were a tight, sunny family, denying each other consolation as a matter of course. A bad cold or a bad mood simply made life difficult for everybody, so best take your lumps and move ahead, sympathy was not on the schedule. As for France, they attacked it, led in the charge by Mrs. Eidenbaugh. They made forays into *boulangeries* and *pâtisseries*, picnicked at the slightest provocation, and descended en masse on museums, carrying away every crumb of available culture. Mr. Eidenbaugh worked long hours, deflected credit to his French colleagues, and was soon enough raised to a position commensurate with his ability and education.

As a family, they liked being different, enjoyed the notion of *living abroad*, and their cheerful optimism seemed to draw pleasant experiences their way. Robert could not remember a time when somebody or other – postman, merchant, parents' acquaintance – wasn't ruffling his hair. With his new position, Mr. Eidenbaugh was able to engage a maid to care for the children, and in this way they picked up the language naturally and effortlessly. At home, they spoke a curious mixture of French and English. 'Where can I have put *l'adresse?*' his mother would say. 'I've looked and looked, but it seems *toute á fait perdue.*'

Robert went to French schools, learned the rudiments of soccer, dressed in a uniform of blue shorts and white shirt, and allowed the requisite Catholic instruction to roll effortlessly off his Presbyterian soul. Family roots went back into Scotland, Wales, and Germany, on both sides, with the first Eidenbaughs reaching America in the mid-nineteenth century and settling on the coastlines of southern New England, where they engaged themselves in the building of ships.

In 1930, with the United States struggling in the Depression and Europe's economy falling apart, Mr. Eidenbaugh's firm won a large contract that called for the refitting of an entire naval battle group, a contract that was to support the firm throughout the early thirties. Thus, that same year, Robert was able to return to the United States to attend Columbia University, majoring in English literature with indifferent success. He was bright enough, but most of what he read seemed distant and remote and he had none of the scholar's passions. On graduation, in June of 1934, he returned to France for two years, working at a succession of small jobs, first around Toulon, later in Paris. He translated business correspondence, taught at small private schools, fell in love with wearying frequency, skated on the edge of Parisian bohemian life, and took to smoking a large, curved pipe.

In 1936, bored with aimlessness, he returned to New York and found a job with the J. Walter Thompson Company in the copy department. With war clearly on the way in Europe, the rest of the family returned in 1938, Arthur Eidenbaugh finding employment at a Boston firm of naval architects with long connection to French shipbuilding interests in Canada.

*　　*　　*

On Sunday morning, Eidenbaugh met Andy Van Duyne for breakfast at a Schrafft's on the Upper West Side. Surrounded by West End Avenue garment manufacturers taking their families out for brunch after temple, they set to work demolishing a basket of soft yellow rolls. The basket was periodically replenished by stern Irish waitresses in black uniforms, who also kept their coffee cups full as they awaited their scrambled eggs.

Andy Van Duyne was his single surviving friend from Columbia. His family owned a petrochemical brokerage associated with Standard Oil and had a season box for the Giants' football games. Clients never seemed to use them, so Van Duyne and his friends had got into the habit of making a day of it on fall Sundays, starting with a late breakfast.

313

Van Duyne looked like an owl, a tall, spindly one, squinting out at the world through round spectacles with thick lenses. At college, he'd been a reliable source for decent bootleg and the occasional real thing, smuggled in from Canada. His family's vacation house on Long Island had a particularly private and convenient beach, it seemed, and, in return for looking the other way, they would at times discover the odd case left behind on the sand – clearly an appreciative offering. Van Duyne had gained some considerable prominence as a college prankster, using a rhinoceros-foot wastepaper basket he'd got hold of somewhere to make tracks in the snow leading up to the Central Park reservoir. This resulted only in a rather tentative news story, never really setting off the *rhinoceros-in-the-drinking-water!* panic he'd imagined, though there were some who swore they could taste it for weeks thereafter. Van Duyne had barely scraped through college and was now ensconced in an oak-panelled office at Morgan Guaranty, where he'd taken to reading *Slade Rides to Laramie*, holding the book on his lap, just below the edge of a polished antique desk.

Robert Eidenbaugh and his friend shared a brotherhood of vocational anguish. Van Duyne had trust funds sufficient to fall into a sultan's leisure, but, as he put it, 'things aren't done that way in my family.' Nonetheless, his restlessness led him to leaving peculiar telephone messages (call Mr. Lyon at Schuyler 8-3938 – which of course turned out to be the Central Park Zoo) for his associates and, once, after a particularly arid day, distributing dry ice in the Morgan Guaranty urinals. He was becoming, he'd said, 'rather too trying at the bank'. But, until Robert met him on Sunday morning, he had evidently seen no way through the briar patch of the Family Obligations.

At Schrafft's, however, his ears were bright red and he could barely sit still, buttering rolls and slurping coffee like a Chaplin machine gone mad. Robert honoured his mood as long as he could, but at last curiosity forced him to pry.

The answer surprised him. Van Duyne was evasive, and offered only a partial explanation.

He was leaving Morgan, had been for weeks on the trail of something that – he could hardly believe it – had actually come from the family. They had taken pity on him at last and, when the proposition had been put, he'd leapt at the chance. 'I'm too young to dry up and blow away,' he said when the eggs arrived, 'and that's an old Van Duyne tradition, unfortunately. We have a tendency to *moulder*.'

Breakfast over, they walked through the stiff wind off the Hudson to Riverside Drive and there took a bus north toward the Polo Grounds. It was a bright, frigid day, December 7, and by the time they boarded the bus their eyes were teary from the cold. They got off at 145th Street and walked east toward Coogan's Bluff.

From the point of view of the Giant fans, it wasn't a very satisfying game. The packed crowds, wrapped up in overcoats and mufflers, their breaths visible in the winter air, groaned more than they cheered. Tuffy Leemans, the Giants' fullback on offence and half-back on defence, their most productive running back, was having a difficult day with the Dodger defensive line, and the fleet Ward Cuff seemed unable to hold the forward passes thrown him. Meanwhile, Ace Parker, the Dodger tailback and safety, was on target all through the first quarter, while Pug Manders was ripping through large holes in the Giant defensive scheme. Late in the first quarter, with the score tied 7–7, a little after 2:00 p.m., Manders took Parker's handoff on a spinner play and galloped twenty-nine yards to a Brooklyn first down at the Giant four-yard line. As the legion of Brooklyn fans made themselves heard, a static-punctuated announcement came from the loudspeaker system: 'Attention, please. Attention. Here is an urgent message. Will Colonel William J. Donovan call Operator Nineteen in Washington, D.C.'

315

The effect of the message on Van Duyne was extraordinary. He sat dead still in his seat, and for a moment Robert thought something was wrong with him. Then he scrabbled at the pocket of his fur-collared overcoat, produced a silver flask, and took an extended swig, passing the comfort on to Robert, who discovered himself with a mouthful of excellent Scotch whisky.

'Well, what is it?' Robert said. 'Have you bet the family bonds on the Giants?'

Van Duyne shook his head.

'Then what is it, Andy?'

'I'm not sure. Something important, I'll tell you that.'

'The announcement?'

'Yes.'

Pug Manders crashed over the Giant middle guard for a touchdown. The Dodger fans roared their approval.

'Now look here, Van Duyne, either tell me what's going on or sit back and watch the game. I feel like a character in a Phillips Oppenheim novel.'

Van Duyne swivelled toward him, oblivious to the crowd rising for the Dodger kickoff. 'Robert, I may be able to do something for you, especially if it's all gone mad in Europe – something to do with our being in the war, at last.'

'Ah-ha!' Robert said. 'You're going to Canada to get into the fighting.'

'No, it isn't that. But how would you feel about leaving Thompson, doing something completely different?'

Robert stared into his friend's eyes through the thick spectacles and saw that he was serious. 'No pranks?' he asked, always a little leery of Van Duyne's elaborate ruses.

'No pranks. On my honour.'

'You're serious.'

'Yes.'

'Then I'm your man.'

'It could be dangerous.'

'No more so than Mr. Drowne.'

316

'Not kidding, Bob.'

'Nor am I,' he said. 'Believe me, Andy, I'm ready for something – how did you put it? – "completely different".'

'I can,' Van Duyne said, 'pretty well promise you that.'

*   *   *

MEMORANDUM

April 19, 1942

TO: Lt. Col. H. V. Rossell
            Office of the Coordinator of Information
            Room 29
            National Institute of Health
            Washington, D.C.

FROM: Agatha Hamilton
            Office of Recruiting – COI
            270 Madison Ave.
            New York, New York

SUBJECT: Robert F. Eidenbaugh

In an interview arranged by my friend, Mr. Carter Delius, Vice President for Personnel, the J. Walter Thompson Company, on March 30, I spent over two hours with Mr. L. L. Drowne, copy chief, in my capacity as Member of the Board, the Manhattan Eye and Ear Hospital. I told Mr. Drowne that the hospital fund-raising committee was seeking a professional copywriter to aid in its fall campaign to build a new wing for the hospital. He mentioned several other candidates before the name of Mr. Eidenbaugh (hereafter RFE) was brought up. Mr. Drowne seems to like him well enough, though he does not believe that RFE will make much of a mark in advertising. Subject was described as 'completely honest' and 'extremely bright', but 'very much a self-starter'. My overall impression was that

RFE's heart isn't much in the Thompson company – they like him, but are not really sure what to do with him.

On April 3, as the parent of a prospective student, I visited the Brearley School and contrived to interview Mary Ellen Walker, RFE's fiancée, who teaches Fourth Form (10th grade) English and History and assists in the coaching of the field hockey team. I came on as quite the 'Bolshy heiress', though her sympathies clearly do not lie in this direction. She was very polite about it all, representing the school as 'more than fair to all sorts of girls, from all sorts of families'. Appearing to be charmed by her (I was not, in fact), I asked a few personal questions. Miss Walker perceives RFE as brilliant and dashing, though not yet situated in a position appropriate to his abilities. I would guess that, following marriage, she has plans to situate him in the family business.

An April 7 digest of reports (Attachment 'A') is enclosed, including credit reports from the following: Consolidated Edison, Chemical Bank and Trust, Sheffield Dairies, Joseph Silverman, D.D.S., and the 414 West 74th Street Management Company. Also appended (Attachment 'B'), RFE's Columbia University transcript and letters of recommendation. (See esp. Professor Horace Newell, Department of English, who praises RFE's intelligence and ability and mentions a tendency 'to stay somewhat in the background'.)

On April 14 RFE attended a party, given at my behest by Mrs. Cleveland Van Duyne, at her apartment at 1085 Park Avenue. I was accompanied by my friend, Mme. Maria de Vlaq, who reports that RFE's French is 'excellent', 'fluent' and 'almost native'. My personal impression of RFE was of a man with a certain charm that comes naturally to him. I flirted with him a little and found him courteous and responsive, though without any interest in pressing his 'advantage'. He is no snake in the grass. He does fade into the background, being slightly built and neither especially

318

handsome nor unattractive. He is the sort of man who will
be liked by all classes of people and who will not engender in
others feelings of spite or envy. He drank moderately at the
party, circulated well, and made no attempt to press himself
forward. I represented myself as the wife of a man who was
about to start a new advertising company and encouraged
him strongly to become interested in the possibilities for his
own career. He did, at last, agree to meet my 'husband' for
luncheon later in the week.

The New York office of the Federal Bureau of Investigation has, once again, been dragging its feet and is as
unresponsive in this project as it has been in all others.
No report from that office to date on RFE, but same will
be forwarded once it arrives – if it ever does. Can't Col.
Donovan do something about this?

On April 17 I telephoned RFE at his office in the guise
of Mr. Hamilton's secretary and arranged a lunch for the
following Monday, April 20, at Luchow's. According to
the headwaiter, he asked for 'Mr. Hamilton's table' and
waited twenty minutes before asking the headwaiter 'if
Mr. Hamilton had called'. (He had been given no 'Hamilton'
telephone number.) He was told that Mr. Hamilton had
telephoned the restaurant, apologizing for the inconven-
ience and requesting that RFE meet him for lunch at the
Coleman Hotel on East 23rd Street and Fifth Avenue. On
arriving at that location and discovering no such hotel,
he consulted a telephone directory and proceeded to
Coleman's, a restaurant on East 25th Street, where he
asked for 'Mr. Hamilton'. Informed that no such person
was there, he made a telephone call (in all probability to
his office, since 'Hamilton's secretary' had reached him
there earlier), then ate lunch at the counter and left the
restaurant, returning to work.

My recommendation is to accept this candidate for further
COI screening.

Signed: Agatha Hamilton
        COI — New York   April 24, 1942

P.S. Hub, my friend Maria de Vlaq is someone you might consider taking to lunch when you are next in New York. She is formerly the Countess Marensohn — Swedish nobility — divorced two years ago, and moves easily in society. She rides and shoots excellently, is lethally charming and of a rather daring disposition. She is of Belgian citizenship and descent, and I believe would be amenable to recruitment. Her connection to Belgian, German, and Swedish circles remains strong, and her relationship with her former husband, and his family, is cordial.

P.S.S. Not to end on a sour note, but here it is April and there is only silence from Washington on my February vouchers. While it is the case that fortune has smiled on me in this world, I cannot by myself assume the cost of the war effort.

*   *   *

In Washington, D.C., Lieutenant Colonel H. V. Rossell leaned his elbows on the scarred wooden desk and stared at the man seated on the other side. Eidenbaugh, Robert F. His fourteenth interview of the day. He knew that if he were charming and likable the candidate would be put at ease, and the consequent forthrightness would help in making a proper decision. But he simply hadn't the strength for charm. He'd been working twenty-hour days since Pearl Harbor, and his initial burst of high-tension energy was long since dissipated. He was out of gas. What he really wanted to do was push his lips into an extended pout and make ishkabibble sounds by flapping them with his fingertips. That would prove *everybody* right.

Since Colonel Donovan had persuaded Roosevelt that America needed an intelligence service, life had come to resemble a lunatic asylum. Rossell had some considerable experience in this work, a career in army intelligence going back ten years. As early as 1937 – when war had seemed inevitable to him – he'd run small preparatory operations when his superiors would allow it, stockpiling European clothing, for instance, by purchasing it from incoming refugees, then storing it in a warehouse under squares of cardboard marked DO NOT CLEAN! Because of his foresight, agents going into Europe would, at least, not be dressed by Brooks Brothers.

But if he knew his way around the profession, few others did. Above him were Donovan and a bunch of Ivy League lawyers, bankers, and Wall Street types. They would, he knew, work out well over time. Once these people got going, the Axis powers would be subject to ferocious trickery of every kind, the sorts of things lawyers and bankers might do if they were able to give in to their cruellest fantasies. Now they were being encouraged to do that very thing. Just that morning, a memo had crossed his desk recommending that a million bats be put aboard a submarine, then released off the Japanese coast in daylight, each one equipped with timer and minute incendiary bomb. They would fly into the dark spaces of a million Japanese homes and factories and, he supposed, blow up, spattering everyone in the neighbourhood with exploded bat. He could just hear one of his superiors giving him the good word: 'Oh, Rossell. Be a good fellow and get me a million bats, will you? By lunch? Thanks loads!'

But that wasn't the worst of it. Donovan – with Hoover and the FBI fighting him every step of the way – was in the process of acquiring an extraordinary zoo of people. 'The successful intelligence service,' someone had said, 'is one which can best turn eccentricity to its own advantage.' Well, they'd have *that*, all right. They'd hired Marxists, led by the philosopher Herbert Marcuse. Playwrights – Robert E. Sherwood and others. Academicians, recruited by Archibald MacLeish. John Ford, the film director. A young actor named Sterling Hayden who would, he thought, eventually be sent to fight with Yugoslav partisans. Then there was John Ringling North, of the circus family, and a large, vivacious woman named Julia Child. There was Virginia Hall, about to be parachuted into occupied France with her artificial leg held under one arm lest it break when she landed. The pile of file folders on his desk climbed toward the sky. Tom Braden, Stewart Alsop, Arthur Schlesinger, Jr., Walt Rostow, Arthur Goldberg. Ilya Tolstoy and Prince Serge Obolensky, the hotel baron married to an Astor. He had them from Standard Oil and Paramount Pictures, he had Mellons and Vanderbilts, Morgans and du Ponts. Union organizers and tailors. He had everything. And more coming in every day.

Meanwhile, they had just been renamed. COI, the Office of the Coordinator of Information, was now to be called the Office of Strategic Services – OSS. Which local wags lately referred to as Oh So Silly, Oh So Secret, and Organization Shush-Shush. Even Joseph Goebbels, Hitler's propaganda minister, had got in on the fun. Knowing that the OSS offices were next to the experimental labs at the National Institute of Health, he had stated in a recent radio broadcast that the organization was composed of 'fifty professors, twenty monkeys, ten goats, twelve guinea pigs – and a staff of Jewish scribblers!' *Hey, Dr. Goebbels*, Rossell thought, *you left out the bats*.

Slowly, his mind returned to business and he realized that the poor soul across from him probably thought he was being tested in a cold-eyed staredown, not a daydreaming contest. Rossell was in his late forties, with grey hair cut in a military brush, big shoulders and thick arms. His tie was pulled down, jacket off and shirtsleeves rolled up in useless defiance of a steam radiator that would grow orchids if they let it. And here it was May. Couldn't somebody get them to turn the goddamn thing off?

'Well,' he finally said to the man across from him, 'say something.' If you couldn't manage charm, discomfort would serve.

322

Eidenbaugh stared at him for a long moment, then, from a face composed in utter seriousness, came a singsong 'M-i-s, s-i-s, s-i-p-p-i.'

'Oh yeah?' Rossell said. 'Is that supposed to get you a job here?'

'No sir,' Eidenbaugh answered, 'that's supposed to help you spell Mississippi.'

To Rossell, the laugh felt better than a week of sleep and seemed to serve the same purpose. He launched himself – *once again, into the breach!* – into the usual interview format. This Eidenbaugh wasn't so bad. He wasn't much to look at, but he had a nimble mind. Would he do the job? Difficult to guess until the situation presented itself. But he found himself enjoying the man, and that weighed heavily in his favour. One of those slippery qualities, hard to quantify, that could really count in the world he was about to enter.

Then there was luck.

It just so happened that while the two of them chattered away, a fly settled on the edge of Rossell's desk. Slowly, he picked up a file folder – it happened to be that of Merian C. Cooper, producer of the film *King Kong* – and swatted it dead.

'See that?' he asked.

'Yes sir.'

'That, son, is technical intelligence at work.

'I always get 'em,' he continued, 'because I know that flies take off backward. So you swat in back of them, see?'

'Yes sir. Will I be allowed to swat Hitler, sir?'

Rossell rubbed his eyes for a moment. *Christ*, he was tired, and he looked like hell. But he didn't feel so bad. He really liked to do the fly trick – it put him in a good mood. 'I think so, son,' he said. 'We just may allow you that privilege.'

*　　*　　*

323

In Paris, in the early hours of June 11, 1940, Khristo Stoianev lay awake in his cell in the Santé prison and planned his 'escape'. Staring at the opaque window with the tiny hole in its upper corner, he smoked up a week's tobacco ration and watched the short, summer darkness fade into early light. In two days' time it would be thirty-six months that he had spent in captivity. He could bear no more.

His had been, he knew, a classic descent. He had braced his mind early on, willed himself to meet imprisonment as he had met other events in his life. 'A man can survive anything.' He did not know where he'd heard it but he believed it, believed in it, a religion of endurance. Thus he had taken his formless days and nights and imposed on them a rigid system of obligations. *Exercise* – physical strength can forestall psychological collapse, a universal and timeless prisoner's axiom. *Use the mind*. He created a private algebra of propositions and wrestled with their solutions, mining his past life for usable circumstance: *How long would it take for a man carrying his own food and water to walk in a straight line from Vidin to Sofia?* From mental images of maps he contrived a route, crossing roads, streams and mountains, estimated the weight of water and food, determined the point of efficiency that lay somewhere between thirst and starvation and exertion of strength: the goal of the exercise was to arrive at the outskirts of Sofia carrying no provisions, crawling the final hundred feet.

Keep a diary. They would give him no paper, so he used the surfaces of opened-up matchboxes he bought from the prison store with his meagre stipend, and kept records in pin-scratched hieroglyphs – a plus or minus sign, for instance, indicated success or failure in the two-hour mental exercise period for that day. *Control is everything*. He permitted himself only one hour a day for daydreaming, which was always erotic, violently coloured, tones and textures scrupulously perfected by his imagination. *Retain any connection at all with the world*. Every moment of his time in the exercise yard he spent talking with other prisoners. Dédé the pimp from Montparnasse. Kreuse the wife-murderer from Strasbourg. He did not care who they were or what they said – to connect, that was what mattered. *Read*. Religious tract or boys' adventure, he sucked them dry of whatever particle of entertainment they could provide. *Regret will kill you*. A concept he embraced to a point where any thought that presented itself for contemplation had to be inspected for traces of hidden anger or sorrow before he would allow his mind to pursue it.

For the first year, as 1937 faded into 1938, the regime worked. He did not think of the future, he did not think of freedom, and achieved a level of self-discipline he had never imagined possible. But time – hours that became days that became months – was a killer of extraordinary stealth, and his spirit slowly failed him. He began to die. He watched it with slow horror, as a man will observe an illness that consumes his life. He would come to himself suddenly and realize that his mind had been on a journey into a violent universe of shimmering colours and bizarre shapes. He understood what was happening to him, but his understanding counted for nothing. Without the daily texture of existence to occupy it, he learned, the human soul wavers, wanders, begins to feed upon itself, and, in time, disintegrates. He saw them in the exercise yard, the clear-eyed, the ones who had died inside themselves. Thus, at last, he came upon the prisoner's timeless and universal conclusion: *there is nothing worse than prison*.

From the gossip in the exercise yard, he knew that Wehrmacht columns were approaching Paris and that the country would fall in a matter of days. In shame, he prayed for this to happen. Bulgaria had joined Germany, Italy, Hungary and Romania in an alliance against Western Europe. He was, no matter the Stateless Person designation of the Nansen Commission, a Bulgarian national, thus nominally an ally of the Germans. When they took Paris, he would send them a message and offer his services. Initially, he would make his approach as Petrov, the former waiter, imprisoned for striking a blow against the Bolshevists. They would approve of that, he knew, despite their treaty of convenience with Stalin, and would more than likely accept him on that basis. If, perchance, they knew who he really was, he would brazen it out. Yes, he had fought them in Spain. But witness, Herr Oberst, this change of heart. Witness this attack on the NKVD itself – could they doubt his sincerity after that? He marvelled at how the past could be refigured to suit the present, at how fragile reality truly was when you started to twist it.

Once he was out of prison, he would return to Spain, a neutral country, by deceit – a notional mission, perhaps, that he would lead them into assigning him – or by underground means: the mountains or the sea. He thought of the little towns hidden back in the hills, with too many young women who could not find a husband after the slaughter of the civil war. They would not look too closely at him, he was sure, if he worked hard. That was how they measured people down there and to that – if the blessed day ever came – he was more than equal.

But, on the night of June 12, everything changed.

At dusk, the mashed lentils and the gritty bread were shoved through the Judas port and his 'quarter' filled up with drinking water. Between the mound of lentils and the tin plate lay a slip of paper.

In roman letters it said BF 825. Then the numerals 2:30.

The shock of it nearly knocked him to the floor.

For the intervening hours he dared not sit down, pacing the small cell and hurling his body about as he pivoted at the far wall. Then the door whispered open to reveal a man in black who stood in the shadowed corridor and waited to enter. Two words, spoken quietly, came from the darkness: 'Khristo Stoianev?'

'Yes,' he answered.

The man stepped forward. He was a priest. Not the prison

326

chaplain, a fat Gascon with a wine-reddened face, but a thin, ageless man with paperlike skin whose hands hung motionless at his sides.

'Is there anything here you will want?'

He grabbed his matches, a few shreds of tobacco folded in paper, his two letters and the matchbook diaries. He had nothing else.

'Let us go,' the priest said.

Together they walked through the darkened corridors, past the night sounds of imprisoned men. There were no guards to be seen. All the doors that would have normally blocked their path were ajar. In the reception area, a long wooden drawer sat at the centre of a rough table. He found his old clothing and all the things that had been in his pockets on the day of his arrest. Also, a thick packet of ten-franc notes.

The priest took him to the front entry of the prison, then pushed at the grilled door set into one of the tall gates. The iron hinges grated briefly as it swung wide. For a moment, the city beyond the prison overwhelmed him with the sounds and smells of ordinary life and, for that instant freedom itself was palpable, as though he could touch it and see it and capture it in his hands. Then his eyes filled with tears and he saw the world in a blur.

'*Blagodarya ti, Otche.*' He needed, in that moment, to speak the words in his own language. Then added, in French, 'It means "thank-you, Father".'

The priest closed his eyes and nodded, as though to himself.

'Go with God,' he said, as Khristo walked through the door.

* * *

In the autumn of 1943, on a cold October night with a quarter moon, Lieutenant Robert F. Eidenbaugh parachuted into the Vosges mountains of southeastern France.

He landed in a field north of Épinal, breaking the big toe

327

of his left foot – by doubling it over against the ground when
he landed with his foot in the wrong position – and splitting
the skin of his left index finger from tip to palm – he had
no idea how. Limping, he chased down the wind-blown
chute, wrestled free of the harness straps, and paused to
listen to the fading drone of the Lancaster that circled the
field, then turned west toward the OSS airbase at Croydon.
From a sheath strapped to his ankle he took a broad-bladed
knife and began digging at the ground in order to bury the
chute. Fifteen minutes later, sweat cooling in the mountain
chill, he was still hard at it. This was not the same turf
he had encountered in practice burials at the old CCC –
Civilian Conservation Corps – camp in Triangle, Virginia,
a few miles east of Manassas, where he had trained. This
grass was tough and rooty and anchored well below the
surface of the ground. At last he abandoned the knife and
began ripping up large sods with his hands – holding his
split index finger away from the work – until he'd exposed
a jagged oval of dark soil. Next he gathered up the silk and
shrouds of the parachute, forced the bulk into a shallow
depression, and covered it with a thin layer of dirt. He laid
the sods back over the dirt and stamped them into place,
then walked away a few feet to see what it looked like. It
looked like someone had just buried a parachute.

Typically, there would have been a reception committee
on the ground and their leader would have bestowed the
chute – the silk was immensely valuable – on one of his
men, a spoil of war bestowed for bravery in a tradition as
old as the world. But this was a 'cold' drop. There were
no *maquisards* triangulating the drop zone with bonfires,
there was no container of Sten guns and ammunition
dropped along with him – to be carried away by men and
women on bicycles – and he had no radio. The mission,
code-named KIT FOX, called for him to contact a loosely
organized group of French resistance fighters in the village
of Cambras, direct their sabotage efforts, turn them into a
true *réseau* – headquarters – for underground operations,

and extend, if possible, a *courrier* – secret mail system – throughout that part of the Vosges. His contact for supply was code-named ULYSSE (after the Homeric hero Ulysses), a senior officer of the *résistance* and his one resource on the ground, based in the small city of Belfort, not far from Switzerland. His only direct line of communication with OSS was to be coded *messages personnels* from the foreign service of the BBC.

His true mission was, in fact, unknown to him.

He was not alone in the area. There were several British communication and sabotage nets nearby, but he had been briefed – twice, first at OSS headquarters in London, then at the MI6 centre in Battersea, located at what had once been the Royal Victoria Patriotic Asylum for the Orphan Daughters of Soldiers and Sailors Killed in the Crimean War – to stay well away from them. Both American and British briefers had been emphatic on that point.

Which left Robert Eidenbaugh alone in a French field with a broken toe and a split finger. His hands were blackened with dried blood and French earth, and he was hobbling badly. A toe was almost a silly thing to hurt, but the pain made him grind his teeth on every step. He thought to bind up the finger with his handkerchief but decided against it. He disliked the idea of a white cloth flashing in the darkness as he moved about. He set off for Cambras – eight miles along a series of mountain ridges – on the narrow road a mile from the drop zone. His index finger throbbed and continued to ooze blood. How the hell had he done that? He leaned on a maple tree whose dry leaves rattled in the night breeze and took off his right shoe, then bound his sock around the finger, cutting off a piece of shoelace to secure the binding. He had, he realized with some horror, nearly removed his left shoe, which would have been an error because his toe had swollen so badly that he would never have been able to get the shoe back on. Limping, he held his zip-up briefcase under his right arm and moved through the darkness toward Cambras.

His hat, suit, tie, shirt, socks and underwear were all well worn, and all of French manufacture. The suit had been altered by a French tailor at the OSS clothing depot on Brook Street in London. His toilet articles were also French, and the pistol in his briefcase was Belgian – a Fabrique Nationale GP35 automatic, essentially a licensed 9mm Browning with a thirteen-round magazine. He had been warned never to carry it in public during daylight hours. His cover name was Lucien Bruer, accented on the final syllable in the French manner, and he was supposedly the sales representative of a Belgian company selling agricultural implements and fertilizers. He had been born on the French island of Martinique, raised in Toulon, a bachelor. His documents were quite good, he'd been told, for examination by French police or German street patrols. Should he fall into the hands of an intelligence section – Gestapo or SD – however, that would be that. *We've learned,* they'd told him, *that the sooner you run after capture, the better your chances of a successful escape.*

He did not intend to be captured. He did not intend to mingle with Germans. He did not intend to be 'brave' – had in fact been specifically cautioned against it. He would move cautiously in daylight, at most another French face in a French countryside, and play the game at night. A few wild souls back in Virginia had been eager to crawl about and slit throats. Their time would come, but for the moment they either trained their days away or disappeared back into regular service units.

For most of the night he walked alone on the road – barely two lanes wide, with no centre line – built of whitish pebbled aggregate with ragged edges bordered by tall weeds. In some places it was frost-rippled from the previous winter; in others, the lush roadside growth had cracked the paving. He saw the brief silhouette of a hunting owl. Something whispered away from his shoe through the tall grass. Then, as the moon waned, he heard a distant engine and hobbled quickly to cover. He listened intently to the two-stroke sputter of the engine and decided it was a motorcycle. He was correct. Watched the German dispatch rider go by, sighting on him with a sockbound index finger and silently mouthing *bam* just at the proper moment, then heard the sound fade into the distance in a symphony of gear changes. No need to shift that much, he thought. The German, alone on the road, was playing with his machine, lying low over the handlebars like a racing driver. But he too, leading the rider for a single perfect shot, had been playing. That would change.

What caught his attention, however, in the reality of that first, nebulous contact with the enemy, was the intimacy of it. The meaning of his job now came to him in bold letters for the first time – what he was really going to do and how it would feel to do it. Professional soldiering he respected – where would the Allies be without a corps of trained officers? – but he could never be more than an impostor in that world, his personality was not made for uniforms. He had, in civilian life, competed in a world of commonplace weapons: typewriters, telephones, perceptions, insights. In that world he had neither won nor lost, but now the battle was rejoined, with the prize for winning or the cost of losing vastly increased.

The British, believing their social system and its exigencies prepared them for clandestine life, had their doubts about the ability of the American personality to adapt to a world where nothing was quite what it seemed. Were these blunt and forthright people capable of subtlety, deception, the artful ruse? Some thought not. But they had not lived and trained with Robert Eidenbaugh and his colleagues. They did not entirely understand that the dark side of the American personality was the adventurer's side and that a time of war was the perfect climate for its flowering.

Maquis meant 'brush', and that was pretty much the story at Cambras. In first light he'd found the chipped stone mile marker on the inner curve of the road, heard, a few

331

minutes later, the sound of a woodcutter at work in the forest – recognition signal number one – then saw a pile of cow dung, confirming the first signal, by a dirt path that wound up the mountainside to the village.

Cambras, backlit by a cold mountain sky, was a mud square surrounded by a handful of stone cottages with tightly shuttered windows and a rust-stained fountain with a tattered hen standing motionless atop the spigot, its feathers ruffled by the breeze. There were several small, brownish dogs, who glared at him unpleasantly from a safe distance, but no people. The village smelled like damp earth and pig manure. Eidenbaugh suddenly recalled a family outing to the mountains of the Var region, north of Toulon, where at lunchtime they had encountered just such a village. He could still see the look on his mother's face as she'd said, 'Not here, Arthur.'

The Cambras *maquis* trickled from the doors of the cottages and formed up, more or less, in the square. There was a period of awkward silence, then they began to introduce themselves. There were the Vau brothers, both tall and hulking with spiky blond hair, clearly the village bullies and, he thought, a little slow. Henri Veul, called Sablé – Sandy – watchful and silent, a shotgun slung, barrel down, diagonally across his back. La Brebis – the ewe – in fact Marie Bonet, a stocky, young woman whose broad forehead and tiny eyes suggested the face of a sheep. And Vigie, which meant 'lookout man', the youngest, perhaps sixteen. The Vau brothers, he thought, were no more than nineteen.

'Lucien?' It was Alceste Vau, the senior brother, who spoke.

'*Oui*,' he said.

He hadn't any idea what they'd expected, but he slowly began to understand that they found him all too mortal. They were disappointed. They had probably anticipated a ten-foot-tall Texan bristling with machine guns and breathing fire. *Well*, he thought, *too bad*. They had instead a rather lean, plain young man, formerly an advertising copywriter, with a sock wound around a bloody finger and a bare right ankle. *Probably*, he thought, *we deserve each other*.

They took him into one of the houses and announced him as Lucien. Breakfast was cabbage fried with fat bacon and hunks of heavy bread washed down with cups of chicory. An older man, Gilbert, and his youngish wife served *l'Américain* and the Cambras *maquis*. After the meal, a grandmother appeared, five feet tall and swathed in black, and examined his finger, sucked her teeth in sympathy, and applied a healing paste of pounded lizards.

Finger rebound with strips of grey cloth, he headed outside to use the stone lean-to in the backyard. As he left, his host mumbled something about the American's learning to *faire le cent-onze* – to make one hundred eleven. He knew the expression, which referred to the marks of three fingers down a wall. But they laughed in vain. The parting gift of his commanding officer had been twenty squares of French newspaper, wedged in his pocket at the moment of their final handshake.

It was a war of mischief.

That became apparent in the week that followed his arrival. Gilbert, in whose house he lived, said one evening that the people of Cambras had 'always hated those bastards down there'. It was the contempt of mountain people for flatlanders, and it would not have been unusual to find such sentiments in parts of Tennessee or Kentucky, similarly expressed. *Down there* meant Épinal, St.-Dié, and the small towns between. *Down there* meant tax collectors and municipal authorities and Gendarmerie and all those blood-sucking leeches who made a poor man's life a misery. Between Cambras and *down there* was a kind of truce, worked out over a long time, the flatlanders silently agreeing to bother the people of Cambras only a little, and the mountain people accepting just about that much botherment. They lived with each other – just.

When, however, you added a heavy-handed Teutonic authority to this chemistry, a certain amount of hell was bound to break loose. The people of Cambras now took it as a divine mission to bother the *schleuhs*, as they called them, while avoiding too much interest from those they called *la geste*. The Gestapo. The French version of the name carried with it a certain amount of irony – bold deed – but it was quite clear to everyone that these Gestapo people were better left alone. They had made that evident early on. Had then taken to strutting about in leather coats and tearing around the roads in Grosser Mercedes sedans. *Here we are*, they said. *Try your luck*.

So, in Cambras, until Lucien showed up, they'd had to content themselves with mischief, testing always to see what the reaction might be. A mistake was painful. When Vigie had somehow contrived to obtain a concussion grenade, Alceste Vau and the others had sneaked inside the perimeter of a Panzer division encampment near Épinal and dropped it into a septic tank that served the officers' latrine – just about the time it was in full use. Judging from the noise level inside the barrack, the result had been spectacular. Fountains. And, better yet, there'd been no response from the Germans.

But when Sablé had become obsessed by an obnoxious poodle – the adored pet of a headquarters *Feldwebel*, who spoke German babytalk to it on the street – and had blown the thing's fluffy head apart with an old army pistol stolen from Gilbert, the local pharmacist and his wife had been stood against a wall. Reprisal. The townspeople took the orphans in, but they had a good notion of who had done it, and Sablé had to visit relatives in another village for a time. They'd learned that angry people are dangerous, that one couldn't be sure what they'd do, especially when the means to a hard lesson were so near at hand – the right word in the right ear was all it would have taken.

*

334

In that same week, Eidenbaugh began to have a feel for the currents that ran beneath the surface of village life. There was a young girl, perhaps fifteen, who lived with Gilbert and his family. Cecille, she was called, a poor thing treated as servant or dishonoured cousin by the rest of the household. Heavy, with a wan, immobile face, she stared at the floor when spoken to. She had come visiting one night, approaching his straw pallet in the corner of the eating room and standing there until he awoke, suddenly, startled by an apparition in a soiled flannel nightdress. He had sent her away – in kind fashion, he hoped – for the briefers had been crystal clear on this point, especially the aristocratic Englishman – known only as Major F. – who had lived for years in Paris. 'Village life is sexually quite complex, dear boy, don't be drawn in,' the British officer had cautioned. And it soon became obvious that he'd been right. Cecille was visited, on successive nights, by Sablé and by Daniel Vau, the younger brother. Daniel, in addition, looked at Gilbert's youngish wife in a quite explicit way. Eidenbaugh hadn't any idea how Gilbert reacted to it – he seemed not to notice.

Meanwhile, he familiarized himself with his surroundings, spent a good deal of his time walking the fields and forests around Cambras, learning the trails from La Brebis and Vigie, and listening each night to the *messages personnels* on the wireless, which held an honoured position on a table in the centre of the room. The volume of traffic surprised him, though a portion of it was certainly dross, designed to mislead the Germans as to the actual level of underground activity. Finally, ten days after he'd landed in the field, the words crackled from the radio: *Limelight, le théâtre est fermé.* His activation signal. He told Gilbert he would be away for a time, and the man offered to accompany him. 'Now that you are here,' he said, 'it is all different. Nothing against the young ones, they are the patriots of Cambras, but I am a patriot of *France*, a veteran of the war. The *schleuhs* gassed me at Verdun.' Eidenbaugh thought about the offer for a moment – by the rules, he was supposed to go alone – but there was something of a test in Gilbert's manner, and he decided to trust the man. 'Unless you are monumentally stupid or terribly unlucky,' the briefers had told him, 'the Germans won't catch you. On the other hand, the chances of being betrayed, for any number of reasons, political or otherwise, are better than one would like.'

But he had to trust somebody, so he trusted Gilbert.

The train ride from Épinal to Belfort was nasty – cold and sweaty at once – and he vowed not to do it again. In the aisle was a great press of bodies, including German soldiers and airmen, making for two hours of sour breath, wet wool, a baby that wouldn't shut up, vacant faces, tired eyes, and icy draughts that blew through spaces between the boards of the ancient *wagon-lit*. Vintage 1914, he thought. A good deal of French rolling stock had travelled east to Germany – to be refitted for the different gauge – then sent on to Wehrmacht units near Moscow, there to vanish forever.

It took them two hours to travel forty-two miles, over oft-damaged and repaired track, shunted aside for flatcars carrying artillery pieces to the Atlantic coast, unable to attain much speed because of coal adulterated by sand and gravel. Gilbert, however, turned out to be a travelling companion of great comfort, prattling away the whole time about the health of his pigs and the price of cheese and 'Lucien's' mother – supposedly Gilbert's sister – and every sort of mindless gossip that made for soothing cover and got the journey over with as quickly as possible. For his part, Eidenbaugh grunted and nodded, went along with the game, and acted as though he were pretending to listen to his boring uncle.

At both the Épinal and Belfort stations – especially the latter, which was close to Switzerland and thus a magnet for just about anything in occupied Europe that wasn't nailed down – *la geste* was much in evidence, pointedly in the business of *watching*. To Eidenbaugh they had the feel of provincial police inspectors, stocky and middle-aged, clumsy-looking in their high-belted leather coats, and very stolid. Their eyes never stopped searching, a stare beyond rudeness that picked your life apart from subtle clues almost absurdly evident to their experienced gaze. Clearly a game but, just as clearly, a game they were good at. It scared Eidenbaugh so badly that a muscle ticked inside his cheek. When they saw something – what? – one of them would snap his fingers and beckon the individual over for a document check, holding the paper up to the white sky above the station platform. Gilbert, bless his heart, faltered not a whit, blabbering him past *la geste* and the usual police checkpoints with the story of his *maman* insisting that the roof be retiled, just at planting time, not a seed in the ground, and rain coming. But, Gilbert shrugged, one must obey the *maman*. What else could one do?

It was not the usual Gilbert who went to Belfort. The usual Gilbert sported a permanent grey stubble of whisker beneath a beat-up old beret, layers of shapeless sweaters, baggy wool pants, and rubber boots well mucked from the farmyard. The Belfort Gilbert, understanding without being told that he was to be no part of the business there, had shaven himself raw and produced a Sunday suit that wore its age proudly. In the street outside the station, he bade Eidenbaugh farewell and went off whistling, with a light step. Clearly, his mission in Belfort was a romantic one.

Contact procedures for ULYSSE called for a visit to the Bureau de Poste near the railroad station. Eidenbaugh stood in line, at last approached the counter attended by a woman in her fifties with two chins, blazing lipstick, and an immense nest of oily black hair. He pushed a letter across the marble counter and requested six stamps in addition. The woman barely glanced at him, weighing the letter – addressed to a certain name in a certain town – and tearing six stamps off a sheet with bureaucratic ceremony. He looked at the stamps, an occupation issue prominently featuring the new national motto that, the Germans insisted, had now replaced *Liberté, égalité, fraternité* – *travail, famille, patrie*. Work, family, and fatherland. In the corner of one stamp was a lightly penned address.

This turned out to be a *boucherie chevaline* – horsemeat butcher – in a working-class neighbourhood an hour's walk from the centre of town. There he was waited on by a girl of nineteen or so, in hairnet and white butcher apron, nonetheless beautiful, her hands bright red from handling iced meat. 'Do you have any *pâté* of rabbit?' he asked, naming a product never sold in such a store. She didn't miss a beat. 'You can't buy that here,' she said. 'Well,' he answered, 'my wife craves it and she is pregnant.' 'Ah,' she said, 'you must return in twenty minutes, we might have some then.' He circled the neighbourhood – it was better to keep moving; hanging about in cafés, if you weren't local, drew too many eyes – and returned on the minute. 'So,' the girl said, 'perhaps we have some in the back.' He went through the door she indicated, found himself in a coldroom amid rows of hanging quarters on ceiling hooks. Ulysse appeared at the other end of the central aisle, his breath steaming in the cold.

Ulysse was in his fifties, handsome and silver-haired, clearly an aristocrat, in a finely cut grey suit with an overcoat worn around his shoulders like a cape.

'Who are you, then?' he asked. It was city French he spoke, each word shaped as though it meant something, not the fast patois of the countryside.

'Lucien.'

'Yes? And who am I?'

338

'Ulysse.'

'And where do I live?'

'At the Château Bretailles, overlooking the river Dordogne.'

'Would that I did,' he sighed. 'Papers?'

Eidenbaugh handed them over. Ulysse spent some time thumbing through the pages. 'Excellent,' he said. He handed back the papers and called out, 'Very well, Albert.'

It was cleverly done. Eidenbaugh never saw 'Albert'. There was some motion to one side of him that caused the red haunches to sway on their hooks, then the sound of a shutting door. He assumed there had been a gun aimed at him.

'Suspicion abounds,' Ulysse said lightly. 'Forgive the surroundings,' he added, rubbing his hands against the cold, 'but it does keep meetings short.'

'Not *too* short, one hopes,' Eidenbaugh said, nodding toward the area where the gunman had stood. He had never, to his knowledge, had a gun sighted on him, and he was faintly unsettled by it.

Ulysse smiled thinly. 'Where better than a *boucherie chevaline*? One leaves this uncertain life with, at least, one suspicion confirmed.'

Eidenbaugh laughed. Ulysse nodded politely, very nearly a bow, acknowledging appreciation of the jest. 'What will it be, then?' he asked.

'The usual. Stens, ammunition – enough for training as well as normal use – *plastique*, cyclonite, taconite, time pencils. A few hand grenades, perhaps.'

'How many *maquis* are there?'

'Five. Probably six.'

'Not enough, Lucien. You must recruit.'

'Is that safe?'

'Hardly. But you'll take losses – everyone does. Say twelve new recruits to start. Ask your people, they'll know whose heart beats for France. What have they right now?'

'Rabbit guns. An old pistol. A few cans of watered gasoline.'

'Dear, dear, that won't win the war.'

'No.'

'You shall have it, but wait for your *message personnel* before you move. Understood?'

'Yes.'

'And the drop zone as agreed?'

'I've been there. It looks good to me.'

'There will be a courier for the date. You won't see him. Anything else?'

'Will I be in radio communication? In the future?'

'In time, Lucien, but not now. The German *radio réparage* is too good. They have mobile receivers that move about the countryside, and they'll find you quicker than you think. Besides, once you are in contact with your base, they will want things, all sorts of things – you'll find yourself counting utility poles day and night. I would suggest that you enjoy your independence while you have it.'

'Very well.'

'I am certain that they are working on the radio problem, and once you have one, it will be something dependable. And safe.'

'I see.'

'By the way, why are you limping? Part of your legend? Or have you injured yourself?'

As far as Eidenbaugh knew, Ulysse had not seen him limp. Most likely he had been watched all the way to the contact. 'Broke a toe,' he said, 'when I landed.'

'Do you need a doctor?'

'No. It will heal by itself – you can't splint a toe.'

'Well, a limp is distinctive, so try and stay off it if you can.'

'I'll do that.'

'Good-bye, then. See you another time.'

They shook hands. At Ulysse's indication, he used a door that opened onto an alley behind the shop.

On the way back, as he waited with Gilbert on the Belfort station platform, the two Gestapo officers made an arrest. How the fellow had got that far Eidenbaugh could only imagine. His clothing was torn, and blackened with railroad soot, his face was drained, white as death, and his eyes were pink from sleepless nights – he was much too obviously a fugitive on the run. They manacled his hands behind his back and he wept silently as they marched him away.

* * *

A mad lady on a bicycle! Most certainly English! All in tweeds!

He had gone down the mountain with Gilbert. Found, hidden in an alder grove, the old truck that was sometimes made to work. Then the two of them had sputtered off to Épinal to buy provisions. When they got back to Cambras, the village was buzzing with the unusual visit. Had she been looking for him? Well, no, she hadn't said that exactly, but she had been in the house of Gilbert and had drunk many cups of tea with the old woman. Tea? There was tea in Cambras? No, the mad lady in tweeds had brought her own tea. In a box made of stiff paper. Really? Might he have a look at it? Alas, no one would expect an *Américain* to be interested in a miracle that *petit*. Where had the box got to? In the rubbish heap, perhaps? No such dishonour. Fed to Gilbert's pigs, along with other delectables stored up in a wooden barrel in the farmyard. Oh Christ. A missed communication – in his trade one of the worst disasters imaginable. That meant an emergency trip to Belfort. He was furious with himself for missing the courier, though Ulysse had told him it would happen while he was away.

When, an hour later, he put on his gloves, he found a slip of paper stuffed down the little finger.

On November 14, a memorable night in the history of the village, the Cambras *maquis* drove to the drop zone, then carried dry wood on their backs for half a mile after hiding the truck well off the road. They triangulated the field with woodpiles and covered them with canvas tarps

341

when it started to rain, a cold, icy misery that fell straight down in drops heavy as pebbles. They tried sheltering under the trees but this particular mountain meadow was surrounded by deciduous forest so that one was merely splattered by raindrops hitting the bare branches rather than nailed directly atop the head. Eidenbaugh was soaked through in minutes. At 3:30 a.m. sharp they lit off the woodpiles, then stood back with ceremony and watched them blaze and smoke in the rain. But there was no sign of an airplane and by a quarter to four their bonfires were no more than smouldering piles of wet, charred wood. They couldn't return to Cambras, so they groped their way into the forest in search of dead branches, falling and bruising themselves in the sodden darkness. The wet branches were piled up on what remained of the bonfires and they tried to light them, using up most of their matches and swearing the blackest curses they could summon.

To no avail. At last, La Brebis came to the rescue. Producing an old piece of rubber tubing from a coat pocket, she siphoned off the gas from the truck, using a wine bottle meant for celebration but drained dry as they sought any available warmth on the mountainside. A bottle at a time, they soaked down the wood piles while La Brebis, who had ingested a certain amount of gasoline in getting the siphon action under way, went off into the woods to be sick. At this point they heard the sound of airplane motors above them in the darkness – coming from the east! The equation for nighttime air supply operations was complex, involving fuel weight, load weight, air speed, distance, weather, hours of darkness, the phase of the moon, evasive flight paths, and fuel allowance for escape tactics in case of pursuit. Thus the bravery of the British pilot, circling above the fog-bound meadow, was extraordinary. He must have used his last margin of safety looking for them and, should he encounter Luftwaffe night fighters on the return trip, was well on his way to ditching in the Channel. They never saw the plane, but they could hear the engines quite distinctly –

he'd come down low to look for their signal. The gas-soaked wood woofed to life and roared against the downpour for only a few moments before the flame turned blue and danced pointlessly along the boughs, burning up the last of the fuel.

But that was enough. The Lancaster pilot must have seen the orange smudges beneath the clouds and signalled his dropmaster, thus the crates with parachutes attached were manhandled out the cargo doors and floated down through the darkness, one of them hanging up in the branches of a tree until Vigie scampered up and cut the shrouds. They loaded the crates into the truck, their excitement obscuring – until Gilbert attempted to start the engine – the fact that the precious gasoline had been burned up. The Vau brothers hiked back to Cambras. At midmorning there were *schleuh* patrols down on the road – someone else had heard the bomber – but it was raining too hard for the Germans to come up into the forest. Nonetheless, the *maquisards* waited most of the morning in ambush by the trail, having voted to defend the arms no matter the cost.

Just before noon, as the rain turned to snow, four of the Cambras women appeared at the edge of the field, pushing bicycles. They had travelled all morning, trading the heavy metal petrol cans back and forth, exposing two extra people to risk in order to make better time.

The entry into Cambras was triumphal. The entire population stood out in the wet snow and applauded *l'Américain, les Anglaises*, and themselves.

Four days later, his Limelight message was broadcast, setting the first attack on the night of November 25. *Seven days!* That was no time at all, but he did what he could. Which meant preparing for the operation – doing the necessary intelligence background – and training his *maquis* in the new equipment simultaneously. To that point, he had followed the Triangle camp teachings meticulously. His instructors and briefers had shown him that the path through danger lay in knowledge of the situation, caution,

343

objectivity, secrecy, planning, and, above all, scrupulous attention to detail. But suddenly he was at war, so he found himself improvising, doing six things at once, making decisions quickly, in the heat of the moment. All the wrong things. But *something* was up, he could feel it in the air – they all could – and he was carried along in the rhythm of it. There were Lancasters overhead every night, the Épinal searchlights crisscrossed the sky, and the *schleuh* patrols were everywhere on the roads. Rumours reached them of stepped-up questioning in the basement of the Épinal Mairie – the town hall, now a Gestapo interrogation centre.

The new guns were a matter of great excitement to the Cambras *maquis*. The Mark II Sten, properly a machine carbine, was *the* special operations weapon of the clandestine war. It was simple: a few tubular components that screwed together quickly once you filed the burrs off the threads. It was light, six pounds, essentially a skeletal steel frame carrying the most elemental bolt-and-spring firing mechanism. And it was fast, putting out rounds in a staccato spray. '*Beau Dieu!*' Gilbert gasped after he had riddled a tree stump with one magazine-consuming burst.

The Stens were less exciting to Eidenbaugh. It came to him, in an idle moment, that the weapon was manufactured by the same armaments industry that produced the Purdey shotgun – a masterpiece. But the reality of the war called for hundreds of thousands of simple death machines to be placed in willing hands. The OSS, in a perfection of that logic, manufactured the Liberator, a single-shot pistol with one bullet and cartoon instructions overcoming literacy and language barriers, then spread thousands of them throughout occupied Europe. It was the perfect assassination weapon, meant for the man or woman whose anger had outdistanced caution to the point where he or she would kill up close.

For Eidenbaugh, the Sten was the least prepossessing of his available tools. It was, for instance, cheaply made

– costing around $12.50 to produce. The primitive firing mechanism tended to jam, thus the thirty-two-round magazine was better loaded with thirty rounds of 9mm parabellum (ball) ammunition to reduce pressure on the magazine spring. In this instance, a special filling device was to be used, but these had not been included in their arms shipment and they had to improvise.

And it was 'short'. That is, the fixed sight was set for a hundred yards. Infantry war tended toward engagement at the extremity of the rifle's efficiency – about a thousand yards, three fifths of a mile. With the Sten, however, you operated at the length of a football field and could see the enemy quite clearly. In essence, a streetfighting weapon. The implicit message was clear to Eidenbaugh: if, as guerrillas, you had the misfortune to engage the enemy on his own terms, the best you could do was to get close enough to burn him badly before he killed you – which he would, simply drawing back out of your range to give himself total advantage.

He had no intention to engage. Their target – identified in code by the courier – was the railroad yards at Bruyères, about fifteen miles from Épinal. Sablé had a cousin who worked in the roundhouse and, on the Tuesday before the attack, it was La Brebis and not the cousin's wife who, at noontime, brought him his lunch of soup and bread. Eidenbaugh found a vantage point on a hill overlooking the yards and watched her ride in on her bicycle, napkin-covered bowl in the crook of her right arm, half a *baguette* balanced across the top of the bowl. The German sentry waved her through. Later, Eidenbaugh was ecstatic to learn there were fourteen locomotives in the roundhouse. He would, he knew, get them all.

It didn't, on the night of November 25, sound like very much. A single, muffled *whumpf* in the roundhouse and some dirty smoke that dribbled from a broken window. That was all. But it would be three months at least before these particular locomotives went anywhere.

Eidenbaugh and Vigie watched it happen from the vantage point, then retreated casually, by bicycle, back to the village.

Eidenbaugh went in alone, with the graveyard shift. They were the brave ones, for they were the ones who would suffer German suspicion after the sabotage. These interrogations would not, Eidenbaugh knew, be of the most severe category, for no occupying power can easily afford to sacrifice skilled railroad workers. The men gathered around him as they trudged into the railyard. To them he was a weapon, a weapon against those they loathed beyond words, and they protected him accordingly. He wasted no time in the roundhouse, simply formed the malleable *plastique* explosive into a collar around the heavy steel and wedged a time pencil into the claylike mass. Then he tied up the two roundhouse workers with heavy cord and moved them behind a wall. He sneaked out the back way, through a well-used dog tunnel in the wire fence. The whole business took less than twenty minutes.

For a mere thud of an explosion and a little smoke. The yard sirens went off almost as an afterthought, the firemen appeared, the French police followed, a few German officers ran about – but there was little to be done. One fireman, reducing the water pressure to the volume of a garden hose, soaked down the area for ten minutes while a yard supervisor nailed a board across the single broken window. A pursuit unit showed up, and the German shepherds went right for the dog tunnel in the fence, picked up a scent that led to the edge of an empty hill above the yards, accepted their biscuits and pats, peed, and went home. A Gestapo *Sturmbannführer* took the rope that had bound the workers as evidence and put it in a leather pouch with a tag stating time, place, and date. Then they all stood around for an hour smoking and talking – bored, more than anything else. It was so insignificant.

346

Apoplectic rage was reserved for the German transport officer, who had chosen that night to occupy a French feather bed rather than a German army cot and thus arrived late. He was the only one there who understood what had happened, for it was, after all, rather technical. It had to do with the way locomotives are turned around in a railroad yard.

In the centre of the roundhouse was what the French called a *plaque tournante*, simply a large iron turntable with a piece of track on it that allowed the crew to turn a locomotive around and send it back out into the yard once it had been serviced. In the interim, locomotives rested in a semicircle around the turntable, which could meet underlying track by being rotated. What the saboteur had done was to blow up the mid-point of the *plaque tournante*. The damage to the electrical system was meaningless – any electrician could · wire around that in an hour. However, the explosion had also damaged the central mechanism of the *plaque*, a large iron casting, and that would have to be reforged. With French and German foundries pressed beyond extremity by demands of the war, replacement would take at least three months. Thus, for that period, fourteen locomotives weren't going anywhere – the *plaque* had been blown in a position directly perpendicular to the outgoing service track.

The transport officer stared at the mess and said *scheiss* through clenched teeth. The gap was less than fifteen feet. It might as well have been fifteen miles. His transportation mathematics were, by necessity, quite efficient. Each locomotive pulled sixty freight cars and, in a three-month period, could be expected to make nine round trips to the coastal defence lines in the west and north. He multiplied by fourteen out-of-service locomotives and came up with something more than seven thousand lost carloads. And this sort of thing, he assumed, would happen throughout the French rail system.

The transport officer wasn't such a bad fellow. In all likelihood he would have appreciated, once restored to his more reflective self, the words of the saboteur's British briefing officer as he reviewed the *plaque tournante* procedure: 'For want of a nail, dear boy, and all that sort of thing.'

* * *

In the winter of 1944, on a night when the mountain was still and silent, when snow hung thick on the pine boughs and white fields shone blue in the moonlight, Khristo Stoianev went to war. As they'd meant him to do.

The priest who had released him from a cell in the Santé prison had barely spoken, but the intent of the action was self-evident. He was free. Free to fight the common enemy. The time and place he must choose for himself. Khristo sometimes thought about the priest: a small, stooped man, unremarkable, invisible. A perfect emissary for Voluta, his church, and NOV, the Polish Nationalist organization. Khristo knew that someone had kept track of him, had known he was in the Santé, but that was no surprise. His training and experience gave him, when the time was right, a certain value, and the NOV priests would be aware of that value. Priests made excellent intelligence officers, he knew; the Vatican was said to have the world's finest intelligence service, calling on the accumulated experience of seven centuries. *Father* Voluta – it seemed a strange idea. But Ilya had claimed it to be so, and Ilya knew things.

Others, certainly, had been set free from French prisons as the German tank columns neared Paris and the fall of France was imminent. Like Khristo, they had been jailed because they were dangerous. Now, for the same reason, they were released. It was one of the first ways a defeated country could fight back. That the French had let him go at the behest of the Poles surprised him not at all. The two conquered nations were old friends, sharing a taste for romanticism and idealism that had got them every sort of misery for a hundred years. But they shared also a near

348

pathological conviction – that romanticism and idealism would in time be triumphant – which made for a battered old friendship but a durable one.

Khristo walked quietly from the bedroom of the old house that had been his refuge, the polished wood floor cold on his bare feet, and dressed from a large closet in the adjoining alcove. Thick wool socks, corduroy trousers suitable for working dogs in the field – a gentleman's roughwear – wool sweater, and an old coat, shapeless but warm. Good high boots that laced up tight. From a peg on the inside of the closet door he took a Hungarian machine pistol – Gepisztoly M43 – on a leather strap. It had cost four chickens, three dozen eggs, and a bottle of brandy, but it made them comfortable to have a weapon in the house. He smiled as he handled it; Sophie had oiled the cheap wooden stock as though it belonged to a fine gun kept on an estate. But then, Sophie had altered the corduroy trousers so that he could wear them, had knitted the sweater and the socks – unravelling fashionable items from better days in order to do so – and, come to that, had polished the floor as well. All her life she had done these things and saw no reason to stop just because of the war. Perhaps the war was all the more reason to do them.

He took four loaded magazines from the closet shelf and put two in each pocket of the coat, then tiptoed down the hall to Sophie's bedroom to say good-bye. Her bed was empty, a heavy comforter folded neatly at the foot. Next door, where Marguerite slept, it was the same. He listened and, very faintly, heard the sound of plates and silverware in the kitchen on the ground floor. Years of service, he realized, had schooled the sisters in the preparation of breakfast without waking the house.

*   *   *

Prison had changed him.

He came to understand that on his first day of freedom. The Nikko Petrov papers were no longer of use, so he walked restlessly about the streets of the city – frantic knots of people on one block, deserted silence on the next – as it waited to see what Occupation might bring. Eventually, he found a young man approximately his height and size and strong-armed him in a doorway, taking his passport. He bought glue in a *papeterie*, then found a café, pried his photograph from the Nansen document and made himself a French passport. The franking marks across the corner of the picture did not quite match, but one had to look carefully to see that. He ordered a steak, ate it so fast he barely noticed the taste, then left the café with the steak knife in his pocket. A few blocks away he found a *mont de piété* – 'mountain of piety', as the French ironically termed their pawn shops – held a knife to the pawnbroker's throat, and stole a small French pistol. He could have bought it, he had money from the priest, but he knew that money meant survival and he intended to survive. Nearby, he saw a finely dressed gentleman getting into a car, held him at bay with the pistol, and drove away in the car, a five-year-old Simca Huit, dark blue, with nearly a full tank of gas. For as long as he was able, he drove south and west. Away from the advancing Germans, headed for the coast or, perhaps, Spain. He would accept whatever the fates offered.

But the farther south he drove, the worse the nightmare. The roads were clogged with people and their possessions, cars had been pushed into the fields when they would no longer run, abandoned cats and dogs were everywhere. He saw a woman pushing a baby carriage with a grandfather clock in it, he saw unburied dead by the side of the road, bloated and flyblown in the early summer heat. The anarchy of flight was exacerbated by Stuka bombing runs on the refugee columns so that people had to run for the ditches and, here and there, a tower of smoke rose into the sky from a burning car.

The Germans had learned the tactic in Spain, refined it in Poland: clogged roads made reinforcement and supply impossible – tanks would simply not drive over their own people, at least not in this part of Europe. So the Stukas' objective was to sow panic and terror among the fleeing civilians, and they buzzed low along the roads for a long while before they used their machine guns or dropped a bomb.

This effort was aided, on the ground, by German agents who spread horror stories and rumours among the civilian population. Khristo came upon such a man at dusk on the first night, holding the terrified attention of a small group of refugees by the roadside with stories of German atrocities. Khristo stopped the car and stood at the edge of the crowd and listened to him, a master storyteller who didn't miss a detail: the screams, the blood, the horror. He was a heavy, blunt-featured man who clearly enjoyed his work and was adept at it. When Khristo could no longer bear the looks on the faces of the listeners, he pushed his way through the crowd and took the man by the scruff of the neck. 'This man is trying to frighten you,' he said. 'Don't you see that?' They stared at him, paralysed, not understanding anything at all. In disgust, Khristo marched the man behind a tree and chopped his pistol's trigger guard across the bridge of the man's nose. The man yelped and ran away across the field, bleeding all over himself. But when Khristo turned back to the crowd he saw that they too had run away. He had frightened them, had only made it worse.

On the second day, somewhere on the N52 where it ran along the Loire between Blois and Tours, the car began to stall. All day it had crept along, in first and second gears, stopping and starting, locked in the stream of cars and bicycles and people on foot. By now, the Simca was full – and heavy: a mother and daughter, the latter having somehow injured her knee, a wounded French artilleryman who sang to keep their spirits up, and an old woman with a small, frightened dog that whined continually. His passengers got out of the car and sat in a resigned group among the roadside weeds while he

351

opened the hood. The smell of singed metal from the engine reminded him of the flight from Madrid, only here no little man on a bicycle showed up to help. *Perhaps it wants water*, he thought, treating it more like a horse than a car. Someone volunteered a bottle and he slithered down the bank to the edge of the Loire, holding the bottle against the gravel and letting water trickle in. It was peaceful by the river; cicadas whirred in the heat, a small breeze stirred the air.

'Ah, monsieur, thank God you have come.'

He turned toward the voice and discovered the woman he would come to know as Sophie. She looked to be in her middle fifties, with anxious eyes and a broad, placid face. She wore a 'good' dress, black with white polka dots, sweated through in circles beneath the arms. He must have looked puzzled, for she elaborated: 'We have been praying very hard, you see.'

'Oh?'

'Please,' she said urgently, 'there's little time.'

Around the curve of the river he found another woman, similar to the first though perhaps somewhat younger – he took them to be sisters – and an old man in a formal white suit laid back against the grassy bank. His tie was undone and his face was the colour of paper. The younger woman was fanning him with his hat. Khristo knelt by his side and placed two fingers against the pulse in his neck. The beat was faint and very fast and the man was comatose, an occasional flutter of the eyelids the only sign of life.

'I'm afraid I can do nothing,' he said. 'This man is dying, he needs to be in hospital.'

The elder sister answered a little impatiently. 'We know he is dying. But he must receive unction, you see, the last rites, so that his soul may rest peacefully in heaven.'

Khristo scratched his head. The women reminded him of nuns, innocent and strong-willed at once. 'I am not a priest, madame. I'm sorry.'

The elder sister nodded. 'That we can see. But my sister

352

and I are Protestant, and we do not know the proper ceremony for these matters.'

He turned back toward the man. 'I cannot say it in French,' he said.

'No matter,' the elder sister replied. 'God hears all languages.' Then, as a slightly horrified afterthought: 'You are Catholic, of course.'

'Of course,' he said.

He was Bulgarian Eastern Orthodox – closer to Catholicism than a Protestant, in theory, but the rites were different and the customs not at all the same. From his training he knew that European Catholics expected 'Hail Mary' and 'Our Father' and an Act of Contrition. What he was able to offer, however, were *predsmurtna molitva*, prayers for the dying. There should have been *soborovat*, elders, present to pray a dying man into the next world, but God would have to forgive this requirement. As for the prayers themselves, they were supposed to be improvisational, in whatever form was appropriate to those present. He therefore leaned close to the man – whispering so quietly that the sisters could not hear him – and asked God to ease his entry into heaven, to forgive him his sins, and to unite him with those he'd loved in this life who had preceded him. Finally, returning to the Catholic tradition, he anointed the man with river water in place of holy oil, touching his face in the sign of the cross and saying, in French, 'In the name of the Father, and the Son, and the Holy Spirit.' The man's lips were cold as snow, and Khristo suppressed a shiver. 'Go to God,' he added, then stood, indicating that the ritual was concluded.

Both sisters were weeping silently, dabbing at their eyes with small white handkerchiefs. 'Poor Monsieur Dreu.' The younger sister spoke for the first time. 'His heart . . .'

'It is the war,' the other sister said.

'Was he your husband?' Khristo asked.

'No,' the elder answered. 'Our employer. For many years. He was as a father to us.'

353

'What will you do?'

They simply wept. Finally Sophie, the elder sister, said, 'Monsieur Dreu intended that we should go to the little house – we would have been safe there. We tried, but we could not make way. Everyone wants to go west. Monsieur Dreu tried to drive the car, all the way from Bordeaux, but the strain on him, the planes, the people on the road . . .'

Something in her voice, in the inflection of *petite maison*, caught his attention. 'Little house?'

'In the mountains, to the east, toward Strasbourg. There is no road there, you see, and no people. Just an old man who chops the wood.'

'Charlot,' the younger sister offered.

'Yes. Charlot.'

'How would you live?' he asked.

'Well, there is every sort of food, in tins. Monsieur Dreu always saw to that. "One must be prepared for eventualities," he used to say. "Some day there will be turmoil," he said, "another revolution." He said it every summer, when we all went up there to clean the house and air the linen. Monsieur Dreu had great faith in air, especially the air one finds in the mountains. "Breathe in!" he would say.' Both sisters smiled sadly at the memory.

East, he thought. No one was going east – perhaps if they took the country lanes between the north-south highways. *No road. Tinned food.* In his mind, the words narrowed to a single concept: sanctuary. But there was his own group to consider; he would not simply toss them from the Simca. 'Have you an automobile?' he asked.

'Oh yes. Up on the road, a very grand automobile. A Daimler, it is called. Can you drive such a car?' Sophie stared at him with anxious eyes.

He nodded yes.

The younger sister cleared her throat, the knuckles of her reddened hands showed white as she twisted the handkerchief. 'Are you a gentleman, monsieur?'

'Oh yes,' he said. 'Very much so.'

'Thank God,' she whispered.

He went up onto the road and inspected the great black Daimler, polished and shimmering in the midday sun. The gas gauge indicated the tank was a little less than half full, but he knew they would have to take their chances with fuel, no matter what, and if his own money didn't hold out, he was certain Monsieur Dreu had provided amply for the run to his mountain retreat.

And if he had any question at all about the change of plan, a visit to his fellow refugees, gathered about the Simca, answered it for him. At the direction of the old lady with the dog, they had pooled their money, purchased a pair of draught horses from a nearby farm, and were in the process of harnessing the animals to the car's bumper. Khristo explained that he would be leaving them and gave the car keys to the old lady, who now assumed command of the vehicle. They all wished him well, embracing him and shaking his hand. As he walked back toward the river, the artilleryman called out, *'Vive la France!'* and Khristo turned and saluted him.

At the river, he waited patiently with Sophie and Marguerite and, as the sun went down, the old man died peacefully. Using the Daimler's tyre iron and their hands, they scratched out a shallow grave by the river and laid him to rest. Khristo found a piece of board by the roadside and carved an inscription with the knife stolen from a Paris café:

Antonin Dreu
1869–1940

The sisters had cared for Monsieur Dreu for more than thirty years, thus Khristo, as his replacement, found himself pampered to an extraordinary degree. The old man had been the last of a long line of grain *négociants* in the city of Bordeaux and the family had acquired significant wealth over time. Dreu himself had been, according to Sophie, something of an eccentric: at times a Theosophist, a vegetarian, a socialist, a follower of Ouspenskian mysticism, a devotee of tarot, the Ouija board, and, especially, séances. He 'spoke' to his departed mother at least once a month, claiming to receive business direction from her. Whatever the source of his commercial wisdom, he had prospered in good times and bad. He had never married, though Khristo had a strong suspicion that he had been the lover of both his servants. Dreu had also believed that a great social upheaval would overtake Europe, and to this end had obtained the little house in the southern Vosges mountains, a long way from anything, and stocked it with food, firewood, and kerosene for the lamps.

Thus in the first months of Occupation Khristo had lived on canned Polish hams, tinned Vienna sausage and brussels sprouts, and aged wheels of Haute-Savoie cheese. The well-stocked wine cellar, he knew from his time at Heininger, was exceptional, and the three of them often got tipsy around the fire in the evenings.

As time passed he ventured out, walking many miles to a tiny hamlet – itself a mile or so from any road – populated by the sort of mountain people who have been interbreeding for too many generations. He became known as Dreu's nephew, Christophe, and was simply accepted as another eccentric from *up there*.

When their tins of food at last ran out, they bought a rooster and several hens, a milk cow, enough seed for a large garden, and replaced staples as necessary at the little village. Khristo journeyed only once into Épinal, the nearest town of any size, to buy a weapon on the black market and to see the Germans for himself. In the sparse, occasional gossip of the mountain village he heard little of *résistance*, so bided his time and turned his attention to matters of daily existence.

By the end of 1941, Khristo and the two sisters had fallen into a rhythm of rural obligations: wood had to be chopped, weeds pulled, animals fed, vegetables canned.

The roof needed repair, a root cellar had to be built, once you had chickens you needed a chicken house and then – local predators were abundant – a strong fence. Given the absence of ready-made materials, improvisation was the order of the day and every new project demanded endless ingenuity. Such demands constituted, for Khristo, a kind of paradise. By turning his hand to unending chores he gradually cured his spirit of the black despair that had descended on it in the Santé prison.

Down below, in mountain villages and valley towns, the war subsided to the numbing routine of Occupation. Twice, in 1942, he left the mountain and contrived to make contact with *maquis* units but in both instances he found himself confronted with the political realities of the early *résistance*. The active groups in the region were dedicated communists, fighting both to defeat the Germans and to obtain political power for themselves. They were suspicious of him – he turned aside their ideological questions, and could find no way to be forthcoming about his past. When further meetings were suggested, in remote areas, he did not attend.

But by the fall of 1942 he had determined to put his caution aside and join the fighting no matter the danger. His conscience gnawed at him, and the peaceful joys of his existence turned bitter. He fabricated a history that could not, he thought, be vetted by the *maquis* organizations and prepared himself to withstand hostile interrogation.

The fabrication was, however, not to be tested. He spent the late fall and early winter in bed; a yellow blush tinged his cheekbones, his kidneys throbbed with pain, and his physical energy simply drained away. The two sisters cared for him as best they could, he would emerge from bouts of fever to find Sophie wiping the perspiration from his body with a damp cloth. He was, during the worst moments, delirious, joining a spirit world where every age of his life returned to him in vivid form and colour and he called out to childhood friends and NKVD officers as they floated

357

brightly past his vision. He was again a waiter in Paris, wept at Aleksandra's absence, rowed his father across the Dunav, and hung his head in shame in the Vidin schoolhouse.

'Who is May?' Sophie asked tenderly when he woke to reality on a winter afternoon.

He whispered that he did not know.

On another occasion – a week later or perhaps a month, he had lost track of time – he came to his senses to discover both sisters huddled against the bedroom wall, their eyes wide with fright. What had he said? Had he confessed to phantom deeds, or real ones? With all his meagre strength he turned himself toward them and held out his hands, pleading silently for forgiveness.

He recovered slowly. It was June before he could properly strip the udder on the milk cow. Rebuilding a sawhorse, he counted twenty hammer strokes before a nail was thoroughly driven. He had all his life taken physical strength for granted and was appalled at how slowly it returned to him. At times he feared he would never again be the same.

Then, in the late autumn of 1943, they had a visitor, a boy from the village down below. After a whispered conference, he was invited in and fed lavishly. The food and wine made him loquacious. He had come to enlist the services of Christophe for the Cambras *maquis*, he said. Everyone could do something, even Christophe. There were Sten magazines to be loaded, bicycle wheels to be repaired. He spoke grandly of one Lucien, who would lead them to glory in forays against the hated Germans. Christophe might well be allowed, after sufficient service, to fire one of the *formidable* Stens.

Khristo only pretended to mull it over. There was a debt to be paid, to a French priest, more particularly to those whose sacrifices had enabled him to appear at the Santé, and Khristo meant to repay it by service in the one trade he knew. Thus, on a clear night in December, he ate fresh bread and warm milk in the kitchen, accepted the tearful embraces of Sophie and Marguerite, and, long before dawn, walked out across the fields with the machine pistol slung over his shoulder. His boots crunched the hard crust of snow and he marched in time, the brilliant moonlight casting a soldier's shadow before him.

*　　*　　*

They operated quietly in the first months of 1944.

The *plaque tournante* operation had been one of an enormous range of Anglo-American actions concentrated over a period of a few days, including operations against railroads, factories, shipping, and communications: an intelligence feint, the first in a series leading up to the Allied landing in Occupied Europe. The Germans knew a major attack was coming but the *when* and *where* factors were critical, and the chief Allied intelligence mission was to create a structure in which deceptions could succeed. At the London intelligence bases, they knew that pins went up on maps in the Abwehr and Sicherheitsdienst (SS) analysis centres – where they understood intelligence feints and deceptions quite well themselves. Thus some of the operations had to be transparent, some translucent, and others opaque. In certain instances, all three characteristics could be combined in a single action. The technique was not new, the tactics of deception and disinformation and special operations behind enemy lines had been well known and used by Hannibal, in the Punic Wars against the Romans. All in all, it was like an orchestra led by an invisible conductor – sometimes the violins played, sometimes the reeds disappeared – and it drove the Germans slightly mad, which it was also intended to do.

Locomotives were not the principal objective in the attack on the Bruyères railyards. This was not Sabotage, General – it was Sabotage, Specific. The actual target was an ammunition train making up in the yards from various parts of Occupied Europe and due to leave forty-eight hours after the attack, bound for the defence lines that protected a span of beaches in Normandy. There would be no major landing in winter, the Germans knew that, but they also knew about dress rehearsals, and the *plaque tournante* action, along with others that week, was ultimately read as a deceptive action, meant to mislead German planners into believing that a dress rehearsal was in progress for a future attack against the sheltered beaches at the edge of the Cotentin Peninsula – precisely where, six months later, they were to take place.

German intelligence in the Épinal region was not able to find out precisely who had attacked the Bruyères yards, but gossip did reach them, was intended to reach them, that it was no more than a bunch of village toughs led by a low-level Special Operations technician. They sent a platoon up to Cambras – one of several villages that interested them – but the *maquis* lookouts on the road passed the word and the group took to the brush with time to spare, cramming themselves into a woodcutter's hut high up on the mountain and waiting it out. Cambras covered by a thin layer of snow was even less impressive than Cambras in its normal condition. The German officer looked in the houses and smelled the smells and saw frightened eyes peering from doorways and the chicken sitting on the fountain and, with Teutonic respect for symbols – of power or insignificance – wrote it off. So, ultimately, in Berlin it was a white pin they stuck in Bruyères and not a red one. The information was wired back from Berlin to counterespionage field units in the Belfort sector and, because a Polish factory worker had stolen a German cipher machine at the very start of the war and Polish and British cryptanalysts had broken the codes, the Allies knew they'd succeeded. And put a pin in their own map.

Eidenbaugh's mission called for ongoing operations at a low level, so, in response to a coded Limelight message, he continued to harass the *schleuhs*. But gently, gently. A telephone pole cut down. Children's jacks with sharpened points strewn about to blow the tyres of the telephone repair vehicle. The occasional tree felled across the road. Which halted supply columns while convoy troops plodded through the snowy woods, making sure there wasn't a nasty surprise around the curve. There was no ambush, just a tree, but it kept the Germans nervous, kept them busy, kept them frustrated. What they were getting, that winter, were pranks, at a level calculated to exclude reprisal against civilians. The Cambras *maquis* blew up the *coeurs d'aguilles*, metal castings that enabled the switching of locomotives from track to track. They pry-barred rails apart so that a locomotive ploughed up hundreds of ties as it derailed, then left a charge behind for the railroad crane that would arrive to put the damage right. But only a small charge, meant to damage a wheel, to keep the huge thing out of action for a week.

They also, under Eidenbaugh's close direction, recruited new members. Ulysse, in their second meeting – at a commercial travellers' hotel between Belfort and Épinal – altered the KIT FOX mission by relieving Eidenbaugh from any further attempt to install a *courrier*. That assignment had been an error – Eidenbaugh had all he could do to operate his own small group and find and train new *maquisards*.

He got all sorts.

There were soldiers of fortune – called *condottieri* in traditional intelligence parlance – former criminals who hoped to make their fortunes in wartime targets of opportunity. There were everyday citizens, who had held themselves out of the fighting until they saw which way the wind was blowing and now rushed to get in on things before it was too late. Service in the underground, they now saw, would count professionally after the war. Such types were called, with some contempt, *naphtalènes* – mothballs. Meanwhile the Cambras *maquis* – the original group in the immediate area, lest anyone forget – strutted about grandly with cigarettes stuck in one corner of the mouth, eyes well slitted, and Stens slung diagonally across the back, mountain style.

Mountain style. Better because it left the hands free, enabling one to move swiftly and safely on the treacherous paths, better for riding a horse or a mule, and better because that was the way it had always been done there, since the time the village ancestors had slung muskets across their backs and gone off to fight as *chasseurs*, mountain troops, in the Grande Armée of Napoleon. Against the ancestors of the very Germans they were fighting in 1944.

You had to learn the mountains. The new recruits, installed on straw mattresses throughout the houses of the village, were certainly patriotic and surely brave, but they were flatlanders, ignorant of the ways of the high forest – the sudden blizzards, the white mist that struck a man virtually blind. They had to be trained, and the Cambras *maquis* were pleased to take on the training mission.

One day in late January, Daniel Vau and La Brebis took two of the new recruits – Christophe, the nephew of the old loon who'd built a house up on a neighbouring mountain, and Fusari, a dark-skinned Corsican from St.-Dié – out on practice manoeuvres. The objective was to teach them some mountain lore and to familiarize them with the network of deer trails that ran through the forest between the road and the village. The day was crisp and cold, the sky bright, a good morning to be in the forest, and Daniel Vau and La Brebis travelled down the path at great speed, testing the stamina of their pupils by setting a fast pace and, consequently, leaving them far behind. A good lesson, let them struggle. They had to learn to be part goat in this region, it could well save their lives. The two *maquisards* would glide down a section of path, then wait for the other two, who would arrive panting and red-faced. Just as they came into view Daniel would say, 'Rest period over. Time to go,' and set out again, leaving the novices to get along as best they could, leg muscles twanging from the shock of a downhill lope.

The German officer – no one really saw his rank – was

bird-watching on his day off. Daniel and La Brebis came around a corner of the path and there he was, attended by a bored *Feldwebel*, probably his driver, who leaned against a tree and picked his nails while his superior alternately peered into the sky through binoculars and consulted a field guide on birds of the southern Vosges. He was in search of a species of mountain hawk often seen in the region, which concerned the villagers only insofar as it competed for the available stock of brown hare. The two Germans and the two *maquisards* saw each other at about the same moment and, for a long second, they froze and nothing happened. It took each of them some time to realize they were in the presence of enemies because they were engaged in innocent pastimes – simply not at war that day. It was less than strange to meet a French boy and girl on a mountain path and all would have been well but for the Stens. The officer, a little to one side of the path for a better view up through the pines, got a good look at the weapons, and it wasn't very long before he came to understand exactly what they meant.

There followed a moment of comedy: the officer scrabbling at the flap of his holster, the *Feldwebel* attempting to grab his rifle – resting butt down against a tree – and knocking it over, Daniel and Brebis having the most difficult time of all, trying to struggle free of their slung weapons. It took them a hopelessly long time to do so and, in fact, they never did manage it. The officer drew his pistol, thumbed the safety off, shot each of them once, then ran away down the trail, the *Feldwebel* galloping after, dragging his rifle along the ground by its strap.

Khristo heard the shots and dived off the path, landing on his belly with the machine pistol pointing in the direction of the gunfire. Fusari he could not see. He heard, below him, the sounds of flight and a series of moans. It took him a minute to sort it out: someone had fired, someone else had run away. Since those who fled were headed downhill, toward the road, he assumed they were the enemy and that

363

the moaning was coming from Daniel or Brebis, one or both of whom were hit.

Both. He circled wide of the trail and came in from the flank; Fusari arrived from the other direction at about the same time. Khristo gestured down the trail and Fusari took off in that direction, crouched, moving quickly and gracefully. It was clear to Khristo that he was not new at this.

The guide to birds of the southern Vosges lay open on the ground, along with Daniel Vau's Sten gun. Daniel lay flat on his stomach. He looked at Khristo, a plea in his eyes: *please help me*. La Brebis seemed worse off, lying on her back across Daniel's lower legs, head hung backward, treading her feet like a nursing cat. She had covered her face with her hands and was moaning softly every few seconds.

'Be careful with her,' Daniel said.

'Are you hurt badly?'

He shook his head that he didn't know. 'She has my legs pinned,' he said. 'It's somewhere down there.'

'Is there a doctor in the village?'

'A midwife.'

He circled Daniel and knelt by La Brebis and gently pulled her hands away. It was very bad. She had been shot in the face. Just below and to the outside of the right nostril, a red bead of flesh extruded from a puffy circle shaded blue at its exterior edge. Suddenly, she grabbed hold of his wrists and gagged. He realized she was swallowing blood, shook one of his hands loose and raised her head. 'Thank you,' she breathed.

'Can you spit it out?'

She tried but couldn't manage, a string of red saliva hanging from her lower lip. He took his other hand back and cleaned her mouth, then wiped away the water that ran from her eyes. 'It is the wound,' she said. 'I do not weep.'

'I know,' he said. Very gently, he opened her mouth. There was a swollen ridge across the top of her palate. He reached around her head and probed gently in the hair

364

at the base of her skull, looking for an exit wound, but couldn't find anything. God only knew where the bullet was, somewhere inside her face.

He realized that Fusari was standing above him, breathing hard. 'They're gone,' he said. 'I heard the car take off.'

Khristo nodded. It meant they would be back in force – perhaps in an hour or a little less. He said to Daniel, 'I don't want to move her. Is she crushing your legs?'

'I don't feel anything,' he said.

'Can you move your feet? Your toes?'

'No.'

His heart sank. Fusari swore softly.

From the trail above him, he heard running footsteps. The sound of the shots had apparently reached them – the cold air carried sound much as water did.

Lucien – the American – and Gilbert came galloping down the path a few moments later. The former was pale and shaken. Gilbert carried a Sten and a tattered old book with its covers missing.

'What happened?' Lucien asked, breathless.

Daniel told him.

La Brebis laid her head back in Khristo's arms. One side of her face had swollen so that her right eye was a slit, and she was beginning to struggle for breath as the damaged passages swelled shut.

Khristo spoke to Gilbert, who was hunting through his book, a medical manual belonging to the village for many years, used primarily to set broken bones and to treat burns. 'Is there a doctor?'

'In Épinal,' Gilbert answered.

'You better get him,' Khristo said. La Brebis was dying.

Lucien spoke. 'We must bring them down there,' he said.

'No,' Gilbert said. 'It's impossible. The *schleuhs* will be all over the place – and they'll be here soon enough. They've seen the Stens.'

'Where is the truck?' Lucien said.

'By the logging. On the other side of the road.'

'Is there gasoline?'

'A little.'

'Let's go,' he said.

'Did you not hear me?' Gilbert asked.

'It doesn't matter. We're going. Christophe and Fusari, take La Brebis. Gilbert and I will follow with Daniel.'

'Lucien,' Gilbert said, grim, 'they'll get us all.'

'No they won't.'

Daniel said, 'I am sorry, Lucien. We didn't . . .'

They waited while Lucien ran back up the path and warned the village that a German search party would be coming. The remainder of the *maquis* and the new recruits took the arms and ammunition and moved up the mountain. Alceste Vau was not told of his brother's wound; he would have demanded to accompany them to Épinal and there were already too many of them for the old truck. When Lucien returned, they carried the wounded down the path, across the road, and loaded them carefully into the back of the truck. They covered themselves with a canvas tarp while Gilbert drove, alone in the cab.

The ride down the mountain road seemed to go on forever. The brakes were virtually useless on the steep curves and every time Gilbert downshifted, the flywheel screamed and threatened to blow the transmission all over the road. The truck swayed and bounced, Khristo lay on his side in the darkness beneath the tarpaulin and tried to keep La Brebis's head from moving with the truck's motion, but it was a losing battle. In the beginning, she cried out when they were jolted by a downshift, but as they went farther down the mountain she made no sound at all, and Khristo could feel her skin growing cold. *Let her die*, he thought. His training told him to sacrifice one in order to save another – and to stop might put all their lives in jeopardy.

But this was Lucien's decision, he realized, and finally he

shifted over next to him and, raising his voice above the truck's roaring motor, said, 'Lucien, Brebis is asphyxiating. She won't make it.'

Lucien's voice answered a moment later. 'Are you sure?'

'No. But feel how cold she is.'

'It could be shock.'

'It could be, but I think it's her windpipe closing up.' When there was no immediate answer, he tried to help Lucien make a decision. 'We can still save Daniel, if we continue.'

'No,' Lucien said. He crawled along the truck bed, then reached out from beneath the tarp and pounded on the rear window of the cab. Gilbert slowed – they could feel him pumping the brakes gingerly – then pulled off the road onto the grassy shoulder. The truck was canted at a dangerous angle, and Gilbert raced the engine so it would not stall. On the other side of the road a German staff car and a truckload of soldiers tore past, but they paid no heed to the truck by the side of the road.

'Hold her head,' Lucien said.

Khristo cradled her head in his lap and pressed his hands against the sides of her face. Fusari crawled over next to him and raised the edge of the tarp to let in some light. Lucien reached into his pocket and brought out a cheap fountain pen. He unscrewed the two halves, then broke off the nib end and cleaned up the shattered edge as best he could with a knife. He pulled his shirttail out and wiped ink from the open tube he'd fashioned. Khristo could see that his hands were shaking.

'Ready?' Lucien said.

Khristo nodded.

'Open her mouth.'

Khristo pulled her teeth apart. He could see Lucien sweating in the cold air as he pressed Brebis's tongue down with his left index finger. When he forced the tube down the back of her throat, the pain brought her back from stupor and she screamed, a hoarse, choking sound that made Khristo shudder. When Lucien withdrew his hand there wàs blood on it.

Lucien wasted no time. He pounded on the cab window again, and Gilbert moved back out on the road while Fusari resettled the tarp and they were in darkness once again. La Brebis tried to move her hand to her mouth, but Khristo held tightly to her wrist. 'Just breathe,' he whispered by her ear. 'Can you?' After a moment, she moved hèr head up and down to tell him that she could.

In Épinal, they heard the sounds of other vehicles and bicycle bells and the truck slowed, bumping along the cobbled streets. At last, Gilbert made as if to park, swinging over toward the kerb. Then, suddenly, he took off quickly, with all the acceleration the old engine could muster. Khristo let go of the wounded girl and found the grip of his machine pistol.

But nothing happened. They drove for several minutes, then rolled to a stop. Khristo peeked beneath the tarp and saw the Épinal railroad station. At Lucien's direction, Fusari checked out the other side and reported that Gilbert was entering the Hôtel de la Gare, which was, Khristo knew, to be found across the street from virtually every railway station in France. Some minutes later Gilbert appeared at the back of the truck and spoke in an undertone. 'There was a *geste* car parked in front of the doctor's office – they know there's been a gunshot wound. I'm going to drive around to the back of the hotel. Once we get there, move quickly and get them inside.'

The truck inched down a narrow alley, cornered, and stopped. They threw the tarp off and saw two men in dark suits with pistols in their hands. Khristo immediately armed his weapon and covered them.

'What's this?' Lucien asked.

'Pimps,' Gilbert answered, climbing up on the truck bed to help with the wounded. 'We're at the Épinal whorehouse. It's the only place in town where the doctor comes – and no questions asked. They've already sent one of the girls to get him.'

They carried Brebis and Daniel through the small bar that adjoined the lobby, then upstairs to a dingy room with faded wallpaper. A moustached man in long underwear jumped out of the bed when they entered the room. 'See here,' he said.

'Take a walk,' one of the pimps answered, showing the man his pistol, 'this is for France.'

A heavy woman in a dressing gown appeared as they lowered the wounded to the rumpled bed. Without a word she handed the customer a sheaf of ten-franc notes. He, in turn, drew himself up to his full dignity, baggy underdrawers and all. 'Never!' he said, with great solemnity. Slapped the money back into the woman's hand, saluted crisply, and marched from the room.

* * *

February, in the mountains, was like a white island. Cut off from time, lifeless, inert. A place where snow showered from the pine boughs, a place where the wind died and the water froze to perfect crystalline ice.

In Cambras, Khristo Stoianev kept to himself. He lived, like the rest of the village, on turnips and rutabagas. Sometimes there was bread. Most of the recruits had been sent home – with instructions to return after the March thaw – because the village food-stocks could not support them. But Khristo and the Corsican, Fusari, were asked to stay.

The shooting of La Brebis and Daniel Vau continued to reverberate in Cambras and not in comfortable ways. They had both survived, for which everyone was thankful. But Daniel had been wounded in the spine, would never walk again, and Gilbert's young wife had taken this very badly. She had been, everyone supposed, Daniel's lover, and her broken heart showed for all to see. This situation oppressed Gilbert's domestic life to a painful degree and he was rumoured to have shifted his sleeping quarters to the bed of the strange servant girl who lived in the house.

The doctor had arrived within minutes that day at the Hôtel de la Gare, a white-haired *professeur* of a man who wore an old-fashioned silk vest beneath his suit. He had patched up La Brebis as best he could, then ordered both wounded removed to a convent near the town of Vittel, some twenty miles distant, and there operated on Daniel Vau. Both had remained and were said to be recovering as well as could be expected. The family of La Brebis – the Bonet clan – muttered continually of revenge on her behalf. Gilbert and Lucien resisted, reluctant to attack the Germans in this way, fearing what they would do to the village in return. The murder of an individual German soldier had elsewhere in France been repaid by the killing of more than a hundred civilians. A high price for the Bonet honour.

But the stalemate could not last indefinitely and late one afternoon an aristocratic Frenchman appeared in Cambras: tall, hawk-faced, silver-haired, even in February wearing a fine topcoat over his shoulders like a cape. He was accompanied by a bodyguard called Albert, a watchful man with lank brown hair parted in the middle, a café waiter's moustache, and eyes the colour of the winter sea. He carried a short-barrelled pump shotgun, a weapon never before seen in the village – what birds you could get with *that* – and wore a Walther pistol in an armpit holster. *The Killer*, they called him, when he wasn't around to hear. He reminded Khristo of his past.

Which now, in February, seemed like another life lived by another man. With war in Russia, he thought, they must all be dead by now. Sascha, Drazen Kulic, all the others from Arbat Street. Perhaps not Ilya. Ilya would always find a way to survive. And he rather thought Voluta was alive somewhere; he was like air, hard to get hold of and thus hard to kill. What, he wondered, would they think of this American who called himself Lucien. For he was surely not

French, no Frenchman ever walked like that, free-striding, body leaning forward. And he was not British. He did not have the British face, that odd, speculative stillness. He was, apparently, what Khristo had been. An intelligence officer, sent, no doubt, to organize and focus resistance to the Germans. And he was approximately Khristo's age. Yet he was very different. His training was different – there was another angle to him. He was nothing like Sascha Vonets or Yaschyeritsa or Ozunov. Nor was he like Roddy Fitzware.

What made him distinct, in Khristo's eyes, was his decision to save the lives of the two wounded villagers. At not so much jeopardy to his life – that was expected – as jeopardy to his mission. That was not expected. And it was wrong. An error. But it was the nature of the error that provoked Khristo's curiosity. The man's component parts, compassion interwoven with aggression, reminded him of Faye Berns, who could be sentimental one moment and entirely practical the next. He had thought her personality to be singular, but he now understood that she was one of a class. To which add Winnie Beale, who had, on the spur of the moment, committed an entirely altruistic act and could have died for her trouble. A wealthy bitch, suddenly swept away by unselfish courage in the face of a machine gun. The combination was attractive, very appealing, but, in the case of Lucien, he had to wonder how it managed to resolve itself to the crueller exigencies of intelligence work.

The French aristocrat, in Khristo's experienced eyes, seemed to be Lucien's superior, but that was not so very unusual; his own experience of being a non-national in another country's service supported that observation. During the three days the man stayed at the village, he spent most of his time soothing one or another of the Bonet family, explaining to them the facts of life in regard to revenge killings. But he also sought Khristo out, chatted with him now and again in the most general sort of way, and finally invited him to have a brandy at Gilbert's house. When Khristo arrived, after a turnip supper, he discovered that Gilbert and his family were absent, as was Lucien.

The brandy was a gift from heaven. He'd spent most of his nights in the mountains as close to a fire as he could get, but it was the first time in many weeks that both sides of him were warm at the same moment. It was private at Gilbert's house. There was only the light of the fire – a big one, Gilbert was liberal with his wood – reflected in the frost flowers that covered the small windowpanes. As Khristo sipped at the aristocrat's brandy and relished the warmth that crept through his body, the Frenchman took a pouch of tobacco from his pocket and rolled two cigarettes. The smell reached Khristo all the way from the man's lap. *Makhorka*. Dark tobacco, strong, and there was no mistaking the aroma. Silently, the man handed him a cigarette, then extended a gold lighter.

'Do you like it?' the man said.

'Oh yes.'

'Just like home, eh?'

Khristo sat for a time and stared into the fire. There'd been no doubt in his mind that this would happen eventually, that he would be challenged to explain who he was. He would never be considered French – perhaps by the villagers but never by someone who knew the world. And you had to be somebody, you had to belong somewhere, you had to have a nationality of some sort. *Even in heaven*, he thought, *where Saint Peter is the border guard*. He discovered that he was angry, not so much at the Frenchman as at the circumstances of his own existence. He looked into the aristocrat's eyes for a moment and realized suddenly that the man was in Cambras not to gentle the Bonet clan, but to find out about him. *Very well*, he thought, *you shall find out*. 'I am not Russian,' he said, holding the *makhorka* cigarette in the air between them to show the man that his tactics were well understood.

'No?'

'No. I am from Bulgaria. A possession of Turkey for centuries, now an ally of the Germans, soon to belong to someone else. It is the bulwark of southeastern Europe – Christian Europe – against Islam. It is a neighbour and, often, an enemy of Greece, your conquered ally. It has always been greatly desired by Russia, your unconquered ally. Romania, its northern neighbour and sometime enemy, was most recently the domain of British interests, even though the Romanian ruling class looks to France for their culture and has sided with Germany in this war. It is also part of the Balkans, and the southwestern area of the country has tended to be sympathetic to the interests of Macedonia – divided between Greece and Yugoslavia, a country presently occupied by Germany, with willing assistance from the Croatian minority, except for those Croats who are communist and fight with Tito, whose father was a Serb and mother a Croat. And yes, I like the tobacco quite well.'

The aristocrat nodded to himself for a moment, something or other had been confirmed. 'You are, sir, something of a politician.'

'I am, sir, a lot of things, but that, thank God, is not one of them.'

The man across from him laughed appreciatively, then leaned forward. 'I am not here to interrogate you, and I am not accusing you. I am only concerned with the politics at hand, not the politics of the Balkans. You must understand that in France there are several *résistance* movements, Catholic, communist, Gaullist, even those who would restore the Bourbon monarchy. We make common cause against the Germans, but the day is coming when the future of this country will be decided – and it will be decided by those who come out of the conflict with the greatest strength. The Cambras *maquis* is something of a Gaullist unit, as much as it's anything, and if you would be happier in a different political setting, well, that can be arranged for you, and no hard feelings. Well, what about it?'

'My war is right here,' Khristo said. A connoisseur of traps, he felt that this was surely the softest one ever laid for him.

'Good. You'll be of assistance – no question about it. On that basis, another brandy?'

'Thank you, yes.'

'Some day, you must tell me your story.'

'I think you would find it interesting,' Khristo said.

They busied themselves with the brandy for a moment. For Khristo, the room grew deliciously warm.

'This war,' the aristocrat said, 'in some sense it makes you happy.'

'That's true,' Khristo said.

'Why?'

'The world turned me upside down a long time ago. Now the world itself is turned upside down. For the moment, we – the world and I – are congenial.'

'But it must end.'

'Some day.'

'And then?'

'I don't know. I don't think about it. For now, a man with a gun can be whoever he likes. With any luck, I'll be dead before the world turns right side up again.'

The aristocrat looked into his eyes for a moment, calculating. 'I don't think you really mean that.'

Khristo sighed. 'No, you're right. I don't mean it.'

'Don't give up hope,' the aristocrat said. 'Everything may be put right in the long run.' He handed Khristo the remaining tobacco, then rose from the chair and tossed a small log onto the fire. Khristo accepted that as a signal, chatted for a few moments more, and left soon after.

He walked across the tiny mud square of Cambras, back to the house where he slept and ate. The night was clear, the ground frozen rock hard. He looked up at the stars, sharp as diamonds in the black sky, and wondered what the Frenchman had meant by saying 'everything may be put right in the long run,' because he had meant something by it.

*   *   *

The thaw came in late February and everything turned to mud as sheets of water ran across the mountain roads. In Épinal, a student named LeBeq was caught writing slogans on a wall. He was detained by the Gestapo and tortured. To make his comrades believe he had confessed – and thus get them running, out in the open – he was almost immediately released. He went home to his family, but was unable to speak. The following day, he walked up to a Gestapo sedan parked in the main square and drove a boning knife – all the blade and half the handle – into the driver's chest. The other officer leaned across the seat and shot him several times. But he had the strength of a madman, and managed to walk several blocks to the doctor's office where he collapsed and died on the front step. Immediately, a number of prominent citizens were rounded up and ten men and women were hanged from plane trees on the main street of the city. The doctor who had attended Daniel and La Brebis was one of them, as was the prostitute's customer who had chanced to be in the Hôtel de la Gare. On the first day of March, friends of LeBeq stretched a wire across the road that passed below Cambras and decapitated – more or less – a motorcycle dispatch rider who had neglected to lie low over his handlebars.

This action produced, in turn, a platoon of garrison troops and some SD officers snooping about at the foot of the mountain trails that led up to Cambras. Nobody would have been foolish enough to commit such a murder virtually on his own doorstep (the Cambras *maquis* suspected a rival resistance group, jealous of their armaments – airplanes didn't come for just *anybody*), but counterinsurgency investigation is given to a kind of plodding momentum, a leadfootedness that will in fact not dismiss, out of hand, the owner of said doorstep.

Vigie, posted across the road, watched the SD officers in conference at the foot of the Cambras trail and began to mistrust his ability to outflank and outdistance them – to warn the village before the troops arrived – so set his fire selector on single shot and popped off a round over their heads. This produced frantic radio calls and an intense *ratissage*, but Vigie melted through the woods like a faun and the only result of the sweep was a few turned German ankles and a good deal of ammunition expended on swaying tree limbs. The fuss was, as well, more than enough to send the Cambras *maquis* scuttling up the mountain with weapons in hand.

Ulysse heard about the business, through his own sources, and the final result of LeBeq's wall writing was that Lucien was pulled out of Cambras. The KIT FOX mission was about to move into a new phase, and Ulysse smelled lots of trouble in the air around Épinal. It was, he thought, the thaw itself, which had melted self-control as well as snowbanks and let loose passions that had remained too tightly wound throughout the winter. KIT FOX was, after all, not a guerrilla campaign, it was a sabotage mission, and there was a feeling in the General Staffs that all-out *partizan* operations, such as the Russians applied to the invading Germans, would lead to the sort of bloodbath that would eliminate a lot of German non-coms – but at the cost of much of the *maquis* leadership. It was not entirely put aside, but was reserved for the week of the grand invasion itself if it was going to happen at all.

At Ulysse's direction, Lucien became the wandering pedagogue of the Belfort Gap, an ancient and traditional attack route up the valley of the Rhine River between the French Vosges and the German Schwarzwald. Two cities, Belfort and Basel, the Swiss border point for France, sit athwart this opening between mountain ranges like stone lions guarding a palace. In the early spring of 1944, the intelligence planners had one objective that led all others: the German high command was now to be exquisitely sensitized to every soft point in Europe that might serve as an Allied invasion route. There was the Balkan route, the Italian route, the beaches of southern France, which led to the Belfort Gap, and the beaches of northern France. Each area had to show heightened levels of sabotage: strategic assets damaged, repaired, then damaged again. Just the sort of thing that goes on before a fleet looms on the horizon.

The Lucien team included Khristo, Fusari, and Vigie, each chosen by Ulysse for a different reason. Khristo, at first, because Ulysse wanted to keep an eye on him. Later, it became apparent that he had a considerable knowledge of the craft in his own right and shared instructional chores with Lucien. Fusari was appointed security chief and bodyguard, their official thug. Dark and suspicious, he looked the part, and in fact had Union Corse connection in his background. He was forever cutting an *X* into the nose of each 9mm round, dumdumming it so that what went in the size of a fingernail flattened out, by the time it exited, to the diameter of the circle made by thumb and forefinger. He was, like many professional criminals, violently patriotic, and focused all his attention on giving the Germans a proper screwing. On the other hand, he made it clear that should Ulysse require the abduction of a bank manager or the interdiction of a payroll, he would be only too pleased to lend his wisdom and experience to the cause.

As for Vigie, Ulysse had recognized his special value early on. He looked younger than his sixteen years and had the scrubbed innocence of an altar boy. He could go anywhere, seemed always a natural part of the environment, and a lie in his mouth was like a hymn. In short, a born lookout. He had, also, an uncanny knack with women – what they did with Vigie didn't really count as infidelity, for some reason, and he returned from his nightly tomcatting with various morsels of pillow talk. These never particularly served the Allied intelligence effort, but they might have, and they did function to keep everybody's spirits up, so Vigie retained a permanent dispensation, denied the other three, from Ulysse. They bitched about that, referring to their leader as 'Mother Superior', but the point of it was later to be driven home in an extremely ugly way.

Like itinerant scholars of an earlier time, the unit crisscrossed the back roads of the Belfort countryside. It was hard, boring work, completely without glamour and very dangerous. There were young Frenchmen who served the Germans as *milice*, militia, and they maintained loose networks of spies and informants who might not themselves wish to be seen collaborating with the enemy. People had their own reasons – sometimes, alas, very good ones – for making backchannel arrangements with *la geste*, thus the possibility of betrayal was constant.

But the mission of the Lucien team was of critical importance. The knowledge they provided turned plain men and women into sharp weapons against the Occupation infrastructure. If you knew enough to cut an electrical plug off its cord – perhaps stuff a piece of rag in the end so the flash wouldn't burn your hand – you could use any convenient wall socket to blow all the power in a building. It could take half an hour to replace the fuses – a long time if, for instance, the building housed ground controllers for the German air defence system.

They taught railroad workers how to spike a *plaque tournante*. They taught teenagers that cutting a telephone line makes it easy to find the break – but that pushing a thumbtack into a signals cable makes it very difficult and time-consuming. They taught the disruption of rail signals. They taught that a single cube of sugar in a gas tank would caramelize on the pistons and freeze the engine solid. If you didn't have a sugar cube, a potato wedged in the tailpipe of a vehicle would choke the exhaust system, blow a hole in the muffler, and could cause carbon monoxide to leak into the driver's compartment. They taught the use of cyclonite explosive, round pellets of *plastique* (invented by Julian Huxley, the biologist) that looked like innocent goat droppings and would blow out a truck tyre. They taught villagers that if they buried a soup tureen upside down, with the silhouette showing up through the dirt, it looked exactly like an inexpertly laid land mine and could stop a column of tanks while a mine disposal unit was brought up. They taught switchboard operators how to disable a teleprinter by wedging a feather in the armature, they taught roadworkers how to blow up a bridge using simple construction dynamite. Every strategic entity – communications, rails, roads, bridges, power – had its weak points, and the French people were taught how to attack them. *But you must wait for the code words on the radio,* they were told. Grimly, they obeyed. Watched the foreign troops marching up and down the streets where their grandmothers had been born, kept their eyes on the ground when *la geste* came by, held on tight to their new and special secrets, and listened every night to the BBC. And waited.

During this period, Ulysse took on the aspect of an omniscient ghost. He would appear at unlikely times, in unexpected places, so far aboveground as to be virtually hidden by prominence. He moved about the Belfort area in a grand, prewar Bugatti, with Albert, in a grey chauffeur's uniform, behind the wheel. The Germans could only assume him to be a Vichy fascist favoured by some very high personage within their own ranks. He had the car, and the gas to make it run, and his hawklike face was the epitome of Gallic aristocracy. If challenged, he radiated the superficial sweetness of the powerful, being so acutely helpful and decent that German officers saluted from the spine. They knew such people, or rather knew of them, and one was well advised to keep out of their path or, if noticed, to make a good impression. They had spent their lives in submission to the gods of Authority, and Ulysse was very godlike indeed.

* * *

They approached the village of Cabejac just before midnight and paused at the edge of town. Vigie rode in on his bicycle to check things out, the other three sat by the side of the road and smoked and talked in low voices. They had bicycled up from the town of Abonne, some eighteen miles away, and they were tired and sweaty from the ride. It was late April, one of those warmish, unsettling nights when sleep, if it comes, is beset by restless dreams.

Staring up at the town, Khristo found himself jittery. Something in the air, the sort of intuition that will cause animals, drinking at water holes, to look up suddenly. Lucien – in his *bleu de travail* worker's jacket and trousers, old sweater and beret, the very image of a small-town garage owner – was slowly assembling his Sten gun, patiently screwing the pipelike parts together. The weapon's use in clandestine operations was in part attributable to the fact that it could be carried in a knapsack and assembled quickly.

From the north, the drone of a bomber flight reached them. All three looked up, but there was only a night sky lit by a quarter moon. 'Good hunting,' Fusari said.

'Amen to that,' Lucien answered, giving the Sten barrel its final quarter turn.

For the last two weeks, the sky above them had been at war. With improving weather, Allied air sorties intensified – American by day and British by night – B-24s and Lancasters flying deep into Germany to bomb factories and railyards. At night, the Lancasters' flight path often took them over the Belfort area, and the sky came alive with probing searchlights and the white flash of antiaircraft burst that illuminated, for one instant, its own halo of smoke. Sometimes German squadrons rose to attack and there were arcs of orange-red tracer, like spark showers from a bonfire, and once there had been an enormous explosion that lit up the clouds – a fully armed bomber had been hit. The following night they had seen the white of a parachute and had watched in silence as it drifted below the horizon.

Vigie appeared from the darkness, coasting downhill on his bicycle, standing with his left foot on the right-hand pedal and coming to an acrobatic skid in front of Lucien.

'Bravo,' Fusari said sourly.

Vigie said something in incomprehensible mountain slang.

'Yes?' Lucien said.

Vigie shrugged. 'Cabejac,' he said, and spat on the road.

Khristo looked up at the dark town but there was little to see, only an irregular roofline of square silhouettes. Cabejac was an ancient village, chiselled into the limestone cliffs that rose above the Leul, a swift, narrow mountain river that ultimately emptied into the Doubs. The road curved along a cut in the cliff, then switched back suddenly and rose steeply into the town. Fusari had told him on the ride up that the place had a bad reputation. Blood feuds. Marriage in the old tradition: abduction, rape, and then the priest to put things right. People carried shotguns and there were too many dogs about. From time to time, a clan of Gypsies had made the village a temporary encampment, but the reputation of the place had nothing to do with them. No matter, Khristo thought, they have a desire to fight, and they have been approved by Ulysse. And all the sayings about strange friends in time of war were true. *Still*, he thought.

'Lucien,' Fusari said, 'we can go back to Abonne.'

Lucien did not answer, stood pensively while the others finished assembling their Stens. Khristo had hidden the Gepisztoly at Cambras – it was a weapon for *partizans* in the forest, not suited to this work at all. He watched Lucien as the American tried to come to a decision. He could abort an operation any time he felt the wind was blowing wrong, but he was also, clearly, under pressure not to do so.

'Vigie,' Lucien said quietly, 'was there anything at all up there? Anything out of place?'

'No,' Vigie answered. 'Nothing.' He slung the Sten on his shoulder and stood on the pedals of his bike, trying to make it stand in place by wiggling the front wheel back and forth. He kept falling over onto one foot, then trying the trick again.

'I am not in love with this place,' Khristo said.

Lucien walked his bicycle forward. 'Nice and slow,' he said.

Vigie sighed, hopped off his bike, and began pushing. 'The women of Cabejac are said to be hairy, like beasts,' he confided to Khristo.

Lucien had overheard him. 'You stay close while we are here, *copain*.'

'*Pfut*,' Vigie said, contemptuous of any suggestion that he could not take care of himself.

They headed into the town, looking for the Gendarmerie, the post of the military police who traditionally patrolled the countryside and the smaller roads. They had met the *résistance* in cafés, schoolrooms, church sacristies, dining rooms, soccer stadiums. Tonight it was to be a police station, not all that unusual.

But they could not find it in the lower town. Unseen dogs barked at them, passing them along from one to the next, and all the houses were dark and shuttered. The April night was warm, yet it seemed that spring had not yet been acknowledged there. *Normal*, Khristo thought. *All is normal.* He pushed his bicycle with one hand and steadied the weapon with his other – just making sure it was there. Looking to his right, he noticed a narrow, stone-paved alley set between high walls. There was some sort of truck parked down there, only the snubbed-off front end visible.

The street dead-ended at a high wall. They turned left up a long flight of white stairs, the centre of each step worn to a sloping valley by centuries of use. Fusari, bumping his bicycle upward, swore under his breath. When they reached the upper town they were high above the road and the river appeared as a winding ribbon, a long way

382

down, its banks suggested by white curls of moving foam. Fusari touched Khristo above the elbow and nodded up the street to a dim spill of light from a partly open shutter. A metal sign, GENDARMERIE, hung from a stanchion above the door and the windows were barred.

'There must be another road down,' Khristo said.

'Why?'

'Who puts a Gendarmerie at the top of a flight of steps? Don't they drive cars?'

Fusari responded with a dismissive grunt. He made a point of being Corsican, claiming often to be puzzled by the French and their logically illogical way of doing things.

The door of the station opened, and a man stood in the smoky light from within. 'Come along then,' he said, 'we've been waiting.' He wore military uniform, red flashes on khaki, and the circular crowned hat often associated with the French Foreign Legion. Broad-shouldered and big-bellied, he had deep anger lines around his mouth and stood with hands on hips, impatient, out of temper.

Down below, the dogs started up again. The French officer had his right hand close by a holstered sidearm. Khristo could hear another sound that lay beneath the excited barking, a muted rumble of some sort. He pushed his bicycle forward until he could see inside the partly open door. There were several men in the room, faces indistinct in the dim light, behind a high wooden counter. Standing, apparently. Waiting to greet them. *The rumbling*, he thought. What was that? The narrow alley. The snubbed-off front end of the truck. The truck? No. Not a truck.

Kummelwagen. The open command car used by the Wehrmacht. No French truck ever idled like that; that was a military engine, tuned, powerful, and this was a trap.

He turned his back to the waiting officer and clapped Lucien on the shoulder and spoke through a laugh, in English, with the intonation of a casual joke between friends. 'We are in trouble,' he said.

All the little wrong things. The counter was what you

found in a police station, not a Gendarmerie. Police rode bicycles. Gendarmes drove cars. Someone had converted a homely Poste de Police – a place where you filled out forms – to a trap. Perhaps there had been a *résistance* cell among the gendarmes of Cabejac, at one time made known to Ulysse, but no more.

Lucien was very quick. The 'gendarme' kept his eyes on the Sten. He was surprised when Lucien's left hand came up from his pocket with a small automatic and shot him twice in the heart. He held his breast with both hands and made the face of a man with indigestion as he knelt down. Vigie leapt for the door and slammed it shut, moving his body to one side of the portal and hanging on to the door handle. Something very fast went off inside the station and chewed a line of holes in the wood of the door. Fusari ran toward the building, got one foot against the rough stone surface and sprang upward, snatching the rain gutter that ran below the eaves, then throwing one leg over the edge of the sloping roof and hauling himself the rest of the way. A second burst came through the barred window – one round struck an iron bar and went singing away into the night. Khristo and Lucien backed up. Khristo put a short burst in the door, aiming well away from the clinging Vigie. Lucien fired at an angle through the window shutter. The sound of an engine changing gears cut through the noise of the dogs, which had changed from barking to howling when the gunfire started. Fusari's dark outline appeared on the rooftop. He pulled the pin from a grenade and short-armed it down the chimney. There was an explosion in the shaft, most of its force directed upward. A muffled bang, then the chimney turned into a cloud of smoke and bricks and, a long second later, Fusari's body rolled off the roof and hit the street like a bag.

As brick shards rained down on the street, somebody inside kicked the door open, sending Vigie flying backward. Khristo fired into the press of bodies that appeared within a rolling cloud of black smoke and soot – mouths wide open,

384

hands pressed to ears, faces squeezed with agony, eardrums apparently punctured by compression from the explosion in the chimney. The door was pulled shut just as the Sten jammed on a dud round – no blowback, no next shot. Khristo swore. Lucien ran past, squatted briefly by Fusari, then stood up and grabbed his bicycle. Khristo got his own bike up and moving. He could hear a man screaming inside the building.

All three of them took off like Furies, pedalling wildly as they reached the stairway. Khristo hung on for the first two bounces, then the handlebars tore away from his hands and he was in the air. He landed on shoulder and hip, the impact knocked him senseless, and the bike clattered the rest of the way down the steps, landing with a metallic jangle in the street below. Immediately, a high-power beam probed the dead-end wall until it found the bike, then went dark. Lucien and Vigie somehow got themselves stopped before they reached the street. The next thing Khristo knew, he was being helped up. Someone yelled in German at the top of the stairway. Vigie pointed at a roof, level with the stairs midway up, and they ran to it, climbing over an iron railing. It was just a step up to the next roof and, as they reached it, the light came back on and all three went flat. Khristo's chest heaved against the chalky stone as he fought for breath. From below, they could hear a whispered conversation in German, only ten feet away. Vigie slithered across the roof, peered over the edge for a bare instant, then scrabbled backward until he lay next to them again. He held all his fingers in the air, opening and closing his hands. Too many to count.

Khristo did not think. He cleared the jam on his Sten, snapped in a fresh magazine from his jacket pocket, and made sure the safety was off. He pointed Lucien and Vigie toward the next roof down, then moved toward the edge of the roof to create the necessary diversion. It was simple training, a lifetime of it. One fires, others escape.

Just before he reached the edge, a hand caught his ankle

and stopped him. He pulled as hard as he could, then, in a rage, turned to see Lucien hanging on to him. He fought to suppress the curses rising to his lips, made a low angry sound instead. Lucien pulled on his ankle with such force that it moved him back a foot. Suddenly, a trap door in the roof opened. Khristo swung the Sten around and tensed on the trigger. A small face appeared. A boy, perhaps ten, beckoned to them urgently, then touched his lips for silence. They moved quickly. The face disappeared.

There was a rough ladder below the door and they found themselves in the front room of a house. In the darkness, they could see a young woman in a nightdress standing terrified in one corner, hands in mouth. The boy materialized from another room, wearing a thin shirt and shorts, with an old French infantryman's helmet on his head. He had to hold it on with one hand. He snatched Khristo by the sleeve and pulled him toward a back door. Then he turned suddenly and whispered, *'Anglais?'*

'Non,' Khristo answered. *'Américain.'*

'Bon Dieu!' the boy exclaimed softly, eyes widening with excitement.

Then he turned and dragged Khristo through the door into a tiny garden plot at the back of the house. The garden butted up against a stone wall topped by a sagging fence of rusted wire. There was a wooden barrel positioned at the base of the wall. The boy let go of Khristo, reached the top of the barrel with a practised leap, then stepped up onto the wall and waved for them to follow. The wall was twelve inches wide with broken bottles cemented down the middle but there was just enough room to get a foot on either side of the jagged glass and the boy scuttled along quickly, crouched low, hanging on to his helmet with one hand. The German troops seemed to be all around them: they heard shouted commands, boots pounding on the street, the sound of a truck shifting between reverse and first gears as the driver attempted to get it turned around in the narrow street. They ran along the wall past four or five houses, then the boy jumped off onto another barrel – no doubt in the backyard of his war-game companion – and onto the ground. The moment Khristo landed, the boy took hold of his sleeve again, they ran forward a few feet, then stopped abruptly. They were at the twin of the alley that Khristo had seen earlier and the soldier game clearly called for scooting down the narrow space and crossing the street. But as they turned the corner the boy's hand quivered and a small cry of fright escaped him. A German officer stood in profile at the end of the alley, waving both hands toward himself as though directing traffic. They flattened back against the wall while the boy thought it over. For a moment, Khristo knew the thing was finished, but the boy peered around the corner, then darted across the alley and, one by one, they followed him. On the other side, they found him straining at a cast-iron grating set level with the ground. Khristo bent to help him and together they pushed it to one side. The boy lowered himself down, then moved forward head first, sliding on his stomach. Khristo followed, listened to make sure Vigie could pull the grating back over by himself, then continued ahead.

The stone beneath him was covered with slime, which eased progress, though the reek of long-stagnant water was nearly overpowering. A storm drain, he thought, with its other end somewhere well east of the Germans if they had any luck at all. He heard the scamper and the tiny squeaking somewhere up the sewer ahead of him – he knew what that meant but forced himself not to think about it. Suddenly, the stone moved beneath him and something roared above his head. He stopped, then realized they were under the street and a truck had just passed over him. He closed his eyes in order to concentrate and resumed crawling, slowly and in rhythm, elbow, knee, elbow, knee, and he could now begin to hear the sound of breathing, his own, and the others', as the motion became an effort. His elbow touched the boy's foot twice before he figured out that the boy was tiring and slowing down. '*Moment,*' he whispered, and lay still. He reached above him, found the ceiling just over his head. The drain had narrowed. He cinched the strap of the Sten tighter and tried to recover his strength.

Behind him, Lucien's voice was barely audible: 'How far? Ask him.'

Khristo did. The boy answered that he didn't know. Khristo passed the word back to Lucien. Lucien asked Vigie if he'd heard. Vigie did not answer. Lucien, in a stage whisper, called out, 'Vigie.' No answer. Lucien doubled his knees up to his chin and managed to get himself turned around. Khristo heard him belly-crawling down the pipe, his breath hoarse with effort. He was gone, it seemed to Khristo, a very long time. Finally, the sound of his progress returned, and Lucien arrived a minute later. He moved as close to Khristo as he could and spoke by his ear. 'He's not here.'

'I heard him. He closed the grating.'

'Closed it behind us.'

'What?'

'Perhaps he was afraid. Close spaces. Rats. I don't know.'

'Goddamn him,' Khristo said.

'He'll get out,' Lucien said.

Khristo whispered to the boy. 'Are you all right?'

'*Oui, Capitaine,*' came the answer, but the voice told a different story. '*C'est le tunnel interdit,*' the boy explained. *The forbidden tunnel*, Khristo thought. Because you will get dirty? Because you will get lost or frightened? Or why? 'You have been before?' Khristo asked. Yes, the boy said. Once. For a few feet only. Never this far.

Khristo thought it over for a moment but there was no alternative. Unless to stay here until the following night, then try to escape through the streets. But Vigie's absence made even that impossible. If he were caught, he would be made to show the Germans where they'd gone. For he had been seen by those in the police station, would not be able to talk his way out of trouble.

On command from Lucien, they continued forward.

For a long time, there seemed to be no end to it. His adrenaline from the attack was long dissipated, and when they stopped to rest he could feel that the skin on his knees and elbows was ripped and bleeding. The dead, oily water attacked the open skin like quicklime. How could the water be so stagnant, he wondered. If water still ran through the storm drain, it should renew itself every few days in the spring rains. Unless a diverter pipe had been removed from the entry and a grating fixed in its place. And the tunnel forbidden. Because its other end was sealed.

An hour later, they came to a grating fixed over the end of the pipe. But the tunnel had widened, and the stone was soft and rotted, and both he and Lucien had knives, so they were able to dig the rusted staples out of the crumbled masonry. Khristo doubled his body back and kicked the grating out. They heard it crashing down a hill.

Crawling out into the tangled underbrush of a hillside, they could hear the sound of the river just below them. For a time, Khristo sat with his head in his hands, breathing deeply, wanting more sweet air each time he exhaled. He was filthy, his trousers soaked with watery slime and, where the cloth had worn away, the skin of his knees showed through, bright red and beaded with blood. Lucien sat down beside him and beckoned the boy to join them. In the faint moonlight Khristo could see tear tracks that ran through the dirt on the boy's face, but he'd made not a sound in the tunnel.

'Where are we?' Lucien asked the boy.

'Below the road,' he said, 'on the hill behind the barn of Madame Rossot.'

'Do you have someone to go to?' Lucien asked. 'Someone

who will clean you up and take you home so the Germans don't see you?'

The boy pondered that for a moment. Then shook his head vigorously beneath the helmet. 'Madame Rossot,' he said, 'though she becomes very angry if we go behind her barn.'

'Are you sure?' Lucien said.

'The *schleuh* killed her husband, in the Great War.'

'You are very brave,' Lucien said. He stood and searched in his pockets.

Khristo thought at first he was looking for money, then realized he wanted something to give the boy – something he could keep. Khristo knew the very thing and fished about for it in his pocket. His good luck charm. That he had kept with him in Spain. That had been stored in Santé prison with his civilian clothes. He stood, then waved the boy to his feet. 'I decorate you for bravery,' he said, giving the boy what he'd taken from his pocket. He extended his hand and the boy shook it formally, very much like a soldier receiving a medal, then looked in the palm of his other hand, at the white pawn resting there.

'*Merci, monsieur,*' he said.

'You are dismissed,' Lucien said. 'Now be careful, will you?' The boy moved off along a trail through the brush, and then he was gone.

They rested for an hour, then, as dawn approached, worked their way cross-country to their emergency fallback position – a downed maple tree a mile short of Cabejac, on the road to Abonne. They waited the rest of the day for Vigie, eating a chocolate bar from Lucien's pocket and, once darkness fell, cleaning themselves by the river. They hid out that night and all the next day, but Vigie did not appear. He was never seen again.

*   *   *

In the town of Abonne there were three small pulp mills that processed wood fibre from the forests of the Vosges into newsprint and inexpensive papers of all kinds. It smelled dreadful, like all the wood-pulp towns of the world, and life there was lived amid a sulphurous haze of rotten eggs. Such conditions the Germans found sharply discordant with their vision of *La Belle France* and they tended to stay away from the place – occupying armies have a habit of discovering strategic value in towns where life is comfortable and pleasant, and the Germans were no exception to the rule.

Left to themselves, the townspeople had organized a particularly predatory and efficient *maquis*, concentrated among the millworkers and led by the local union boss, a tough old bastard called Vedoc. When the remnants of the Lucien team walked back into Abonne, hollow-eyed and exhausted, they were taken immediately to Vedoc's house. His wife and sister cleaned out the larder to feed them while Vedoc himself provided an ample supply of that year's basement wine, aged all of eight months and considered pretty good for what it was. The one called Lucien was too quiet, too much inside himself, so Vedoc, who had seen this sort of thing before, kept him reasonably drunk and sent an old lady off on a series of local trains to Belfort.

The Bugatti pulled up in front of Vedoc's house a week later. Ulysse, shadowed as always by the cold-eyed Albert, was his usual elegant self: calm, aloof, an island of Gallic sanity in the stormy seas. Winter was gone and the pearl-coloured topcoat with it; a stylish raincoat now served as cape. Only Khristo, perhaps, noted a tiny razor nick to one side of his Adam's apple and inferred that Ulysse himself was having to withstand a storm or two.

They were debriefed at length – first separately, then together – on the trap at Cabejac. Ulysse showed them a series of photographs, which Albert then carefully burned in the fireplace. They could identify only the 'gendarme', and he was, they both believed, likely dead. They talked for hours over a two-day period while the room turned blue with smoke. They told the story again and again. Ulysse listened with infinite patience, Albert took notes in some private code of his own.

During this time, Khristo gained some understanding of the aristocrat's character. He was obviously an acute observer of human beings, their strengths and weaknesses, what they could take and what they couldn't. It was as though he had long ago ceased to judge behaviour and had, instead, given himself over to the pure study of it. Further, it became clear to Khristo that war was this man's time, that war ran in his blood, heritage of an aristocracy that had led men in battle for centuries and continued to do so. And that it was precisely this comprehension, this set of instincts, that Ulysse had put at the disposal of the American intelligence services in order to defeat his traditional enemy.

Thus he was not at all surprised when Ulysse suggested a walk in the woods behind Vedoc's house on an afternoon when the weather was cold and grey. Lucien had been sent off on a small errand. Albert, shotgun in hand, waited at the edge of the trees.

Ulysse strolled slowly, hands clasped behind his back, and his mood was soft and tentative. With a rather arch apology for the lack of *makhorka* ('My tobacconist stocks it only once in a great while'), he offered Khristo a Gitane and lit it with a snap of his gold lighter.

'Of course I must not ask you about Lucien,' he said as they walked.

'No,' Khristo responded.

'Loyalty to a comrade-in-arms is everything.'

'Naturally, that is so.'

'Americans, Americans,' he said, despair in his voice. 'They do not accept casualties at all well, do they. They take it to heart, and they blame themselves. A kind of false pride, surely, yet one must admire them for it. Do you?'

'Yes,' Khristo said, 'I do.'

'Yet a man of your experience must also see that it is their weakness.'

'Perhaps a weakness. Or a strength. Or both at once, perhaps.'

'Yes,' Ulysse mused. 'Still, not an ideal trait for an officer class, you'll admit that.'

'I suppose not,' Khristo said.

'Lucien has done very well, you know, in the way these things are judged. Quite a number of trains, and one must add what other groups have been able to do with his assistance, and what they will do in the future. Considered altogether, a most gratifying boil on Hitler's backside. But, we ask ourselves, can he continue? I've not told Lucien, by the way, but the village of Cambras has been entirely decimated.'

Khristo winced and shook his head in sorrow.

'Yes, I'm afraid so. A servant girl betrayed them to the Gestapo, and they were taken by surprise. She had been made pregnant by Gilbert, poor thing, and was terrified she would be cast out of the village, to live in the woods, and in her state of mind the Germans seemed like saviours, who could rescue her from her predicament. I don't look forward, I must tell you, to the moment when Lucien learns of this.'

'He has no lack of courage,' Khristo said.

'Not remotely in question,' Ulysse said. 'But do you suppose he would be willing to sacrifice the lives of others, should it become necessary?'

Khristo was silent.

'Please forgive me,' Ulysse said, 'for having to ask you that.'

'The world will go on,' Khristo said.

'It will.' He paused to light another cigarette. 'And then, where will you be?'

'God may know that,' Khristo answered honestly, 'I do not.'

'In your homeland, perhaps? To marry and make a life? It is what most of us will do, in time.'

'No,' Khristo said, 'I do not think so. Though there are times when I would give anything to be back where I was born, even for one hour. But I have seen the world, and whoever runs that country will want to start fresh – they won't have much use for people who have seen the world. It will be under the Russians, I think, and there won't be anything we can do about it. Our history is a sharp lesson on the subject of borders.'

Ulysse nodded in sympathy. 'We're going to exfiltrate Lucien to Switzerland, in a day or two. Would you like to come along?'

They walked along the path through the mist; the sound of dripping trees filled the silence. 'Yes,' Khristo said.

'You'll be interned, in a sort of way, so that our understandings with the Swiss will be, at least, nominally observed. But your circumstances can be most comfortable, and, who knows, you may just make some new friends. American friends. Would you like that?'

'Yes,' Khristo said, 'I would.'

Long before dawn, the horse-drawn carts began lining up on the French side of the Vöernstrasse bridge. There wasn't all that much produce to take into the Saturday market – you got little variety in early May – but the farmers brought what they could: cabbage, broccoli, spinach, wintered-over carrots, and early greens of every sort. Across the bridge, in the well-swept squares of the city, the housewives of Basel awaited their French vegetables – one more Swiss cauliflower might well have driven them mad.

The border guards came in two versions: the Vichy French, theoretically still in charge of their own boundaries, and the Germans – Gestapo or military – who considered the Swiss border far too sensitive to entrust to French authorities. In any event, there were far more Germans than French at this particular crossing and they milled about ceaselessly, sharp-eyed and suspicious – there was always some wretched idiot hidden away under the produce and fishing him out meant extra leave. So they took their time, while the horses stood patiently, and checked the farmers' well-worn passports long before the wagons actually reached the bridge.

Khristo held the reins loosely in his hand while Lucien appeared to doze at his side. Behind them, the old wooden cart was piled high with cabbages. The German corporal who approached them was no more than eighteen, a country boy with red cheeks and a stiff shock of blond hair who licked his callused thumb to turn each passport page. He looked from faces to photographs – up and down, up and down – a dozen times before he was satisfied.

But he could find nothing amiss because the French passports were in every way perfect, legitimately issued to real French citizens and full of exit stamps from previous market Saturdays. He next turned his attention to the two farmers, forcing them to empty their pockets onto the seat of the cart and pawing through a collection of string, wire, horseshoe nails, a few strands of pipe tobacco, half-used ration cards, and a miscellany of French and Swiss coins – all gloriously redolent of horse manure. But the corporal was a farmboy and did not mind at all.

At last, he turned his attention to the huge whitish-green mound of cabbages piled in the cart. He lifted them up, rolled them aside, peered down among them, and seemed intent on spending the rest of his days in contemplation of a pile of cabbages. Finally, the driver turned halfway round in his seat and called out to the corporal in a loud voice, his market German cut by a strong French accent:

'Hey back there! What are you doing? Counting the farts?'

The Germans roared with laughter and waved him ahead – any mention of such matters hit them hard in the funny bone.

And somebody knew that too.

* * *

In December of 1944, Robert Eidenbaugh was transferred to administrative duty in the United States, with a thirty-day furlough to precede his appearance at the OSS offices in Washington, D.C. He flew from Croydon airfield on a MATS C-47, landed at a military air base on the eastern seaboard, and made his way to Boston to see his family.

It was a happy, emotional reunion, lacking only his younger brother, who was serving as a gunnery officer on a destroyer in the Pacific. The family had devoted themselves to the war – his father's firm now entirely taken up with designs for a new battle cruiser, his mother managing blood donor drives for the Boston Red Cross, various cousins and uncles spread across the globe in a variety of uniforms. One of his mother's Wiscasset nephews had died in New Guinea but they were thankful that, otherwise, the casualty lists had not touched them, and the grace said before meals was no longer the casual mumble it had once been.

The family found Robert leaner, stronger, and a good deal older than when he'd left, and they made a considerable fuss over him. Privately, Arthur and Elva Eidenbaugh thought their son had changed. He seemed lonely, edgy, isolated and, sometimes, angry for no discernible reason. They decided that what he needed was to raise a little hell and, to that end, slipped ten ten-dollar bills in a new wallet and shooed him off to New York.

Before he was even out of Grand Central Station he'd treated himself to an elaborate dinner at the Oyster Bar. He managed to promote a special serviceman's room at the Biltmore and was given, a privilege of uniform, a ticket to a Broadway show. For two days he wandered around midtown Manhattan, bought a few Christmas presents, and enjoyed the anonymity of being part of a busy city; looking at faces, listening to conversations, trying to pick up the thread of American life. Walking down the street he was only one uniform among many, yet now and again he did sense the quiet approval of strangers.

He called some old friends, but most were not around. Dropped in at the OSS office on Madison Avenue, where Agatha Hamilton, the genteel lady who had been involved in his recruitment, treated him to the lunch at Luchow's he was supposed to have had three years earlier. Walking back up to the Biltmore – it was a sunny, cold day – he ran into one of the J. Walter Thompson telephone operators, and she invited him to the big Christmas party that Thompson was throwing late that afternoon.

When Eidenbaugh arrived, just after five, there were already more than a hundred people milling about. The Thompson staff had made a major effort for the party. By marshalling their considerable design resources, they had managed to make the rather utilitarian space seem festive and seasonal. There were no balloons – latex had been declared a strategic material for the duration – but there was everything else: streamers of coloured crepe paper, red and green Santas driving paper-bag cutout reindeer across the walls, and a huge Norfolk pine tree cut from the Stamford property of one of the senior partners – so fulsomely decorated its lower boughs touched the linoleum floor. There was every sort of liquor and large trays of sandwiches, cookies and fruit cake – the entire office had pooled sugar rations for the party. The opaque green glass that divided the cubicles was decorated with posters done by Thompson for various wartime campaigns: recruiting, blood donation, war bonds, aluminium collection, and the cautionary ones advising defence plant workers not to talk about what they did.

When Eidenbaugh arrived, they made him very welcome indeed. He felt like a hero. He was kissed and hugged and slapped on the back, a triple-strength Scotch and soda appeared in his left hand, a giant Christmas cookie in his right. Looking about, he could see several uniforms moving through the crowd. He was in the midst of earnest conversation with a young woman from Barnard, who did something in the production department, when Mr. Drowne, his old boss, stood on a desk at the centre of the room and banged on a drinking glass with a knife.

'Oh Gawd,' his new friend said, 'here goes Drownie.'

Mr. Drowne cleared his throat. 'On behalf of the J. Walter Thompson Company, I want to take special notice of some of our fighting men and women who are here with us tonight. Some of them are former employees, their friends, whoever you may be, all are welcome! We think it would be fitting if each of you would step up and say a little something and give us folks on the home front a chance to express our appreciation.'

This announcement was received with cheering, and the parade began. Marine Captain Bruce Johnson from the billing department, who had lost a leg at Tarawa. Army Lieutenant Lee Golden, former account executive, now instructing pilots in Oklahoma. Naval Lieutenant Howard Bister, from the copywriting department, who had participated in the D-Day landings the previous June.

Bister, looking sharp in his dark blue officer's uniform, faced the crowd and waited that brief moment which usually signals that the speaker has something significant to say. As prelude, he thanked Mr. Drowne and the Thompson management for one helluva fine party, as well as for their hard work in bond drive and recruiting campaigns. Then he placed his drink on the desk next to him and took off his glasses.

'On D-Day,' he said, 'I found myself aboard the U.S.S. *Bigelow*, an APA, which, for the uninitiated, is an attack transport that loads assault troops into landing craft for their final run to the beach. We were carrying several hundred reserves, whose job it would be to replace casualties taken in the first day of the attack. My job – it sounds important but let me tell you people that every job is important in an operation like this, from the mess stewards all the way to the admirals – my job was flag signals officer to Rear Admiral Orville G. Brants. At dawn, the sixth of June, I brought the admiral his coffee on the bridge, where he was standing with the ship's captain as we circled out in the Channel. Just as I reached the bridge, we were bracketed by two shells from a shore battery. I won't say it was close, but I did get some spray on me. "Careful, Lieutenant," Admiral Brants said to me, "don't spill that java." Not a word, you understand, about the shore batteries. Well, I spent most of the day up on that bridge, while the battle raged ashore, and I just want to say that I've never been so proud to be an American. Thank you.'

Applause thundered out for Bister's speech. The young woman from Production, standing next to Eidenbaugh, squeezed a cocktail napkin tightly in her fist and her eyes followed Bister as he walked away from the table. Mr. Drowne cleared his throat before he was able to speak again. 'Thank you, Howard,' he said. 'We are all very proud of you. Next' – he peered out over the crowd – 'I think I see Bob Eidenbaugh. Bob?'

Eidenbaugh moved slowly to the front of the room, then turned and looked into the expectant faces before him. 'I'm Captain Robert F. Eidenbaugh,' he said. 'I used to work in the copy department. And I want to thank the Thompson people for a terrific party. As for my war, well, I was involved in staff work in London, lots of details, nothing very glamorous I'm afraid. Anyhow, I do want to wish everyone a merry Christmas.'

There was a scattering of polite applause as he made his way through the crowded room and Mr. Drowne stepped in quickly to fill the gathering silence. 'And I'm sure that work was important!' he said firmly as his eyes sought the next speaker.

Eidenbaugh returned to his new friend as a Marine corporal described the landing at Okinawa. 'Well,' she said, much too cheerfully, sensing his mood, 'someone's got to do the paperwork.'

Robert Eidenbaugh stayed at the party for a half hour, then he went back to the Biltmore.

* * *

In Basel, Khristo Stoianev lived in a rooming house on the Burgenstrasse and walked to work every morning on little streets shaded by lime trees. Legally, he had been interned in neutral Switzerland for the duration of the war. In fact, he read Bulgarian newspapers and transcripts of radio broadcasts and fought the Germans with scissors and paste.

His task involved abstracting the truth from the Nazi-controlled Bulgarian press and radio. If they said a certain fact was true, he was to comment on the degree of falsity in the claim. Would the Bulgarians believe it? Which ones would know it to be false? Did he think it true? His English improved as he wrote copious, longhand answers to these questions, and he became adept at working through systems of lies: the shades and tones, the subtleties, the tiny crumb of truth that sweetened the digestion of a falsehood. He dealt also with the 'hammers' – designed to bash the population on the head with information until some of them at least believed that two and two made seven and weren't they the lucky ones to have so much.

This particular approach – studying newspapers and transcripts – had been severely maligned by the NKVD instructors at Arbat Street. At the direction of Comrade Stalin himself. All worthwhile intelligence, *razvedka*, had to come from secret channels, undercover agents, and suborned informants. The rest – the use of open sources – was deemed mere research, women's work, not befitting the heroic Soviet intelligence *apparat*. The dictum, as put by Western intelligence services, ran, *we only believe what we steal*.

For Khristo, the work was boring and repetitive – a long,

400

difficult test, he rather thought. He worked for a former college professor from Leipzig, a gentle soul who watered his plants every day, and neither praised nor criticized – simply accepted his work as though it were, each day, each time, a happy surprise, saying 'Ah!' when he appeared in the doorway to hand in a thick batch of reports.

But it was clean where he lived and where he worked, quiet, Swiss, and it would be warm, he knew, in the wintertime. He had a casual woman friend who entertained him on Thursday nights. He had become entirely addicted to *Rösti*, a crisp pancake of fried potatoes and onions. He lived in a room of his own, and he had a radio. When the people he worked for asked him questions – about his former life and work – he answered them. As the summer turned hot and silent, he burrowed to the centre of his circumscribed life and nested safe and sound. He thought about Aleksandra only now and then, when the summer nights were too quiet for sleep.

In late August, communist *partizans* rose in Bulgaria and threw the Germans out. Bulgarian fascists were executed. The Bulgarian Communist party immediately allied itself with the Soviet Union, and the newspapers and radio transcripts took an entirely different line – the propaganda remained much as it had under the Germans but was, Khristo felt, more artfully developed. The massed children's choirs who had 'spontaneously' sung carols in Hitler's honour the previous Christmas now sang anthems dedicated to Joseph Stalin. By the ninth of September, 1944, the change of government had been completed. Parades were held. A news photograph from Vidin came across Khristo's desk. The old Turkish post office, on the same street where his brother had been murdered by fascists, was hung with two-storey banners: portraits of Lenin, Stalin, and Dmitrov.

Then, as the summer ended and the German armies of occupation fled east from Paris, a curious thing happened. A coincidence. He opened a folder of news clippings and saw that a mistake had been made. This folder contained news items not from the Balkans – but from the United States. He glanced at the clipping on top of the pile and saw a photograph of Faye Berns.

The article was taken from the business page of a newspaper in Manhattan, and it said that Miss Faye Berns had been appointed fund-raising director of the New York office of the World Aid Committee, which would seek to assist Displaced Persons in returning to their homelands once the war ended. The article was brief, but it did give the address of the World Aid Committee, and he copied it out on a piece of paper.

In the photograph, a three-quarter angle, he could see the changes. Her hair was shorter, there was a line to her jaw that hadn't been there before, and she had smiled for the photographer in a way that he didn't recognize. It was an artificial smile, posed and official.

For a long time he stared at the photograph, shocked by the degree to which memory had betrayed him, deceived him. Because he had always remembered her as she was in Paris, on the afternoon they had met by accident in the bookstore. He had, unwittingly, frozen her in time, kept her as she had been on a June day in 1937. He remembered her as she cried for Andres, remembered her as someone who would dare to love a man like Andres, who did not desert him, who paid the price of that love, and then survived. He remembered her as a girl who had flung herself against the world without caution, without a care for her safety. Now she was a woman who had grown up to accept the artifice of a smile, poised and confident, for a newspaper.

He remembered, particularly, both times they had touched: when she had slept on his shoulder in the car parked at the Bilbao docks, and when she had held his hands while they waited for the train to depart at the Gare du Nord. Did men and women ordinarily remember the times when they'd touched each other? He did not know.

Once again his eye ran over the article. *Miss* Faye Berns.

So she had not married the man she had mentioned in the letter that had reached him in prison.

He decided to write to her, and spent the better part of an hour at his desk, composing in English. But it was not to be. The letter seemed to him, when he drew back from it, strange and wrong: a man she had once known, briefly, writing poorly in a language not his own and apologizing for it. He tore it up. The girl he had known in Paris might respond to such a letter, but the fund-raising director of the World Aid Committee would, he feared, find it awkward, even pathetic.

He took the folder into the professor's office. 'This is not for me,' he said in explanation, setting the folder on one corner of the desk. 'Ah!' the professor said, surprised that such a thing could happen.

And why, he wondered, returning down the hall to his little room, *are they toying with me?* The 'misdelivered' news clipping was no coincidence. It was a provocation. It was their way of letting him know that they were aware of his relationship with Faye Berns. What could that matter to them? What could they mean by it? And how had they known about it? More important, what did they expect of him now that he'd seen the clipping?

He didn't know. And decided to ignore the incident. If this were something truly significant, they'd press him further. He turned his attention to other matters, determined to put the entire episode out of mind. He bore down on his work for the rest of the afternoon, then, since it was Thursday, went off to visit his woman friend.

She was, as usual, responsive, falling in with his mood and treating him with a certain casual tenderness that he'd always found very comforting. Yet he was not his best self, distracted by the image of a woman with a professional smile in a grainy photograph. He imagined himself a great realist, and that passion without sentiment suited him perfectly. But at work on Friday morning he experienced a surge of emotion, more gratitude than love, and sent his friend a bouquet of flowers. For which she thanked him, with a certain casual tenderness, the following Thursday.

In Basel, the autumn came on quickly, and by October the mornings were frosty and clear. One such morning he arrived punctually for work and, on opening the vestibule door, came upon Ulysse and Albert and two other men he did not know. They were rolling down their sleeves and putting on their jackets and yawning – he had the impression they had been up all night and working hard. Ulysse's eyes lit up when he saw Khristo and he smiled broadly. 'Well, well,' he said, in perfect American English, 'look what the cat dragged in.'

Khristo grinned sheepishly, a little taken aback, and they shook hands warmly. Ulysse turned to leave, his overcoat, as always, worn capelike over his shoulders, and his bodyguard followed. As Albert moved past, he winked at Khristo and banged him affectionately on the shoulder with his fist.

'Hey buddy,' he said.

Bessarabia

In December of 1944, at the Utiny gold fields on the Kolyma River, in a far southeastern corner of the Siberian USSR, Captain Ilya Goldman sat before a table of unpeeled birch logs in one of the interrogation rooms of Camp 782. Alone for the moment, he held his head in his hands, closed his eyes to shut out the world, and listened to the timbers creak and snap in the frozen air. A light wind blew in off the East Siberian Sea, sighing in the eaves, rising and falling. Otherwise, there was nothing.

On the table before him were two stacks of files, which represented prisoners already processed and those yet to be seen. A bare bulb dangled from the ceiling on a long cord. At his feet, a malevolent cold flowed up through the floorboards, seeping through his boots and socks, a kind of icy fire that caused the skin to itch and burn simultaneously. This he accepted. Travelling the Utiny camps, he had come to admire the cold, a cunning predator that used the human body as a wick, crawling upward in search of the centre of warmth. The heart – that was what it wanted.

And welcome to it, he thought.

He took a deep breath, closed his mind to anger, and tried to concentrate on the notes he had just completed. They were scratched on the stiff, waxy paper native to Soviet bureaucracy – wood-flecked, pale brown stuff meant to last for a thousand years. The millennium, therefore, would know that at least one inmate of Camp 782 had claimed that the bread ration was more than adequate, perhaps excessive, and gone on to suggest that food allocations be reduced, so that the heroic men and women of the patriotic Red Army might better strengthen themselves for the fight against the fascist invader. So said Prisoner 389062, a nameless yellow skull that had sat nodding and trembling before him, twisting a cap in his hands in the ancient gesture of the peasant and attempting, toothless mouth stretched to its limits, what could have been taken for a smile. The statement had been dutifully recorded and signed by Captain I. J. Goldman, Office of the Inspector General, Bureau of Labour Camps, Fourth Division, Sixth Directorate, NKVD.

Thus, in bureaucratic terms, he had been buried alive.

Since the inception of his service in Spain, Ilya Goldman had moved exclusively in the upper echelons of the NKVD – First Chief Directorate, Fifth Department – the prized Western Europe posting. Ideologically, he was trusted. Professionally, he was considered clever and sharp-witted, a man who played the game and avoided the pitfalls: protecting his friends and protected by them, gaining influence, banking favours every day. Words of thanks were, casually, waved away. *Some day*, he would tell his newfound friends, *you can help me out*.

But when the great day came – a punitive transfer to the office responsible for the labour camps – his friends did not answer their telephones, and down he went. Into an abyss where grace and wit counted for nothing. Here you needed only a steel fist and an iron stomach, though it helped to be blind and deaf. He despised himself for allowing such a thing to happen, for not comprehending that it could happen. He had stood so high in his own opinion: brilliant, deft, an intelligence officer who *belonged* in Madrid, in Paris, in Geneva. A smart little Jewboy from Bucharest – he mocked himself – sophisticated and urbane, in NKVD argot a *cosmopolite*, deserved no less. The service would never send such a fine fellow off to the Gulag, to listen to memorized speeches from a parade of exhausted skeletons. Oh no, they'd never do that.

But he had failed them, had tried to deceive them, and they'd found out and punished him.

His downfall had come about in Romania, of all places, the homeland he had not seen for ten years. Sad, wretched place, backwater of southeastern Europe with its ridiculous decayed nobility and peasants who had believed, truly believed, Iron Guard leader Codreanu to be the reincarnation of Christ. Their leaders had sided with Hitler, and the Romanian divisions had fought bravely enough, in the Crimean peninsula and elsewhere, before the massive Russian counterattacks had inevitably rolled them back.

The country had surrendered early in September. To the United States, Great Britain, and the USSR, theoretically, but the Russians were little interested in the diplomatic niceties of shared power and, within days, had presented their bill to the Romanians. Then sent NKVD personnel, Ilya Goldman among them, to make sure it was paid. In full. And on time.

It was, for a country that had just finished fighting four years of war, a bill of some considerable magnitude. Seven hundred million lei – about fifty million U.S. dollars – easily exceeding the contents of the Romanian treasury. But this was merely the first item on the bill. The government had to provide, in addition, the following: all privately owned radios, 2,500,000 tons of grain, 1,700,000 head of cattle, 13,000 horses, and vast tonnages of vegetables, potatoes, and cigarettes. All telephone and telegraph lines were to be torn down and shipped east in boxcars – once the latter had been refitted to accept the Russian rail gauge. Twelve divisions to be formed immediately to fight the Germans and the Hungarians. The list went on: ambulances, doctors, gold, silver, watches, timber – whatever they had, the entire national wealth. Further, the USSR would now control all means of communication, the merchant marine, all utilities and industries, all factories and storage depots, and all radio stations. If the Romanian population couldn't listen to them, with all the radios shipped east, foreign monitors could.

The directives went out and the peasants, by and large,

obeyed. Ilya saw them shuffling into the villages and market towns with their livestock and the contents of their granaries and root cellars – even next spring's seed grain. God had directed their leaders, they seemed to feel, now God had forsaken them. Ilya watched their faces, and the sight broke his heart. To his superiors, of course, he was not a Romanian, he was a Jew – that was a nationality, a race – and they saw no reason he should feel allegiance to a country adopted in the distant past by some wandering pedlar and his family. He was supposed to know these people, their little tricks and deceits, and he was supposed to squeeze them.

Not that his bosses meant him to do any of the rough stuff himself. No, they had special personnel for that, many of them former Iron Guardsmen who had now 'seen the light' of progressive socialism. No more than thugs in uniforms, but they served a purpose. When there was shooting to be done, they did it. But Ilya heard it, and saw the bodies sagged lifeless on the posts behind the barracks. Sometimes one didn't have to shoot, a simple beating would suffice. When the peasants were beaten, they cried out for mercy from the lord of the manor – an old tradition. Clearly, they did not understand what was happening to them, protested their innocence, swore it before God.

Most of them, however, did as they were told. Brought in everything they had, garlanded their beasts before they were led away so that they might make a good impression on their new masters and be treated with kindness. One old man, parting with his plough horse, slipped a carrot in Ilya's pocket. 'He's a stubborn old thing,' he'd whispered, believing Ilya to be the new owner, 'but he'll work like the devil for a treat.'

For the first few weeks, as the Carpathians turned gold in early autumn, he had steeled himself to it, took it as a test of courage, inner strength. But his superiors had not been entirely wrong about him; he did know these people, their little tricks and deceits. In fact, he knew

410

them much too well. He knew the look in the eyes of a man who sees a lifetime's labour flicked away in an instant.

So he cheated.

Just a little, here and there, principally sins of omission, a matter of not reporting what he saw. But, as the weeks went by, the accounting was turned in and the numbers rose up through the apparatus to those whose job it was to compare, to set unit beside unit in order to judge production. And the showing of his group grew poorer and poorer until somebody caught on and sent somebody else down there to see what the hell was going on and it only took a little while before they got onto him.

The transfer followed immediately. He tried making certain telephone calls. But they'd marked him, and his friends knew enough to leave him alone lest the virus touch them as well.

*   *   *

At Camp 782, the procession of inmates continued all through the winter afternoon as the wind sang in the eaves. One left, another entered. Each prisoner had been judiciously selected by the camp commandant, so their statements were well rehearsed. It was all to do with self-sacrifice, patriotism, hard work, shock brigades that laboured through the night to meet a production norm. And, of course, undying faith in the Great Leader. Ilya Goldman wrote it all down and signed it, an automaton, playing his assigned role in the ritual. The mute agony of these places – themselves lost in the silence of the endless, frozen land – would finish him if he permitted himself to feel it, so he had, by self-direction, grown numb, and now felt nothing about anything. There was no other defence.

By early evening, only one file remained to be processed.

411

503775.
Admitted: 20 December 1936
Labour Classification: Clerk
Present Function: Office of Task Assignment
Security Notation: Reliable
Charge: Articles 40, 42, 42A, 45 and 70 of the
Judicial Code
Release Date: 20 December 1966

There was no name on the file, no age, nothing of
503775's life before admission to the camp system. Such
information was classified and held elsewhere, no doubt
in the files of the resident NKVD officer. But Ilya could tell
by a glance down the page that this had, at one time, been
somebody, somebody snaffled up in the purges of 1936, too
important or favoured to kill, thus consigned to the Utiny,
a nonperson. The man was a trustee, with a good deal of
power – clerk's power, but power nonetheless – so had
apparently contrived to ingratiate himself with the camp
administration. When he entered the room, Ilya felt a slight
prickle of recognition.

.To look at, he was no different from the others – hesitant,
nervous, with humility suggested in every motion. He
dragged a foot as he walked – a soft scrape on the
floorboards – his head was shaven against the lice, camp
rations had shrunken his features, and his eyes were slitted
from years of the Kolyma weather, sun glaring off the ice
fields. His shoulders were stooped, his beard long and lank
– a man perhaps in his late fifties, though one could never
be sure about age in a camp.

Ilya nodded him to the chair; he sat down, then launched
himself into a speech of such patriotic frenzy that it became
clear to Ilya why the commandant had placed him last
on the day's schedule – a theatrical flourish to send the
inspector general's little man off happy to his next camp.
The phrases flowed like oil. 'Let it be remembered' and
'hour of the nation's need' and 'strayed from the true

412

course' and 'dedicated more than ever to sacrifice'. All that year's favourites – the man was something of a poet, working in the genre of political cliché.

My God, Ilya thought, *I'm talking to Sascha Vonets.*

He lurched forward, face lit by recognition. Opened his mouth to speak. Sascha's hand shot across the table and Ilya felt a rough finger pressed briefly against his lips in a plea for silence. Ilya was caught with admiration. Sascha didn't miss a beat – 'inspired by the Great Leader' – as he pointed back and forth to the far wall and his right ear. Ilya nodded his complicity. The camp commandant was evidently making sure that nobody said *the wrong thing*. The interrogation room had been cleverly constructed within a maze of administrative offices, essentially three partitions built against an exterior wall. It was windowless, as all interrogation facilities were supposed to be; one wanted to avoid even the implicit suggestion that the prisoner had any way out of the difficulties in which he found himself. The camp commandant, Ilya realized, would likely have some flunky sitting next to one of the walls and taking verbatim notes in shorthand.

Sascha, having wound up his introductory remarks, now began the recitation of a poem entitled 'Red Banners', a reference to the NKVD medal of honour that could never be worn in public. This poem was, apparently, a personal contribution to the war effort. From the first stanza it became clear to Ilya that it was to be a kind of modern epic, an inspirational hymn of praise to the security services:

> Arise!
> O patriots of the shadows –
> who do not see the flight of cranes,
> whose red banners fly in darkness only –
> we salute you!

It went on for quite some time, stern images of struggle and heroism marching forward in a grand parade. Then, as he ended the recitation, Sascha came around the table and thrust two slips of paper into the front of Ilya's uniform jacket. When he moved away and sat down again, Ilya slowly exhaled the breath he'd been holding. Up close, the smell of mildew and stale sweat had nearly gagged him.

'Might one ask, comrade Captain, your opinion of my humble poem?'

'Laudable,' Ilya said. 'I will certainly inform the appropriate agencies of the existence of this work, you may depend on it.'

'Thank you, comrade Major.'

'Thank *you*, 503775. You are dismissed.'

Sascha stood. For one instant his eyes were naked, and Ilya saw the truth of the eight years he had spent in the camps. Then the man drew back inside himself, his eyes dulled, and he became again a clerk in a Kolyma gold-mining facility.

Ilya found himself wanting desperately to reassure him, to offer at least a gesture of human fellowship, and so patted the place where the slips of paper rested over his heart. Sascha closed his eyes in a silent gesture of gratitude and bowed his head, then turned and left the room, his dragged leg scraping softly over the floorboards.

Before Ilya could be alone to read the letters, there was a great deal to be got through: a formal meeting with the camp NKVD officer, followed by a painfully formal exchange of 'confidences' with the camp commandant's principal assistant, during which Ilya made sure to communicate his great satisfaction with all he'd found. Followed in turn by an endless, vodka-sodden dinner given in his honour by the commandant and attended by senior staff and their wives. He was seated next to a fat, red-faced woman with merry eyes, stuffed into a gown from the 1920s, who rested a hand on his thigh beneath the table and leaned against his shoulder. 'You are eating breast of wolf,' she giggled in his ear, 'is it not delectable?'

At long last, late at night, he was returned to the two-car train that sat chuffing idly on the rail spur that serviced Camp 782 and took its gold away. He entered his private compartment – in an old boxcar that rode high over its cast-iron wheels – and told his adjutant he did not wish to be disturbed, then turned up the flame on an oil lamp that lit the rough wooden interior of the car.

He felt the first shudder of motion a few minutes later when, as the couplings clanged, the train slowly began to make way. Outside, the endless snowfields shone white and empty in the darkness, and the slow, steam-driven rhythm of the engine sharpened the sense of being lost in vastness.

The first letter was scrawled – apparently written in great haste:

Ilya Goldman: I observed you entering the camp this morning and realized that we have known one another. If I have not been able to approach you, I will identify myself as Colonel A. Y. Vonets – Sascha. We met briefly while serving in Spain in 1936. In March of 1943, a man named Semmers came to this camp, sentenced under Article 38 (Anti-Soviet Statement). He told me of a conspiracy known as BF 825 that existed among the Brotherhood Front of 1934 in the training facility on Arbat Street. He claimed to have been approached by Drazen Kulic, and that others were involved, including Josef Voluta, Khristo Stoianev and yourself. Semmers attempted to escape in March of this year, was discovered, and shot.

I will inform no one of your complicity in this conspiracy as long as you undertake two actions on my behalf: (1) The accompanying letter is for Josef Voluta, I believe that you are able to transmit it to him. (2) Within the next sixty days, I must be transferred to Camp 209, in Belgorod-Dnestrovskij at the mouth of the Dniester on the Black Sea. I know you have the ability to do this within the labour camp administration. If you choose not to do it, or to reveal these communications, I will inform local NKVD of the existence of BF 825, and your participation within it. Forgive me, Ilya. I will not live out another year in this place.

The second letter did not have a heading and was printed in tiny letters crammed together on a small slip of brown paper:

On 12 April I will be in the Romanian village at Sfintu Gheorghe, on the southern arm of the Dunărea, where it empties into the Black Sea. I have extraordinarily valuable information for Western intelligence services. The information is recorded in a document I will carry, but it is usable only with my personal assistance. For example, the agent known as ANDRES (Avram Roubenis) was murdered in Paris in 1937 with a slow-acting poison clandestinely administered in a café at the direction of Col. V. I. Kolodny, of the Paris *rezidentura*. The above is one item among many hundred. I will remain in Sfintu Gheorghe from April 12 on – until I am discovered or betrayed. I will then confess to the BF 825 plot and all else I know. Signed: An NKVD Colonel.

Ilya sat back and stared at his reflection in the dark window. He saw a taut, colourless face above the green NKVD uniform. By inference, he pieced together what he took to be Sascha's intentions. The mouth of the Dniester was less than a hundred miles from the Romanian delta of the Dunărea – the Danube. Since the surrender, converted

416

ore steamers moved constantly back and forth between the two areas, sailing empty into Romania, returning with wheat, vegetables, horses, and God knew what else. Sascha intended to escape from the camp, then he meant to stow away on a Black Sea steamer that left from Odessa and called at Belgorod, where a chemical works was being built by Gulag labour. He would hide aboard the ship at Belgorod, then disembark secretly at Izmail, the Soviet port on the Danube, after which he would make his way to Sfintu Gheorghe – nominally in the nation of Romania, but in fact a part of the ancient region known as Bessarabia, a remote corner of the world, so lost as to be nearly unknown.

If the letter were delivered to Voluta, he would use the NOV apparatus to move the letter to a Western intelligence service, and Sascha believed he would be exfiltrated from the little fishing village of Sfintu Gheorghe. The letter had to go to Voluta because Sascha was aware that Voluta knew him personally and that he, as well as other members of the BF 825 conspiracy, were in a position to confirm his value to the Western services.

It was, in its own way, a reasonably clever plan. Escape from a camp in the Kolyma was nearly impossible – the land itself was a prison. And no Allied intelligence service would want to attempt this sort of covert action in the country of a nominal ally, thus Sascha had placed responsibility on himself for leaving Russian soil. Romania, on the other hand, was in a condition of political flux that might facilitate an operation to remove a desirable asset.

But, Ilya realized, years of training and practical experience said no. The scheme had virtually no chance of success: too many steps, too many assumptions, a blind thrust from a doomed man. In effect, it sentenced Sascha to death and, once he escaped from Belgorod and someone checked on how he came to be transferred there in the first place, sentenced Ilya Goldman to death as well.

Unless by April 12, Ilya thought, listening to the slow beat of the wheels, *I am somewhere else*.

But if the exfiltration scheme was wishful thinking, the part of the plot that touched *him* was close to perfect. Considered objectively, Sascha Vonets had built a fine trap. In it, Ilya realized, he could move in only one direction; there were no exits along the way and, at the end, it sent him where he wanted to go. The white face in the window smiled ruefully. Truly, you couldn't ask for a better trap than that.

*   *   *

Christmas, *Rozhdyestvo*, was no longer a holy day in the Soviet Union, yet somehow, on the night of December 24, the duty roster at the Fourth Division of the Sixth Directorate was seriously depleted. The inspector general's central bureau in Moscow was on Ulyanovskaya Street, in a turn-of-the-century building with vast marble hallways that had once housed the czar's Corn Tax *apparat*. Ilya Goldman was very nearly alone in the building on Christmas Eve — most of the senior officers seemed to be down with the flu or engaged in important business outside the office. Perhaps, Ilya thought, they were engaged in the surveillance of *Dedushka Moroz*, Father Frost, as he visited children on the night before Christmas. In any event, Captain Ilya Goldman was a Jew and, as such, found it productive not to have the flu or important business elsewhere on Christmas Eve, and had volunteered to work a double shift and assume the responsibility of night duty officer.

He dug away at his paperwork until a little after midnight, then strolled down the corridor to the office of Major General Lyuzhenko, whose chief responsibility was the suppression of the occasional uprising within the camp populations. He'd chosen Lyuzhenko, a particularly nasty brute with a savage temper, rather carefully, for the man was, in Ilya's scheme of things, about to commit the single honourable act of his life. One could, when the fat was in the fire, hear him all over the seventh floor – screaming on the telephone, cursing, almost weeping with rage.

Lyuzhenko had locked his office door, but to Captain Goldman, trained as he was by the NKVD, that did not present a serious problem. Ilya turned on the office lights and rummaged through the files until he found a packet of transfer forms. He put one in Lyuzhenko's secretary's typewriter and filled it out, making all the proper marks in the appropriate boxes. Under the heading *Reason for Transfer* he wrote: 'By order of Major General Lyuzhenko.' That had been reason enough in the past, it would be now. He found a letter signed by the general, slid it beneath the transfer and traced out the signature, using a pen from the desk drawer. He turned off the lights, locked up the office, and proceeded down the hall, collecting three countersignatures in precisely the same manner in three other offices. He then deposited the transfer in the Action box on the desk of the commanding officer's secretary and Sascha Vonets was on his way to Belgorod-Dnestrovskij. How quickly, Ilya thought, the Soviet bureaucracy could move when it wanted to.

He left the building, walking along Ulyanovskaya Street for several blocks, then turning north toward one of the buildings given over to the Ministries of Transport (Internal). The door guard, seeing his NKVD uniform, let him in without question. Who knew what business these people might be about, even on what used to be Christmas Eve.

The hallways of this particular ministry were even grander than his own, and each floor had its own cleaning lady, traditional Russian *babas* in kerchiefs who spent the long night down on their knees with buckets of soapy water and hard brushes, rubbing away at the heelmarks of the previous day's boots. On the third floor, Ilya walked carefully along the wet marble, his footsteps echoing down the empty corridor. He found the third-floor cleaning lady just outside an office door marked Bureau of Streetcar Maintenance – Assistant to the Deputy Director. She was all in black, large breasts swaying within an old cotton dress as she scrubbed, humming to herself, absorbed in this work that would go on night after night, apparently forever.

She saw him approach and stand before her but took no notice of him, he was just another pair of boots. When he handed her a slip of brown paper with tiny printing crammed on one side and the coded name of an addressee on the other she took no notice of that either, simply tucked it away somewhere inside her dress with one hand while scrubbing away with the other.

Back on Ulyanovskaya Street, Ilya walked slowly toward his office. The night was icy cold and clear, a million stars overhead.

At 6:30 on the morning of December 25, Natalya Federova, a cleaner at the offices of the Ministries of Transport, waited at the Usacheva tram station for the number 26 trolley, which would take her back to the flat she shared with her daughter and son-in-law and their children. By coincidence, her sister's husband, Pavel, took this same route, and six days a week they greeted each other as she got on the trolley to go home and he got off to go to his job. It was snowing lightly, a fine, dry snow of the sort that often went on for days.

The trolley was twenty minutes late, but Natalya waited patiently with the other night workers heading home, all of them standing quietly in the falling snow. When the trolley finally did arrive, Pavel was among the last to get off, so they kissed hurriedly and he murmured a salutation – *Shrozedestvrom Kristovim*, Christ is born – by her ear as their cheeks brushed. He clasped her hand warmly for a moment, then tucked the slip of brown paper away in the pocket of his infantryman's coat. He had lost an eye in the fighting at Stalingrad and wore three ranks of medals on his chest.

The brief greeting kept her from being early on the tram, so she had to stand for the hour-and-a-half ride back to her flat. She shifted her weight from one foot to the other and gazed pensively out the windows at the passing city, looking forward to the dinner she would have with her sister and Pavel that night. She planned to bake a Christmas bread for the occasion. It would have to be made without eggs, sadly, and raisins were out of the question, but Pavel had received a little packet of powdered sugar at his job, so there would be something sweet for the Christmas meal.

A few minutes before seven, Pavel arrived at the Usacheva Street offices of the temporary Belgian mission, where he worked as a porter. Humming to himself, he took out the garbage cans – the big, dented one with food scraps and other 'wet materials' would be picked up by a garbage truck. The small wooden one, 'dry materials', was mostly office waste, paper trash of all sorts generated by the night shift of communications clerks at the mission, and it was picked up by two men in a black car who never spoke to him.

Next, he made a round of the mission offices, making sure the ashtrays were clean and emptying the pencil sharpener shavings into a piece of newspaper. The tiny office at the end of the hall was used by a junior diplomat – a devout Catholic, the grandson of Polish immigrants to Belgium – and after Pavel emptied his pencil shavings on the paper he left him a little something in return: a slip of brown paper, folded once, inserted in the barrel of the pencil sharpener before the canister was wiggled back into place and left upside down, a signal that the mailman had visited.

On January 10, a Canadian war correspondent was driven west from Moscow to the suburbs of Warsaw, to be on hand when Marshal Zhukov's First White Russian Front, accompanied by units of the Lublin Polish Army, marched in to take official control of the city. Zhukov's divisions had been waiting across the Vistula since August of 1944, while the Polish Home Army under General Bor fought it out in the streets and sewers of Warsaw with Hitler's Totenkopf (Death's Head) Division. Some quarter of a million Polish *partizans* had died in the fighting – only occasionally supplied by the Russians. Thus there would be no resistance from the Poles when the Lublin Army, representing the Polish Communist party, took over the administration of the country. The Canadian reporter was entertained on the night of January 15 by a group of Zhukov's aides. There was great good fellowship and many toasts were drunk. As a cold sun rose on the morning of the sixteenth, the correspondent walked down to the Vistula and stared out at the haze of grey smoke hanging over the burnt-out city. When he returned to the old manor house that served as Zhukov's headquarters, the little slip of brown paper had been removed from the bottom of his sleeping bag. He was glad to see it go. The tiny Cyrillic printing had been beyond his ability to read, but he'd taken special care of the thing while it was in his possession. These little 'favours' he did for his Belgian friend made him nervous, but in return he was sometimes permitted to send solid background material off to Canada in the Belgian diplomatic pouch, thus evading the heavy-handed Russian censorship. The newspaper was delighted with these transmissions, spread the material about to protect their source, and had advanced him three pay grades since August. He was glad of that, for he was very much a man who wanted to do well at his work.

* * *

Josef Voluta had returned to Occupied Poland in the summer of 1944, along with two other members of NOV, the Polish Nationalist group made up of loosely affiliated army officers and Roman Catholic priests. They had been ordered to Warsaw to be on hand when their country returned to life but, instead, had witnessed its death.

By the end of July, the Poles could virtually taste freedom. July or August, that was the prevailing view. Pessimists spoke in favour of October. The German troops were giving ground, retreating from occupied territory throughout Eastern Europe, leaving behind terrified colonies of German 'settlers' put in place by Hitler to bring civilization to the 'barbarian' lands he had conquered.

By July 31, even the pessimists were heard whistling on the streets. The First Byelorussian Front under Rokossovsky was ten miles from Warsaw, but Hitler could not seem to bear the thought of losing his beloved Poland – his first conquest by force of arms, his first *amour*. NOV intelligence nets photographed the arrival of the SS Viking and Totenkopf divisions, the Hermann Göring Division, and the 19th Panzer Brigade. They were the best – the worst – that Hitler could bring to bear.

But this did not deter the Polish Home Army, under General Komorovski (known then by his nom de guerre, General Bor), from rising against the Germans. The Poles had known the Russians for centuries and were indifferent to the distinctions between czars and Bolsheviks. Thus, when Rokossovsky took the city, the Poles had planned to greet their Russian allies as saviours and liberators, but not conquerors. And not occupation forces.

It went quite well in the first weeks. Panzer tanks, induced to enter the narrow alleyways of the old city, discovered themselves unable to manoeuvre and were then set alight by gasoline and soap bombs with potassium permanganate wicks. When the crews ran from the burning armour, Polish snipers knocked them down. Moscow radio celebrated the uprising, calling out in a September 5 broadcast for all patriotic Poles to 'join battle with the Germans, this time for decisive action!' Throughout the city of Warsaw, partisan units attacked German positions, often at night: lively, sudden, short-range ambushes by running shadows who melted away into the darkness as German reinforcements arrived.

By the middle of September, however, the Poles were running out of supplies: food, ammunition, weapons, and especially anaesthetics for the wounded. The Russians, still ten miles away across the Vistula, gave permission for British and American supply drops, using Russian airfields for refuelling. Thus for four days, beginning on September 14, supplies reached the Polish fighters. But, on September 18, Russian permission was withdrawn. In the next three days, SS units inflicted terrible casualties on virtually disarmed *partizan* groups. Then, on September 21, a massive resupply effort was initiated – more than two thousand missions flown in a seven-day period. But, on September 30, with Polish units fully engaged, the Russians withdrew permission for a second time, and at that point the supply effort ended permanently.

By then, 250,000 Poles had died in the fighting. The Polish Home Army ceased to exist as a unified fighting force and, on October 19, Hitler determined to destroy that which he could not possess: under his specific orders, German engineers methodically blew the city to pieces. The Lublin Committee – the Soviet-sponsored government-in-exile – condemned the uprising, calling it 'futile'. On the first day of 1945, the Lublin Committee declared itself the legitimate government of Poland. On January 17, the Russians finally crossed the Vistula and the First White Russian Front under Zhukov marched triumphant into the city.

Voluta had stayed on in Warsaw long after it became clear that the city was doomed. There was always one more thing that had to be done – wounded to be cared for, German positions observed, gasoline bombs to be manufactured, last rites offered. The *partizans* lived like rats in a city of ghosts, a city that burned for three months and immolated its own dead. Voluta picked wheat grains from the mud to keep from starving, loaded machine-gun belts, performed an operation on a wounded man with a tailor's needle and thread, using wood alcohol as an anaesthetic because there simply wasn't anything else.

On January 3, Voluta had been able to reestablish contact with his base in Vatican City, sending a coded radio message to the NOV communications centre. A commercial frequency was used, with a letter code based on Chapter Twelve of the Book of Daniel. The German *radio réparage* had almost caught up with him, because he was exhausted and slow on the keys of the transmitter and the sending had taken him much too long. But the driver of the German radio truck had become disoriented in the dense pall of smoke that lay over the city and a few teenagers had come up out of a sewer and turned the truck over, lighting off the gasoline with a strip of shirttail run into the tank.

Voluta's contact was answered on January 9. A fifty-second transmission in Book of Daniel code, ordering him to wait for 'an urgent letter' that was moving toward him via the NOV courier system and telling him where and when he could receive it. The latter half of the transmission ordered him to forward this message to 'KS' and informed Voluta of his whereabouts.

Thus, on the morning of January 17, he made his way to a shattered tenement on the edge of what had once been the Jewish ghetto, where a group of youngsters was busily breaking down – emptying sandbags, tearing apart a wall built of paving stones – a machine-gun emplacement that had somehow survived the destruction of the city. A girl of thirteen greeted him and handed over a small slip of brown paper. They stood together at the edge of an enormous hole that had been blown in the street by a German 88 round. Voluta could see down into a sewer, where black water flowed sluggishly past, sometimes carrying a body in its current. From the distance, the sound of a Russian marching band could be heard, brassy and discordant. Voluta read the slip of paper quickly, then put it in his pocket.

'Thank you,' he said to the girl. Then nodded toward the blare of the music and added, 'You must be careful now, you know.'

She smiled at him, face grey with soot and ash, hands wound with rags against barrel burns from the machine gun, feet lost in a preposterously large pair of Wehrmacht tanker's boots. 'I shall be, Father,' she said to him, 'you may be sure of that.'

'You had no trouble across the river?'

'No, Father, no trouble. They were all snoring like *krokodil*, and, anyhow, I have learned to be invisible.'

He nodded, said good-bye, then touched her face for a moment. His heart swelled with things to be said but he could say none of them.

At nightfall, he left the city, dressed as a labourer. The following morning, dressed as a priest, he crossed through rear-guard elements of the retreating German divisions, giving his blessing to those soldiers who requested it. After that, he headed south and a little west, meaning to deliver the slip of brown paper to the 'KS' named by the NOV officers in Rome. The message could have been moved unobtrusively into diplomatic channels – far more efficient than a priest walking by daylight through the battered and frozen countryside – but the NOV officers knew the ways of bureaucrats, knew the fate of paper that sat on desks.

So he walked, sometimes riding a little way with a farmer who still had a horse and cart, day after day, often through snow, moving always southwest, along one of the many escape routes – some so old and well used that they were marked by fugitive's huts – that led out of Poland.

*　　*　　*

They had come to Khristo Stoianev in December of 1944 and asked him to undertake the FELDSPAR mission. They had not threatened him – they were the OSS, not the NKVD – but neither had they relieved him of any obligation he might place upon himself. They were all very well dressed, these people, and they spent money like water, taking him to lunch or dinner over a three-week period and sliding Swiss franc notes from leather wallets and dropping them atop the check on its little plate and not waiting for change. 'We don't want you to feel we're putting pressure on you,' one of them said in the grand dining room of the Hotel Schwarzwald in Bern, putting extraordinary pressure on him at precisely that moment. 'It would,' the man said ruefully, knocking cold ash from the bowl of his pipe by smacking it against his palm, 'be very dangerous work.'

'Where is it?' he'd asked.

The man put the pipe in his mouth and made a whistling sound by blowing into it a few times, making sure the stem was clear. 'Prague,' he said.

'I cannot speak native Czech,' Khristo answered.

'No, you can't,' the man said, 'but you'll do for a Yugoslav. Perhaps a machinist, forced labour, you know the sort of thing.' He began to pack tobacco into his pipe from a leather pouch as a waiter came gliding to the table like a swan and began the exquisitely laborious process – silver urn, gleaming hotel china, silver cream pitcher, sugar bowl and tongs – of serving coffee.

Who could say no?

Who could bear the subsequent weight of Episcopalian disappointment, unvoiced but not uncommunicated, the dreadful undercurrent of icy sympathy extended to those who have proven themselves, at last, cowards and failures. *We don't blame you, of course, it's just not in your nature to accept danger*, they would say. Or, rather, much worse, they *wouldn't* say.

Yet the approach could be resisted and often enough was – by those to whom survival really was paramount – but

Khristo was not among them. His dining companion's eyes twinkled as he sipped his coffee and looked over the rim of his cup. 'I'm proud of you. I really am,' he said as he set the cup down. 'Once this Nazi business is done with' – he lit the pipe at last, and the table was wreathed with drifts of sweet-smelling smoke – 'well, there's always the future to consider.'

It was said as an afterthought, almost, *we know you don't require an inducement, but here's one anyhow*. The man's expression, in that moment, had something of the philosopher about it, suggesting he knew all too well that people accepted such missions for reasons of the heart, and that material rewards were of no consequence once the real danger was considered. Thus Khristo found himself bribed and flattered in the same moment. *Wily old bastard*, he thought, enjoying the performance for the pure virtuosity of it. 'Someone has to do it,' the man said, shaking his head in wonder at what the world seemed to demand of both of them.

And the restaurant bills were nothing compared to what they spent on him after the operation got under way. The NKVD, he thought, would have woven an elaborate conspiracy to achieve the same results, using coercion, ideology – whatever human pressure point could be laid bare. The Americans, on the other hand, fought with money and technology, and they were extravagant with both.

They flew Khristo down to OSS headquarters in Bari, Italy, and trained him in the use of the new J-E radio. The Joan-Eleanor communications system had been the brainchild of Lieutenant Commander Steve Simpson, an engineer from RCA, who named the invention after a certain Joan, a WAC major he quite liked, and Eleanor, the wife of his associate, DeWitt Goddard. Clandestine communications to that point had depended on the self-descriptive suitcase radio. The J-E radio was six inches long, had an aerial that unfolded to one foot in length, and transmitted to a receiver in a British De Havilland Mosquito – a fast little two-man fighter-bomber with a range of 1800 miles – circling above the transmission point. And the German *radio réparage* could not locate a J-E radio.

On a quarter-moon night in early January, Khristo Stoianev was parachuted into the Czech countryside south of Prague, the insertion achieved by a B-24 Liberator specially modified for agent drops behind enemy lines. The bomber was painted matte black, making it nearly invisible, even when tracked by German searchlights. The exhaust flame was shielded, the ball turret normally found on the belly of the plane had been removed – altering its silhouette – and a hinged plywood panel installed in its place to serve as exit hatch for the parachutist. The navigator's compartment in the nose of the airplane was sealed off in such a way as to create the total darkness required for visual navigation at night. On a normal bombing run, great numbers of planes flew over a target at 20,000 feet, protected by fighter squadrons.

Agent insertion technology demanded that the plane fly alone, 500 feet above the ground, at the slowest possible speed – sometimes less than 120 miles per hour – the sort of contour aviation that demanded some moonlight and a cloudfree night. The navigator followed roads, or moonlight reflected from rivers or lakes. Some of the runs used German concentration camps as beacons, since they were lit brightly all night long to discourage escapes.

Khristo landed without difficulty, in the proper location. His papers were excellent forgeries, typed on German typewriters, stamped properly with German inks, and the legend created for him – a fictitious life cycle from birth to present – was indeed as the man with the pipe had suggested it might be. He was a Yugoslav conscript worker of Croatian origin, a machine tool expert and drill-press operator, a valuable asset to the Reich. He carried a thick wad of German Reichsmarks and Czech crowns and an additional sum in gold coins. His map was perfect, guiding him into Prague along the Vltava River in something under six hours once he had stolen a bicycle. He made his way to a safe house, owned by a mathematics teacher, where he was received with cheese dumplings and eggs.

The objectives of the FELDSPAR mission were not complicated: he was to collect and transmit data on bombing effectiveness and war factory production in Bohemia, the region of Prague, and prepare for the reception of additional agents. The J-E radio would work very nicely from a roof, and the Mosquito would be circling 35,000 feet above him at certain prearranged hours of the night, unseen by German antiaircraft crews. There had been no arrangement made for exfiltration; General Patton's Third Army was headed that way at a good clip and they would come to him. If he got into trouble, the Czech underground could move him to the protection of units fighting in the Tatra Mountains to the south.

Hundreds of man-hours had clearly been spent on this mission and, to the extent possible, the nature of the operation shielded him from excessive peril. That gave him a certain confidence, reinforced by his NKVD schooling and experience, which trained one to rely on guile and ruthlessness because there was no J-E radio and not enough aviation gasoline for an airplane to fly in circles over the communicating agent.

Concentrate, the briefers told him. Know where you are and whom you are with every second of every day, and if you experience fatigue, treat it as you would a dangerous sickness. Keep incriminating evidence as far away from you as possible – hide *everything*. When you are out in the streets of Prague, you must *be* a Yugoslavian conscript worker. They used chemicals to remove the nicotine stain from his index finger because cigarettes were sufficiently scarce in Occupied Europe that the yellowish discolouration was now rarely seen. The Czechs you'll be working with, they told him, are *very good*, espionage has been a high art in

430

Central Europe for hundreds of years. FELDSPAR certainly was, he thought, a mission guaranteed for success as much as any operation of that type could ever be.

Perhaps his nerve slipped.

He accused himself of that more than once, as January became February and Prague lay under a blanket of dirty ice in the coldest winter in Europe for forty years. He'd left the teacher's house after three days. He had no objective reason to do so – it was simply that the neighbourhood felt wrong. He moved to a burned-out warehouse on the eastern edge of the industrial district, a place where barrels of cooking oil had been stored. The building stood three storeys high, scorch patterns flared out on the plaster walls above and below the broken windows, and when the rains came in early March, oil that had leached into the cinder loading yard over the years returned to the surface and the smell of it, singed and rancid, hung in the wet air. He lived in what had once been the warehouse office, where a small stove still functioned, bought black market coal at an exorbitant price and lugged it back to his hideout in a metal bucket. And, anytime he went anywhere, he carried a small snub-nosed VZ/27 he'd picked up from his coal supplier. That was something no Yugoslav conscript worker would dare to have, but he had no intention of being taken alive here, not by *these* Occupation troops, not by *this* Gestapo. It was a cheap, shoddy weapon, a 7.65 automatic with a miserly eight-round magazine and a plastic grip, produced under Occupation, with Böhmische Waffenfabrik Prag replacing the usual Czech manufacturer's mark. *This pistol was made in German Bohemia* – the inscription implied – *there is no such thing as Czechoslovakia.*

But there was. The Czechs had insisted on that.

And the well-dressed people in Bern and Bari who had paid for the lunches hadn't told him about Prague. Oh, they'd told him, in so many words, in rather cool, unemotional language, what the *situation* was, describing the political climate, analysing the cultural and economic conditions, characterizing weather, food, religion, local customs – all the empirical data you could want.

But Prague, in the winter and early spring of 1945, would have required a chorus of the damned to do it true justice. Khristo, when he was out among the people, believed he could actually feel it, like a sickness, a cold, gestating rage that swelled toward the moment of its birth. And the harder the Germans bore down, the more they whipped and tortured and executed, the more it grew. 'The day will come,' one of his agents had told him, 'when we will hang them up by the feet and soak them with gasoline and set them alight. Upside down, you see, so that they do not die too quickly from breathing the smoke. You will be here,' the man said. 'You will see it.'

Khristo believed him. It was not a fantasy of the oppressed, it was a plan, a lucid, thought-out ritual of justice, and the day of its reality was not far off. In the Staroměstské Square, in the old part of the city, there was a medieval clock high on the façade of the town hall. When the hour struck, a painted Christ and twelve apostles would appear one by one in a little window below the clock, followed by the figure of hooded Death, whose bell sounded for the passing of time, then the Turk, the Miser, the Vain Fool, and, at last, the Cock. The Germans found it fascinating – Bohemian folklore displayed for their pleasure – and they would gather below the clock when it struck the hour and point and smile and take photographs. They seemed able to ignore the faces of the Czechs who surrounded them: taut, watchful faces, pale amid the dark clothing that everyone seemed to wear, pale in the perpetual dusk of cloudy days and coal smoke that hung above the city.

His principal contact with the Czech underground was named Hlava, a stolid, heavy man who wore eyeglasses with clear plastic frames, a man whose hoarse, measured breathing seemed, to Khristo, a kind of audible melancholia. They sat one seat apart in movie theatres, bumped shoulders in the street as they made brush passes – a scrap of paper moving invisibly from one to the other – urinated side by side in metal troughs in railway stations, shook hands like old friends in shopping streets just after dark. In one week in February they saw the same German newsreel three times: Hermann Göring, having just shot a bison in his private game preserve, distributed the meat to refugees on the road as they streamed in from Soviet-conquered territories in East Prussia.

Hlava was employed as chief bookkeeper in a factory that repaired shot-up Messerschmitt fighter planes. Now and then they were able to meet in a situation where actual conversation was possible, and Hlava revealed himself to be a man who told a certain kind of joke. 'Three Czechs – a Bohemian, a Slovakian, and a Moravian – meet in heaven. The first one says . . .' He never laughed at the jokes, simply gazed at Khristo, awaiting a reaction, his breath rasping in and out in a slow, methodical tempo.

There were, at any given time, about a dozen other agents. Khristo spent his days bicycling around the city, hard-pressed to make his *treffs* – as the Russians called clandestine meetings. There was a violin teacher whose pupils were mostly the children of German officers, and she had a way with papers – letters, reports – left lying atop desks in studies. There was a police detective, apparently enough trusted by the Germans to see marginal intelligence distributions. Four or five factory workers, a factory physician, a clerk in the electric utility who fed him data on the daily rise and fall of power usage in certain industrial facilities critical to the German war effort.

But then, on March 20, he was offered information of a very different sort. It reached him in bed, amid a jumble of sweaty blankets in a hotel room that rented by the hour, reached him as he smoked a cigarette and stared at the waterstained ceiling above him, numb and mindless for the moment, in a blank daze that passed for tranquillity.

Magda, she was called, buxom and fat-hipped and

exceptionally pink, with a thick yellow braid that fell to the small of her back. Had his controllers known about her, they would have told him he was signing his own death warrant. And she was not the only one; there were others, who drifted into his life, then disappeared: one was dark and looked like a Gypsy, another was very young and brought him small gifts. There was a seamstress who scented herself with lilac water, and a soldier's widow who dressed all in black.

Together, they constituted yet another step into the forbidden zone. Like the burned-out factory where he slept. Like the pistol beneath the horsehair pillow on the hotel bed. He'd been driven to it, somehow, he did not understand why, but something had its fist in his back and forced him into acts which, in his particular circumstances, amounted to dancing blindfolded at the edge of a cliff. The women he knew were not prostitutes, they simply needed money and needed to make love and weren't averse to going to bed with a generous man. And he was generous. 'Here,' he'd say, 'make sure and eat a good dinner tonight, you look worn out.' He knew that he was calling attention to himself, easily the worst thing he could do, but he couldn't stop. Maybe, he thought, his nerve really had slipped. Or was it, perhaps, some premonition about the future that compelled him to a kind of greed, compelled him to take from life anything it might give him. *Christ*, he thought, *you are acting like Sascha Vonets*.

'Hey you, dreamer,' said Magda, rolling onto her ample stomach and propping her chin on her hands. 'I met an old friend of yours. He said, "That black-haired fellow you see, we used to be pals."'

Magda was much given to fancy, he didn't take it too seriously. 'Oh?' he said. 'What did he look like, then?'

'Mm, like Death in a play.'

She was evidently going to spin a tale. Amused, he turned on his side to see her face. 'How strange. He carried a scythe, perhaps?'

'No, you stupid man. He was thin as a skeleton, with staring eyes and long, bony fingers. A scythe indeed! I was at the Novy Bor restaurant, at the buffet. He just came right up to my table and spoke to me. "Say hello to him for me," he said.'

She moved her face close to his. 'Now give me a great big kiss,' she said.

The truth of it began to reach him and his body tensed. 'What are you saying?' he asked, eyes searching her placid face.

She made popping noises with her lips. 'Kissy,' she said, running a fingernail down his flank.

'Is this true? What else did he say?' His voice was quite different now.

She pouted for a moment and rolled her eyes — she'd got his attention, but it wasn't the sort of attention she'd wanted. 'Some silliness about a postal box. B, F, uh, eight something. I don't remember. But there is no such address in Prague. We don't use the alphabet, just numbers. One of your black market friends, no doubt. *Now*, ungrateful man . . .'

'That's it, all of it?' he said, every nerve in his body humming.

'Yes, my little king,' she sighed, sorry now that she'd bothered to bring it up, 'that's all of it.' She snuggled against him and cooed on his chest, her hand walking on two fingers down his belly.

He made himself respond, and the cooing became mock-surprised, then appreciative. 'Witch!' he said softly by her ear, 'you turn a man into a tomcat.' He reached across her shoulder, pressed his cigarette out in an ashtray on the bedside table, stroked her back. *Novy Bor restaurant*, he thought, *at the buffet*.

'Meow,' she said.

Lunch and dinner at the Novy Bor on March 21.

A long, narrow room, windows white with steam so that

people in the street passed like ghosts, black and white tiles of the floor awash with water from muddy boots, over a hundred people talking in low voices, the clatter of trays, a portrait of Hitler on the yellow wall above the bubbling tea urn.

And again on March 22, this time aborting a pass from Hlava scheduled for noon.

A pass successfully managed at the fallback location on the morning of March 23, a page torn from a copybook pressed into his hand:

1. *New plant directives specify that workers absenting themselves from the factory for any reason shall be charged with economic sabotage against the Reich and hung without trial, such hangings to take place directly outside the factory as example to all workers.*
2. *Two N40 milling machines down after gears sabotaged with emery grit.*
3. *Repair of six ME-109 fuselages delayed by oxyacetylene shortage. Resupply promised for week of 9 April. Old-fashioned metal brazing techniques used instead of welding and parts shipped.*
4. *ME-110 wing trucked in on 18 March appears to have taken intensive ground fire from small-bore weapons. Number 7705-12 on wing.*

Lunch on March 23 at Novy Bor. Khristo sat against the wall opposite the buffet counter. As he was stalling through the last of his beer, Josef Voluta appeared at the table with a bowl of soup on a tray. Almost immediately after he sat down, two old men joined them at the table.

'Salt, please,' Voluta said, handing him a slip of paper beneath the table. Khristo passed him the salt.

'Thank you,' Voluta said.

Khristo waited a few minutes and sipped his beer in silence, then rose from the table and went into the toilet, locked the door, and read the small slip of brown paper.

When he emerged, Voluta was gone. He sat back down at the table and finished the beer before leaving.

Could this be the man, he wondered, that he had known at Arbat Street? His face was grey and lean, features sharpened, eyes too bright. The backs of his hands showed patches of glossy red skin, the mark of recently healed burns. He had eaten his soup hunched over, face close to the bowl, holding the spoon in his fist, moving with a steady, constant motion – a man servicing a machine. Khristo fought the sudden urge, nearly a compulsion, to find a mirror and look at his face.

On one edge of the message from 'An NKVD Colonel' a different hand had written the word *Sascha*. In writing that Khristo took to be Voluta's, a message had been pencilled on the back of the paper: *Jiráskův bridge, March 24, 8:05 p.m., then 9:15, then 10:20. If not, good luck.* The message was written in Russian.

My God, Khristo thought. Sascha.

On the night of March 24, 1945, a De Havilland Mosquito circled at 35,000 feet above the city of Prague. All armament had been removed from the airplane, marginally increasing its range. Even so, the plane would land at the OSS field at Bari with its fuel tank nearly empty, the round trip between the two cities barely within its capacity. The pilot and navigator wore fur gloves and sheepskin jackets and breathed from an oxygen tank – their problem was altitude, not hostile anti-aircraft fire. Even if the Germans could hear them, they couldn't see them that high up.

A four-minute message from the FELDSPAR operative, crouching somewhere on a roof down below, was recorded on a wire-spool machine and flown back to OSS headquarters in Bari. The FELDSPAR committee, responsible for oversight of the operation, was waiting anxiously for the recording. They spent fifteen minutes discussing the information, then sent it on to the typists and clerks. Data on German war production capabilities in Occupied

Czechoslovakia was immediately prepared for distribution to various analysis groups. A rather peculiar addition to the message, concerning an NKVD colonel offering material on Soviet intelligence operations in exchange for exfiltration from someplace in Romania, was only briefly discussed. Someone said it sounded like a provocation, somebody else wondered what the hell the FELDSPAR operative was doing with stuff like that – who was he talking to?

The Soviet contact was something of a sore subject, because the OSS had had its problems with the NKVD. In 1943, they had made attempts to cooperate with their allied service, sending them cryptographic materials, miniature cameras, miniature microdot-manufacturing devices, microfilm cameras and projectors, as a gesture of good will. But the good will was not returned. On a trip to Moscow in 1944, General Donovan, head of OSS, had been prevented from leaving the USSR for ten days. In the first months of 1945, reports from intelligence officers in Bucharest, Sofia, Warsaw and other territories recently occupied by Soviet armies indicated that the NKVD was hard at work against its Western allies. Then, in response to a broad pattern of Soviet actions, Donovan had proposed to the Roosevelt administration that the United States continue to maintain an intelligence agency after the war. But J. Edgar Hoover – Donovan's mortal bureaucratic enemy in Washington, D.C. – had learned of this proposal and leaked word of it to several newspapers that shared his views and the American people had been informed, in banner headlines, that a postwar 'American Gestapo' was under consideration. There were those in the OSS who now believed – correctly, it turned out – that the agency had received a mortal wound, and the time of its dismantling was only months away.

Information relevant to Soviet intelligence operations was therefore handled by a special committee, so the FELDSPAR product was duly forwarded amid the daily traffic of memoranda, reports, personnel actions, requests for clarification of policy, and proposals for new operations originated by the Bari station.

As for the FELDSPAR operative himself, the March 24 message was his final transmission. Mosquito missions were flown above Prague on March 29 and on April 4, 5, and 6, but he was not heard from on those dates and the mission was therefore terminated with the notation that the agent had been neutralized — believed killed or captured by the enemy. The FELDSPAR committee ceased to meet, its members assigned to oversee new operations. It was considered a lousy break. The FELDSPAR operative had been erratic at times, but during his active period he had furnished significant product to the intelligence effort and those who had known him personally had generally liked him.

*   *   *

In Prague, the night of March 24 was cloudy and overcast and there was no wind to stir the dead air. Moving through the blacked-out city, Khristo found it difficult to breathe. Coal smoke poured from the chimneys of the ceaselessly operating factories and hung in the streets like a fog. There was other burning as well: two hundred miles to the north the Russian armies were massed for an assault on the eastern borders of Germany, firing twenty-two thousand field guns in barrages that lit up the evening sky and set whole cities on fire. The distant rumble could be heard all night long and a haze of acrid smoke drifted south, covering Central Europe and blackening the roofs of Prague with a fine, sooty layer of ash. People scrubbed themselves with lye soap but the grime was stubborn and would not leave them, so they tried to live with it, spitting incessantly when the taste of the war in their mouths grew too strong to bear.

The 7:50 p.m. radio transmission from the roof of the warehouse had cost Khristo his first opportunity to meet with Voluta, but there was nothing to be done about that. He just barely managed to make the 9:15, trudging along

439

the winding streets like a tired man on his way to work, but Voluta did not appear. Khristo moved away from the bridge, found an unlocked door, and settled down to wait in the narrow hallway of an old tenement, listening to a loud argument in the apartment on the other side of the wall. It was a mother-daughter fight, something to do with money, punctuated by banging and bumping as the two women cleaned the house while they fought.

Heading toward the 10:20 meeting, he found the streets nearly empty – Occupation rules of curfew specified that only those with stamped permits could be on the street after 9:00 p.m. As he walked, a Tatra automobile slowed to have a look at him. Gestapo, he thought. He came almost to a halt and stared apprehensively at the car, like a man about to have his papers checked. This tentative act of submission apparently satisfied the Germans, because the Tatra accelerated and drove off toward the river.

At the edge of the small square that faced the Jiráskův bridge, he heard running footsteps and moved quickly against the wall of a building, fingers touching the outline of the pistol in his belt. A heavy man, panting hard, came jogging around the corner and stopped dead when he saw Khristo, his eyes lit with fear. 'Run!' he whispered, waving him away with both hands. 'There's been a shooting.'

Khristo ran forward into the square, peering into the darkness. There was something midway across the bridge – a dim shape wedged between the roadway and the side-walk, a man, he realized, sprawled face down in the gutter, the soles of his shoes resting together at an angle, one arm flung forward, the hand white against the grey pavement.

Across the river, a car without lights raced south on Dvorakovo Street, its engine noise rising as it gained speed.

He took a deep breath, then sprinted across the open square, the pounding of his boots echoing against the building façades. Suddenly, a pair of headlights turned a corner at the other end of the bridge, the beams narrowed and intensified by blackout slits. Light fell on the man lying in the street and Khristo knew it was Voluta. The vehicle – he could see it was a Wehrmacht armoured car – rolled to a stop and a searchlight mounted atop the roof probed at the body. Khristo heard himself make a wordless exclamation, a small sound of disappointment. He simply stood there for a moment, frozen, unable to think. The shape on the bridge lay still in the spotlight. Finally, he turned his back and walked away, not bothering to run until a static-laden voice crackled from a loudspeaker on the armoured car across the bridge and a white beam swept across the deserted square.

*   *   *

As master sergeants, SS Sturmscharführers, Geiske and Helst did the work while the officers took the credit. That was generally the way of the world, and certainly the way of the Gestapo, so you lived with it and kept your mouth shut. There were compensations. In 1934, when they'd joined the Nazi party, they'd been poor men. Now they had a little put by – there were ample opportunities in counterintelligence work, it only remained to have the courage to take advantage of them. The war, they acknowledged, was the best thing that ever happened to either of them. Sturmscharführer Geiske had been a prison guard in Leibnitz when he got the call, while his partner Helst had worked on the Hamburg docks; they'd both risen quite a way up in the world since then. They were heavy, well-fed men; dark and stolid, and they both smoked cigars, so that when they sat side by side in the black Borgward the car sank low on its springs and the interior turned blue-grey with smoke. Their particular war – interrogation cellars, executions – tended to smell bad, and the cigars were a common man's way of dealing with that. The worst corpse in the world hadn't a chance when Geiske and Helst lit up.

The battle between the Gestapo and the Czech resistance

had been a savage one, and they'd both played a role in its major actions. In 1942, Geiske had taken part in the pursuit of the assassins Gabcik and Kubis – parachuted in by British MI6 – who had murdered Reinhard Heydrich, the chief of the Gestapo intelligence service, by rolling a hand grenade under his car. Heydrich had survived the initial wounds – fragments of leather upholstery and uniform buried in his spleen – then died of gangrene. Geiske had helped to organize payment of the $600,000 bounty to the Czech who had betrayed the assassination ring, while Helst had assisted in the interrogation of the young man whose confession had ultimately led to its capture – the boy's collapse under questioning having been facilitated by the presentation of his mother's severed head. The Gestapo had staged a strong reprisal for Heydrich's murder, arresting ten thousand people, executing the entire population of Lidice, then levelling the town with explosives.

From their Borgward, parked discreetly just off Jiráskův Square, Helst and Geiske had observed with interest the unfolding of events on the night of March 24.

A man had loitered briefly on the bridge just before the 9:00 p.m. curfew, then melted away quickly into a side street.

A second man had walked into the square at 9:15, looked about, then retreated much as the first one did. 'Better and better,' Geiske remarked. Patiently, they waited for the fallback meeting. Entirely unprofessional to have it at the same location, but the two sergeants had seen stranger things in their time. Perhaps a poorly contrived black market exchange, perhaps a situation where extreme necessity had outdistanced caution. Either way, a plus for them.

Geiske grunted with satisfaction when the first one showed up again at 10:10.

This time he walked onto the bridge with great determination, ignoring the fact that he was alone and there were no crowds to protect him, carrying it off as best he could. Then the Tatra appeared, moving slowly into the square.

Geiske and Helst sat forward expectantly – the chemistry of the situation had altered with the addition of the car. 'Ah,' Helst said, 'he gets in.' But he did not. The Tatra slowed to a crawl as it reached the man on the bridge, someone in the back seat rolled a window down an inch or two. The man on the bridge glanced at the Tatra and there was a muffled report inside the car and he collapsed, falling forward. He made no move to shield himself as he fell; the marksman had been perfect.

The Tatra accelerated, then turned right at the end of the bridge. Helst snatched the radio handset from beneath the dashboard and reached another unit almost immediately. 'For you, my friend,' he said in a low voice, 'a Tatra headed south on Dvorakovo.'

'I'll go see to the other one,' Geiske said, hauling himself out of the car. He trotted toward one of the side streets and, sure enough, here came the second one, right on schedule. Geiske didn't want him in the square. The Wehrmacht clods in their armoured car at the other end of the bridge would likely shoot him, and he didn't want him shot – not just yet. 'Run!' he called out. 'There's been a shooting.'

But the second man was as much of a fool as the first, for he went charging off into the square without hesitation. Geiske shrugged and let him go, stepping back into a shadowed doorway and waiting to see what would happen. But the Wehrmacht boys held their fire, simply squawked at him over their loudspeaker and tried to pin him down with a searchlight. Lately, he had noticed, they were all teenage recruits, green as grass and barely trained. He breathed a sigh of relief as the man came back out of the square in a hurry. Perhaps not such a fool after all.

Geiske counted slowly to sixty, then sauntered on after him. He had little hope of being able to follow the man for very long – not alone, not in a city where the streets veered and twisted in a devil's maze – but his professional instincts were challenged and he decided to give it his best effort. Helst would understand, you had to take chances now and then, and he was extremely curious about this one, about where he might be headed. He could have arrested him on the spot, but these bastards worked on a certain principle: *if I don't come back on time, they've got me*. That made it damned difficult to find their friends, no matter how hard you worked in the cellar.

But Geiske was lucky. The man ahead of him appeared to be in some sort of daze. He just went slogging along for a time, street after street, taking no elusive action at all. There was one bad moment, when he climbed down a ladder onto a disused spur of railroad track that headed out into the factory district, but Geiske counted again and climbed down after him, then followed at a distance, picking his way along the track among the weed-choked ties. The man in front of him never stopped dead, never turned around, seemed to believe he was alone in the world. Geiske gave himself a bit of credit for that – he could walk like a cat when he had to. But it was the man himself who made the pursuit possible. When Geiske halted for a moment to listen, the sound of his footsteps never faltered. Geiske the sergeant was delighted by such stupidity, though Geiske the hunter, he admitted to himself, was perhaps a little disappointed.

As he entered the factory district at the eastern edge of the city, the smoke and fog seemed especially thick and, at the point where the man ahead of him suddenly left the tracks, the smell of burning was particularly bad. They were really catching it tonight, Geiske thought, up north on the Oder where the Russians were working their massed artillery. The entire eastern border was likely on fire, judging from what drifted south. Worse yet, he was below a loading dock that served some sort of warehouse and the stench of rancid oil in the burnt air very nearly made him gag. He patted a row of cigars in his breast pocket, but of course that was out of the question. The sound of footsteps had disappeared, *subject having entered said warehouse*. The warehouse part was very encouraging, however, so Geiske tried to take shallow breaths and concentrated on great caches of Czech hams and automobile tyres. That would make the whole business quite worthwhile.

He stood at the base of the loading dock for a time and listened carefully to the silence. Now he missed his partner. He was going to have to go groping around in there alone and he didn't look forward to it. He took a moment to steady his nerve – he'd done this sort of thing many times before. If you kept your wits about you, nothing much could go wrong. He unholstered a Walther automatic and worked the slide, made sure of the pen flashlight in the pocket of his coat, then vaulted up onto the dock.

Getting in quietly turned out to be easy: a sliding door had been left partly open. And, once inside, he realized that finding the man wasn't going to be a problem either. The first floor of the warehouse was empty – apparently the place was no longer in use – and a faint glow at the far end indicated a candle burning behind a windowed partition in what must have once been the shipping office. But, candle or not, a sea of darkness lay between him and his quarry and he would have to cross it blind – a flashlight in this black hellhole would shine out like a beacon.

He decided to have done with the whole nasty business and walked forward across the warped floorboards at a normal pace. The man in the office might come out at any moment, he too might have a flashlight and a weapon, and Geiske could move quickly as well as silently.

There was no warning. One moment he was walking, the next he was in space, falling head first, arms flailing. At the basement level, his head struck a charred beam-end that before the fire had been part of the flooring. The blow reversed his rotation so that when he hit the concrete subbasement he landed full on his back. He never screamed, though it took a long second to fall thirty feet, but when he hit the concrete the force of landing blew the breath from his lungs and made a sound like the roar of an animal in an empty cavern. He understood what had happened, understood that a fire had caused the warehouse to be abandoned, had burned through the first floor and the basement, and he called himself several kinds of fool just before he died.

* * *

'And did you think, perhaps, that just because I let you play between my legs that I was not a patriot?'

Magda did not look at him, her eyes never left the mirror as she prepared to go to war. She had arrayed, on the dressing table, every weapon in her armoury: paints, powders, creams, brushes, pencils, tweezers, miniature bottles of scent, and a frightful device that curled her eyelashes upward. Hands darting here and there, she worked like an artist in a frenzy of creation. 'That I might refuse you this? That I even *could?*' she went on. She pressed the end of her finger against the mouth of one of the scent bottles, made a dot on her wrist, shook her arm in the air, sniffed herself, waved some more, sniffed again, made a face, then went on to the next bottle and began the process all over again. 'Whatever else you may be, you are a thorough idiot about women,' she said, pausing to colour an eyelid blue, 'about Czech women certainly.'

He had stood outside Magda's flat in the early hours of the morning. Her husband, she had once told him, was a postman. When he saw a postman – a strutting little man with a cavalry moustache, something of the old Austro-Hungarian bureaucrat about him – march off to work, he'd taken the chance and knocked on her door. Explained to her what needed to be done, telling her as little as possible about himself, but insisting on the danger of it. 'You could regret it,' he had said.

She was affronted that he did not *know* she would do what he asked of her. As would her friends. A neighbour boy had been dispatched with what amounted to a queen's message to her most favoured ladies-in-waiting. When the boy returned, to accept a half-crown piece and a kiss that widened his eyes, the answer was yes in every case.

At which news she turned to him triumphantly and said, 'So!' Gimlet-eyed, cheeks rouged in circles, lips carmine, something like a witch in a pageant, he thought, she announced, 'Now you see what we are made of!' When her hair was brushed out in a wild blonde spray, she began the lengthy process of pinning it up, driving each hairpin home with a determined thrust of her index finger. Next she ran about in her underwear, rummaging through her wardrobe, a final show for him before he left Prague. No matter what else might be going on, she wanted him to suffer a little for giving her up.

They gathered at midafternoon on March 25, a strange exfiltration team indeed, he thought, Uta and Erma and Marie and Bibi – he never knew which one was which – in a staggering variety of feathers and scarves and little hats and tail-biting fox furs slung carelessly around their powdered necks, and the little balding cab-driver called Rudi, who was already drunk and lurched between hysterical lust, surrounded by so much delicious flesh, and quaking terror, in contemplation of what he was about to do. His taxicab was a modified Skoda – a barrel of kerosene mounted on struts where the trunk had once been, a pungent black cloud boiling from the exhaust pipe when he started the thing up.

Because the taxi had no trunk, they put Khristo on the floor in front of the back seat, covered their laps and him with a giant eiderdown quilt, and rested their feet on his back. Thus he went to Bratislava.

They had told him, in Bari, that he should get out if he thought the Germans were on to him. 'You might last a week,' they told him, 'on the roofs and in the alleys, but it's just a matter of time.' They had told him, if he was betrayed or identified or under suspicion, to go south to the Tatra Mountains, to join a *partizan* group and wait for Patton's Third Army.

Well, Bratislava was south, at the foot of the Little Carpathians. And Voluta had died because there was more

447

to the message than could be written on a slip of paper, so he had to ask himself what it might have been that could not be committed to writing. A request, he thought, *please do this*. And *doing this* did not just mean passing the information on to an intelligence service. Voluta, he believed, had been in Poland. When the Russians took over – people in Prague had spoken of it with fear in their eyes – he'd had to run. There was no plan, no technical arrangement, for him to go from Warsaw to Prague – the old escape route for Protestants fleeing religious persecution, across the Krknoše Mountains in northern Czechoslovakia. He had just set out to walk it. And the Russians had got onto him. It was not the Gestapo in the automobile he had seen driving away from the bridge, of that he was sure. Then, there were the mechanics of the meeting itself – poorly planned, the work of a sick, exhausted man. He realized that Voluta, a lifelong craftsman of clandestine practice, had acted, in his last hours, like an amateur. No matter. Voluta, through his friends, had contrived to give him his freedom from prison and, years later, had died trying to tell him, *tell* him, in human words and not in secret notes, that Sascha Vonets had to be collected.

He could, perhaps, defend the decision to terminate FELDSPAR. The man who had fallen into the subbasement had been an SS Sturmscharführer, a Gestapo sergeant. He would do as a reason if reasons were, sometime, to matter. And, somewhere, well back in the chain, was Ilya Goldman – for who else could have reached down into the Gulag system? BF 825 had finally become real, had taken on a life of its own, and he was now a prisoner of its obligations. That did not much worry him. What did was that Voluta *had known where he was*. The system that had contrived and supported the FELDSPAR mission had been somehow penetrated – by a friendly service, it was true, but who in turn might have a view of their operations? They were brave, the Americans, and ingenious to a fault, but they neither liked nor understood security. That took an iron fist, and they and their forefathers had fled the iron fists of the world since the beginning of their country.

He did not know what the OSS would think about it, would think about some colonel who said he would be in Sfintu Gheorghe on 12 April with what he claimed to be depth intelligence on NKVD personnel and actions. There were a million pieces of information every day in a war, like fish in the sea. Which one is the right fish? Someone, somewhere, would make a decision, a practical decision, a logistical decision, a *political* decision, finally, based on who had what power at any given moment, based – because the USSR was an ally – on the levantine politics of alliance, based on the positions of the planets and the stars. If it were one sort of a decision, they would be at Sfintu Gheorghe.

If not, not.

In the mad taxi, the first bottle of plum brandy was long gone by the time they got to Vlašim, the second well down before they reached Brno. German roadblocks stopped them every few miles because they were headed east, headed straight into the war, headed into Malinovsky's Second Ukrainian Front that had swept up from the Danube and fought its way across the Dukla Pass in the Carpathians to attack the town of Nitra, only forty miles north and east of Bratislava.

Magda, in the front seat next to Rudi, took charge at the roadblocks. 'We are on our way to a party, to see our Wehrmacht friends in Bratislava.' One last bash, apparently. The Germans saw no good reason to stop them. Khristo lay beneath the eiderdown and listened to the exchanges, his nose full of the mingled aromas of powder, scent, sweat and the alcoholic fume of the brandy. Driving away from the roadblocks, Rudi's taxi left a pall of kerosene smoke as it went weaving back and forth across the road, making Khristo slightly seasick with unexpected swerves he could not balance against. Time and again, German military trucks and tanks drove them off the pavement while the women screamed with laughter at all the bouncing and jouncing and Rudi swore like a little madman.

Encountering them, some of the German sentries laughed wildly and shouted their approval in very graphic terms. They knew that Malinovsky was coming, they knew what would happen to them, yet behold these bosomy Czech girls, off to *ficker* their German boyfriends one last time. Twilight of the gods – spring, 1945. It appealed to their sense of doom.

Waved through the roadblock, the Skoda sputtered to life and off they went again, the women screaming at Rudi, insulting or praising his manhood. Rudi drove the taxi and they drove Rudi, singing dirty songs and working their way through a third bottle, pouring some down the driver to keep his courage afloat as the road began to curve and climb.

At one of the last sentry posts, a hand reached in through the back window and lifted the edge of the quilt where it lay over the knees of the woman closest to the door. Khristo froze, stopped breathing as the upper corner of his hiding place was peeled back. Then came the sound of a hand being slapped, six inches from his ear, followed by a raucous bedroom chuckle. 'Bad Fritzi!' said a voice above him. 'Trying to look up my dress? Shame on you and your naughty eyes, what would your dear *Mutter* say if she knew?' There was more laughter, both within and without the car; the window was rolled back up and the taxi rumbled off, swerving back and forth across the road to Bratislava.

In Bratislava, they had boys strung up on the lamppost standards. These were not the old-timers, the ones who'd been in Russia and learned to survive anything; these were conscripts, sixteen and seventeen, and they'd faced the Russian guns and realized that Hitler was finished and nobody wanted to be the last one to die in the war. So they'd scampered over the nearest hill, planning to live

450

in the woods like boy scouts until all the scary stuff was over and they could go home. The Gestapo caught most of them. Bound them hand and foot and hung them on short ropes from the lamppost standards, their shoes only six inches from the ground, each one wearing a hand-lettered paper sign around his neck on a string: *Der Überläufer*, 'I am a deserter' – in the same way they used to make them wear the *I am a dunce* sign in school. Their eyes were wide open.

What worried Khristo in Bratislava was being dragooned by the Wehrmacht, given a rifle, and told to hold a position. His papers might be good here if he talked fast and convinced somebody that he didn't need a travel pass outside Prague, but he wasn't willing to chance it. They were getting ready to die in Bratislava and it had made them very serious. The city was much too quiet. He found an alley behind a bombed-out house, crawled down a hole into a watery basement, and waited until after midnight to move any farther.

The city was blacked out and deserted. Now and then he could hear the whine and rumble of tanks changing positions; the Second Ukrainian Front was shelling Nitra, forty miles away, colouring the night clouds with a reddish cast, but that was all, even the insects were silent here. He worked his way through the darkness, past German street patrols, and discovered an abandoned shed at the western edge of the docks where he had a clear view of the river.

By a slight shimmer of moonlight he could see the slow eddies and whorls the river made when the current ran full in the spring. This was the Czech Dunaj; it would be the Hungarian Duna in a few miles, then the Dunav in Yugoslavian Serbia, the Dunărea in Romania, then the Dunaj again, in Bulgaria, but it was all the same river, the Danube. He recognized this water, the rhythm of its slow, heavy course, the way it gathered the night's darkness and ran black. For a long time he leaned against a wooden beam in the shed and watched it flow past him.

He was isolated – for the first time in a very long time, he realized. The J-E radio he had destroyed according to specifications – smashed to bits and distributed piecemeal along a mile of canal in Prague. For the moment, Magda and her friends knew where he was, but he would leave here soon, and then no one would know. He needed a boat – the low shapes of hulls along the dock were just visible in the quarter moon – almost anything would do. He would make it, he told himself. He knew the river and, if he survived the initial part of the journey, he would know people along the river. He was a thousand miles from Sfintu Gheorghe; he had seventeen days to get there. He checked the current again, watched the white curl of water at the foot of a pier stanchion. A spring current. He could do it.

He would have to cross the Russian lines, would have to go through the white water at the Iron Gate, where the Duna came crashing down onto the Wallachian plain to form the border between Romania and Bulgaria. He would have to negotiate the delta, up in Bessarabian Romania, a thousand square miles of meandering, reed-choked channels. He would have to go past Vidin, past his mother and father and sister, if they were alive, without seeing them. For their own safety he would have to do that. But from the river he would send his spirit to see them; it was something, better than nothing. *Probably*, he thought, *I should not permit myself to feel this way, to feel this hope.* There were German soldiers hanging from lampposts in the streets of Bratislava, and the outlines of the riverport cranes were broken, twisted skeletons from the American bombing, but he knew this river, he had left a part of himself with it all these years, and he was surprised to find that it was still there waiting for him.

He must have dozed, for he snapped into consciousness as a drone rose higher and higher until it became a full-throttle roar. The hour was barely dawn, the river ran silver in the greyish light, and just east of his vantage point a tug was pulling a barge upstream. It was a heavy barge, and the tug was only just making headway against the current. The two planes flew side by side up the river – the gunports on their wings twinkling briefly as they passed over the barge – then broke off the attack, climbed steeply as their engines screamed, banked into tight, ascending turns, and headed back for another pass. He knew the silhouette: they were P-39 Airacobras, fighter planes of American manufacture with the red stars of the Soviet air force on their wings.

To see what they were shooting at, he narrowed his eyes and stared into the faint light: grey bundles, tight ranks of them pressed together on every available foot of barge space. As the Russian pilots made their second strafing run, one of the bundles rolled over the side and vanished in the river. They were German wounded, he realized, probably casualties of the fighting in Nitra, barged down the river Nitra into the Danube, now headed west to Austrian field hospitals. The fighter planes' guns mowed from the stern of the barge to the foredeck of the tug as he watched. Just as they broke off the second attack, a fountain of ack-ack tracer flowed upward from the dock area, falling far short of the climbing planes, and a figure in black ran from the pilothouse of the tug and began swinging something at the towing bitt on the aft deck. His motions were frantic, and Khristo realized he was chopping at the towline with an axe. As the Airacobras came around the third time, the barge broke free and began floating backward, downstream in the current, and the tug headed toward the bank, attempting to crawl in under the protection of the antiaircraft fire.

He broke from the shed in a dead run as the planes harried the tugboat, headed for the river. The cold of it exploded in his head as he dived in, and the shock caused him to take a sickening mouthful of oily water – the iridescent sheen was all around him. Keeping his face out of the river, he struggled toward the tugboat, the weight of clothing and shoes dragging him down. The roar of the incoming planes rang in his ears, then they were gone.

He had tried to calculate a safe angle of intersection – heading well upstream of the tugboat when he entered the water – but the river was taking him. He dug his arms in as hard as he could, told himself he was getting it done, slicing through the current. A look at the boat showed him he was wrong. He was losing ground with every stroke. He ducked his head below the surface and kicked like a maniac to keep his body straight, driving the hard water beneath him as he brought his arms through. When his air was gone he came up gasping and tasted oil in his throat. The tug was near, he'd gained a few feet, but he was sliding past it and the hammering pulse of the propeller shaft felt as though it was on top of him. He lunged through the water, flailing his arms, then kicked his weight upward and got one hand through the rope lashing that looped along the hull. Dragged against the swell, his body created a wave that almost drowned him. He fought above it, snatching the rope with his other hand and holding on for his life. The motion of the boat drove him against the hull and he tried to thrust himself farther up the rope by shoving his feet against the wood, but it was slippery as wet ice and he couldn't do it. *Oh well*, he thought, amused by his predicament, a grand euphoria rising within him. Then he realized that the cold had invaded his mind, that he could die snagged on the hull, the strange dreamy death that came from immersion in cold water. In terror, he hauled frantically at the rope and his body sprang loose from the river, and then he had the rope under his arms and was inching his way up the loop, struggling toward its height and getting one hand hooked like a claw on top of the deck bulwark. He looked up, noted casually that blood was welling from beneath his fingernails, running pink as it mixed with water, then hung all his weight on the hand in order to swing one foot up on the bulwark. He pleaded for strength, then rolled himself over, falling three feet and landing deadweight on the planking of the deck. He lost himself for a time, then discovered the fading drone of airplane engines and the throbbing of the tug's pistons and returned to the world. The night before, he had studied the river from a distance, finding consolation in its slow, dark motion. A man of the world, who had walked the streets of Paris. Now he remembered himself as a little boy, guided by the lore of older kids, throwing a few crumbs of bread in the river before he would even dare to put a foot in the water.

Gun in hand, he crawled along the curve of the bulwark until he reached the pilot's cabin, which was set just forward of the small deckhouse that served as the tug's living quarters. Inside, a woman was at the helm, adjusting the large spoked wheel, watching the water ahead of her with unmoving eyes.

A bearded man in a black uniform sat against the far wall of the cabin, eyes closed, knees pulled up, hands clasped across his stomach, chest moving slightly as he breathed. An old-fashioned machine gun – a *pepecha*, with rough wooden stock and pan magazine – lay at his feet, and a trickle of blood ran across the deck from somewhere beneath him.

The pilot glanced at Khristo, then returned her attention to the river. She was immense, a solid block of a woman in carpet slippers and black socks and a flowered print dress that hung down like a tent. Above the socks, her white ankles were webbed with blue veins – the result, he realized, of a lifetime spent standing at the helm. Her face, in profile, featured an enormous bulb of a nose, a massive, square jaw, and salt and pepper hair scissored in a line across the nape of her neck. She was, he guessed, well into her fifties.

She spoke to him briefly in a language he did not at first understand, then realized was Hungarian. Next, she tried him in rapid German. He shook his head dumbly and started to shiver in the cool dawn air. 'Who is he?' he said in Czech, nodding at the man on the floor.

'Hlinka,' she said. The Hlinka, he knew, was a Slovakian fascist militia that fought alongside the Germans.

'Your guard?' he asked, purposely vague. A guard could protect you or hold you prisoner.

She declined the trap. 'What do you want?' she said in Czech. 'Here it is forbidden to refugees,' she added. With authority, just in case he was something the Germans had thought up to test her loyalty.

He did not answer immediately. She shrugged, went back to work, changing course a point or two to avoid a whitewater snag some way upriver.

'I want to go east, mother,' he said, using a term of respect.

'I am not your mother,' she said. 'And they are fighting east of here. And if you try to shoot that thing it will piss on your foot.'

He looked down to see water dripping from the barrel of the Czech automatic. He stuck it back in his belt, then reached into his pocket and brought out the gold coins — there were sixteen, each a solid ounce — and sprayed them across the metal shelf by the helm so that they made a great ringing clatter.

She moved her lips as she counted them, then gave him a good, long look, taking in his worker's clothing — wool jacket and pants, heavy boots, peaked cap stuffed in side pocket — and staring him full in the face before she went back to watching the river.

'Who are you, then?' she said. 'And spare me the horseshit, if you don't mind.' Her tone was courteous, but bore the suggestion that she could throw him back overboard anytime she felt like it. He looked at her arms. She could do it easily, he realized.

'I am from the river, like you.' He said it in Bulgarian.

She nodded and thought it over. 'That is a fortune,' she said, switching into Russian, knowing he would understand it. 'A lot of gold for a river boy.' She paused for a time, ruminating on things, as the tug slid past the snag. She'd

456

given it just enough room for safety, not so much as to waste fuel.

'What is your name?' he asked.

'My official name you don't need to know,' she said. 'On the river I am called Annika.'

'If you turn your boat around, Annika, they will think that you are going back downstream for the barge, and they will not send a patrol boat out from Bratislava.'

'Smart, too,' she said, 'for a river boy.'

He did not press her further. She picked up one of the coins and studied it front and back, then tossed it onto the shelf. She mumbled to herself in Hungarian for a time – curses, he suspected, from the choppy rhythm of it, aimed at Germans, Russians, gold, rivers, boats, him, and likely herself and her fate as well – then spun the wheel toward the far bank. The rudder responded and the tug swung slowly in the direction of the shore, the course change preparatory to coming about and heading east.

'My Hlinka/watchdog,' she said, 'he still lives?'

Khristo looked at the man. 'Yes,' he said.

'He crawled in here for company while he died,' she said. 'That much we give him.' He nodded his agreement.

'When he's gone,' she continued, 'pitch him overboard. On my boat, you must work.'

She was a small tug, so wide-beamed in the middle and high in the bow she seemed half submerged. Her current name, *K-24*, was just barely visible amid the rust stains and moss green patches on her hull. She had been designated *K-24* in 1940, when Hungary had joined the Axis powers. Aside from a few gunboats and a small fleet of tugs and barges, Hungary had no navy. It had no coastline and no access to the sea, though it was governed by an admiral, Miklós Horthy, throughout the war.

The tug had been launched in 1908 at a dockyard near Szeged and christened the *Tisza*, after the river on which the city was located. She was forty feet long, built low

457

to the water in order to slide beneath the old Danube bridges. Her steam engine was Austrian, a simple boiler that put forth 200 horsepower on a good day and would burn coal or wood but in its time had run on straw, hay, cotton waste or anything else that could be set on fire. When the Americans were bombing up and down the river – hitting the Romanian oil transfer points at Giorgiu and Constanta, finally taking out the oilfields at Ploesti – she had been regularly strafed, something about the slow progress of a tug inciting turret gunners to a frenzy as they passed above her. One fighter pilot – 'a splendid idiot' was the way Annika put it – had spent the better part of a half hour machine-gunning a bargeload of gravel, to no particular point, having first nearly melted his barrels in fruitless attacks on the *Tisza*'s pilothouse, which was covered by a two-inch sheet of iron plating painted to look like a wooden roof. The *Tisza* had, in four years of war, taken its share of hits at the waterline, in the engine boiler and the smokestack, but these were easily enough patched.

She was, Annika admitted, an old lady and a noisy one. Her pistons hammered relentlessly as she ran, and you could hear her coming a good way off, ticking like a clock gone mad. 'A *dirty* old lady,' Annika's husband had called her, in the days before the war. Her stack – chopped off a few feet above the roof level of the pilothouse because of this or that bridge – trailed sooty clouds of smoke into the sky, black, grey, or white, depending on what they had to burn that day.

Leaving Bratislava, the smoke was black as they used up the last of the Czechoslovakian coal. 'From here on, it's brushwood,' Annika told him, casting a meaningful eye toward the double-bitted axe that stood in one corner of the pilothouse. 'She'll run on trash, if she must.' The Danube grew its own fuel, abundant softwoods – alder, willow, big-leaf maple – that lined its banks and drank its water. It was light, fibrous stuff that grew up in a year and burned up in a minute but it was abundant, and the *Tisza* had never minded it. 'Thank the Lord for the current,' Annika said, 'and for a load of one river boy rather than a barge of sand.'

Just south of the Bratislava docks, the river became the north-south boundary between Czechoslovakia and Hungary, passing entirely into Hungarian territory at the town of Štúrovo. In mid-afternoon, Khristo hid below decks, behind a coal bin next to the boiler, where he at last dried out while the Hungarian border guards came aboard to joke with Annika and consume several bottles of beer and a tin of jam. When they'd gone, Annika came down the hatchway and showed him how to stoke the boiler and manage the primitive gearing system that changed propeller pitch. 'Three speeds,' she said, 'all slow. And if we have to go backward, I come and show you. You must be a little bit the mechanic.'

But for most of the day, not much was demanded of him. He stood by Annika's side and watched the shore as they moved through the vast Hungarian plain. It was a March afternoon on the river as he remembered it, cold and grey, with racing clouds above and occasional moments of sunlight passing into sudden rain squalls that roughed up the surface of the water, then disappeared. They went past odd little towns full of bulbous shapes and steeply pitched roofs with storks' nests woven into the eaves. Deserted towns, they seemed; only a few skinny dogs came down to the water to bark at them. Perhaps the people had fled as the fighting moved toward them – west to the German lines or east to the Russian. He did see the barge of wounded Germans, what was left of them, being towed upriver by another tug with whom Annika exchanged a greeting of whistle blasts. Sometimes the sky cleared, revealing the low Carpathians in the northern distance, sun shafts piercing the cloud and lighting the ridges a pale green.

In the late afternoon they pulled into the harbour at Szöny and tied up next to a line of tugs, some of them

459

joined to empty barges. Annika went off visiting, hopping nimbly in her carpet slippers from deck to deck, stopping at each pilothouse to gossip and exchange news. It was dark by the time she returned. They sat together by a miniature parlour stove in the kitchen area of the crew quarters – two hammocks and a battered old wardrobe chest – while Annika added water to flour and rolled up *csipetke*, tiny dumplings, boiled them in a pot of water, and added some dense tomato sauce from a tin can, then a single clove of garlic – 'to make it taste like *something*' – squeezed flat between thumb and forefinger before ceremonial addition to the stew.

'Oh, for an egg,' she said sadly, 'or a pinch of rose pepper. You would love me forever.'

In Prague, Khristo had lived on bread that was part sawdust, and horsemeat stewed with onions to hide the spoiled taste, and he wolfed down his portion of dumplings in sauce. 'I'm in love with you already,' he said.

'Well, there's enough of it,' she said, referring to a stack of zinc-coloured cans of tomato sauce piled up on a shelf. 'There used to be fish,' she said, 'but the bomb concussions have done for them. Big ones, catfish with whiskers. *Strong* – but cooked in milk they were sweet. Ach' – she shut her eyes and grimaced in sorrow – 'this stupid war is a curse. It took my husband, both sons, most of the men on the river. The winter of '43 got them, retreating from Moscow in the snow, so cold that when they took their pants down by the side of the road, they froze up back there and died.' Her mouth tightened at the thought and she crossed herself. 'One or two came back. Husks. Good for nothing after that – they'd seen too much.'

She cleaned her bowl with a thumb and licked off the last of the tomato sauce. 'They are fighting east of us, just as I warned you. Near the prison at Vác, downriver from the bend at Esztergom. The Hungarian Third Army, they say, what's left of it, and the Sixth Panzer, facing the Third Ukrainian. Mongolian troops, river boy, they fight on vodka and if you're a woman, God help you die quick. They haven't been here for a thousand years, yet we've never forgotten them. They surrounded forty-five thousand German troops up by Lake Balaton, and *pffft*, that was that.'

'What are people saying?' Khristo asked.

'Well, the Russians have got Budapest, so that's the end of the government. No great loss. Some say the thing to do is cross over the lines, surrender to the Red Army – others want to wait here. The Russians will need us. They'll pay something, at least, to have their supplies move on the river.'

'And so?'

'Some of us are going to try to sneak through tonight. Maybe they stop fighting and have a snooze.'

'I doubt it.'

'So do I. How far east are you going?'

'I'll tell you when we get there,' he said.

'So I guessed.'

'Have you got anything black? Like paint?'

'Paint! You are crazed. Some tar, maybe.'

'It will do,' he said.

They chugged slowly out of Szöny harbour just after midnight, eight tugboats moving in single file along the dark river. Since they could expect to be under observation by Hungarian and Wehrmacht rearguard units, each flew the flag of the collapsed Hungarian regime on the short pole astern. The best navigator of the group, a stooped old man called Janos, took the lead in his boat, followed by *Tisza* and the others. The moon was fully risen, but the spring westerly had increased its force and a low scud of cloud obscured the light, leaving the river in drifting shadows. Difficulty of navigation was increased by a drop in temperature that brought a heavy mist off the water, swirling in the wind as it blew downstream. This made Janos's job harder, but turned the

461

boats into ghostly, uncertain outlines from the perspective of the shore.

Of Janos, Annika said, 'He is half blind, so the darkness will not bother him. He navigates with his feet, he says. By the run of the water under the keel he knows his way.'

'Is that possible?' Khristo asked.

'He is on the river since childhood. Thus he is a good navigator, also a good liar. Take your pick.'

Standing in the pilothouse, Khristo could feel only the rapid pulse of *Tisza*'s engines. Yet the boat ahead of them moved slowly back and forth from the centre to the starboard bank of the river, as though it were avoiding hazards, and the rush of water passing over a sandbar shoal could be heard to one side of the boat as they moved around it.

'A sandbar,' Khristo said. 'He has taken us away from it.'

'*Ja, ja,*' Annika said, unimpressed. 'A famous sandbar, one that everybody knows. What you and I must worry about are the new ones. Danúbio – the god of this river – stirs his mud up every winter and leaves it in different places, so that we may find it with our propellers.' She made a small correction with the wheel, apparently following some motion of the lead boat's stern that was invisible to him. 'A way down from here, there are granite blocks under the water, quarried by the Romans as piers for a bridge. The emperor Trajan desired to build a military road, from Spain to the Euphrates River, but he died. He left us his granite to remember him by and, when the water is low and there is sand on both sides of the river, it will peel the bottom of a boat clean off. I have seen it.'

They were silent for a time, staring ahead of them through the drifting fog. 'Do you want me down below?' he asked.

'No,' she said. 'Stay up here with me and keep the *pepecha* handy. We are going full slow as it is, and if something happens you don't want to be belowdecks.'

He thought of steam under pressure and what it could do and was thankful for the dispensation. 'What use will the *pepecha* be against field guns?'

She shrugged. 'Not much.'

The river meandered north and south at Esztergom, then swung around in a sharp bend by the Vác prison and headed due south, toward Budapest and eventually into Serbian Yugoslavia. They could hear the fighting well enough, like an approaching thunderstorm, and the sky flickered a dull orange with artillery and tank barrages, but most of the action seemed to be centred north of the river.

Moving along the northward curve toward Esztergom, a searchlight cut through the fog and raced forward from the last boat to the first, then pinned Janos's tug in its beam. A loudhailer, sounding eerily close over the water, called out a command in Hungarian. As Janos, shouting in a cracked voice, answered the unseen officer, Annika translated into Russian:

'Convoy leader, identify yourself.'

'*K-38* and seven K-class tugs – out of Bratislava.'

'Where bound?'

'Vác prison.'

'Say again, *K-38*.'

'Vác prison.'

'Have you gone mad?'

'Long ago.'

'The Russians are up there. Are you under orders?'

'Yes, sir. To remove special prisoners to the rear.'

'Written orders?'

'Verbal orders. From the SS. A German colonel accompanies us, would you like to hear it from him? I can wake him up for you.'

'Proceed, *K-38*.'

'Thank you.'

'God help you.'

'One hopes.'

The searchlight blinked out, and the running lights of

the patrol boat faded away as it returned to station in midstream.

The convoy steamed on into the darkness, its slow progress taking them toward the steady beat of artillery exchanges in the hills above Vác. They could now see yellow muzzle flashes on the ridgelines, and a piece of burning debris arced gracefully above them and hissed into the water. At first, the bass thudding of the gunnery was a massive rumble, low and continuous, that rolled and echoed above the river. But as they drew closer, the sound resolved into separate parts: the low thump of field mortars, the whistle of Wehrmacht 88s and the sigh of Russian field-gun rounds, the rhythmic crackle of machine-gun fire and the muffled impacts of exploding shells.

As they steamed around a bend in the river, the horizon glowed brighter and brighter and the sound swelled in volume. Then they were in the middle of it.

It was like a nightmare, he thought, because he wanted to run but could not move. His eyes streamed with tears from the billowing smoke – suddenly every object was blurred and misshapen. The prison on the far bank was burning, towers of flame from the roof and cell windows rolling into the sky as though sucked upward by an immense wind. The air around him buzzed and sang, and he thought he could hear voices from the near bank, calling out in a strange language, and a huge shower of sparks rained down on the boat. Then the water exploded, a white wall, and the river rocked backward. The window glass trembled and water sprayed across it, a prism refracting clouds of tracer, the fiery prison, the shore ahead stuttering from white light to blind darkness and back again. He went deaf. Braced himself against the pilothouse wall and felt the *Tisza* taking fire, like an animal kicking the hull. The stern of *K-38* began to move away from them and Khristo tore himself from the wall and ran crouched along the deck, throwing the hatch back and jumping six feet into the hold. He opened the boiler door with a bare hand – saw the red stripe across his palm but felt nothing. He piled armloads of brushwood through the opening, kicking it into the roaring furnace as it snagged on the rim, bowed and resisted as though it did not want to burn. The *Tisza* rocked again. He slammed the door with his boot and leaped up the ladder onto the deck. An enormous yellow flare went off above him and a wind knocked him flat on his face. He scrambled to his knees, ready to swim, then saw that it was the boat behind them. Its pilothouse was gone, stack bent over to the deck with white steam spraying from one side. As he watched, the boat yawed out toward midriver, a line of little flames licking along the bow. He scurried toward the pilothouse, like a rat in a burning barn, he thought, and saw human shapes onshore, running with the boat, their arms raised in supplication. One of them tried to swim out, then vanished.

What they did in Budapest, two days later, seemed entirely ingenuous. That was necessary. Had the tracks of planning and calculation showed through, it would have raised *questions*. But what he contrived was just simple enough, naive, to have about it a taste of the peasant's innocence, and Khristo well understood what the Russians thought about that – especially those Russians whose job it was to think about things. It made them sentimental, for they saw their former selves in it.

Budapest was eighteen miles downriver from the Vác prison, just far enough behind the front lines to be, by then, choked with *apparat* of all sorts. The tugboat captains feared that as much as Khristo did, and river gossip confirmed their fears. There would be no sneaking through a web of those proportions – it had to be confronted.

Once the fighting was well behind them, Janos led them into a narrow stream which, at first, did not appear navigable, then widened suddenly and ran four or five miles into the empty countryside. What a dark alley was to a criminal, he thought, this byway to nowhere was to

465

the boats. 'When we have no customs stamp, we unload here,' was how Annika put it. 'We are all smugglers, of course,' she added offhandedly, 'some of the time.' The tugs tied off to trees on the bank, then everyone fell into a sleep of exhaustion.

The following morning, he joined the crews in chopping brush. Annika had applied lubricating grease to the burn and bound it up with an old engine rag, and the right hand slid up and down the axe handle anyhow, so he was able to manage it. He relished the work, labouring under a pallid sun with his jacket and shirt off, the sweat running down his back. Both blades of the double-bit axe were sharp, and he could take a two-inch trunk down with two or three wallops. Softwood was like that, of course, but he fancied himself a great woodsman nonetheless, the darkness of Prague and the terror of the previous night sweating itself out of him as he hacked at the brush.

They made a fire and burned the Hungarian flags, then patched the hulls with canvas and tar, which would have to do until they got to a boatyard. There, he was told, fabled craftsmen could saw out a damaged section of wood and then, almost unbelievably, reproduce the precise curve and size of planking to be tamped back into place with mallets. Then, using a long file called a slick, they would bring the new planking to a perfect harmony with the old hull. And it would never leak.

At sunset, they stood in a circle with caps in hand and Janos spoke a short prayer for the lost crew and tugboat. Many of them had been slightly wounded going past Vác – a steam scald, a broken wrist, two minor shrapnel injuries, Khristo's burned hand – but they all felt themselves fortunate to see the sun go down that night. They were close to Budapest, there were those who wanted to go on right then and have it over with, but Khristo made a short speech, translated by Annika, and they eventually decided to trust his perception of Soviet bureaucracy – which by nightfall was wobbly at best and sometimes surly, from a

466

full day's vodka ration, and didn't much like the darkness in the first place.

The next morning, Annika chose a young, whippy birch and Khristo felled it and trimmed the branches. About his further preparations she was less than pleased, but admitted glumly that it would be for the best if a strong effect were achieved. 'It is hard to know with that sort of army,' he explained. 'Maybe they hug you, maybe they squeeze off half a magazine in your belly. They themselves don't know what they're going to do until the mood takes them.'

'*Ja, ja*,' she said, not really convinced he was right. Khristo's preparations had made a grave dent in her supplies, and she felt she might regret that in the future.

But she was proud of him later on that day, as they steamed downriver through the centre of Budapest, he could see that. He was standing forward of the pilothouse with a ten-year-old boy borrowed for the occasion from another boat – *Tisza* was the leader of this convoy, and everybody, Annika included, knew they had to make an impression. Khristo turned at one point and looked in the pilothouse window and saw a sly and appreciative grin on her face.

The noise was overwhelming. There must have been thirty thousand of them – Mongolian troops with European Russian officers – lining the quays of the city as they moved through it. They cheered and waved, raised their *pepechas* and their old rifles with long bayonets. Some of the officers came to fervent attention. The child next to him, Khristo realized, was meant for the theatre. He thrust his little fist into the air with revolutionary passion and scowled patriotically as though he were about to cry with all the emotion of it. Or perhaps, Khristo thought, he came suddenly to believe it. That was surely possible. It was exciting, thrilling, those tens of thousands of voices roaring in unison as the seven boats passed, their crews standing atop the cabins and saluting fiercely, their steam whistles hooting in celebration. The roar increased to thunder as they sailed past the elegant old parliament building that faced the river, the soldiers inside apparently so excited that desks and chairs and a snowstorm of papers came sailing out of the windows.

This was Khristo's finest moment. Annika handed him the *pepecha* through the pilothouse door and, in perfect imitation of a thousand posters, he held it high in one hand – the bandaged one, forearm bulging – shaking the weapon with revolutionary fervour: *fuck with us and this is what you'll get!* The soldiers on shore, recognizing their very own weapon, the PPSh M1941, cheered even louder. And when he climbed up the iron ladder onto the roof of the pilothouse and repeated the gesture, using the flag for background, the cheering reached a glorious climax. On both banks, voices were raised in spontaneous singing – the Red Army anthem.

A real Soviet flag would not have worked, he knew; it would have puzzled them, made them curious. *Where did he get it? Who is he?* But the huge square of canvas, four feet high and six feet long, roped to a birch pole nailed into the back wall of the pilothouse, then stretched forward by a rope wound around the smokestack, as though it were flying stiff in a fast breeze – that took them past curiosity. That sort of gesture took them in the heart.

It was a grand flag: red with tomato sauce, hammer and sickle crudely painted with black tar. On both sides, so that all could see it.

Russian press dispatches, for March 29, 1945, would include a mention of the incident: 'In Budapest, elements of the Hungarian navy overthrew their fascist officers and joined forces with the victorious divisions of Marshal Malinovsky's Third Ukrainian Front in a display of patriotic solidarity.'

They were arrested, of course, but it was the mildest sort of arrest. Around a bend in the river, a Russian patrol boat guided them into a dock and the military intelligence people were sent for. Papers were produced, examined, held up to the light – but they had already 'confessed', in the most public way imaginable, to the worst of their crimes: being part of a supply system that served an enemy fighting force. Thus the intelligence people found little to provoke their interest. They had the 'crime', which satisfied one of their instincts, and they had the 'penalty', which satisfied the other. The penalty was a form of conscription: these tugboats and their crews would serve the Occupation garrison, which desperately needed a way to get back and forth across the river. The retreating Germans had blown every single bridge in Budapest, whose twin cities, Buda and Pesth, were divided by the Danube. In return for faithful service, they would receive Red Army food rations, which amounted to a generous ladle, twice daily, from a cauldron into which all appropriated food was thrown. The stew boiled twenty-four hours a day, a fatty broth of onions, roosters, rabbits, dead horse, turnips – whatever they happened on in the course of their collecting forays – the Red Army essentially lived off the countryside. Vodka rations, supplied from the east, might come later, the Russian officers said, if they worked hard and kept their noses clean.

The tugboat people found this an excellent arrangement. They had their lives and their boats, they would be fed, and they were keenly aware that captured enemies of the Soviet armies rarely fared that well. After a few hours, they were sent back to their boats and told to await further direction.

Khristo was taken to a room. For him they had two captains with the top buttons of their tunics undone. One was tall, with colourless eyes, the other short and not happy about it. So, they started in, he was a Yugoslav conscript worker who had escaped from his masters in Prague. A curious tale. How had he done it? Describe a milling machine, please. And what was the lubricating procedure for a lathe. Had he ever used a router plane in his work? Where was the factory? What did it do? Where did he live? What was his mother's maiden name? The street on which the factory was located – what did it look like? What was he paid? Had anyone helped him in his escape? How had he got from Prague to Bratislava? Transferred? Who had signed the order? The German supervisor? What was his name? What did he look like? The papers had been destroyed? How convenient. We know you're an American spy, they told him. One of the tugboat crewmen had suspected it, had told them he was carrying gold. Where was it? Where was the radio? Where were the maps? Make a clean breast, they said; all we want is for you to work for us, surely you see you would be too valuable to be shot. Come on, they said, all three of us are in the same profession, if we don't stick together the higher-ups will shaft us all, we know it, you know it, let's make an arrangement, let's make each other comfortable. Some of these bastards would poke your eyes out if we weren't protecting you. *Mongolians!* You're lucky it's us and not them. We understand your problems.

No, no, he told them, you've got it all upside down. He was a member of the Yugoslavian Communist party – he'd destroyed the card ten minutes before the Germans got him or it would have been lights out for him. He was a worker. All he wanted was to go home, eat some real food if he could find it, see what his old girlfriend was up to. He'd repaired German aircraft at a factory in Prague. The production schedules were set weekly, based on an anticipated workload known to three foremen. The day before he left, an ME-110 wing had been trucked in with damage from small arms fire – the number on the wing was something like 7705-12. The German security officer in the factory was called Bischau. Production norms were not being met. He had committed several acts of sabotage, using emery grit and other materials. The name of the Communist party secretary in Kralijevo, his hometown, was Webak, but he believed it to be an alias. German casualties were being barged down the river

470

Nitra, then up the Danube to Austria. *Flies for Yaschyeritsa,* he thought.

He spooned it into their mouths as they slapped him and kicked his shins. Something to write down. Names, numbers, addresses. He never met their eyes and made them work for every bit of it. Dried up several times, was driven back to the subject. At last, he began to bore them. He'd taken the edge off their appetites and seemed to them less and less like anything resembling a banquet. Would he, they wanted to know, just in case he should some day be allowed to return to Yugoslavia, keep in touch? Nothing formal. Just the odd observation on life and circumstance in his homeland.

Such a request caught him entirely unaware. He blinked stupidly, paused for some time, mulling it over like a machinist's problem. Well, he told them, this was not anything he'd ever considered, but he could find little wrong with it. The fascists in Yugoslavia had nearly destroyed the country, they must in future be resisted. If he could help in such an effort, be of some value, he saw nothing wrong with it. Any patriotic Yugoslav would do no less – he was sure of that.

Well, they said, they would see him again. And they let him go.

He returned to the *Tisza* and told Annika the sad facts of life. 'Too bad,' she said sorrowfully, staring off into the darkness as though she could see her lucky gods heading downriver.

'I am sorry,' he said.

They stood at the rail together. From the streets of the city they could hear drunken singing and shouting and the occasional shot fired. 'Be grateful that you are alive, Annika,' she said to herself sternly, pulling her sweater tight against the night chill rising off the river.

'What now?' she asked him.

He nodded east and said, 'One way or another.'

'You are a funny sort of an American, river boy, that speaks Bulgarian and Russian and God knows what else.'

'American?'

'You run from the Germans and fool the Russians. What else could you be?'

'Just a man going home.'

'Very well,' she said, 'I shall remember you so.'

They were together in silence for a time, he was reluctant to leave her. She patted him twice on the shoulder and went below-decks. When she returned, she handed him the Czech automatic that she had hidden for him, two tins of jam, a clasp knife, and a few ten-florin Hungarian coins.

'You are kind, Annika,' he said.

'For luck,' she said. 'You cannot give a knife without a coin.' She leaned out over the bulwark and unknotted a kerchief that held the small fortune he had given her – they both knew she dared not keep it.

'Farewell, my little friends,' she said sadly. 'Once upon a time you were a rich man's pride. You have made a great journey, but now you stink like old cheese, and the Russians will smell you out.' One by one, at first, then all together, she let them fall from her open hand, gold coins lost in a river.

He walked up a ramp onto the quay and made quickly for the side streets. He had intended to steal a rowboat and drift silently away from the city, but there wasn't an unguarded craft of any description that he could see – not with all the bridges down, there wasn't. So he walked south, making his way to within sight of the river from time to time to be sure he wasn't wandering off course.

The city had apparently seen many weeks of street fighting. A few blocks were mounds of stone and dirt and splintered wood, but it took bombs or artillery to do that. Where he walked it was mostly building façades pocked with mortar shells and sprinkled with the whitish chip marks of small arms fire. There was hardly an unshattered windowpane to be seen – glass crunched continually beneath his boots – and the clouds of flies and the smell of unburied bodies nauseated him. He clamped a hand over his mouth and nose and breathed against his own skin and that seemed to help a little.

There were no Russian officers to be seen, just a few drunken troopers trying to make their way back to wherever they thought their units might be. At one point, a Mongolian corporal rushed out of a doorway and, embracing him with a clasp like iron, lifted him completely off the ground, put him down, and began singing wildly and dancing him around in a bear hug. The man was only an inch or two above five feet tall and his breath reeked of turpentine. Khristo danced along and sang at the top of his lungs – he knew that when you are that drunk, everyone else had better be too – whooping and yowling like a lunatic. After they had sworn friendship for life and Khristo had gravely accepted the hand of his sister in marriage, the man went staggering away and disappeared into an alley.

He spent the better part of the night reaching the outskirts of the city. When first dawn began to lighten the road, he wandered into a neighbourhood of little shacks, crawled under a piece of tin sheeting at the back of a roofless house, and fell asleep.

It took him four days to reach Yugoslavia. There was nothing moving downstream – no opportunity for stowaway or expropriation presented itself– so he walked, on a road that meandered down the eastern bank of the river for some hundred and ten miles. He had to guess the distance; only a few mile markers remained and some of those had been altered to deceive invading armies, but it was at least that far.

He was not alone on the road. Small knots of refugees, old people, women and children, walked along with him or passed him going the other way, their possessions rolled in blankets on their backs or pushed along in handcarts or baby carriages. There seemed to be equal numbers of them headed in each direction, and this puzzled him. In his experience, refugees moved only in one direction: away from war. But this was different, he thought. This was something he had never seen before.

In 1940, when he'd fled from the German armies down clogged French roads, the air had been filled with wild rumours and the electricity of unfolding events. That had been a terrible time, but despite its sorrow and confusion there'd been a perverse ecstasy to it – the struggle of ordinary people, caught in the open by a moment of history, to survive. This was far worse. These people were the defeated, the uprooted; hopelessness and despair hung about them like smoke. They walked slowly, hypnotized by exhaustion, and their eyes never left the ground.

He began to suspect, after a time, that the refugees on the road might not have a destination. Perhaps they had no papers or permits, perhaps when they tried to stay somewhere they were chased away. He did not know the reason, but the people walked without purpose, as though walking itself was now all they could do, and they meant to walk until they dropped or until some authority appeared and told them what was required of them.

On the first day, he caught himself walking too quickly, with too much purpose. He cut a stick from an exploded tree and, after that, fell naturally into the appropriate limp. By the second day he was covered with a fine, gritty soil that blew in the wind, and he was tiring, and there was no longer any difficulty at all about blending in. He walked past empty villages where open shutters banged in the wind, past burnt-out farmhouses seen at a distance across fields of unploughed mud, past blackened tanks with guns pointing at the sky. At night he slept on the ground, waking damp and sore, and the brief flurries of rain meant that he never really dried out.

He had started out in reasonably good shape. In Prague he had spent so much time on the move, hurrying from meeting to meeting, always behind schedule, that the walking of the first two days did not bother him overmuch. His shins ached where the Russians had kicked him, but that would pass, he knew, and he had unwrapped his hand to let the air heal the long, white blister that had formed on it.

But he now began to comprehend what had happened to Voluta, how he had come to make the critical error that had nearly killed them both. To meet after curfew, in the open, at a guarded bridge, was a reasonable definition of suicide, an extraordinarily stupid mistake for a man who had spent his adult life in the shadows, for a man who crossed borders like the wind.

Yet it had happened, and Khristo finally understood how it had happened. Moving across the countryside made one prey, over time, to a series of small mishaps, none of them serious in and of itself, but cumulative over time. A few hours of sleep when one could manage it, a meal now and then, the insidious chill of the early spring, the constant forcing of the mind into a state of vigilance when all one craved was numbness, when not to think about anything seemed the most exquisite luxury the world had to offer.

He woke on the morning of the third day to find that he was soaked to the skin and the back of his throat was on fire. In panic, he forced himself to a sitting position, then swallowed obsessively until the burning subsided. He was thirsty, dry as dust. The only water available collected in shellholes or farmers' ponds or, in extremity, there was the river. But each time he had to drink he was in fear of cholera, so permitted himself only a few sips, imagining that his body would fight the bacteria better if it was limited to small doses. *An old wives' tale*, he told himself. Yet something primitive within him insisted that it be done that way even if he knew better. The body runs on liquid, he thought, I must have it. *No*, said another voice, *only a little*.

Out on the road, a small group of old people in black clothing was already on the move, though it was barely light. What did they eat? he wondered. He'd had a tin of jam the previous day. Had slid down an embankment onto the shore of the river, where he could hide in order to eat it. Like an animal with its kill, he thought. Plum jam. The most delicious thing there could possibly be. He'd sawn the tin open with his knife and spooned the jam up with his fingers. *Walk*, he told himself to stop the reverie. *Walk and you will feel better*. And there would be more jam tomorrow. Maybe the sun would come out and dry him off. Maybe the Americans would swoop down in one of their special planes – they seemed to have no end of them – and whisk him off to Switzerland, to Basel, to the Gasthaus Kogelmann. Where they served a thick pancake of fried potatoes and onions and, for those who took full board, Frau Kogelmann would make sure there was a second pancake for you if you were still hungry. When you drank some water, in the little dining area set off from the parlour, a boy came with a yellow pitcher and refilled your glass. You didn't have to ask.

Of the fourth day he remembered little. The villages of Ercsi and Adony and Dunaföldvár seemed deserted. He would wait at the outskirts for a group of refugees and walk through with them, so as to pass unnoticed. But he was not challenged. Russian military police sat in American Jeeps and smoked cigarettes, watching him limp past. At Fajsz, a woman came out of a house and gave him a cup of water. Her face beneath the black shawl was seamed and windburned, yet she was young and seemed very beautiful because there was pity for him in her eyes. He drank the water and handed the cup back. '*Köszönöm*,' he said, his voice a dry whisper. She nodded in acknowledgment, then a voice called from a house and she went away.

Some miles before the town of Mohács, he left the Great Plain and entered the swampland of southern Hungary. Now it was not so far to Yugoslavia. Soviet troops had been there longer, river traffic would be closer to normal. It was a guess – information abstracted from Czech newspapers by Hlava and reported to him twice a week – but a reasonable guess. The German censors did not want the population to know where the lines were, but they could not resist reporting Russian atrocities against civilians – an attempt to stiffen public resistance as the time of invasion approached.

Good guess or not, he would have to find a way to get back on the river, he could not walk much farther. The hunger had stopped gnawing at him, but his mind was running in odd channels, wandering through images of the past. There was no sense to them; they were simply moments of other days, things heard or seen with no reason to be remembered. He would, from time to time, snap awake, recall who he was and what he was doing, but then he would drift away once more. A woman in Fajsz had given him a cup of water. Or had she? Had that happened? At one point, somewhere south of Mohács, he came to his senses to discover that he was on his knees by the river, water cupped in his hands. There were black specks floating on the surface. He bent his head and sipped at it, but it was foul with dead fish and the taste of metal and he spit it out.

'Serves you right.'

Startled, he scrambled to his feet. The voice came from a small skiff not twenty feet away, its bow partly grounded on the sand. A man in the uniform of a Russian enlisted soldier was watching him intently. Then he realized, through a mist, that the man had spoken in Serbian, a Yugoslav language close enough to Bulgarian that he understood it easily. Had he left Hungary? Contrived to walk blindly through a frontier post?

'Here,' the man said, 'try this.' He held out a canteen, the flat kind used by the Red Army, its canvas cover dripping from being hung over the stern of the boat in order to keep the water cool.

He waded over to the boat, accepted the canteen and

took a brief drink. The water was cold and sweet. Handing it back, he saw that the man was wearing several ranks of medals on his jacket. He was young, nineteen or twenty, with service cap pushed back on his head to reveal hair chopped short in military fashion. The bottoms of his trousers were tied in knots just below the knees and a pair of homemade crutches was resting on the bow seat, their tops cushioned with folded rags.

The man waved off the canteen. 'Go ahead,' he said.

Khristo drank more water, rubbed his lips with his fingers, and returned the canteen. 'Thank you,' he said, using the Bulgarian expression.

'Bulgarian?'

'Yes,' he said.

'Where are you going?'

'Home,' Khristo said. 'Downriver from here. Near Silistra.'

'Can you row a boat?'

He nodded that he could.

'Come on then,' the man said.

Khristo climbed carefully over the side, balancing his weight so he would not rock the boat. The soldier changed seats, moving to the bow by using his hands to shift himself along the gunwales. Khristo took the oars – facing the 'wrong' way, downstream, a river tradition that allowed the oarsman to keep an eye out for obstacles – and rowed out to midriver, his hands rolling over each other, oar blades chopping up and down in the water.

'Good,' the soldier said appreciatively. 'I see you've done this before.'

'Oh yes,' Khristo said.

'Just as well. It's a bastard out here – you'll break your back trying to keep this bugger pointed downstream.'

'We have the current,' Khristo said, thankful he didn't have to put his back into it.

'More like it has us. You'll see.' He twisted around and watched the river for a few moments, then turned back to Khristo. 'I'm Andrej,' he said.

They shook hands. 'I'm called Nikko.'

He rowed for several hours as the rain sprinkled on and off. Andrej spoke casually of his time in the army. His father had been a great admirer of the Bolsheviks and had sent him off to enlist with the Russians in 1940. He had fought at Stalingrad as a machine-gunner, then come west with the Second Ukrainian Front, seeing action at the forcing of the river Prut and fighting through the Oituz Pass in the Carpathians. Wounded in the back by mortar shrapnel, he had served with a second-rank unit as far as the town of Szarvas, in eastern Hungary, where he'd stepped on a German land mine and lost the lower parts of both legs. He was philosophical about it. 'At least they didn't get anything important,' he said with a wink. After a time in a field hospital, he'd taken off on 'night leave' and caught a ride to Budapest. Nobody there wanted to hear about his problems – a harassed clerk took a moment to stamp his mustering-out papers – so he 'borrowed' a skiff from a drunken guard and headed toward home, a little town to the east of Belgrade.

They crossed into Yugoslavia late in the afternoon and a Yugoslav patrol boat came alongside to take a look at them. Andrej tossed a salute, then waved his crutches. A sailor returned the salute from the foredeck while Khristo waved and smiled.

'Home,' Andrej said.

'Your Russian uniform,' Khristo said. 'They don't seem to mind.'

'Why should they? We are allies. Tito will be running things down here and we'll be much better off. You'll see when you get home to Bulgaria. The Russians bring us peace.'

Khristo nodded polite agreement. 'No more politics and feuding.'

'That's it,' Andrej said vigorously. 'Everything nice and quiet, a man will be able to get on with his life.'

*

The tempo of the river was steady and constant and, after a time, Andrej's head lowered to his chest, his body rocking gently with the motion of the skiff as he dozed. Khristo rowed on, riding the current, working the oars as rudders to keep the prow pointed east. It required all his attention, and the repetition of effort soon crept into the muscles between his shoulders and resolved into a sharp, persistent ache. It was hard labour – Andrej had been right about that – the spring flood toyed with the skiff, tried to spin it in eddies or knock it sideways with a quartering swell, but Khristo used the force of the water to his advantage. He knew the techniques in his bones, having learnt the job as a child. And he had gained strength when Andrej had shared white cheese and bread with him. He was astonished at what a little food could do for a man.

In the skiff, he was much closer to the water than he had been on the *Tisza*, and he could see the war coming down the river – a grey sludge that floated on the surface, smashed tree trunks, dead birds, the tangled remnants of a feather mattress, a strip of German camouflage cloth wound around the end of a stick. What could that have been, he wondered.

The barge was close to the point where the Drava entered the Danube, near the town of Osijek, on the inside of a tight curve to the north. In the fading light he could see that it was a very old barge, half sunk in the water, half settled into the mud of the shoreline. There were white gouges in the wood at the stern – it was obviously something of a hazard to navigation, abandoned there long ago and never removed. An old man was sitting on the stern, fishing with a line on a pole and smoking a pipe. The barge's former markings were still visible, whitewashed numerals that appeared to have faded into the rotted hull over time.

БФ 825.

He closed his eyes for a moment, but when he opened them again it was still there. Someone had reached out for him. He took a deep breath and let it out very slowly.

Resisted the urge to leap out of the boat then and there and swim wildly toward the barge.

In the bow, Andrej dozed on. He should be killed, Khristo thought. Because whatever cover story might be contrived at this point was going to be so thin that a light would shine through it. This close, the Czech automatic would do the job, and one more pistol shot on this river wasn't going to make a difference to anybody. But he hadn't the heart for it. The soldier's life had been spared in battle, he did not deserve to be shot dead in his sleep a few score miles from home. Khristo waited until the barge was out of sight, scooped some water onto his face, then shipped oars.

Andrej woke up immediately. They were rotating slowly in the current, drifting toward the rocky profile of the near bank. 'Can't do it,' Khristo said sorrowfully, breathing hard, wiping his face. 'Just can't do it.'

The soldier rubbed the sleep from his eyes. 'What?' he said.

'I tried,' Khristo said, and by way of explanation extended his blistered hand.

'You can manage,' Andrej said. 'I saw you.'

Khristo shook his head apologetically.

'Very well,' the soldier said, his expression resolute and cheerful. 'I shall take over the oars for an hour, then we'll pull in for the night. That will fix you up, you'll see, by the morning you'll have your strength back.'

'No,' Khristo said. 'It's best that I go on by foot, out on the roads.'

'Nonsense. Stand up and we'll trade places. Keep a lookout in the bow for your share of the work.'

'I cannot allow it,' Khristo said, putting the oars back in the water and guiding the skiff into the near bank, making a great show of hauling at the water.

'Don't be a proud fool,' Andrej said. 'We must all work together now, remember, and take up the slack where we are able. I am able.'

'Rowed halfway home by a legless man? Not me.' The

bow skidded into the mud and Khristo hopped out, then pushed the boat back out into the water.

The soldier worked his way down the gunwales to the rowing seat. 'To hell with you, then,' he said bitterly, rowing the skiff toward the middle of the river, chopping angrily at the water with his oars.

By the time Khristo worked his way back through the underbrush along the shore, the old man had lit a lantern. He clambered up on the barge and called out a greeting. The old man nodded in response, not bothering to turn around.

'Any luck?' Khristo asked.

'No,' the old man said, 'not much.'

'Too bad.'

'Yes. There used to be pike here.'

'The markings on this barge – I used to have a friend whose boat had the same numerals. Quite a coincidence, no?'

The old man nodded that it was.

'I'd like to see him again, this friend,' Khristo said.

'Then I'll take you there,' the old man said. He stood slowly, taking the line from the river and wiping the muck from it with thumb and forefinger, then kicked an old piece of canvas aside and, with his other hand, retrieved a Browning Automatic Rifle, the American BAR, much battered and obviously well used. 'Your friend is my son,' he said, shouldering the heavy weapon, gripping it so that his finger was within the trigger guard. 'You carry the lantern,' he said, 'and go on ahead of me, so that he may have the pleasure of seeing his old friend arrive.'

They walked for a long time, climbing into an evergreen forest where the sharp smell of pine pitch hung in the evening air. This was the land called Syrmia, lying between the rivers Danube and Sava, the edge of the Slavonian mountain range that ran north into the Carpathians. The trail reminded Khristo of Cambras – a steep, winding approach with potential for ambush at every blind turn. His lantern sometimes showed him a gleam of reflected light at the edges of the path. Weapons, he thought. But these sentries did not challenge him or show themselves, simply passed him on silently, one to the next.

After an hour of hard climbing, the old man melted away and Khristo was alone in a clearing. He stood there patiently while, somewhere, a decision was made. Above him, an ancient fortress of weathered stone was built directly into the face of the mountain. There were hill forts scattered all across northern Yugoslavia, he knew, some of the sites already in use at the time of the Greeks and Romans and, the story went, never vacant for one day in all those centuries. From the top of the hill, the river would be visible for miles in both directions once daylight came.

At last, a silhouette moved toward him from the darkness, a man who walked with great difficulty, his weight shifting violently with every step. Khristo raised his lantern so that his face could be seen and the man advanced into the circle of its light. Perhaps it was Drazen Kulic, he thought, or perhaps not. This man wore the blue jacket of a Yugoslavian army officer over a torn black sweater. He walked with the aid of a stick in his right hand, his left arm dangling useless by his side, the hand cupped and dead. A black patch covered his left eye, and the skin on that side of his face was ridged and puckered all the way to the jawline, pulling the corner of his mouth into an ironic half smile. The man stared at him for a time, searching his face, then said, 'Welcome to my house.'

'Drazen Kulic,' he answered formally, 'I am honoured to be your guest.'

They walked together through a pair of massive doors made of logs cross-braced with iron forgings, into a cavelike room with a fire that vented through a blackened hole in the ceiling. There were some thirty people in the room, half of them sprawled asleep in the shadows, the other half occupied with a variety of chores: loading belts and magazines, cleaning weapons, repairing kit and uniform. They spoke in low voices, merely glanced at him, and ignored him after that. The women had bound their hair in scarves and wore sweaters and heavy skirts, while the men were dressed in remnants of army uniforms. The room smelled of unwashed bodies and charred wood and the fragrant odour of gun oil. The sound of working bolts, metal on metal, formed a rhythmic undertone as the guns were reassembled after cleaning.

Kulic took him to a trestle table set against one wall, and an old woman appeared with two tin cans made over into cups and filled with home-brewed beer, a bowl of salt cabbage and a slab of cornmeal bread. Khristo used his knife to put pieces of cabbage on the bread.

Kulic raised his beer. 'Long life,' he said.

Khristo drank. The taste was bitter and very good. 'Long life,' he repeated. 'And thanks to God for letting me see the signal on the barge. I could have missed it.'

The right side of Kulic's mouth twisted up in a brief smile. 'You have not changed, I see,' he said, 'forever fretting over details.' He paused to drink. 'At that bend in the river there is a cross-current, and if you do not see the barge you will hit it – though I take nothing away from God, as you can see.'

'How did it happen?'

'A mortar shell, in a graveyard in the Guadarrama, the mountains west of Madrid. I'd been a bad boy, and the NKVD "arranged" for it to happen. They meant for me to die, but I was only – well, you can see for yourself.'

'I'd heard that you were captured. Also that the Russians got you out.'

'Who told you that?' Kulic asked.

'Ilya Goldman.'

'Ilya!'

'Yes. Years ago, you understand. In Paris, before the war.'

Kulic took two cigarettes from the pocket of his uniform jacket, gave one to Khristo, struck a wooden match on the table, and lit them both. 'In Paris, before the war,' he repeated, a sigh in his voice. He did not speak for a time, then said, 'It's true. They did get me out. If I'd died they wouldn't have cared, but I was alive and I knew too much, so they couldn't leave me where I was. Then, after they'd sprung me, they tried to send me back to Moscow, but I vanished.'

'Have you made it right with them?'

Kulic shook his head *no*, exhaling smoke from his nostrils. 'Bastards,' he said briefly. 'Do you know what went on here, in Yugoslavia?'

'Some,' Khristo said.

'Communists fighting Chetnik fascists, centrists, monarchists, the Mihailovich units, and all of us, excepting the Chetniks, fighting the Germans. Some groups with OSS support, some with the British MI6, some with the Russians. Believe me, it is beyond imagining. We shot our wounded, Khristo, to keep them from the Gestapo. *I* did that, with my own hand, sometimes to friends I'd played with as a child.'

'This war . . .' Khristo said.

'This war was worth what was done only if we come out of it a nation. Forgive the speech, but it's true. When the Russians got here in force we'd already taken control – they could not do to us what they did to the Poles. But for that we paid a price.'

'I know,' Khristo said. 'I saw it in France.'

'This was worse,' Kulic said simply.

They were silent for a time. The sounds of the great room – the hiss of damp wood on fire, the cleaning of weapons, subdued conversation – flowed around them.

'And now,' Kulic said finally, 'it begins again. Only this time we are alone, or soon will be, and the NKVD begins to nibble. Assassinations, kidnappings, false rumours, the press manipulated, officials bribed, the destruction of reputations – you know their methods, I'll spare you the bedtime stories – but there is no misreading their intentions. They want Tito for a puppet. If they can't have him, they'll throw him out a window and try someone else. Meanwhile, our American friends are still here, and they help if they can, but they are about to fold up their tents and steal away into the night.'

'I doubt that,' Khristo said.

'You'll see.'

'Drazen,' Khristo said after a moment, 'the numbers on the barge.'

'Still a mystery?' Kulic smiled with the right side of his mouth.

Khristo waited.

'I believe you sent a radio message to the Bari station. Some strange ravings about an NKVD colonel who is supposed to materialize in Sfintu Gheorghe on the twelfth of April. Well, you wanted a contact, now you have it.'

'You are to help?' Khristo leaned forward, a little amazed.

'Help.' Kulic repeated the word to himself and laughed. 'How is your English?'

'Good enough.'

'I believe it went: "*Find out what that crazy son-of-bitch does.*" You understand?'

'Yes.'

'Well.'

Khristo took a moment to assemble his thoughts. '*What he does* is bring Sascha Vonets out of Romania, with information, probably very good information. Ilya got Sascha's message out – from the camps. Voluta delivered it to me. It cost him his life. In Spain, Sascha told me what was coming – in the *Yezhovschina* purge of the security services – and Ilya warned me when I had to get out. Then, in Paris, I was trapped by the British, in an émigré operation against the Soviets, and sent to prison. For life. Voluta's organization set me free, just before the Germans took Paris. So, because of these people, because they endangered themselves on my behalf, I sit here drinking beer with you. One could simply walk away from such responsibilities. Is that your suggestion?'

'These friends . . . are all NKVD friends.'

'And you, Drazen.'

'Perhaps someone wonders just what really goes on with you, where your heart is. You walked away from the Russians in 1936. Or maybe not.'

'Horseshit,' Khristo said.

'Yes? Could be. All apologies, and so forth, but explain to me why you are not the bait in an NKVD trap? You go up into that godforsaken Bessarabia – some little fishing village, a place beyond the end of the world. Romania now belongs to the Russians, so what you are trying to do is draw OSS operatives onto Soviet-occupied soil. Where they will be gobbled up and put on show. Somehow, heaven only knows how, American newspapers learn of this. "Oh-ho!" they say. "This bunch of wild asses in the OSS now spies on our great ally in the war. Off with their heads!"'

Khristo stood up. There was silence in the room.

'Sit down, sit down,' Kulic said, making calming motions with his hand. The old woman returned and poured beer into his tin can from a pitcher. 'Very well,' he went on, 'you are a virgin.'

Khristo sat down on the bench. His hands were shaking so he put them between his knees.

Kulic leaned forward and spoke very quietly. 'It is politics. The American government is going to shut down the OSS. The minute the Axis surrender is final – that's the end of it. Some sections will be moved around to other departments, some of the networks will be salvaged, but . . .'

'And so?'

'So there is no guarantee, even if you should manage to slip through the Russian nets on this river, that there will be anybody to help you in Romania.'

'Even if you tell them that I am not a traitor?'

'Even then. You could be unknowing, no sort of traitor at all, yet still bait. You've seen such operations.'

Khristo was silent. It had happened in Paris: he had been drawn into a scheme to stir up the Soviet intelligence *apparat* in Western Europe, and he had never known about it until too late, until Aleksandra was gone.

Kulic's expression changed. There was suddenly discomfort in his face, regret, as though he had determined to do something that he did not want to do, but that he knew he had to do. 'Khristo Nicolaievich,' he said quietly, 'you are my old friend. I know your heart. But we are both part of something that is larger than two individuals and sometimes, in war, individuals cannot matter. There are times when a sacrifice has to be made. But, for one time, maybe we should try to let friendship win. Let us take you south, through the mountains. We'll put you on a boat, give you a passport of some kind, and leave you in Trieste. It's not a bad place, you can live there if you like. Or go to Paris and drive a cab. Live your life, stop fighting, have your politics over a coffee if you must have them, but for God's sake do not delude yourself about Americans. They change, Khristo. One minute they are excited, the next cool. What point is there in having two useless corpses in Sfintu Gheorghe instead of one? They may decide to leave you sitting there like a fool, untrusted, a provocateur for the Soviets, and such a thing would be too sad for an old friend to see. I will get you down the river, if you feel you must go, but my heart tells me that tragedy is waiting for you there.'

Khristo lay on a blanket in the corner of the room but he was too cold to sleep. From time to time someone got up and fed the fire and he stared into the flames and wondered what to do. Lying next to him was a girl, perhaps seventeen, with a blanket pulled over her head like a shawl. Awake, she would be soft and pretty, he knew, but in sleep her face was aged and frightened. Her eyelids flickered, then her lips moved as though she were speaking in a dream.

He was so cold. He had lived a cold, wasted life, he thought. Blown about in storms from Vidin to Moscow to Spain and then Paris. Santé prison had put an end to that, a white blank in his life. And what was the point? To end up dead in some little Bessarabian village? Was that why he had been put on this earth?

The end of the war was coming; it would be like a dawn, the living would sigh with relief and set about to change the world. He wanted to see it. He wanted to live. It would be the best of times to start a new life. *Trieste*. A part of Aleksandra's fantasy. Something about the place had always intrigued her. Perhaps she had been right. In Trieste, he knew, there were Slavs and Italians living side by side – he would not have to be an émigré, an alien, he could just be a man.

Looking into the fire, he could see it. Little streets with radios playing behind shuttered windows, bakeries, dogs napping in the sun. He could walk beside the Adriatic with a newspaper folded beneath his arm. He could stop at a café and read the news. About the mayor and his deputies and the scandal over the contract for the repair of the local streets. Out at sea, a freighter would move slowly across the horizon.

The girl sleeping beside him mumbled some words and, for a moment, her face was touched by sorrow.

In the morning it was raining and wisps of fog hung in the tops of the pine trees. Someone gave him a cup of hot water flavoured with tea and he felt much better after he'd drunk it. Then Kulic took him some way up the mountain – they had to walk very slowly, and Khristo helped him in the difficult places – to an open meadow, a sloping field with mist lying above the long grass and a row of wooden boards set in the ground. One of them was marked *Aleksandra – 1943*.

Khristo stood with his hands in his pockets, his face wet

in the rain. 'She came down here in '37,' Kulic said. 'When Ilya got her released, he bought her a ticket and put her on a train. He sent along a letter. "Keep her out of sight," he said. "Encourage her to live quietly." She did just that. Stayed in a village and worked in a shop, kept to herself. She was someone whose fire had gone out, though you could see, every now and then, how she'd been. But she seemed to have promised herself to be that way no more, to make the world pay for what it had done to her by withholding her light from it. Then we were invaded and went to war. In the strange way of things, it brought her back to life. She fought with us, first as a courier, then with a rifle. We took a German supply column in October of 1943 – mules with mortar rounds strapped to them. And when the thing was finished we found her curled up behind a tree and she was gone. The magazine of her rifle was empty, Khristo, she bore her share of it and more.

'While she was with us, she used the cover identity that Goldman had provided for her. But then, as the war went on, she began to call herself Aleksandra. So, when we brought her up here, we marked her grave with that name only, as we believed she would have wished. From Ilya, I knew her story, but she never spoke of you, or of Paris, but neither did she take a lover.'

'Thank you for bringing me here,' Khristo said.

'I spoke to you from the heart last night, about Trieste, but I could not let you go away without seeing this. It is another side of things, something between you and me, only that.'

'It's better for me that I found out,' he said.

'There are meadow flowers this time of year,' Kulic said. 'I'll wait for you if you like.'

Three days later, he went east on the river.

Kulic found him a berth on a tug called the *Brovno*, bound for Belgrade to pick up a bargeload of iron pipe destined for the rebuilding of the transfer station at Galati, in Romania, the final staging point for oil going to Soviet Black Sea ports. Obtaining export stamps for the pipe had been, according to the pilot of the *Brovno*, 'like a fire in a whorehouse – everybody running around in circles and screaming at everybody else.' The city of Belgrade had been virtually levelled by the Wehrmacht, and whatever pipe they did manage to fabricate was, they felt, better used to supply water for Yugoslavian toilets rather than fuel for Soviet tanks. And as for the Romanian state trading company, which had to be pounded on the back until it coughed up the *import* papers, well, that was even worse. A fire in a whorehouse on a Friday night. 'All spies up there,' the pilot said. 'Romanians.'

For Khristo, there was little to do aboard the *Brovno*. Ivo, the pilot, stayed in the wheelhouse while his brother-in-law, Josip, ran the engine down below and his son, called Marek, served as second engineer. The *Brovno* was a big, powerful river tug, built just before the war. They'd run her up an inlet in 1940, built a shack around her, dismantled the diesel engine and hidden the parts in three separate attics, then gone off to the hills to fight the Germans.

Khristo spent most of his time leaning on a railing and watching the land go by. Kulic had taken him off to the Osijek town hall and obtained, using forged identification papers, a Yugoslav work permit as a deckhand. So he was officially part of the *Brovno*'s crew, but the captain wanted no part of him as a worker. 'What do you want me to do?' he asked as they got under way at dawn.

Ivo thought for a time. 'Coil a rope,' he said.

'And then?'

Ivo shrugged. 'Put it in the rope locker, if you like.'

He did neither. The river was taking him home, and he wanted to stand at the railing and gaze at the countryside. The hundred and twenty miles from Osijek down to Belgrade passed quickly, and by nightfall they'd pulled into the river Sava and tied up while Ivo went off to the dockside office of the harbourmaster. He was gone for a long time. When he returned, he rang for three-quarter power and nosed the *Brovno* through a forest of tugs and barges with such speed that their wake drew curses all across the harbour. 'What did they say?' Khristo asked.

'He said he'd throw me in the river. I said I'd throw him in the river. Then he signed over the barge.'

'That took three hours?'

'We said it many different ways.'

They located the pipe-laden barge and tied up to it, positioning themselves at a point just forward of the stern on the starboard quarter, then, at Ivo's direction, resecured the load, tightening the cables down with a Stillson wrench. It was after midnight by the time they pushed the barge out of the Sava and back onto the Danube, turning east by north into the foothills of the Carpathians. How you came across the Hungarian plain, and then into the Serbian mountains, on a river that ran downhill, Khristo had never really understood, but the mountain shapes rose bulky and dark on either side of the river and the air grew sharp as they moved through the night. Ivo navigated by the beam of a powerful searchlight that swept the river ahead of him, revealing shoals and sandbars where the water foamed white. Somewhere past the giant fort at Smederevo, the light fell upon a pair of bodies, a man and a woman, joined together at the wrist by rope or wire, shifting slowly downriver on the current. 'Collaborators,' Ivo said, his cigarette glowing red in the darkened pilothouse.

Khristo slept for a time, after Marek relieved Ivo at the helm, swaying in a hammock in the crew cabin, waking at dawn to a moment of panic as he tried to remember where he was. On deck, he saw that the *Brovno* had tied up to a small dock, for customs and passport stamps and to take on a Romanian pilot, a small man in a suit and tie. 'For the Iron Gate,' Marek explained.

'Who is this?' the Romanian said, staring at Khristo.

'Deckhand,' Marek answered, winking at Khristo above the man's head.

Taking the hint, he went off and coiled a rope in the stern. Ivo, rubbing the sleep from his eyes, appeared and took the helm, and they were off at slow speed through the Kazan pass into Romania.

It was the strangest piece of river he'd ever seen, sculptured columns of rock thrust up in midstream and the mountains closed in like high walls. There were sudden dips and falls in the river, and the *Brovno* and its barge plunged and bucked past rocky outcrops that looked close enough to touch and echoed back the throb of the pistons above the water. As morning came, the passage filled with strange light. He kneeled in the stern, a piece of tarry rope forgotten in his hands, and watched a line of sunlight crawl up the slope of a mountain, turning the mass of dark shapes into a forest of evergreen trees, their branches hanging with the weight of morning rain, droplets glittering as the sun caught them.

The Bulgarian border station was a sagging dock at the mouth of the river Timok. Two army captains came on board and sat at a table in the crew cabin. Glasses and brandy were produced. One of the captains was dark-skinned and wore a thick moustache, the other was fair-skinned, with black hair and blue eyes. When they had finished their brandy, Khristo and Marek were brought in together to have their papers stamped. The pale captain looked at him curiously. 'He's new,' he said.

'Yes,' Ivo said, 'a hard worker. My sister's boy.'

The man glanced down at the Yugoslav papers, then back up at Khristo. 'He looks like a Bulgarian,' he said. 'Who'd your sister marry?'

Ivo shook his head. 'Do not ask,' he said, voice filled with mock sorrow. They laughed together.

The captain stamped his papers. 'Good luck to you,' he said, using an old-fashioned Bulgarian idiom. Khristo smiled uncertainly and nodded his way out of the crew cabin.

*

Under way once more, they drew close to Vidin, and when the river turned south at the chalk cliff hollowed out by curving water, he was home. They chugged past the shacks by the river with grapevines that looped over the reed roofs, the pole-built docks, the minarets, and the Turkish fortress on the beach. He stood like a sailor, leaning on his elbows, one foot hooked in the lowest rail, and a woman in black waved from the shore. He waved back. Then the town receded in the distance, a small place lit by a weak April sun, the river turned east again, and it was gone.

The days and nights blended together on the river, it was as though the rules of ordinary life were suspended and hours no longer mattered. There were high guard towers on the Romanian shore – sometimes the glint of binoculars – and twice they were boarded from patrol boats and searched. But there was nothing to be discovered, only some Yugoslav river sailors and a load of iron pipe on a barge. Europe was lost behind them – after the Iron Gate they were in a different land, a different time, running along the great plain that reached to the edge of the Black Sea. At Silistra, the *Brovno* left Bulgarian territory and moved north toward the Romanian delta. A day later, they crossed the southern boundary of the strange land known as Bessarabia. Officially it was Romanian territory, called Moldavian Romania, lying south of the Ukrainian SSR, which was part of Russia. But the name Bessarabia was older than the official borders, and it had always been a lost place, home to ancient Russian religious sects expelled from the interior, home to Jews and Turks and Gypsies and Tatars and tribes so lost they no longer had any name at all. It was a place for people that nobody else wanted.

The spring wind blew hard from the west and the sky shifted grey and white and blue above them. Along the shore, birch and poplar groves were leafing out, softening the empty fields that ran to the horizon and vanished in the distant hills. At dawn, herons worked at fishing in the shallows. Khristo felt he was sailing on the edge of the world, east of the Balkans. At dusk, the mountains of Transylvania were silhouettes, backlit by the setting sun, and where the land fell away from the river he could see lakes that turned violet as night came on and great clouds of birds that rose from the shore and wheeled across the evening sky. The nights were black, with not a single light to be seen. Late one night they saw a bonfire on an island, with human shapes dancing slowly before it. Ivo shut the engines down but there was no music to be heard, only the sounds of insects and water sweeping by the hull and a deep silence.

*   *   *

In April of 1945, in Palestine, Jewish refugees arriving by freighter from Cyprus came first to the northern port of Haifa, where they sat on benches in a large shed and waited to be processed. They were called by number, and each held tightly to a worn scrap of paper and waited, patiently or impatiently, to see one of several men and women who sat at old school desks facing the benches. They came from everywhere – from Jelgava in Latvia, from Wilno in Poland, from Strasbourg in France – everywhere. They had survived Hitler in a number of ways. Some had spent years in an attic or a cellar – having never seen the sun for all that time. Others had lived in the forests like animals. Still others had hidden themselves by the use of deception – assuming non-Jewish identities, sometimes resorting to blackmail or bribery of officials to ensure that identity checks confirmed their false papers.

It was hot under the metal roof of the shed and there were flies, and the people waiting on the benches were exhausted. Heshel Zavi tried to be kind, to be patient, but he was not young anymore and these were difficult people, suspicious, often hostile. They had saved their lives, a miracle. They had reached Palestine, another miracle. They had dreamed of oranges and joyous rabbis. Now they were confronted with Heshel Zavi, an old man with a short temper who had to ask them questions and write things down on paper. To the people on the benches, those who sat behind desks and wrote things on paper were enemies.

Heshel Zavi didn't look much like an enemy – he was a burly old man in an open-neck shirt with a yarmulke set precariously atop stiff, woolly curls – but some of their other enemies had not looked like enemies either. *Well*, he thought, *it's to be expected*. He glanced at the chalkboard in the corner and saw that the next number was 183. He called it out in Hebrew. There was no answer. Too much to hope for, he thought. He grumbled to himself and tried it in Yiddish. Again, no answer. What next, Polish? Russian? He tried Russian. *Ah-hah*, he said to himself.

This one was youngish, with a week's growth of stubble on his face. He wore the long overcoat and the traditional hat and shuffled to the desk, shoulders stooped, eyes lowered, much the usual thing, yet Heshel Zavi was not so sure. This one looked like a *yeshiva bucher*, a dedicated student of the Torah, yet there was more to him than that. He had small, clever features, there was something of the rat in him. Not quite a bad rat – Heshel Zavi amended his impression – a good rat, a wise rat, a rat in a children's story. But not a mouse. Definitely not a mouse.

'Sit down,' he said brusquely. 'Welcome to Palestine. You will see me, then a doctor if you need one, representatives of the *kibbutzim*, and so forth. We are here to help you, please be patient with us. Do you understand?'

The man nodded that he understood.

'Very well. Your name?'

'Itzhak Gold.'

'Your name truly?'

'Not really.'

'Never mind. We don't care. Itzhak Gold it is. From where?'

496

'Kurland.'

'I'll write Lithuania.'

'If you like.'

'From a village?'

'The city of Kaunas.'

'Very well. I'll write Kaunas. Next, occupation.'

'Clerk.'

Heshel Zavi wrote the word in Hebrew. Another clerk, he thought, just what they needed. He glanced at the man's hands, uncallused and soft. Well, they would fix that. 'You would, no doubt, like to be a clerk in Palestine.'

The man shrugged, as though to say he knew nothing else.

'It's farmers we need,' Heshel Zavi said. 'Someone who can fix a tractor. Clerks we have.'

Again the man shrugged. 'Perhaps there is a civil service.'

'Like me, you mean?' Amazing how many of them wanted *his* job – two hours in the country and they were ready to shove him aside.

'No, not exactly like you. You have a small defence force, I believe.'

'There are several, all with grand names. Night watchmen is what they are.'

'Ah,' said the man, his small, ratlike face lighting up with a smile, 'the very thing for me.'

'You're sure? You can always change your mind. You *will* change your mind – that's mostly what we do here, we are preoccupied with it. People who have not been able to change their minds for two thousand years tend to make up for lost time once they have the opportunity. As for being a night watchman, well, there's not much future in that, is there.'

'A little, maybe. Where there are night watchmen, there will soon be someone to suggest what they should watch at night.'

Nimble, Heshel Zavi thought, and ambitious. He found

himself liking the man, soft hands or not. He leaned forward across the desk. 'Look,' he said, 'if you can bear waiting a little longer, maybe I have a friend who might help you. But it will take time. I have you to finish, and many others.'

'I don't mind at all,' the man said. 'I'll wait.'

* * *

The people of Sfintu Gheorghe would never forget the events of April 1945. The stories were told again and again – never the same way twice, of course, everybody had their own version of it, depending on where they'd been and what they'd seen and what they wished they'd seen. They weren't liars, exactly, they just liked to make a good story better. Who can blame them? After all, Sfintu Gheorghe wasn't much of a place. In the old days, five centuries earlier, it had been a port of call for Genoese traders, but now it was just a fishing village, a few hundred souls perched out on an arm of the Dunărea that reached to the sea. They were of Greek origin, descendants of the Phanariot Greeks who had once served as the bureaucracy of Turkish and Boyar rule. Those days were gone, of course, now they were simply fishermen who took their boats out on the Black Sea.

The sea *was* black, a curiosity of nature, teeming with life just below the surface, then, fifty fathoms down, a dead place with a bizarre chemistry of water. The normal oxygen had, in some ancient time, been replaced by poisonous hydrogen sulphide and nothing could live in it. So whatever died in the surface waters drifted down to the lower depths where, because there was no oxygen, it did not decompose. Think of it, they would tell the rare visitor. Sailors, great fishes, boats, sea monsters – *it was all still down there*.

They had a slightly peculiar vision of life in Sfintu Gheorghe, but that served them well during the second week in April because peculiar things went on. First, there was the madman. There were those who claimed the whole business started right there. Others disagreed. The Fortunate One, they'd say; the madman had nothing to do with it, he just happened to be around when the Fortunate One made his grandiose gesture. Nobody, however, denied that the madman had been there first, showing up on the tenth of April and hiding in the church.

Hiding really wasn't the word for it. Everyone knew he was there. A fellow with a bald head and a scraggy beard, clutching a piece of burlap that held a sheaf of soiled paper. Well, they thought, since the war some very odd people had shown up in the village, the madman was just one more, and he didn't bother anybody. He spent his days in the tiny loft inside the onion dome atop the church, coming out at night to relieve himself. The priest would leave him a little something to eat, and they all waited to see what he would do. A few of them had hidden up there themselves, when some dangerous person from the government came looking for them – it was the official village hiding place, and the madman, for the moment, was welcome to it.

Then, on the morning of April 12, the magnificent gift was made to appear – as though by sorcery. A fisherman discovered it on the beach, crossed himself, prayed to God, then ran like the devil to spread the news. He brought with him the note he found, and read it aloud as people gathered to see what was going on:

> To the Good People of Sfintu Gheorghe, Greetings and God's Blessing. For those who sheltered a man when he was cold, who fed him when he hungered, and who consoled him in the darkest hour of his life, a gift of appreciation.

He signed himself *The Fortunate One*.
Who was that?
Many candidates were suggested – the villagers combed their memories for lost travellers or storm-beached sailors

that they'd helped – but no one of them was considered a certainty. His gesture, on the other hand, could easily enough be explained. The wicker hampers came from Istanbul, almost due south of them on the Black Sea, and they were clearly marked with an address in Turkish – a certain shop on a certain street, obviously the grandest of places. This man, whoever he might be, had been helped by the village – nursed back to health, some said – then travelled on to Istanbul, where he had made his fortune. Now, later in life, he had determined to make peace with his memories and acted lavishly to repay an old kindness. He must be, they decided, a very fortunate one indeed, for there were twenty hampers. Half the village gathered around them as their contents were revealed. Fresh hams. Purple grapes. Tomatoes. Squash. Even eggplant, the most treasured vegetable of all Romanians. Pears. Peaches. And Spanish champagne – at least thirty cases of it. How, someone asked, could you even *have* an eggplant in April? Where did these things come from? Not from any farmer they'd ever heard of. *Grown in a glass house*, others said, shaking their fingers up and down as though they'd been burned – the universal sign language meaning *very expensive*. It was all perishable, would have to be eaten that very night, so preparations for a great feast were immediately undertaken.

There was, in the otherwise joyous proceedings, one sour note. Sometime on the afternoon of the twelfth a few Bucharest types, tough guys in city clothes, showed up at Sfintu Gheorghe accompanied by a big, nasty-looking Russian in a leather coat, with his hair sheared off so you could see the big nasty bulge at the back of his skull. They were looking for the madman, though they weren't very specific about it. This threatened to put a severe damper on matters, for if they took the madman they would also, clearly, take those who had aided him. But the people of Sfintu Gheorghe had not survived the horrendous regimes of their country for nothing. The city types weren't going to be a problem – their eyes lit up when they saw the bounty and they immediately went to work on the peaches. The Russian was another matter. He was the sourest thing they'd ever seen, so they determined to sweeten him up in a very traditional way. A couple of dark little girls with black eyes took him off somewhere and fucked him senseless. To begin with, they teased him into drinking a bottle of champagne which, instead of slamming a lid down on his feelings or making him explode like a bomb, as the vodka tended to do, rendered him giddily lightheaded and merry as a goat. He took a little black-haired girl under each arm and vanished in a swirl of giggles and wasn't seen again for two days, at which time he was discovered sitting in the mud in his underdrawers, holding his head with one hand and his balls with the other.

* * *

At 8:30 on the evening of the twelfth, the *Brovno* pulled into Galati harbour and Khristo walked up a long ramp onto the quay, Ivo at his side. The docks were lit by dazzling floodlights, and he could see a small army of welders crawling around in the skeletons of newly raised cranes, showers of blue sparks raining down through the girders.

'Good luck,' Ivo said. He reached into a pocket and handed over a thick packet of Romanian lei.

Khristo was a little taken aback, it was a great deal of money.

'From your friends,' Ivo said. 'It's a cold world without friends.'

'It is from Drazen Kulic?'

'Him. And others.'

'You will thank him for me?'

'Of course. There is also this: it is suggested that you take a taxi to Sfintu Gheorghe – no need to walk with all that money. Best to show the driver that you have sufficient means for the ride. Then, on your way back, use the same

501

taxi. Lake Murigheol is one place you ought to see, as long as you've come this far. Quite beautiful in the spring, it's said. And you should have it all to yourself – tourists are not expected.'

'Is it close to Sfintu Gheorghe?'

'Some few kilometres. The man who drives the taxi ought to be able to find it.'

They shook hands. 'Thank you,' Khristo said.

'My pleasure. Now the work begins – a hundred papers to be stamped by idiots, then we'll have to shove this wretched pipe all the way back to Yugoslavia. *Up*stream.' He grimaced at the thought.

'No. Really? For God's sake, why?'

Ivo shrugged. 'We need it more than they do. Let them be satisfied with a fraternal gesture.'

'A lot of work for a fraternal gesture.'

'Yes, but there's nothing to be done about it.' He nodded back toward the pipe-laden barge, his expression a parody of helplessness. 'Wrong gauge,' he said.

There was a bonfire in Sfintu Gheorghe. Four men in shirt-sleeves, ties pulled down, were dancing to the music of a violin, each holding the corner of a white handkerchief. The men were very drunk, and it was not a large handkerchief. But the violin was rapturous, the crowd was banging knives and forks and tin pots, and the dancers made up in gravity what they lacked in grace. Two of the men were wearing tinted glasses, and all had holstered pistols beneath their armpits.

Khristo Stoianev, still vibrating from a three-hour taxi ride over a cart track, stood quietly at the edge of the crowd. A heavy woman turned partway toward him and stared uncertainly. He smiled warmly, clapped his hands to the rhythm with broad enthusiasm, and was rewarded with a shy smile in return. He spent some time in this way, letting them notice him, letting them accept him as someone who did not mean them harm. Villagers, he knew, could communicate without speaking – a subtle defence mechanism – and somehow come to a silent decision about the intentions of strangers. You had to let them read your character.

When they began to lose interest in him, he looked over the crowd and picked out the village priest. There would be, in such a place, a triumvirate of leadership: a headman or mayor, a queen of wives, and a local priest. Any one of them would know where Sascha was – if they did not know of him, he was not there. When people grow up in a small village, they learn all the hiding places.

The priest was not hard to find. He was a young man, with hair and beard worn long in the Greek Orthodox manner, and his black cassock fell to the tops of his shoes. Khristo circled the crowd casually until he stood next to him.

'Praise God, Father,' he said, using very slow French.

'My son,' the man acknowledged.

He was flooded with relief. He could not speak Romanian, but he knew that most educated people in the country had a second language – German or French. 'A feast,' he said. 'Is there a wedding?'

'No, my son,' the priest said. 'The village has been blessed today. A good deed has returned to us.'

'And you have guests,' he said. The men with the pistols, sweating in the night air, moved with slow dignity as the violin encountered a brief period of melancholy.

'We are all countrymen,' the priest said. 'Praise God.'

Khristo heard clearly the relief in the latter statement. 'Is there one guest missing?' he asked gently. 'A man with dark hair? A man who has seen the world?' Now he had put himself at the priest's mercy and feared what he would do next. One shout would be sufficient, he thought, yet who would shout at a feast?

The priest's eyes sharpened in the firelight and Khristo knew that Sascha was somewhere in the village. His fingers dawdled for a moment by the pocket where the money nested, but instinct told him that such an offer would not

503

be well received. The music picked up and he shouted 'Hey!' and clapped his hands.

'Are you a believer?' the priest said.

'I am, Father,' he answered matter-of-factly, 'though I have strayed more than I should these last few years.'

The priest nodded to himself. He had been forced to make a decision and he had made it. 'You should attend church, my son,' he said, and pointedly broke off the conversation, walking forward a pace or two to be nearer the dancers.

Khristo could see the church; its silver-painted dome reflected light from the bonfire. He moved slowly away from the crowd in the opposite direction, then circled around behind a row of little houses, climbing over garden fences and groping ahead of him for beanpoles and twine. The local dogs loved a feast as well as the villagers, for which he was thankful – the last thing he needed was a dog to wear on his ankle and these yards, he knew, were their sacred territories.

The church was dark and silent. He watched it for a time but it told him nothing – an old mosque, built under Turkish rule, with a cross mounted atop the dome when Christianity returned. He opened the door a few inches, then stepped inside and let it close behind him. It smelled musty, like old straw, and there wasn't a sound to be heard. 'Sascha,' he whispered.

There was no answer.

He regretted, now, leaving his little automatic on the *Brovno*, but his cover would not allow for it. A Yugoslav river sailor just might turn up in Sfintu Gheorghe – an armed Yugoslav river sailor had better not. There was the faintest trace of light in the church, filtering in from a high window. He moved slowly down an aisle between wooden benches until he reached the altar. 'Sascha?'

There was no answer.

To the left of the altar, out of the sightline of the benches, was a pole ladder. He walked to the base of it, slowly, and looked up to see the edge of a loft. 'Sascha, it's Khristo.

504

Stoianev. I've come to take you away, to take you to freedom,' he said in Russian.

There was no answer.

Had he left the church? Perhaps the meaning of the priest's statement had been innocent, the man simply telling him to go to church more often for the good of his soul. He took a step back from the ladder, his thoughts settling on the taxi that waited for him at the edge of the village.

'Sascha Vonets.' He said it in a normal voice. 'Are you in this church?'

There was only silence, the muffled sound of the violin, a shout of laughter, barking dogs. He was going to have to climb the ladder. He put one foot on the bottom rung and bounced to make sure it would take his weight, then moved up a rung at a time. 'I'm coming up to talk to you,' he whispered into the darkness. A fool's errand, he thought. The man was likely a thousand miles away while he whispered nonsense into an empty church loft. Still, he kept climbing. He reached the point where he could see over the edge of the loft, but it was very dark, walled off from the high window. He went up another rung and swung one foot onto the boards of the loft. He kicked something, a plate by the sound of it, which went skittering away across the floor. There was an orange flame and a pop and he fell backward, landing on his back and taking the ladder down with him. 'Oh no,' he said. He got to his hands and knees and crawled past the altar, down the aisle between the benches, shouldered the door open and rolled himself down the three steps to the dirt street, then wedged himself between the steps and the wall of the church.

He tore at his clothes until he found it. He couldn't see very well, but it was midway up his left side, just below the ribs, a small hole like a nail puncture, with blood just beginning to well from the centre. As he watched, the blood made a droplet that swelled until it broke loose and ran slowly down his skin. He covered the wound gently with a cupped hand, as though it embarrassed him. It hurt a little, like a cut, but there was a frightening pain on the left side of his chest and he realized that he was gasping for air.

From within the church there was a crash, then the sound of running footsteps. *Here they come*, he thought. But there should have been more of them – in the houses, among the crowd, everywhere – the NKVD used scores of people to set a trap. A man threw open the door and ran down the steps into the street, a pistol in his hand. His hair and beard were wildly disarrayed, his motions frantic and abrupt. 'Satans! Where are you? Murderers!' he mumbled, as though to himself. Suddenly he discovered Khristo, ran toward him and peered into his face. 'Is it Khristo?' he said, seemingly stunned at finding him crumpled between the steps and the wall of a church.

'You killed me,' Khristo said, voice sorrowful and tired. The pain in his chest was fierce and there was no air to breathe. In the distance, the violin began to play a new kind of song. It was a jazz song, one he'd heard before, but he could not remember its name.

The man knelt above him. 'Oh God,' he said. 'It is you.'

He shrugged. He no longer cared about anything.

'Why did you speak Russian? You frightened me.'

He coughed, spat something on the ground. 'Sascha?'

'Yes?'

'Look what you did.'

From his kneeling position, Sascha fell backward and sat on the ground and began to sob, clutching his face in his hands.

He began to have a dream, and in this dream Lake Murigheol was violet, like the lakes he had seen from the deck of the *Brovno*. Such a place seemed to him remote, difficult to approach. The driver of the taxi would argue and say there was no road and the rest of the money would have to be given to him and still he would not go and finally Sascha would put the gun against the back of his neck – the old place – and call him names in Russian until he turned the key in the ignition. Then later Sascha would remember that the 'Red Banners' poem had been left in the church and they would have to go back and then start all over again. Then they would drive across fields on flat tyres with the driver howling and swearing and Khristo bleeding and Sascha crying and waving the gun around and finally they would reach Lake Murigheol. There would be a seaplane, of course, with the usual freckle-face American pilot and some gangly fellow in a blue three-piece suit and tie, and eyeglasses that made him look like an owl, standing there like a diplomat and holding a submachine gun away from his side so the grease wouldn't get on his suit, and he would be tense as the pilot fired up the engines and they began to move across the darkness of the violet lake, and he would ask if the villagers of Sfintu Gheorghe had enjoyed the party which he – fortunate one indeed – had given them. And he would see that Khristo was shot and he would be concerned and Khristo would pass out and come to and pass out again and wake to a moment when the plane quivered and roared and made white plumes of the violet surface until they lifted up and just barely over the tops of the trees and he realized that he was going home now on a new river and that only when he got there would he find out where home was and what it was like and how that river ran and the last thing he thought was that he hoped he would like it there.

In late September of 1945, in Manhattan, Muriel Friedman walked from her apartment building on West End Avenue up to Cake Masters bakery on Broadway, where she purchased two dozen jelly doughnuts, then hailed a cab and returned to West End Avenue, where Estelle Kleinman was waiting in front of her building on the corner of Eighty-third Street. The cab was then directed

507

south, to Forty-sixth Street and Twelfth Avenue, the area of the docks. The two women were volunteers for the USO, the organization which, among other things, greeted servicemen returning from overseas on troop transports, serving them coffee and doughnuts as they disembarked. In most cases, the transports carried hundreds of troops and the doughnuts were trucked in from commercial bakeries in Long Island City.

But Muriel Friedman had been telephoned the night before by her USO supervisor and told that the next day's arrival, the *Skögstaad*, would be disembarking only four or five passengers, to go ahead and buy a few boxes of doughnuts at the store, for which she would be reimbursed. She could have gone up to Gristede's and bought box doughnuts, but she had decided to do something a little grander than that and absorb the cost herself. The money didn't matter. Vanity Frocks, her husband Mort's company, was once again manufacturing dresses, having spent most of the war producing uniforms for the army. A jelly doughnut baked that morning was a much friendlier greeting to a returning serviceman than a plain old box doughnut and, in Muriel Friedman's view of the world, such small gestures were important.

The *Skögstaad* was an old Norwegian freighter caught by the outbreak of the war in the Spanish port of Algeciris and used as a Liberty ship thereafter, successfully making the convoy run from American harbours to Murmansk — the chief supply port of the Soviet Union — many times during the war. Now she was nearing the end of her days. She'd carried a cargo of Jeeps and medical supplies from Baltimore to Athens, then called at Istanbul for a load of jute destined for rope factories in the southern United States, stopping at several ports on the way home to take on a few military passengers as well as sixty coffins — fallen American servicemen whose families had requested they be re-interred in military cemeteries in their homeland.

In the back of the cab, Estelle Kleinman glanced at the

two Cake Masters boxes tied with string and lifted an eyebrow. 'Cake Masters?' she said.

'A few jelly doughnuts,' Muriel said. 'The world won't end.'

Estelle's disapproval was silent, but Muriel didn't care whether she liked the idea or not. Estelle Kleinman disapproved of almost everything, and it was much too nice a morning for an argument. Riding down West End Avenue, Muriel could see it was the first real day of autumn, the sky was bright and blue and the wind off the Hudson River made the city streets seem clean and fresh. When the driver took them up on the elevated West Side Highway they could see the river, sun sparkling on the water, surface ruffled by the wind.

They paid off the cab at Pier 48 and busied themselves in the USO office with a large coffee urn that had to be coaxed into action. A bridge table was carried out to the street entrance of the pier by a burly longshoreman with U.S. Navy tattoos on his forearms. He pinched his finger setting the thing up and swore under his breath, then declined the quarter Muriel offered. The jelly doughnuts were laid out on paper napkins in front of the coffee urn and the two women waited patiently for the ship, sharing a few bits of gossip about friends in the neighbourhood.

At 12:30, the *Skögstaad* was just docking, the river tugs that had hauled her up past the Statue of Liberty nudging her gently against the old wooden pier. There was a pause, perhaps a half hour, while customs officials boarded the ship, then, at 1:15, the handful of passengers began to appear. A naval ensign exclaimed over the jelly doughnuts, and both Muriel and Estelle flirted with him in their own particular way while he sipped a mug of coffee and kept an eye on the street, apparently waiting for someone. Two businessmen, perhaps Turkish, declined the jelly doughnuts with elaborate courtesy, then hurried off toward the rank of taxicabs that waited at the docks. An army major ran right past them, swept up in the arms of a blonde woman and an old man – wife and father, Muriel thought. Then, finally, one last passenger appeared, walking slowly from the great dark structure that covered the pier and blinking at the bright sunlight.

There was something different about this one, Muriel thought. He had black hair set off by pale skin, and deep blue eyes over high cheekbones. Striking, she thought, if you liked that Slavic type. He walked slowly, with a slight limp, and once touched a place on his left side as though it hurt him. Wounded, she realized. Wounded in the war, and now coming home.

Or was it home? He appeared to be very nervous, stopping at the pier entrance and tugging at the jacket of the light grey suit he wore. With dark blue shirt and yellow tie he was clearly what Muriel would call a 'greenhorn', a newcomer, an immigrant. She could see it in his eyes – how he looked and looked, trying to take in everything at once, struck with fear and joy and excitement over finally setting foot in America. Well, she thought, he would learn what it was, he would find his place in it. They all had. When her father had come to Ellis Island from Latvia in 1902 he must have looked something like this. Overwhelmed, for the moment, as the dream turned into reality before his eyes.

The passenger in the grey suit never noticed the coffee and jelly doughnuts on the bridge table with the USO sign tacked to its edge. Estelle started to call out to him, but Muriel put a restraining hand on her arm, and for once in her life she had the sense to shut up. The moment was too private for intrusion. Let him be with his thoughts. For a few seconds Muriel shared his feelings, seeing it all for the first time, taking the first step along with him as he moved from the shadow of the pier.

Then, from across the street, a young woman appeared, climbing out of a cab and walking briskly toward the entrance to the pier. She had short, chestnut-coloured hair and green eyes. Jewish, Muriel thought. Wearing a very good wool dress from — Saks? Lord & Taylor? Was she perhaps meeting this immigrant? Maybe he was not so alone and friendless as he appeared.

Her eyes searched the crowd, then the young man in the grey suit waved his hand and called out 'Faye!' and her face lit up with pleasure. Muriel watched carefully as they approached each other and shook hands. *So formal?* she thought. All the way from God only knows where, by what means she could not even imagine, to be greeted by a handshake? She found herself vaguely disappointed and started to turn away.

But then, as they crossed toward the waiting taxicab, sidestepping the honking trucks and cars that filled the busy street that served the docks, she took his arm. *There,* Muriel thought, *that's better.*

ACKNOWLEDGMENTS

Research on this book involved a considerable range of source material, but I want to mention particularly R. Harris Smith's history of the OSS as having provided, on page 241, the conceptual key for the novel. I am grateful for the attention and care of Louise Noble, art director, Luise Erdmann, manuscript editor, and Ann Stewart, book designer. I want to thank Michael Speers, for advice and encouragement; Melanie Jackson, for her faith in me and in this project; and my editor, Robie Macauley, for the kind of support that, in a perfect world, every writer would have with every book. A special word of thanks to William Curran, a great friend to this novel and a man who knows about maps and borders and the rivers that cross them.

The Alan Furst Collection

Fourteen gripping novels by the master of historical espionage thrillers

'An addiction' *The Times*

Available now from W&N in paperback and ebook

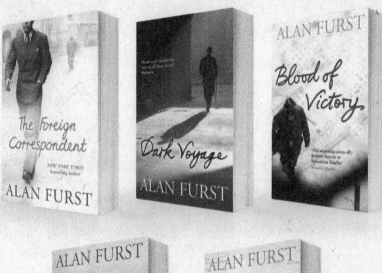

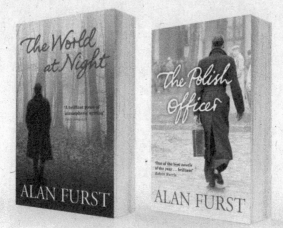